KINGDOM

of

ASH and SOOT

BOOK ONE OF *THE ORDER OF THE CRYSTAL DAGGERS*

◊ ◊ ◊ ◊

C. S. Johnson

Dedication

First and foremost, this is for my darling children. The world needs more brotherly love and sisterly affection such as yours, and you are my inspirations.

Second, as always, this is for Sam. I have never forgotten your questions or our conversations, and I hope in some small way, you'll read this and allow them to live on.

And finally, this is for all my favorite people I fangirl over.

To my favorite podcasters: Ben, Michael, and Drew. I love you all. And my video playlists are filled with Ravi, Dinesh, David, Dennis, and Nabeel. Thank God for you! I would not be anywhere close to who I am without all of you, and I am tremendously grateful for your wit, wisdom, and insight over the years.

As a special note, I would like to add Michelle and Ayah to my list. I am sorry for the late tribute to Nabeel, but I am grateful you are able to carry on his life's work.

For the translation help, I must thank Riad El-Choueiry. Small as it is, your words have helped me so much.

Prologue

◊

My father's hands, stained with darkened sunlight and roughened sores, were cold as I touched them for the last time.

As he lay still in his coffin, I rubbed my small hands over his, much as he had done to mine before I went to sleep each night when he was home.

"Night-night, *Táta.*" I said my final goodbye softly, my lips barely moving to form the words. Not even my hair stirred, the ebony curls stilled out of solemnity.

My gaze turned to his face, as the church's robed pallbearers, silently but surely, came up beside me. I felt them surround my father's body more than I saw them, as I continued to watch his face, searching for any sign his eyes might open and wink up at me once more.

A sleeve tickled my neck. "It's time to let go, miss," one of the pallbearers whispered into my ear.

"Not yet!" I objected.

"Eleanora." The sharp voice of my stepmother, Cecilia—officially Baroness Cecilia Haberecht Chotek Svobodová of Bohemia—snapped loudly and harshly against the quiet sea of silence inside the church. "Let the men do their job."

Only after I turned to face her did her hard expression melt into one of concern.

"Please," she added more sympathetically, but I knew from the hard line of her jaw she was more concerned I would make a scene in front of the whole kingdom.

How impudent it would be of me to embarrass her with my grief.

"But Ben didn't get a final chance to say goodbye," I said, my nostrils flaring.

At the sound of his name, my brother, at twelve years of age, shifted uncomfortably on the hard pew bench. In the last few days, Ben had transformed from the smart and silly, fun-loving boy I grew up with into a cynical, unrecognizable man.

I did only what I could—I waited for his response. There was a long moment where the crowded church returned to its stifled silence, before finally, *finally,* Ben coughed discreetly, and spoke.

"It's fine, Nora. I've already said my farewells to *Otec.*"

I grimaced at his tone; it was brusque and formal, and nothing about it suggested Ben was as heartbroken as I was.

"Come sit down, Eleanora," Cecilia insisted once more. "Father Mueller is waiting to perform the last rites."

"I'll not come down until Ben comes and says a proper goodbye to our father."

"You are embarrassing yourself in front of our family and neighbors. Even His Grace has come from Moravia to be here at your father's Mass." Her voice was low and deadly.

Briefly, I glanced over at the stern-faced man who was standing next to Cecilia. The Duke of Moravia, Lord Franz Maximillian Chotek, was a cousin to both the Emperor and my stepmother. His thin, dark mustache twitched in irritation as Cecilia and I battled over the right to grieve.

"It is the honorable thing to do," I argued.

My brother sighed. In his lap, I could see his fingers clench into a fist.

"Benedict, go. If it will let us move on before Adolf's body starts to smell, then by all means, appease your sister."

I held my breath, wondering what I would do if he did leave me to send *Táta* off all by myself.

I relaxed a moment later when he reached over, almost as if he was mentally reconsidering his reluctance, and grabbed his crutch; glaring angrily at me, he hobbled less than gracefully up to the altar. I was relieved when no one muttered anything about my brother's crippled right leg.

"I can't believe you're making me do this," he whispered to me. "You of all people know how I feel about *Otec*."

I frowned. "*Táta* was a good man. Even the king said he was a good man who protected him during the Revolution."

"Kings are quick to reward those who would die for them."

"Not all of them."

"Nora, what do you know of war or any soldier's duty?" Ben hung his head at my childishness. "It doesn't matter anyway, does it? The Germans are still in control of the Diet, and the Emperor is in his palace in Vienna, while King Ferdinand is playing with his posies all day long."

My brother was clever. In ducking his head, it looked from behind as though he was sad or even crying. The church's audience murmured a quiet approval as Ben grasped onto his crutch with one hand and put his other hand over mine, while I continued to rest it on *Táta's*.

As we stood there, I saw there was a bluish tint to my father's stiffened hands, and I wondered if death had chilled him even in the afterlife, so much that his veins had swelled. I looked back up at his face, surprised to see there were similar lines around his lips, although his beard and mustache helped to hide the unsightly marks.

"There." Ben squeezed my hand. "Are you satisfied?"

"Yes." I nearly choked out a response. "He was all we had, Ben, no matter what you say."

I slowly released my father's hands and whispered one last prayer toward the heavens for his soul as I headed back to my seat in the pew.

But when I turned around, I suddenly stopped, as a flurry of sound and movement in the back of the church caught my attention. Ben, with his uneven steps, bumped into me from behind, and I heard his mumbled curse.

Fortunately for Ben, everyone else, including Father Mueller, was too busy staring at the back of the church to chastise him.

My own mouth dropped open as I saw a kingly procession entering the chapel. Men wearing fine livery made from shining threads, woven with the proud red and white colors of Bohemia, dotted the small crowd.

It was only when they parted that I saw the king.

King Ferdinand V, the former leader of the Austria-Hungarian Empire and King of Bohemia, and a string of several other titles, had arrived.

"His Majesty!" Cecilia gasped. I might have laughed at her expression at any other time, but she was right to be surprised.

The king did not come out in public very often, and at once I could see why. My eyes took in his large forehead, his wide-set eyes, and his aged, enlarged face. His robes were grand, and his jewelry ornate, but there was nothing ostentatious enough to hide his shaking discomfort. He walked slowly, with a cane in hand and two young attendants immediately behind him for support. I, along with everyone else stared as the elderly figure proceeded toward the front, where my father's casket was waiting.

I had heard the rumors of the king's precarious mental state—of his simplemindedness, his mental fits. I wondered as he passed, only giving me a light glance, if he was here against his doctor's wishes.

King Ferdinand V used to be our king. In 1848, the same year Ben was born, Ferdinand had been forced to abdicate his throne to his nephew, the current Emperor, Franz Joseph I.

But, as the king bowed down before the altar and made the Holy Cross over my father's corpse, I remembered King Ferdinand's informal title, Ferdinand *Dobrotivý*, or "Ferdinand the Good."

It seemed to suit him.

I blinked back tears, remembering *Táta* telling me that even kings had to bow to something greater than themselves in the end. Many of them submitted to God, in life and in death, while King Ferdinand had submitted to the power of the people. My father had remained at the king's side, protecting him from physical harm during the Revolution of 1848, when King Ferdinand's power was revoked.

Maybe that's why the king decided to come down out of his castle in the city to see him.

Father Mueller continued with the Funeral Mass, reciting the familiar lines of liturgy, along with the occasion's additions for the deceased. I barely listened to the service for my father. While grief was not preferred, it was familiar; Ben, *Táta*, and I had all been through it four years prior, when my mother was lost at sea.

As we responded to Father Mueller's reading of the twenty-third Psalm, I glanced back over at the king. My grief was great, but my curiosity was proving itself the more demanding of the two.

"I can't believe the king came," I whispered to Ben.

"He didn't come for *Máma's* funeral," he whispered, "and she was the better one between the two."

"*Táta* is with *Máma* now. They are together again at last."

"If *Otec* even made it to heaven," Ben retorted.

"Ben! That's terrible to say."

"He was a terrible man."

"To you, maybe."

"Exactly."

At the bitterness in his tone, I decided to discontinue the conversation.

But I stopped for other reasons as well—two of them, to be more precise. Priscilla, my stepsister, was earnestly tugging on her mother's skirts as she glanced over in our direction, and my stepbrother, Alexander, glared menacingly at Ben.

How can they be the same age as us, but act like such little children?

It was not hard for me to make that deduction; they had never known pain as Ben and I had. It seemed that for every burden my family had borne, our stepsiblings had only brushed theirs aside.

In addition to our mother's death, there was Ben's injury. *Táta* never forgave Ben for getting crippled two summers past, falling off the stable roof after trying to fetch one of my cats for me.

Priscilla and Alex's father, Cecilia's second husband and the one before my father, had died serving in the armed forces abroad. Even at our first meeting, Alex had been eager to boast of how his father's shield had saved the baby prince, Leopold, and his mother, Queen Victoria, and subsequently, the entire kingdom of Britain, from death and destruction. When I asked if his father was acting as a nursemaid, he nearly cried.

I think that was the moment when he began to hate me.

Quickly, so Cecilia would not see, I stuck my tongue out at Alex and glared a warning to Priscilla, before turning away from them completely.

Ben shifted in his seat uncomfortably again. I looked up to see he was giving silent warnings to our stepsiblings himself. Their derision toward us since the day we had met had never been more inappropriate. Some part of me blamed Ben for that; he had been angry, angrier than ever, the winter after his accident, and gaining a new family was the last thing that could have cheered him up.

"Stop fretting, Ben," I told him, placing my hands over his as I had done to *Táta's* just moments before.

"I can't. I have to watch out for you now."

I wrinkled my nose. "Cecilia's *children* don't scare me."

"Lucky you," he said. "There is no one to stop them from taking our inheritance now. Indeed, Cecilia has already begun raiding *Otec's* estate. How else do you think she was able to get such a fancy dress made up from the seamstress before his funeral? And how else do you think she was able to get clothes and shoes for Alex and Priscilla? I also overheard her ordering a new carriage in the English style. She fancies herself to be Queen Victoria or Empress Elisabeth, cast out to far and foreign lands."

I glanced over to see Ben was right; Cecilia's dress was indeed much finer than my own. The gown was cut in a fashionable style, though from what I remembered of *Máma's* wardrobe, I would have said it was French rather than British. The stitching was fine, and even from where we were sitting, I could easily make out the sheen of expensive silk.

"We didn't get any new clothes," I said.

"Clothes are one thing, Nora. But how will you be able to get married? You have no dowry to your name now."

"I'm not even ten years old yet."

"I knew after my accident I would never marry," Ben said. His words were stilted, as though he had to chisel them off his chest. "But you, Nora. You could have had any suitor in the kingdom, just as *Otec* said *Máma* did."

"I *did* inherit *Máma's* looks," I said, straightening my posture, momentarily forgetting my pain as pride took over.

"You dream of a family."

"No." I shook my head firmly. "*You* are my family. It is enough for me. I need no husband to be content."

"I would not let you be alone with me if you could do better."

"For all your trouble, there is no one better than you," I said. "You have always watched out for me, even before Cecilia and the demon twins came to live with us."

A small chuckle was smothered in his throat, but I heard its echo nonetheless.

"You've got *Máma's* humor too, it seems. Hopefully you'll have her strength as well," Ben said. "Because these next few years may be hard."

"*Máma* taught me to be brave, Ben. As long as you'll face them with me, we will survive." My hands tightened in his.

"We may survive, but we will not be free."

"One day we will," I vowed. "You'll see."

He could only grip my hand back in reply before Father Mueller, finished with the eulogy, harkened us once more to prayer.

" … And so, let us pray for Adolf Svoboda, a regal nobleman in the court of His Imperial and Royal Apostolic Majesty, the Emperor of Austria, Apostolic King of Hungary Emperor Franz Joseph I, of the House of Hapsburg-Lorraine, his kind and generous legacy in service to His Majesty King Ferdinand V of Bohemia … "

Upon hearing his name, I glanced over at the king once more. He had his one hand resting on his walking stick, and the other nudged between his legs underneath a thick blanket.

I tilted my head, watching him. Was he cold? I wondered. It was getting close to the end of summer.

When he began to twitch and moan a moment later, I felt my own body go still. "Ben, look!"

The congregation began to whisper voraciously as the king fell over in his pew, convulsing fitfully. Father Mueller faltered mid-prayer, and I saw another man, one I recognized as my father's friend and medical doctor, Dr. Sigmund Artha, hurry forward to help.

"Your Highness," Dr. Artha said. He patted down his bushy wave of gray-streaked hair, and I wondered if he had only just remembered he was in the presence of the former king of Bohemia. The faded, familiar rosary beads from the Church of St. Nicholas, the *Kostel svatého Mikuláše*, jangled against his small medical bag as I watched him hastily make a quick bow. "Let me assist you."

I had seen Dr. Artha in our manor enough to know that he was deathly afraid of the silliest things, from spiders and dusty books to messy rooms and babies. On several of his visits with my father, he would excuse himself to go to wash his hands, and he would rub down his hair in both a nervous and necessary habit. I found it amusing and endearing that Dr. Artha had no fear of approaching King Ferdinand.

"We're here, too, sir." One of the young attendants, the shorter one, behind the king, stepped forward.

The first attendant, the one with black hair, began to issue orders to the king's men. Meanwhile, the other one who had spoken with Dr. Artha, a slightly shorter boy with copper hair, stepped up beside the king and began to tend to him, whispering into his ear. I saw he had a small decanter in his hand.

"Stay calm, Nora," Ben whispered beside me, as the king let out a loud moan.

"Father." The second assistant suddenly yelped as the king fell to the side.

I frowned. King Ferdinand had no children.

"Father Mueller," the black-haired boy called, his voice more confident and urgent, and I quickly realized my misunderstanding. He was calling for the priest. "Please, continue on. His Imperial Highness would benefit from your godly prayers."

The other boy nodded, and the reverend complied. I saw Father Mueller's face was white with slight panic as he stepped back up to the pulpit.

As the normal prayer resumed, this time louder and clearly more strained, I kept glancing over at the king.

"Oh, merciful infant Jesus! I know of your miraculous deeds for the sick. How many diseases you cured during your blessed life on earth … "

I made the sign of the cross over me, still watching as the king slowly reverted to his previous state; there was less jolting and gasping, and his eyes, even though they were still blinking fast, seemed more alert. He watched the copper-haired attendant with a tepid smile on his face.

That was when the attendant boy caught my eye. He was dabbing the king's head with a handkerchief, carefully and calmly, almost lovingly, before the king whispered something. Then the boy turned to see me staring at him.

Remembering my father's affection for the disposed king, I gave the boy a kind smile.

He went still, staring at me.

I stared back.

Just as I noticed he seemed to be close to Ben's age, the other attendant stepped in front of him.

"Guard," I heard him call. "Prepare His Highness' coach for departure. We will be leaving shortly. The king needs his rest."

A guard saluted him and headed down the back of the small church.

The dark-haired boy suddenly narrowed his gray eyes in my direction. From his expression, I could tell he expected me to turn away or bow my head in feigned prayer.

Rather than submit to his wishes, I stared back at him, arching my brow at him, letting him know, in my own small way, he had no moral authority to shame me. As a citizen, I had just as much concern for our king's health, even if he was no longer our ruler.

Our imagined conversation did not seem to be going as smoothly as he might have hoped. The boy at least seemed unnerved by my response, blushing quickly and then turning back to say something to Dr. Artha, who seemed to be asking him a question.

"Nora," Ben whispered. "Stop causing trouble."

"I didn't do anything," I said.

"Just be quiet and focus on the ceremony, would you, *ségra*? Maybe it was nice of the king to come, but it seriously doesn't matter."

I was tempted to pinch him for his flippancy, but hearing his pet name for me softened my resolve. It had been awhile since he had called me *ségra,* and I was glad to hear it again. I took his hand in mine, holding it as I returned my focus to Father Mueller.

" … Extend your most holy hands, and by your power take away all pain and infirmity, so that our recovery may be due, not to natural remedies, but to you alone … "

I sighed. Father Mueller's prayers were appropriate, I supposed, but they were as dead to my ears as the words were to my heart. I knew they were for my father's heavenly ascent, but I felt Ben and I needed prayers more than our father did.

I tightened my grip on Ben's hand and prayed. *Please, Holy Father, help Ben and me. Help us to find a way to be happy once more. Please keep us together and keep us safe.*

As my father's casket was finally removed from the church, as Cecilia wept loudly, kneeling before the benign king of Bohemia, as I sat helplessly next to my brother, I beseeched God again with a barrage of earnest prayers.

It would be many years before I believed God had heard me—and even more before I realized that he had bigger plans than I could have ever imagined, and he had already set them in motion.

1

◊

"Nora."

The call to wake up was never a pleasant one. Ben's voice, though it had grown deeper over the years and changed according to his moods each day, was constant throughout the last decade of our lives; it was the precursor to the endless rounds of chores and errands.

It was a comfortable kind of discomfort.

My slumbering barrier against the real world was breached again, this time more urgently.

"Come on, Nora, wake up."

I could hear the mix of impatience and compassion in his tone as Ben sighed.

"Cecilia's coming."

At that, I shot up, sitting upright on my small pallet. I groaned as I pushed back the loose tresses of my hair, allowing my eyes to find sunlight. It was a wasted effort; the sun had not yet risen. "Already?" I asked, rubbing my eyes. "Why is she even up this early? You'd think that after so many evenings of dancing till dawn she would never again rise from sleep before noon."

"Why else?" Ben asked. "She and Priscilla have rounded up more treasures that used to belong to our father, and she wants us to trade or sell them at the market before the neighbors can see how shabby they look."

"Oh, no. Not more of *Táta's* things!" I turned my face away from my brother and flopped back onto the small, soft bag I had stuffed with cotton and feathers to use as a pillow. "I thought she'd finished searching for his stuff years ago."

"*Otec* collected a lot of junk from his travels for the king," Ben said. His formal use of "*Otec*" snapped in the air between us, also reminding me of his animosity toward our father. "*Máma's* stuff is nearly gone, too. Including all her lovely books from Paris."

From the look on his face, Ben mourned the loss of those books more than I did, and it was likely only a little less than either of us missed our mother.

"I know, but still. It's been over ten years since *Táta* died," I moaned. "Cecilia wasn't married to him that long."

Ben gave me a small smile. "I know it hasn't helped Cecilia that we've hidden some of *Otec's* things. And there is her party tonight, don't forget."

"How in the world could I forget about the party?" I held up my hands. "My palms have been raw all week from the extra scrubbings she's had me and the other maids do."

"That's probably how she managed to find some more of *Otec's* collectibles."

"She didn't find anything under the floor in the pantry, did she?" I asked, my eyes suddenly wide with fear. "I put *Máma's* locket there, along with *Táta's* pocket watch."

"I'm sure we'll find out," Ben said. "I just saw her hanging out the east tower window, yelling at the gardeners, and when I went to go pilfer some bread earlier, Betsy told me 'Her Ladyship' has to check on the barn's repairs on her way over here to us. She'll come for us last."

"Of course."

"*Of course.*" Ben mocked my tone. "So you'll have time to shake the soot out of your skirts."

"Huh?" I looked down and sighed. I had stayed up late reading by the fireplace, and my skirts were covered in a light coating of soot.

Why was it so hard to find the time to read, and then to have the joy of reading itself tampered with the cost of Cecilia's anger?

"Ben, help me." I began jumping up and batting the ashen dust off my apron. "She'll kill me if she sees my dress like this. She hates doing laundry any more than she has to."

"You mean she hates it when *we* have to do laundry any more than she wants us to. It's laughable to think she does any real work herself."

"She does all the accounting work. I've seen her doing it, even very late into the night in the library." I suddenly laughed. "Oh! I forgot to tell you. The other night, I actually saw her wearing her spectacles."

Ben smiled as he pushed my pallet and homemade pillow inside a small chest and grabbed a broom while using his crutch to push aside the rug. "I'll bet that was a sight," he said. "What did they look like?"

"They were wire frames," I said, "and they were perched on her nose like a chained bird, trying desperately to fly free. They made her nose look so big! I'd never noticed how long it is."

"We'll have to keep that in mind if we ever need emotional blackmail," Ben said.

"Yes, most definitely—"

"Ouch!"

I flinched as Ben's weak leg tripped over the book I had managed to hide under my pallet; once I recovered, I hurried over and picked it up, quickly thrusting it behind my back.

"I see you were in the library looking for books again," Ben said.

"I can't help it," I insisted. "Life is so dull without books."

"Life also gets much worse when Cecilia realizes you're reading these by the fire, getting them dirty, and demands we work more to earn back the cost."

I lowered my eyes. "We only have each other, Ben. Can't we have books, too?"

"Not while they're technically hers, and we have to pay for them."

The door snapped open with a melodramatic creak. "Pay for what?"

Instantly, we snapped to attention before our stepmother. While ten years had passed since our father died, and it had been eleven years since her marriage to him, Cecilia's face was nearly as fresh and fair as it had been on their wedding day.

Unless, of course, she was frowning, as she usually was when she looked at us.

After the long years of working as her servants, Ben and I were well acquainted with the flash of her temper and the guilt of her sermons.

"Good morning, my lady," I murmured delicately, curtsying in the fine manner *Múmu* had taught me.

"Save your curtsies," Cecilia snapped. "I have no time for your disruptions today. Tell me, what are you going to pay for?"

"A new dress," I said. I did not think God would mind the small misdirection. "I heard that Madame Balthazar down at the market has a bolt of new silk in from the East, and I'd like to try to earn some money to pay for it."

Between dresses and books, I was more than happy to let Cecilia think I wanted the dresses more. She was appalled at the thought of servants knowing how to read, let alone actually reading.

Her nose reflexively sniffed. "I doubt you'd be able to afford it, Eleanora. It would be a poor investment besides, considering you ruin the dresses you have now by sleeping close to the fire." She prowled around the room as she shook her head. She let out a disapproving *tsk, tsk* as she looked up and down at my servant's outfit.

I turned along with her, keeping the book behind me and out of sight.

Ben coughed, effectively distracting her.

She turned her gaze on him. "Benedict, are you ill?"

"No, ma'am," he said, bowing his head down to her ever so slightly.

"I have some items I need you to take to the market." Her eyes narrowed. "I'd like for you and Eleanora to take them today, and quickly. I also have a list of things you will need to pick up before His Grace arrives for the party tonight."

"Yes, ma'am," he said.

"See to it that you are both back in time to help with the dinner preparations," she said. "Betsy and Mavis are going to be extra busy, and we need all the hands we have to make sure the day is sufferable."

"Yes, ma'am."

"Stop that," Cecilia barked. "Don't use that tone with me."

Ben said nothing.

Part of me waited to see if Cecilia was going to give the same old lines to Ben:

You're lucky I am able to keep you, as a cripple wouldn't last long in the market streets or out in the fields.

I am more than willing to do my Christian duty to your father's memory, but you're enough of a man to know I could turn you out if you would ever indicate that was your desire.

You have no place here anymore; it is fortunate for you that you can be of some *help, given your regrettable condition.*

I should think you would be grateful to me, to keep you here with your sister, rather than thinking you deserve more.

Life does not guarantee you anything, and it's time to stop acting like I should feel sorry for you, rather than embracing what my good choices have brought me.

It was almost as if she had branded those words on Ben, deforming his heart as much as his leg. A moment passed, and from the small smirk on Cecilia's face, just barely peeking out from the thin layer of wrinkles, I knew we were all thinking the same thing.

I guess she knows that she doesn't have to say it anymore.

Still, I held my breath as she turned to face me. Over the years, I had learned to stop flinching; the one time I stopped her, back when she was more apologetic about the state of "poverty" my father left her in, she had me flogged. "As a servant girl should be," were her exact words on the issue.

"See to it that you have at least one clean outfit to wear tonight, Eleanora," she said. "I will need you to help with our guests."

Her impressive skirts swept around her, and before I could ask her who else besides the Duke was coming to dinner, Ben cut me off with a stern look.

I shut my mouth and nodded to him.

"You'll find the items to trade gathered in the back of the main house," she called back. "Go, and hurry now."

I finally allowed myself to wince. "She's getting shrilly," I said to myself.

"Old age comes to us all," Ben said. "Hopefully, we won't have to deal with her too much longer."

"How is our goal coming?" I lowered my voice by several degrees. "Are we any closer to Liberté?"

"Nora." Ben sighed. "We will need another year, at least."

I wanted to pout. But I gave Ben my best smile. "Only a year doesn't sound so bad." I almost hid my roughened hands in my skirts, before I recalled I was hiding the book I had taken from the library.

"Do you want me to return it for you?"

There was a playfulness behind his grin, and seeing it, I could not help but give in to the temptation to run and pretend I was far away from home. "I'll race you," I said. "Just let me get my shoes."

"If I win, you have to go to town yourself," he said. "I want to stay and help with the cooking."

"Help yourself to the cooking, more likely."

"The rich and fancy have people taste their food before they eat it," Ben said. "They aren't like us, Nora."

I ignored the part about the fancy. Ben and I had known our share of a comfortable world, before *Máma* was lost at sea and *Táta* died. "Are you hoping you'll get the job?"

"No, and that's a shame. It might help us get to Liberté faster."

"Ha!" I rolled my eyes. "I doubt Cecilia would let you be hired, even if it was the Duke of Moravia that wanted you as his personal food taster."

"Yes, where would she be without us?" Ben rolled his eyes. "She wouldn't be able to get on her high horse and claim she's doing her duty to our father's memory."

"I can't imagine her on any horse at all," I said, trying to add some levity. "Not in those gowns, with those horribly voluminous skirts. It's worth it to be a servant just so I can walk without falling over and drowning in a puddle."

Ben laughed, and I cheered at his mirth as I grabbed my shoes and laced them up. My brother knew little of joy in his life, outside of caring for me and working on his machines. It was only right that I tried to provide him with as much happiness as I could.

Especially since Cecilia seemed so determined to take it away, just as she had taken our inheritance away.

"Ow," I muttered.

"What is it?" Ben asked.

"My shoe." I held up the small slipper. "It has a hole in the bottom."

"I'll see if I can repair it while you're out on the town, you klutz." The smirk on his face might have made me mad if I did not know we relied on making each other laugh and keeping each other fighting.

"Ha!" I stood up. "You really think you'll beat me to the library?"

"*While* I'm holding the book." He lifted up his right pant leg to show me the latest brace he had designed for his crooked leg. "This model helps my balance a lot more. I used some spare iron from the blacksmith's shed. I don't even need my crutch to run."

"Run, maybe," I said, "but I'll still be able to beat you climbing into the kitchen windows!"

And before he could stop me, I tore out of the small servant's house and headed for the main house, laughing all the way.

Ben quickly managed to catch up to me. I could see his twisted leg moving with a straightened limp, and he had been right; his balance was kept in place as he ran.

As soon as I could feel him catching me, I twisted about, skipping through the pig's pen.

The mud and muck would surely slow him down, I thought, not too thrilled to be so competitive that it made me less than compassionate.

Ben did not seem to mind.

"Ha, nice try, Nora!"

As I watched, he pulled out the feeding trough and used it to slide through the muck. The pigs did not even see him.

And I did not really see them. I stumbled right into one, only managing to jump over him at the last moment.

Furious Ben had found a way to beat me, I grappled with the ivy vines, thick from years of growth in the Bohemian clime, and pulled myself up to the second floor of my father's mansion.

"Ha, yourself!" I called back, teasingly waving as I headed down the stone battlement.

Ben grunted in response, but I saw the smirk on his face as he trotted up a small tower of hay bales and hurried into a nearby window, only catching his leg briefly on the outer trim.

"Hey!" I rushed toward the door.

Only to be immediately stopped by my stepbrother.

"Where are you rushing off to?" he asked, as he lazed about in the doorway to the inner keep.

"I'm just going inside, Alex," I murmured, avoiding his eyes.

He looked too much like Cecilia that I did not like to look at him in general, but he had inherited her vanity along with her looks.

As I glanced up at him, waiting for him to move, I caught sight of the leer on his face, and I felt the sudden urge to hit him. He was looking down his nose at me, as though I was beneath him.

Which, considering my role in his household, even I had a hard enough time doubting. But I was a lady, a true one, just as my mother had been, and my father made me a knight's daughter.

"That's Lord Alex to you."

"Well, then it's Lady Eleanora to you," I spat back.

"I'd hardly bow to a servant, especially a hoyden such as you," he countered. "What kind of lady romps around on the battlements just before breakfast? One returning from an illicit, romantic tryst, maybe?" His gaze wandered down my dress, and I gave in to my hateful temptation.

My fist balled, and I struck him in the stomach before he could move.

"*Ack*." He gasped before doubling over in pain.

"Serves you right," I said, kneeing him in the face. I could feel the stark bluntness of the impact, and I was not surprised a moment later to see droplets of red slam against the stony walkway.

"You'll pay for that," he vowed, as his nose began to bleed.

"Oh, what are you ever going to do? Tell your mommy on me? She'll hardly think you're man enough to marry that countess then."

"I'll find a way to make you pay," Alex grunted, "if it's the last thing I do."

"I would gladly let you try, if it was indeed the last thing you would ever do," I yelled back, already moving past him and out the door of the next room.

It was no secret my stepbrother was a monster; Ben and I had caught him trying to coerce Betsy and some of the other younger maids into dark corners of the house a few years ago, and ever since then we made sure he was constantly watched.

All of *Táta's* playing around when we were younger looked more and more like a wise investment, I thought, as I arrived at my destination. Ben and I had learned to hit and fight as well as any siblings who shared the ups and downs of our lives, mostly thanks to each other, but plenty of others as well.

The halls around me were quiet and still. I burst through the double doors of the library and threw up my arms in triumph.

"Take that, Ben!" I twirled around and flopped into a chair. I decided it was the perfect place to greet him as he entered and found himself in second place.

There was just one problem with that.

"Take what?" Ben asked, all too innocently, from behind me.

I jumped up and swiveled around, the mud on my shoes making my feet more slick. "Oh, no."

"Yep, that's right. I'm the winner." The innocence was gone, and the arrogance had come.

My shoulders slumped over. "I guess this means I have to go into town by myself."

"You know it." Ben grinned. A moment later, he softened. "It might be for the best," he said. "If you go by yourself, you'll take longer. That'll give me some time to get the work done around here."

I sighed. "Anything to get away from Alex. I ran into him out on the battlements. That's why I lost."

"Then it is better you go," Ben said. "So when I beat him, you won't be around to take the blame."

"I already took care of it," I said, before diving into the details, telling Ben the story of how I had fought off our wicked stepbrother.

"In all seriousness, we need to practice your fighting some more," Ben said when I was done, and he was done laughing. "He'll be the master here soon, Nora."

"Not for some time, surely. Even if he gets this manor when he's married, they're only announcing the engagement tonight. It'll be at least another year before they get married and move in. That's plenty of time for us to get the funds we need for Liberté and then get out of here."

"I hope so. But that also gives him plenty of time to terrorize us." He came up and patted me on the shoulder. "I don't want anything happening to you, *ségra*."

Since I coveted his approval and affection, I quickly hugged him, before brushing off his concern. "We'll be fine, *brácha*," I assured him, using my own endearment for him in return. "Now, let me go. If I'm supposed to be back from town before tonight, I'd better get going. Alex might be a terror, but he's still nothing compared to his mother."

2

◊

If I had any other reason to be there, going into the city would have been my favorite chore. Over the last few years, I had grown accustomed to the sadness I felt when I sold my father's possessions, but I never tired of the wonder I felt when I wandered into the city.

As I packed up the small carriage and flicked the horse's reins, I breathed in deeply, tasting freedom's forbidden elixir. I had nothing of my own, except the time that was given to me, and I was reminded of this nearly every day since my father's passing. Going into the city was a respite from my reality, and like anyone who hungered after something so secretly and desperately, the tendency to hoard it and hide it came naturally.

It doesn't come senselessly, though.

That was why I pulled on Dox's reins, stopping at a small cottage not far from my home.

I hopped down from the carriage perch and knocked on the door. After waiting patiently for a long moment, I cupped my hands against my cheeks and hollered, "Tulia! It's me!"

The door creaked open, and one-half of a half-wrinkled face appeared before me. Despite her annoyed look, I grinned at the surly figure. "*Dobré ráno,* Tulia. I need a companion today."

Tulia rolled her pretty topaz eyes, gesturing toward the sun and curling her fingers, making a motion like she was checking the time.

"I know it's early," I said. "Cecilia's party is tonight, remember? She is on a tirade, preparing for His Grace's arrival."

Tulia had worked for my mother as a nursemaid and companion for several years. After *Máma* died, she took up residence at her cottage, keeping watch over Ben and me as best as she could. I was sure it was hard for her, especially because Tulia was never permitted inside our manor after Cecilia moved in. Cecilia hated "crippled folk," as she called them, and she seemed to have a particular animosity toward Tulia, who was a mute.

But Tulia was like a second mother to me—or maybe because of her age, more like a grandmother—and I sought her company as much as I could, even if it meant trouble.

From her doorway, Tulia shot me another bitter look, and I gave her my best smile.

"I'll bring you more tea next time," I promised, as she came over to the carriage, finally ready to head toward the heart of Prague.

Tulia climbed up beside me on the wagon's perch, bumped against me companionably, and waved her arms toward Dox. It was her way of signaling to me she was all ready to go, and there was no need to keep her waiting now that I no longer had to wait for her.

At her spirited movements, I laughed; Tulia was perpetually silent, but she had a way of speaking that left me in little doubt of her exact thoughts.

I jostled Dox's reins, and together we set off for the city.

Prague was the crown jewel of the whole kingdom of Bohemia, and I did not need to travel great distances to see that reality. The city skyline misted over with clouds, keeping itself steady on the edge of my dreams while it remained grounded in the roots of my blood.

The November fog cleared as the sun rose, leaving the city sharp at its edges and shimmering at its core. I breathed in the fresh air deeply as I surveyed my surroundings. The mishmash of newer housing clashed with the cramped townhouses in color as much as in design, further juxtaposed against the darkness of the old city walls. It was a strangely beautiful thing, ugly but still mesmerizing, to see the city growing even as it remained the same.

I knew convenience and change came with a cost, just like the new sewage system that was installed a few years after the Revolution. I did not know if it was always a fair exchange, and I did not know if the Lords and lawmakers always acted in the best interest of anyone but themselves. The political wars between the Bohemian Diet and the German Diet were legendary, and I considered myself too young and too poor to care as much as I might have.

When I had been younger, my father mentioned once that there used to be much more violence in Prague, but more effort was culled into political maneuvering than anything else. When I told *Táta* that sounded like a good thing, he said the expended effort was better going into the arts.

"Always remember, art is upstream from politics," he had once told me at bedtime, before pulling out a new book for us to read.

"What do you mean?" I asked.

"Art is supposed to inspire the highest level humankind has to offer. Politics is only agreeing on rules that one might use to engage with others, and slowly changing them with the hopes no one else will notice."

"Is that really how politics work?"

He cupped my cheek and smoothed back my hair lovingly, in that way he had always had with me. "Always so curious," he said. "Just like your mother."

Then he would kiss me goodnight, before reading to me until I fell asleep.

Tulia suddenly clapped her hands, and I blinked. "What is it?" I asked.

She nodded toward the city, urging me to go faster.

"Dox can only go so fast," I said, briefly reaching forward to pat my faithful steed. "Besides, you're the one who took her time this morning. Are you getting older and slower naturally, or were you just moving slowly on purpose?"

Tulia flicked her nose at me.

"Careful. God still knows you're cursing at me."

In reply, Tulia made even more obscene gestures at me, and I laughed. I was pleased to have had inherited her friendship.

Tulia waved her hand again, and I looked to see she was greeting a man with his own *leiterwagen* full of grain. She gestured to me, cupping her hands and rounding them out in a small oval.

"I should have enough to get some bread from the baker's." I glanced back at the goods in the carriage. "There's enough here that Cecilia won't miss a *koruna* or two."

Tulia gave a silent cheer, and my stomach concurred with her, giving a hungry rumble of its own.

I knew I should have eaten more, especially after fighting with Alex and racing with Ben.

"Alex is just terrible," I told Tulia, recounting my earlier tale of bravery and triumph. Even though I had lost the race to Ben, I held my head up high. I had stood up to my terrible stepbrother, and that was no easy task. Over the past ten years, Alex had grown much taller and with his schooling at Oxford complete, he had become even more insufferable.

And Alex was barely human before he went to London. Ben was right to worry about him.

"I can't wait until the day Alex goes too far," I told Tulia. "I'd really love to see him squirm."

Tulia grinned, and I could see her full smile, complete with its gaps of missing teeth.

My hands tightened carefully on the reins while Dox's feet hit the bridge stones hard and steady as we headed over the river.

"I wonder if this is how Aeneas felt," I mused aloud, "crossing into the Underworld."

Tulia pretended to yawn; she knew of my love for books, but she always insisted I read too much.

As soon as we entered into the heart of the city, heavy traffic and crowded streets forced us to a momentary stop. Carefully, I stood up on the coach box, only to see there was a funeral procession heading down Kaprova Street.

Tulia tugged on my skirt. "There's a funeral," I explained, surprised when she stood up herself. As she looked down the street, her expression changed from one of interest to something much darker.

"What is it?" I asked.

She held up a hand to me, telling me to wait. It was strange of her to be so blunt with me.

I heard angry yelling, the words mixed with German and Prussian. From the little German I knew, the man was yelling about the funeral.

"Sounds like a politician died," I said as we passed by, heading deeper toward the heart of Prague, where the markets were located.

Beside me, Tulia nodded. She was a mute, but I had a feeling she knew six or seven languages herself. When I was younger, she had caught me trying to learn how to swear in Italian, and when I switched over to Slovak and then Spanish, she had still known what I was saying.

Then, like any good mother figure, she had me learn to curse in French properly, telling me in her own way that if I was going to curse, I was going to curse like a lady.

"Who was it?" I asked her, and she used her secret language to spell out the man's name.

"Sigmund Artha?"

Tulia nodded again, and I was shocked I recognized his name. "He was *Táta's* doctor. He was close with the king, too. He came to my father's funeral. How sad that he died."

Tulia frowned angrily. I saw her fists clench and her eyes narrow with dangerous tears. When I asked her what was wrong, she responded with a vitriolic message.

He did not deserve to die.

"What happened?" I asked. Something was unusual about her demeanor, and I was suddenly worried. "Tulia?"

Tulia did not respond, as she was still looking over her shoulder, distraught at the sad scene. As we passed by the *Betlĕmskĕnàm* church, I saw Leopold Artha, Dr. Artha's brother, the former Minister-President of Austria. He wore his finest clothes and a stoic expression, but, even from where we were, I could see his eyes were blurry with tears and tiredness.

"He was a good man," I said. From what I remembered, Dr. Artha had been a polite man, even with all his strange idiosyncrasies. I could not imagine him as a politician, but his brother had likely compelled him to accept such a position.

Tulia was obviously upset about it.

"I will pray for his soul's peace." I made the sign of the cross over my heart, silently sending love to my mother and father as well.

Tulia joined me in the motions, but much more slowly. She kept her eye on the funeral as we turned down the street and headed for Old Town Square.

As we approached the market, I forgot the funeral and Tulia's frustration.

I was not indifferent to her confusion and pain, it was just very easy to get lost in the city and its beauty. Prague Castle dominated the background as we rode through the crowded city streets. We passed by the Old Town Hall, where the *Pražský orloj*, the Prague Astronomical Clock, continued to push the shadow of its dial around its concentric faces in an age-old dance. The *Kostel Matky Boží před Tynem* church, flanked with its high twin steeples, sounded with echoes of pipe organ music, mixing with the angry shouts, the hurried people, and the busy, face-freckled crowds. The city radiated a life and heart of its own.

I looked back at the goods Cecilia had ordered me to sell, the ones that let me reach back into my past, when my father was alive. I was carrying out a hellish task in the middle of my imaginary heaven, and I suddenly felt the weariness of the world sink into me even more at the irony.

"Well, Tulia," I said with a heavy sigh, "I hope this doesn't take too long."

I worked my way through the various traders and sellers, negotiating deals for hours as the sun passed overhead. It took no more than a couple of hours to find buyers for the things my father had spent his life collecting.

As I passed the last of the furniture pieces to their buyer, Tulia tossed me a warm roll.

"You did pay for this, right?" I asked.

She rolled her eyes again, but nodded. As she took a bite out of her own loaf, I saw the earlier sadness I had witnessed was not completely gone, just hidden.

Is she upset at Dr. Artha's death because he was friends with my parents?

It was possible Tulia had known him, although I could not remember ever seeing them together.

Still musing over her strange reaction, I took a bite of my bread. The warmth ran over my tongue and I felt a spiritual sense of strength return to me. "This is great. Who made it?"

Tulia nodded toward a baker delivery cart, and I frowned. *No wonder this is so good. French bread is expensive.*

"How much was it?" I asked, and Tulia made a few gestures.

It took me a few moments longer to realize what she was saying, and then I blushed. "You didn't have to trade your … amorous favors for the bread. I could have paid for it."

She grinned before she puckered up her lips and blew a few kisses toward me in reply. It was her way of saying that she did not mind having to allow a merchant a stolen kiss or two, knowing it was a gift for me.

"Still," I mumbled, embarrassed, "*Máma* would be upset with you for teaching me such behavior."

Tulia shrugged, and it was as if I could hear her tart reply. *You asked, didn't you?*

As much as I hated to give her credit, I ate the rest of the bread.

When I was finished, I turned back to the carriage. There was a small chest left, and that was it. Despite the nourishment of the bread, I felt my spirits plummet once more. There were only a handful of things that could be in the chest.

As I opened it, I saw my hunch had been correct. Two books, editions in prime condition, were carefully placed inside, and I despaired at the sight.

Táta's books were each small pinnacles of civilization, and only a bookstore could give me a good price for their treasured contents. I wept when Cecilia sold his first edition copy of *Le Morte d'Arthur*.

I carefully pried the two books out of the soft velvet lining. One book I recognized easily; it was one of my father's favorites, *The Prelude*, by William Wordsworth.

The other made me pause. It was an intricately carved book, with a strange symbol on the front. I opened it up to see a script written in unusual, foreign scrawl.

I sighed. My father's books were very precious, and very expensive. He would not have kept these two side by side if they were not of high value, but I hated to have to haggle with a bookseller not knowing what I was trying to sell.

"Well, I hope Cecilia's not hoping for a fortune," I said, noticing the small notes along some of the margins. "I'm not sure if I'll be able to sell this at all."

We approached the small bookshop, Wickward Bookseller and Publisher, with its name branded in golden gilt across the top of the building. I could only sigh at the oncoming headache.

I jumped down to the ground, eager to get the business over and done with. In my haste, I landed hard on the stony streets, and the small chest I had held went crashing down to the ground and fell open at the feet of a man.

"*Prominte*," I said quickly, rushing to hide my embarrassment. "I'm so sorry … " I felt my voice trail off as the man turned around.

I felt bad for staring, but there was something about him that demanded my full attention. Beneath his white turban, I saw his glossy black hair was combed back in the London fashion, and he had a trimmed mustache that would not have been out of place in a

Spanish court. His skin was a deep tan with a bronze undertone, hinting at his Turkish blood and bringing out the darker chestnut of his irises. From his own stare, he seemed just as surprised to see me, although I had to wonder why. I was perfectly average in Prague.

"*Naděžda*," he whispered, and I had to wonder what language he was speaking.

"*Pardonnez-moi*," I tried again, hoping the French would work. The Ottomans and the Turks had significant trade deals with France, and I could only hope he would know enough French to realize what I was saying.

I was gratified when he replied, "*Je vous pardonne, mademoiselle.*"

At that, I smiled, and then hurried forward to grab my fallen books. "*Merde.* They're covered in dirt now. Wickward better still give me a good price on these, or I'm going to be upset."

I hurried to wipe the books off with my skirt, making a face when I could not get a scuffmark off *The Prelude.* I caught sight of the man's Hessians as I stooped on the ground.

Why is he just standing there? He was still staring at me with a shocked look on his face.

Realizing I was staring at him again, he suddenly knelt down next to me. He produced a handkerchief, and when he held out his hand, I realized that he was offering to clean it. I handed him *The Prelude*, and he kindly wiped it off.

Behind me, Tulia was throwing a fit, pointing at him and waving her arms.

"Wait a moment, Tulia," I said to her, glancing over my shoulder. I had to wonder if she was afraid of him, or if she suspected him to be dangerous because he was a Turk. "He's almost done. He has the other book now."

As I turned around, there was suddenly a small, curved dagger in my face.

"*Merde*," I cursed again, this time much more loudly, as he lunged forward. I was terrified he was going to hit me, so I put my hands up.

I felt something pound against my chest, and I ended up falling into Dox.

I saw the Turk's dagger slice through one of the reins. At the sudden movement, Dox reared, almost sending the carriage toppling over.

"Tulia!" I called, but I watched as she leaped down and grabbed a hold of Dox's bridle.

I looked down to see *The Prelude* in my hands.

The other book was gone.

Meanwhile, the Turk headed down the streets. Anger suddenly boiled within me. "Stay here, Tulia! See if you can fix the wagon. I'm going to get my father's book back."

Before Tulia could signal to me not to go, I went.

As I was chasing the Turk through the crowded city streets, I mentally cried out to Ben, hoping he had managed to find someone to fix my shoes for me. The ones that I had borrowed from Betsy seemed to pinch more with every step.

"Come back!" I raked my mind for the German, French, English, and Czech words for "thief," as I began to pant.

I saw him round a corner ahead of me and instantly brightened.

I've got you now. There's a shortcut ahead.

I ducked through a small alleyway, skirting around sludge, piles of trash, and fallen laundry from one of the upper floor apartments.

When I came out on the other side, I pressed against the crowd.

I had taken a risk, and I was rewarded.

The Turk came barreling right into me. The second before he collided with me, I saw his eyes go wide.

My own face might have betrayed my fear, because a moment later, I felt him latch onto me. Together, we whipped around, and a second later, I saw we were back in the small alleyway, pressed between the buildings and in a fight.

"Give me my book back," I demanded, punching him hard. My left hand burrowed into his side, and he fell back against the wall.

"I just want my book." I stood over him, panting quietly. "I won't report you if you just give it back."

The curved dagger glinted off the small light of the alleyway. I could not say if I stood my ground out of bravery or fear.

"*Non, mademoiselle,*" the Turk replied, before he jumped up.

He feinted, and I lashed out a quick kick. He managed to land a quick blow to my leg.

"Whoa!" I lost my footing and stumbled, desperately trying to keep my balance.

Just as I managed to steady myself, I felt the chill of his blade next to my throat. In the seconds I had been distracted, he wound his arm around me and held me at his mercy.

"If you're going to take the book from me and threaten my life over it, I should at least be told why you want it so badly, shouldn't I?" I snapped, unable to stop myself from fighting even if I was only left with words.

He sighed. "*'Anti la tafhamin.*"

I frowned, angry and flustered, frustrated and embarrassed. "That's not telling me anything," I said. "I don't understand what you're saying."

Before he could respond, a new voice stepped into the conversation.

"*Ma aldhy yajri?*"

The Turk stilled behind me, shifting his focus from me to the young man who stood in front of us, blocking the entrance to the alleyway. I sighed. From his clothes, I could see this young man was clearly a street urchin, possibly homeless.

I was wondering if he would try to rob me too when he gave the Turk a quick bow, pulling off his cap in a gesture of respect. "*Ymknny musaeadatuk fi dhalik.*"

The Turk shook his head and said something else. The boy nodded and responded easily, and I grew more frustrated as their conversation continued.

"I don't understand either of you," I said. "But I will scream until someone comes to help if you don't let me go and if he doesn't give me my book back."

The street urchin smiled at me, before giving me a quick wink. "I'm sorry, my lady," he said. His voice was unusually calm and cheerful, despite the tense situation, and I was loathe to trust him.

"What is he saying?"

"It seems this gentleman believes that book to be his."

"It's not," I snapped. "It was my father's. I want it back."

He nodded in understanding before he talked to the Turk some more, who shook his head. Their arguments grew more terse, before finally the Turk seemed to give in.

The street urchin smiled as he turned to me again. "He will let you go. He wasn't expecting you to give chase."

I wrinkled my nose, ready to respond with a tongue-lashing that would have replaced any public execution when the Turk pushed me away, hard. My pinching shoe caught on the cobblestones, and I fell forward.

My scream was late, and because it was late, it was muffled. The other man jumped to my rescue, catching me close to his chest. I tasted the streets on his scarf as I gripped onto him. Behind us, the Turk disappeared.

"*Merde*," I shouted.

3

◊

I stood there, paralyzed with simultaneous shock and rage, as the young man tightened his grip on me. He seemed to be steadying himself as much as he was helping me.

"Let me go!" I insisted, suddenly realizing he was keeping me from any chance of pursuit. "He took my book."

"I rather think you should be grateful you survived the encounter, even if you lost the book."

I thought of the book, of how my father must have cared for it, protecting it after he procured it. "You don't understand."

"Why? It's just a book. And from how you dropped it earlier, it was a dirty one at that. I doubt you would get much for it, especially if you were going to see Wickward. He would have been unwilling to buy it, and he would have lauded every defect as he looked it over."

It was too tempting to hate him for the blatant superiority in his words at that moment.

"You wretch!" I finally came to my full senses and shoved myself out of his arms. "My father is dead. His books are among the last things I have of his."

I was a little infuriated to see the young man smile.

"Your father would be happier, I think, that you are still alive. So it was good that I saved you."

"What was the point in saving my life if you just made it harder?" I glared at my so-called rescuer, and I only grew more upset as he began to laugh.

"What's so amusing?" I asked through gritted teeth.

"Your logic. A hard life is still better than death."

Cecilia briefly came to mind. I did not know whether or not to agree with him.

He saw my hesitation, and I stopped to study him. Under his sloppy hat, he had darkish brown hair, with kind eyes the color of lightened shadows, a strange but lovely gray layered with silver. I was still unsure whether or not he was going to rob me, too; I was glad I had given *The Prelude* to Tulia. As his hand reached out for mine, I eyed him suspiciously.

"Well, if that is not enough to convince you that I have done you a service, perhaps I can make your life easier in another way."

When I did not allow him to take my hand, he gave me a deep bow instead, and I softened ever so slightly at his manners. A thief did not need to use manners.

As far as I know, at least.

"It only seems fair I help you once more, since I made your life harder, after all."

He did not push for me to accept his offer, but his politeness seemed to insist upon it.

"You can call me Ferdy," he added, as he straightened.

"Ferdy?" I wrinkled my nose. "That's a strange name."

Ferdy did not seem to take any offense. He laughed, before giving me a slightly crooked smile. It was, despite my attempts not to notice, quite charming. His whole face seemed to light up, and I was momentarily dazzled.

I was suddenly aware that we were still very close, standing in the small alleyway.

"You can blame both Bohemia and my family for that one, although 'Ferdy' seems more fitting for a poor man such as myself, rather than my proper name," he said, ignoring my discomfort. "'Ferdinand' is a Bohemian favorite, thanks to the king, and in my family, we have the same two or three names that get used again and again, and each generation is expected to surpass the greatness of the previous one."

I looked down at his slovenly clothes again, reliving the smell of what I suspected was tobacco smoke on his scarf. "I wish you the best of luck in that regard, then."

"Well, I have proven my worth for today at least," he said, looking back to the far end of the alleyway, where my assailant had slipped away. "After all, I saved a damsel in distress."

I could not stop myself from scowling at him. I had been protecting myself for the last decade, only occasionally with Ben's help, and I did not appreciate being reminded of my failure.

But he was obviously poor, and he was right; he had stepped in to protect me. If I let myself, I could still feel the cool edge of the Turk's curved blade held against my neck. Pushing that thought aside, I decided that Ferdy had earned some merit.

"Well, then." I gave him a grand curtsy, mimicking his own introduction. "You have my thanks. I'll remember you in my prayers tonight. Surely the Lord himself will repay you for your trouble. Now, if you will pardon me, I must go."

"God might reward me later, but I'd prefer to collect now, if you please."

I knew it! I felt a rush of vindication. He was just after a reward.

I steeled myself against him. "So you would have me reward you?"

"*Absolument.*" The cheeky smile was back, and I was suddenly aware that he was flirting with me. I did not know whether to blush or scoff. While I was a servant in my home, I was still born a lady, and I knew better, even if he did not.

"Well, unfortunately, Mr. Ferdy," I said, emphasizing his name with all the power to dismiss him, "I do not have anything with which to pay you—"

"Ferdy, please."

"—so you will have to leave it up to providence for your remittance. Good day." I turned away from him and headed down the street. Already, I could see Tulia maneuvering Dox toward me. She waved eagerly, placing her hand on her heart and taking a deep breath.

"I was not talking about money," Ferdy said from behind me. "In return for my services, I request only to know your name, my lady."

Groaning silently, I turned to face him once more. "Why?"

"Why not?"

"It hardly seems proper." Tulia arrived behind me, and upon seeing Ferdy arguing with me, immediately leaned down to better hear our conversation.

"I imagine it's very improper in some circles to interrupt a thief about his business, too," Ferdy pointed out. "But here we are."

I turned back to Tulia, frustrated and confused. I needed to get home soon or Cecilia would have me beaten again, although she would probably do that anyway.

The thought disappeared as I realized Tulia was suddenly smiling sweetly at Ferdy. She nodded her head toward me in that manner of hers, compelling me to give in.

No, I thought, recalling the kisses she had given earlier to the baker as payment for our bread. *She cannot possibly be on his side in this matter.*

"My lady?"

Glancing back, I eyed Ferdy suspiciously. He did not seem to be sorry in the least for making me uncomfortable. And while there was nothing inherently wrong with him, something did not seem right. I could not explain what it was. Behind me, I heard Tulia start to fuss.

I resigned myself to my fate. *I cannot believe I am doing this*. My hands tightened around my skirt.

But before I could properly introduce myself to Ferdy, he nodded to the book lying beside Tulia on the perch. "What book is that?" he asked. "It seems that you still have some left after all."

"That one? It's a first edition of *The Prelude*, by Wordsworth." I almost told him it was my one of my father's favorite books, but I decided not to mention that. While Ferdy had saved me, there was no need to pretend we were close.

"I can get you a good price on that, if you're interested in selling it," Ferdy said.

His offer briefly distracted me from my suspicion. I arched my brow delicately. "Do you even know who Wordsworth was?"

"I happen to know what 'first edition' means, if that is what you really want to know," Ferdy replied. "And that if it's a book, Clavan will probably like it."

"Who's Clavan?"

"A friend of mine. He collects rare books. Including first editions. I can assure you, he pays much better than Wickward, too. Wickward is as tight as a drum, but Clavan's especially cheerful, especially if you get him full of liquor first."

"Does your friend perchance have a drinking problem?"

"Why, yes he does," Ferdy said, so guilelessly I almost laughed. He straightened his cap. "But he's familiar enough with me that I think I can use that to your advantage."

I bit my lip. I needed a good price on the book, especially since the other one was gone. Cecilia would be upset if she thought I did a poor job selling our goods. "Where is his shop?" I asked. "Is it near?"

"It's further east of the bridge, down by the Vltava."

"In the Jewish Quarter?" I asked.

For the first time, I caught him off guard. His eyebrows raised a little, but he nodded. "Yes, my lady. Clavan works out by the *Josefskà,* the Jewish Quarter."

"I see." It was a little further than I would have liked to go; I had to get back to the manor soon.

"Does this offend you?" Ferdy asked. His voice was careful and his tone was casual, but he was suddenly less at ease.

"Oh, no, that's not it," I said, blushing. "I was just worried about the time. I have to return home soon."

"Well, let us not waste any more time on it," Ferdy said, his quick smile returning. "I'll take you there, and Clavan will buy your book, and then you can head back to your home. Here, let me help you up."

He held out his hand to help me back up into the carriage.

After all the trouble I had gone through, I was tired. Tulia was nodding at me, giving me her stern looks to tell me to accept. And I needed a good price on *The Prelude.*

That is why I allowed Ferdy to take my hand—or so I told myself. But I laid it down gently in his, intending to suffer through it, his hand wrapped protectively around mine, and I found myself unable to resist twining my fingers into his.

As I sat down on the carriage box, I looked down at him again, suddenly nervous. "My name is Eleanora."

Ferdy bowed properly once more. "It is a great pleasure to meet you, Lady Eleanora." He gave me a thoughtful look, before he frowned.

"What is it?"

"Your name is too long."

"Hey!" I objected. "It is not."

"You're the one who said mine was strange. I can say yours is too long."

Beside me, I could tell Tulia was amused. She seemed even more amused when I scowled at him and he laughed.

"I'll call you Ella instead. It's a lovely name for a lady—suitable for a princess, in fact. Now, give me the reins. I'll lead the way to Clavan's shop."

I decided not to bother to tell Ferdy that my family called me Nora as Tulia eagerly tossed him Dox's hastily repaired bridle. He intrigued me, but that did not mean I had to give him any intimate details.

"If you are too lazy to say my name properly," I said, "it's unlikely you'll be able to accompany us to the Jewish Quarter. It is several blocks away."

"Maybe I am trying to conserve my energy so I can make the effort. Besides, it is only proper for a lady to be escorted. And you are very concerned with what is proper, aren't you, Lady Ella?"

Tulia nudged me with her arm. She wanted to hear the details of what happened, but I said nothing as we made our way through the various streets. Ferdy did not need to hear how angry and frightened I had been during the whole encounter with the Turk, and I did not want to admit I was still skeptical of Ferdy himself. Several minutes passed as I watched him, more curious than I wanted to admit.

It was only as we came upon the Vltava that I began to ask him questions.

"How did you know I was a lady?" I asked, scooting forward on my seat as we faced the edge of the Jewish Quarter. "I'm dressed like a servant."

In front of me, Ferdy shrugged. "Everyone lies about something. Once you figure that out, it's easier to figure people out."

"Oh."

He glanced over his shoulder, his eyes sparkling like lightning across stormy clouds. "Don't worry, Ella. Your secrets are safe with me."

I was about to assure him I did not need him to keep any of my secrets when he added, "Clavan's place is just up ahead. I'll pull over here. Does your grandmother want to stay with the cart?"

"Grandmother?" I suddenly realized he meant Tulia. I was surprised to see the amused look on her face, but I was glad she was not insulted. "Oh. She's not my grandmother. She's my companion. And she is going to come with me."

"My apologies." He held out his hand, waiting for me to take it.

My stomach suddenly twisted into knots. I jumped down on my own, brushing passed him, ducking my face away from his. I told myself that if he was going to call me by half of my given name, he could not expect me to take his gestures of gallantry seriously. But, as I watched him help Tulia down in the same manner of a gentleman attending to a proper lady, I felt a layer of shame settle on me.

Tulia handed me *The Prelude* firmly; it was her way of reminding me to be brave and kind, as my mother would have wanted, and that sometimes it required more bravery to be kind.

"Clavan works here," Ferdy said, pointing to the sign above us. "The Cabal."

"The Cabal?"

Ferdy nodded. "He enjoys the absurd and the eccentric, like all the elites. But he is a good man, and you'll see what I mean, the more you get to know him."

Ferdy led us into the tavern, and at once, a new world reached out to welcome me. It was dark inside, with homey colors and elegant fixtures; the air clashed with a battle of smells and moods, with food cooking and foreign spices, the taste of fine alcohol, and the distinct cloud of tobacco smoke—all of it converged together to give a strange and immersive sense of otherworldliness.

As Ferdy led me to the bar, a dark and rich oak, polished to a shine, I felt my eyes wander around, trying to take in the small tables and plush chairs, the silk wallpaper, and the quiet rattling of newspapers.

"Josef Clavan, you old kook," Ferdy called. "Where are you? In the kitchen, busy under your wife's skirts, looking for something to do?"

I blushed at his insolence and intimate joking. I felt Tulia twitch with silent laughter beside me.

"If you're distracting Helen from her cooking, your customers are going to be upset."

Seconds after Ferdy's taunting, a door opened and a man walked out. The lights of the tavern glistened on his bald head and twinkled off the small, round glasses on his slightly crooked nose. He rolled up his shirtsleeves as he walked over to us. "Well, if it isn't Ferdy," he said. "Should I even count you as a customer, since you have yet to settle your tab?"

"You know my word is as good as gold," Ferdy said with a friendly chortle. "And speaking of my tab, I'm going to help take care of it with your help today."

Clavan cocked an eyebrow and gave Ferdy a smirk. "Is that so? Enlighten me, you knucklehead."

"Let me start by introducing you to Ella here." Ferdy reached out and took my arm, pulling me forward. "She's a lady I rescued earlier today, when a thief was after her books."

"Well then, it sounds like she's had a hard day." Clavan took my hand in his over the bar and bowed over it. "Lady Ella, is it?" he asked. "I can't imagine which was worse for you—dealing with the thief or getting stuck with this rogue as your hero." He gestured toward Ferdy, and I could not help but laugh.

"I'm not done deciding," I replied, and Clavan nodded approvingly.

"Smart lady, Ferdy," he said. "You're already not worthy of her."

"Don't I know it," Ferdy agreed. "Which is why I can at least buy her a drink. Put it on my tab, won't you? And one for her companion, too."

"I would say it's only appropriate." Clavan hurried to get us our drinks. "Perhaps too appropriate."

"And yet, not proper at all," I muttered, before Tulia nudged me.

Clavan handed me a small glass of beer, and it struck me just how inappropriate this whole scene was. I was a lady, I was not supposed to sup with my vendors, I was not supposed to allow myself to be led around by a street urchin, and I was not supposed to visit any taverns.

I was not supposed to chase down any thieves, either.

For all Ferdy captivated me, I finally allowed myself to see the absurdity of my situation with a smile.

Tulia put her hand on my arm, giving me a reassuring pat. I was not comforted as Clavan handed her a shot of French whiskey, telling her he knew a connoisseur when he saw one, but I decided I could relax.

Not senselessly, though. I put my glass down after a small sip, just in case. I recalled Ferdy saying that Clavan had a drinking problem—and indeed, he probably did, working in an establishment such as his, with temptation all around. I was not going to lose my wits as Ferdy attempted to coax Clavan free of his.

If Ferdy was actually going to do that at all. I was already starting to see Ferdy joked about any number of things, and it was hard to tell what he was serious about and what he was not. His irreverence was as dizzying as it was fascinating.

"Where's Jarl?" Ferdy asked, looking around. "I was hoping to see him today. I found a new pipe merchant he might like, one that trades with a plantation in San Salvador."

"Jarl's working, since he has a steady job, unlike you," Clavan said, sitting down across a table from us.

"Only because that was your requirement for him."

"Well, if he's going to marry my Faye, and Faye says he is, and since she and her mother are their usual, insistent selves on the matter, he has to keep a job. I won't have him standing out on the streets, waving a sign around, asking for a new job every other day."

"That means you're allowing some poor businessman to take the risk and employ him, though."

"Is that why you have yet to get a job and keep it?"

As Clavan and Ferdy talked and laughed together, I tightened my grip on *The Prelude.* Was this really worth the trouble?

Before I could wonder too long, Ferdy said my name, and I became the focus of the conversation.

"We're boring Ella with our discussion," Ferdy said. "And since it was hard enough to get her to come here, let's talk business, Clavan."

Clavan gave me a smile—a genuine one, not the smirk he had given to Ferdy. "Well, Lady Ella, if I did not know Ferdy here as well as I did, I would wonder what kind of woman would associate herself with him. But I'm sure I can help you free yourself from him if needed."

I eyed Ferdy carefully. "Well, I'll be sure to hold you to that then, Mr. Clavan."

He chuckled. "Ferdy mentioned books earlier. I assume he's brought you to me in order to see if I am interested?"

"I gather that is the reason. He said you collect rare books, as my father did before he died. This is the latest book in his collection I've been ordered to sell." I carefully reached out and handed him the copy of *The Prelude.*

He shifted his glasses up to the bald crown of his head as he studied it. "Beautiful etching," he observed, and I decided I already liked him.

As if Ferdy read my mind, he nodded. "See, Ella? I told you Clavan was a better buyer than Wickward."

"Wickward?" Clavan huffed. "I'm surprised that ancient blowhard is still in business, considering how well he treats his customers. Not to mention his books."

"I admire any man who has the courage to make his love of writing and books into a business," I said softly, thinking of my own dreams of Liberté, the small bookshop Ben and I wanted to open once we made enough money to escape from Cecilia. "Even Wickward."

"True enough," Ferdy declared. "What else would the alcoholics and addicts do to relieve themselves from the stress of their addiction, if not write? It's best that we keep them in business, so Clavan can stay here in business, too."

Clavan put his glasses back down on his nose. "You're in a rare mood today, Ferdy. I see Lady Ella is acting as a tonic for your own addiction to trouble."

"A tonic to which I might well find myself newly addicted," Ferdy agreed, and I blushed. He glanced over at me, suddenly thoughtful and sincere, as he added, "If for no other reason than she's too easy to tease."

I decided to ignore him. He was unsettling me, and I did not like it. Or at least, I did not like that I liked it so much.

"Well, Mr. Clavan, what do you think of the book?" I asked, shifting my focus back to sales.

"I'd love to add it to my collection. And as I'm partial to Wordsworth, I'll even settle Ferdy's account here at the bar as his finder's fee."

"Much obliged, my good man," Ferdy cheered, lifting his cup in celebration. His eyes met mine over the rim of his glass. "And my good lady, too."

Moments later, Clavan handed me a small pouch of *koruna*, and upon feeling the weight, I felt much better about my decision to follow Ferdy to the Cabal.

"Thank you, Mr. Clavan," I said. "I hope next time I will be able to bring you another work you will like."

"I do not merely like Wordsworth. His work is among the most prized in my collection. His wisdom and insight are too keen to miss, for all the poetry he hides even in his prose." He glanced over at me. "Have you read his work?"

"Some," I said. "More of his poetry than his prose."

"There's magic to be had in his poetry," Clavan said. "But there is more freedom in his prose."

I saw the reverence he held for the book and its writer, and smiled. *Táta* would be happy with my choice of buyer. And Cecilia would be happy with the money, even if it came from a Jew.

"Then I will have to read his other work," I replied, and Clavan's eyes twinkled warmly at me.

"You long to be free?" he asked, and it was almost as if he had spoken into my soul.

I nodded. "Yes."

"From what, if I might ask?"

"My stepmother would be a good start," I admitted, half-watching as Ferdy chatted away at Tulia, trying to figure out some of her silent signals. "She is the one making me sell my father's books in the first place."

"I wish you luck in that regard," Clavan said. "I know the pain that comes with dealing with a tyrant, especially one who is a parent. But freedom is found in truth and the struggle for it, and if you are as determined as you seem, I believe you will find it one day."

"Thank you," I said, touched and humbled. Clavan had a way of speaking that seemed to release calmness and hope into the world.

"You're welcome. It was a pleasure meeting you, Lady Ella. Take care—especially if you're going to go around with this *schlemiel*." He nodded toward Ferdy, and I laughed again.

"There are far worse people than me running around Prague." Ferdy grinned. "And you know it, Clavan."

"Speaking of which, did you hear anything new about the Artha case? Eliezer sent me a message asking for more details."

Behind me, Tulia went still. I caught her concern and quickly leaned in closer.

Ferdy sighed. "A runner saw him leaving the Church of Our Lady of the Snows after taking confession. He was stabbed by a man wearing a servant's coat as he was leaving and then left for dead."

Dr. Artha was murdered? My eyes, wide with shock, met Tulia's. She did not seem surprised at all to hear the news.

"Hmm. That doesn't give a thief a lot of time to ask for money." Clavan frowned. "Anything else?"

"I've talked to a few sources, but nothing else odd or suspicious," Ferdy said, his voice grim. "The former Minister-President blames the Jews for his brother's death, but the king's guard suspects the Nationalists."

"You are talking about the politician who was buried today, aren't you?" I asked.

"My apologies, ladies," Clavan said. "I forgot it is hardly proper conversation."

I waved my hand, brushing it aside, knowing Tulia would appreciate the chance to hear more. "No, no. I am interested in hearing about what happened. What can you tell me?"

Clavan and Ferdy exchanged a quick glance, before Clavan shrugged. "Sigmund Artha was a medical consultant for the king before his brother promoted him to a political advisor. He and I were friends, since we shared several interests. He sent a message to me a few days ago, declining his weekly invitation to the Cabal. He mentioned he had reason to believe he was being followed. He was killed only a day later."

"This is not entirely unexpected, unfortunately," Ferdy said. "Several politicians in Prague have been threatened of late. Even Dr. Artha's brother received a threat, which is rumored to be the real reason he stepped down from his position as Minister-President. There have been two murders like his in the last several months, where it appears to be a hasty mugging or a gruesome accident, and the Jews have been blamed. Others have died, too, but under less unusual circumstances."

"Less unusual circumstances that seem much odder when considered who gains from their death, anyway," Clavan murmured thoughtfully.

"That sounds terrible," I said, suddenly very glad I was a servant in my own home, rather than one to the lords of Bohemia. As much as Cecilia could rail and wail, I doubted she would ever try to kill me.

God forbid she would have to do her own laundry or hire someone else to do it for her.

"It is terrible." Ferdy gestured toward the Cabal. "Eliezer, our other friend, has been gathering information on the cases. If the murderer is Jewish, he wants the Jews to see to it that this person is caught and tried. But so far, we have not found any solid leads."

Clavan sighed. "When something like this happens, the Jews need to be the ones to take care of it, or our silence will be seen as support."

"Why would a Jew kill Dr. Artha?" I asked. "Was it because he was Catholic?"

"Jews and Catholics do have a terrible history. However, Sigmund was good friends with me and Eliezer. That is why others, like his brother, condemn us in this matter," Clavan said with a shrug. "Sigmund also worked with Eliezer's wife, who is a midwife, several times. He was her source for a lot of her herbs and medicinal supplies."

"That is hardly fair for the Minister-President to blame the Jews."

"Many things in life are not fair," Clavan reminded me. "With increased tensions between the German Diet and the Bohemian Diet, many prefer it that the Jews are to blame for things like this. I am not surprised to hear that the king's guard actually suspects the Bohemian Nationalists."

"It is a sad story all around," Ferdy said. "The runner said Dr. Artha died calling for Father Novak, one of the priests at the church."

I thought of the rosary beads Dr. Artha had kept on his bag. "I'm sure he had enough patients who requested the same thing."

Beside me, Tulia was rigid with muted anger. I pressed against her, offering a small gesture of comfort while we said our farewells.

Clavan saw us out, inviting us to come again as he gave us a kind smile and a small wave, before disappearing behind his doorway.

As we made our way to the carriage, Ferdy grinned. "Well, that was a nice visit, even with that last little bit."

I nodded. "Yes, it was very nice. I enjoyed coming to the Cabal."

"See, Ella? You sold your book. I've made your life much easier now."

"According to your friend, that's quite a risk I took." I had been suspicious of Ferdy's kindness before, but after the visit to the Cabal, I knew that it was quite genuine. I gave him a smile of my own and allowed him to take my arm as we walked toward Dox and the carriage.

"Any lady who would follow after an armed thief can surely summon the nerve to gamble every once in a while." Ferdy offered Tulia his hand and helped her up to the carriage perch.

"Gambling is a sin."

"Well, that's why it's so fun then, right?" Ferdy laughed. "But you know that some would say it is just misplaced hope and faith. Sometimes it is occasionally rewarded."

"Are you one of those people?"

"It was a gamble earlier, stepping between you and your book thief." Ferdy leaned against Dox comfortably, taking a long moment to stare at me.

I stared back, before I felt the unbearable heat of my blush. "Ever the charmer, aren't you?"

"I would be happy to give you a further chance to see just how charming I can be," Ferdy said. "Next time you come to the city, ask for me. Most of the merchants in Old Town Square know of me and can point you in the right direction."

I saw Tulia heave a silent sigh at my hesitation.

"You should come back here when the others are around," Ferdy said. "Between Jarl and Faye, and Helen and Eliezer and Eliezer's wife, it is always a riot."

"It was very enjoyable meeting your friend, Mr. Clavan." I had never planned for this kind of conversation, and it was frustrating that I liked it.

"We can see each other again, then?"

I bit my lip. I knew Cecilia would only be too happy to forbid me to go into the city if she found out about Ferdy.

He took my hand again. "Come on, Ella. Be brave and take a risk."

There was something about him, I thought. Something that made me nervous and excited, somehow certain and completely unsure at the same time.

"Sometimes when you gamble, you lose," I said quietly.

"I haven't lost yet, where you're concerned." Ferdy leaned closer to me. "Will you come and see me again?"

I could not refuse him—or myself.

"I'd like to," I finally admitted. "But I really must be going for now. I have to go home and help get ready for tonight. My stepmother is throwing a party for a special guest."

"So, you like parties? Are you going to the Advent Ball this year, then?"

"Advent Ball?" I shook my head. "I've never heard of that one."

"Empress Maria Anna celebrates the Advent each year. A lot of the nobility and aristocracy come to the castle to join her for mass and celebrate afterward. It is the only ball that the royal family still hosts every year for Bohemia."

"That sounds lovely, but I have never been to one before."

"Here." Ferdy pulled a scroll out of his pocket. He jerked the wax seal off the letter and tore off the heading. "Take it. I'm sure your stepmother would love to be invited."

I glanced down at the crinkled sheet of vellum. It was indeed an invitation to the Advent Ball, hosted by their imperial highnesses at Prague Castle.

"How did you get this?" I asked.

Ferdy smiled. "Sometimes I work as a runner, which is why Clavan still lets me come in out of the cold every once in a while."

"Then won't someone else be missing an invitation?" I ran the torn stationary between my fingers where the recipient's information had been ripped away. There was an ugliness to the frayed edges, but I could not tear my eyes away from the fine lettering. "You'll get in trouble for this, won't you?"

"It will be worth it all if you will come."

"But—"

"Just take it, Ella, please. And come."

"But I wasn't invited."

"They won't turn you away. You're a lady, Ella," he insisted. He gave me an assessing gaze. "Aren't you? You weren't lying before?"

"Well, no, I am a lady, but—"

"Excellent. And since that is the case, I swear on my life, and all of my honor, you will not be turned away. So, come. I will see to it that you have fun."

"Will you be there?" I asked.

"Yes. I've also worked as a server before, at different soirees."

"I thought Clavan said you didn't have a job."

"I don't have a job. I have several."

As much as Ferdy intrigued me, I still felt unsure. "I know we have met under unusual circumstances, Mr. Ferdy—"

"Ferdy, please, Ella." He flashed me one of his charming smiles, and I was distracted enough to stop talking.

Despite his impudence and relentless flirting, something about him made me look twice and still left me curious. I stared at him in the dimming sunlight, transfixed and mesmerized, and I felt angry I was not free to enjoy myself, that I was not free to allow myself to feel happy at his attentions.

As the clock tower struck the hour in the distance, Tulia tapped me on the arm, letting me know it was time to go. She probably thought she was saving me from embarrassing myself—or from Cecilia's wrath, should I be late in returning.

I sighed. "I have to go," I said.

Ferdy nodded. There was an understanding, if unsatisfactory, look in his silver eyes. "It was truly my great pleasure in meeting you, my lady." He gave my hand a final squeeze before stepping back. Ferdy bowed gallantly as I flicked the reins and we headed off.

As we were about to turn back toward the bridge, I glanced over my shoulder to look at him once more.

Ferdy was gone, and I already missed his cocky grin.

Sighing, I rolled up the torn scroll in my hand and pressed it deeply into the hidden pockets beneath my skirt. Tulia left me to my thoughts, and it was only as we pulled up to her cottage that I wondered if she was still upset at Dr. Artha's passing.

As much as the day felt like a very strange dream, I needed to focus in order to get through Cecilia's party. The Duke of Moravia was coming back into town for the first time since my father's funeral, in order to finalize the engagement between his daughter and Alex. Of all nights I would have to be prepared, it was this one.

4

◊

Hours later, I was still mulling over the events at the market. Mostly, I kept reliving my time with Ferdy. Part of me hated how much I thought of him and his irresistible, irreverent smile.

But thinking of Ferdy was a welcome distraction. My feet were aching in the newly repaired shoes Ben had brought me, my back was sore from walking all over the castle, and I could feel my hair falling out of its pins as I changed out linens, scooped up laundry, and mopped up messes.

I was just about to head to the kitchens to check on dinner when Ben came up beside me in the hall.

"I heard Cecilia was pleased with the money from the market," he said as he matched his pace to mine. "Even though she was upset it took us so long."

"It's money. Why would she be upset at all, other than when there's too little?" I asked, blinking away Ferdy's face from my thoughts. "Wait. Did she know you were home while I was gone?"

"No." Ben grinned. "I've been running around the castle, gathering information."

"You've known the Duke of Moravia was coming since Alex finished his last semester at Oxford," I reminded him. "What more do we care? What more *should* we care?"

"If we're going to survive here with Alex in charge, I thought it would be best to make sure we have the upper hand. And a lot of that includes collecting information that is not readily shared with us—or anyone else."

"You only make people angry when it comes to blackmail. Cecilia's glasses are one thing. Business with the manor is another."

"We have both been spying on Cecilia's movements for years, between your unauthorized trips to father's dwindling library and my midnight forays into the kitchen. Besides, how did you think I found

Betsy giggled, seeing my apparent confusion. "It's the family of the general who defeated Napoleon."

"Oh. Yes, I see."

"They're a prominent family in England, thanks to the Duke of Wellington's service to the Crown," Betsy said. "I wonder why they've come."

The question of their arrival stumped me as well. I watched as others alighted from the carriage. Among them were two men wearing greatcoats and hats. Because of the rain and shadows, I could not make out their features much more than to know they were gentlemen.

I tapped my fingers together thoughtfully as Graves opened the door. From the angle I was watching, I saw they entered with very little hindrance, despite the butler's attempts to prove himself one.

"What do you think?" Betsy whispered.

"Nora, what's going on?" Mavis asked. Her brown eyes, the same shape as Betsy's, blinked back unshed tears. "Her Ladyship never told us she had more guests arriving. What do we do?"

"Do only as you are told," I said in a hushed voice. "I don't think these are guests of Cecilia's."

"She's going to be so upset with us!" Mavis pouted. "She's going to punish us severely after this."

"You will be fine," I assured her. "The responsibility is mine."

"I don't think we can be sure," another maid said softly. "Madame Cecilia is very clearly upset by the sight of the new arrivals."

Scooting toward the hall entrance, I saw that she was right; the hall was chittering with the small talk between my stepfamily and our guests one moment, and in the next, everyone went silent and still.

I watched as Cecilia stood up, prepared to do battle. "Who do you think you are, coming here without an invitation? And you, Graves, how could you let them in?"

As far away as I was, I could still see Graves' throat convulse with stress.

Before he could answer, the lady reached up and removed her dark veil. Her gray hair was piled up onto her head in an intricate style, and I could see her high forehead and classic British features; her heart-shaped face became an ironic quality as I watched her. She had the face of a lady, but wore the smile of a viper. And when she spoke, I felt the vibrations of her words echo throughout the whole castle.

"Perhaps the better question, Lady Cecilia, is who do you think you are, and what makes you think you can keep me from entering at all?"

The small party began to murmur uneasily amongst themselves once more. I slipped out of the kitchen another step, careful to stay in the shadows of the servants' entrance.

I could not stop watching Cecilia attempt to stare down her uninvited guest. She was fighting a battle she would never win, and I found myself looking forward to the coming spectacle.

"I am the mistress of this manor," Cecilia insisted. "My husband died and left it to me. It is mine by right of inheritance."

The lady's smile curved, suddenly even more dangerous than before. "Well, if that is what you think, let me answer your first question and introduce myself properly."

She inclined her head, only by mere degrees. "I am the Dowager Duchess of Wellington, Penelope Ollerton-Wellesley, in service of Her Majesty, Victoria, by the Grace of God, of the United Kingdom of Great Britain and Ireland Queen and Defender of the Faith."

"That means very little to me." Cecilia looked to the Duke of Moravia in a hurried manner. Her sallow cheeks brightened with fury. From Lord Maximillian's expression, I could see he was no longer annoyed by the interruption. Rather, he was now looking at Lady Penelope with undeniable interest and curiosity.

"Wellesley, did you say?" he asked, and Lady Penelope gave him a shrewd nod.

I put my hand over my mouth, trying to hide my smile. I did not know why a dowager duchess from the other side of Europe would come and visit Cecilia, but it was nice to see someone displace her.

"Well," Lady Penelope said, her voice tight, "it meant considerably more to my son-in-law, who was your husband as well as the husband of my daughter."

My world began to crumble at that moment, as I realized who Lady Penelope was.

"Grandmother?" My mouth dropped open in shock as I heard myself speak.

Behind me, I could feel the stares of Betsy, Mavis, and the other maids all turned on me, while Lady Penelope shifted her gaze in the direction of my hiding spot.

A memory of my mother, back when I was only five, came back to me. I remembered her as she worked through brushing my hair, lamenting my knots, even as she awed over my Bohemian curls. "Grandmother would adore you, just for your curls," she whispered, before telling me stories of how her mother would always brush her hair, long and straight, each Sunday before church.

The memory faded, and I found myself still concealed in the shadows of the servant entrance. My grandmother was searching for me, and I suddenly felt completely trapped as her eyes slid over the darkness around me.

"Who is there?" she asked.

My hand covered my mouth. I felt foolish, I felt trapped; I was unsure of what to do, or if indeed, I should do anything at all.

I was not the only one who seemed beyond words. Cecilia stared at her, the wrinkles on her forehead piled with stress lines and her mouth flapping open and closed, as though she was trying to say something, but God in his goodness was refusing to let her words sully the earth and its atmosphere.

It was only when Cecilia finally found her voice again that I was released from my indecision.

"That's no matter. You are trespassing in my home, and I will deal with you."

"Unfortunately, you are wrong on both accounts," Lady Penelope replied. "This is not your home, and my man of affairs shall take business with your man of affairs. In the meantime, while we settle the details that have been neglected since the death of my daughter, I will take up residence in the manor's west wing."

Cecilia sputtered, unable to form a coherent response.

Dismissing Cecilia, Lady Penelope turned to Lord Maximillian. "It is a pleasure to make your acquaintance, Your Grace. I apologize for the intrusion. Perhaps over the next few hours we will be become better acquainted as you begin to search for new lodgings."

Lord Maximillian blinked. "Beg pardon, Your Grace," he began, "but is this a very opportune moment to make your acquaint—"

Cecilia found her voice in time to object. "Max, I beg your patience in this matter."

"You cannot expect one such as His Grace to stay here while the ownership of this estate is being debated by men of law," Lady Penelope said. She added enough abhorrence to her voice to suggest that it was among the most scandalous of activities. "Why, the very thought is appalling. Indeed, it would be very unfortunate for His Grace. I imagine the rumors alone would destroy his reputation among his business partners and his daughter's potential suitors."

"My son is his daughter's suitor!"

"But surely that was before the integrity of his estate was questioned?" Lord Maximillian said, and I almost laughed at the sputtering rage on Cecilia's face.

It made me wonder if the Duke was looking for a way out of their agreement on his own.

Lady Penelope shook her head, before turning back to her two guards—companions?—behind her. "I fear we are indeed a long way from London, if this is the sort of practice we find in these places. And I remember Prague as such a refined city, too; it is a shame how its stock has fallen since I last visited."

Cecilia's face burned. She turned back to the Duke. "I seem to have some unexpected business I need to see to immediately, Max. Pray, continue with the celebration while I handle these *unfortunate* matters. Then we will discuss our arrangement."

"Nothing would please me more, Cecilia. It seems we will have to renegotiate."

With her nostrils flaring, Cecilia beckoned Lady Penelope to follow her out of the great hall.

I was not surprised when Lady Penelope remained where she was. "I believe I will be the one to dismiss you," Lady Penelope said. "I will confer with you in tomorrow morning, in the library in the west wing."

Cecilia scowled, so furious her face was twitching. "You assume too much, Lady Penelope."

"And you are playing a very dangerous game," Lady Penelope replied. She took a menacing step toward Cecilia, and Cecilia immediately backed down.

Priscilla, my stepsister, finally decided it was her turn to speak up. "Does this mean our party is over?"

I groaned, but I knew that if Prissy said anything, it was sure to be something ill-timed or completely ignorant. She was Cecilia's doted daughter, and I never knew her to take anything serious except for her food intake and daily exercise routine. Like Empress Elisabeth, she often spent days fasting. If we could have afforded it, Cecilia would have set up a gymnasium right next to Prissy's room. It was the only thing I had ever heard Cecilia deny her.

"It is very unfortunate that I did arrive in the middle of your celebration," Lady Penelope said, talking more to everyone in the great hall rather than just Priscilla. "By all means, continue on. The good Lord knows that there might not be anything at all to celebrate tomorrow."

"Is that a threat?" Cecilia hissed.

Lady Penelope gave her a dazzling, devious smile. "Of course it is, Lady Cecilia. And a very credible one, would you not agree?"

"We could have you arrested for that!" Alex finally stood, angry and ready to fight.

Lady Penelope turned her eye to him. "I see I have been too quick to assume that Lady Cecilia was the lady of the household. My apologies. You have my attention, young sir."

I saw him wince at her wry tone, but Alex held his ground. "You should leave immediately, Madame."

"You have my apologies for my assumptions," Lady Penelope said, "but hardly for my logic. The orders I have issued will go observed, despite your bravado, young man."

"You cannot—"

"You would be most wise not to tell a lady what she can or cannot do. Consider that lesson a welcome gift. Now, sit down and return to your silence. I would hate for you to embarrass yourself even further."

Alex was not used to having his wishes denied, let alone his intelligence or authority questioned. Like a dog with his tail tucked between his legs, he sat down and slumped over in his seat.

"My son is right," Cecilia said.

"Hardly. I assure you, Madame, I have come well prepared for any amount of force, legal or otherwise, that you could possibly muster against me."

"No one can verify who you are," Cecilia insisted.

Lady Penelope walked up to her. Each step was a slow, deliberate act of pure intimidation. Cecilia flinched as Lady Penelope reached into her cloak.

I watched, unblinking, as she produced a letter, shut with an elaborate wax seal.

"No one less than Her Imperial Highness, Queen Victoria, can provide the details of my person." Lady Penelope handed the letter to Cecilia. "She was kind enough to ask for your willing assistance in settling our legal matters. She recalls your previous husband's kindness to her and her son, Leopold. She remembers how, during the week of German and Prussian reception, he once caught Leopold as he fell out of a tree, no doubt saving him grave injury, and she wishes you well."

Cecilia's fists were shaking as she tore open the letter and read it. When she was done, I could tell she was having a hard time not screaming.

It's true.

The murmurings continued, more awkwardly. Lord Maximillian looked over to Cecilia, uncertain, as Teresa Marie asked about her marriage contract to Alex, and Alex only looked viciously appalled.

"If you are satisfied, take your seat and finish entertaining your guests, before I relieve you of that duty as well." Lady Penelope waved her hand, and slowly, ever so slowly, Cecilia backed away, her resolve as neutered as Alex's bluster.

Lady Penelope nodded approvingly, her contempt apparent even as she remained calm. "Now, I will excuse myself and see to the details of my stay."

Before I could do anything else, Cecilia turned and stormed out of the great hall, headed right for me. Her fluffy skirts whipped against me as she passed, and fury suddenly boiled into her eyes.

"Eleanora, this is unacceptable!"

"It is hardly my fault that the grandmother I did not even know existed came to call tonight," I said.

"You mark my words," she bit back, wagging her finger at me, practically mad with rage. "You will pay for what you have done tonight."

Anger simmered inside me. "But I didn't do anything!"

"That's enough." I looked over and saw Lady Penelope standing just behind Cecilia. "You have been dismissed to your room. I can have a guard escort you, if you insist on making this more difficult."

Cecilia cursed before flying down the hall.

Lady Penelope looked at me, and for the first time she seemed visibly discomforted. "Eleanor."

"Eleanora," I corrected her.

She winced. "Apologies … Eleanora. You … you look so much like your mother."

I could only nod. *What else am I supposed to do? Curtsy?*

Lady Penelope also seemed at a loss for what to do, as all of her earlier gusto disappeared. It was not a look that suited her, and she seemed to agree; a moment later, she cleared her throat. "I request you join me in the library in the west wing shortly."

"Should I bring Ben, too?" I asked.

"Ben?"

"Benedict. My older brother."

Her somber expression further saddened. "I see. Yes, bring him as well. We will talk then."

Lady Penelope turned away and headed off, and I heard small footsteps as they shuffled behind me. "Are you feeling well, Nora?" Betsy asked, putting her hand on my arm.

Almost as a reflex, I patted her hand, comforting her even though I was the one who needed it more. "I have to go and get Ben," I said, deflecting her question. "Excuse me."

I have to tell Ben about this.

That thought was the only thing that propelled me forward. As I headed toward the stables, where Ben would likely be, I felt another strange sense of absurdity take hold of me, much as I had felt earlier in the Cabal with Clavan and Ferdy. Only this time there were so many more questions I had—questions that hurt to even think, let alone ask.

Why is our grandmother coming to see us now?

Táta had been gone for ten years. She had not come to the funeral. I thought of that day in the church, with Father Mueller, with Cecilia, Priscilla, and Alex. Even Lord Maximillian had been there, along with Ben and me.

Ben was truly the only family I had left. Our father had no other siblings, and he was the last of his line. I knew that well enough—that was the reason Cecilia was able to gain control of his estate so well. Ben was neither old enough, nor deemed fit enough to challenge her.

In all that time between the funeral and now, I had never even thought of our mother's family. But *Máma* had been gone for even longer than *Táta*, and it was possible I never thought of her family because no one from her family came to her funeral mass.

Of course, she had been lost at sea, so there was no burial. It was possible that Lady Penelope had received the news too late.

I had so many questions, and there was so much I did not know if I was ready to face. I did the only thing I could, which was the same thing I had done all those years ago, on the day of my father's funeral in the small church.

My steps slowed to a stop, and I leaned against the hallway wall for support. I clasped my hands together, bowing my head down to my chest. "Please, Lord," I prayed softly, "help me."

Tears threatened to come, and despair momentarily choked me as I stood there, surrounded by uncertainty and darkness.

But the moment, like all moments before it, passed, and I was able to take comfort in my faith. It was a bedrock of my life, having sustained me through the loss of my family. It kept me going through the hard times, silent during Cecilia's floggings, and hopeful that Ben and I would one day find our freedom.

Maybe this was the day. Maybe this was the day my life would change forever.

At the thought, the memory of my mother's bright laughter sang through me. *"Dear Eleanora, my lovely one, your life can change at any moment; you need only be brave enough to let it."*

I clung to that thought—that wish—as I continued onward, looking for my brother.

5

◊

Seemingly hours later, I watched Ben as he mindlessly picked at the dirt underneath his fingernails. We were stationed outside of the library, both of us silent.

I had a feeling Ben was going through the same emotional turmoil as I was; as I gave him an overview of what happened in the dining hall, his expressions shifted constantly, ranging from amused to angry to suspicious.

“Do you think she’s really our grandmother?” I finally asked Ben.

“No one with that kind of coach and team would come to our manor in Bohemia if it were not for real,” Ben said. “Besides, it makes sense. She is British, as *Máma* was, and she’s clearly a member of the higher social circles. And remember, when *Máma* left us, she was headed for London.”

“And then her ship went down,” I remembered. “*Táta* was devastated.”

“We were *all* devastated, Nora. *Táta* wasn’t the only one.”

The door opened behind us, held open by one of Lady Penelope’s companions wearing a long cloak. He shuffled back, keeping his face hidden under the hood, and I was just about to ask him what he wanted when I heard Lady Penelope call out from inside the room.

“You may enter.”

Ben and I exchanged a quick glance, and then the two of us walked into the room.

The doors shut quickly behind us, and my attention was immediately focused on the lady sitting at my father’s desk.

Up close, Lady Penelope had even more formidable features. The wrinkles around her eyes complimented her resolve, while her high forehead suggested intelligence and insight. Her lips, though they were thin with age, curled into a small, somewhat welcoming smile as she looked at us. “It is good to see you.”

Ben and I bowed and curtsied respectively, unsure of what else to do.

She waved her hand, brushing our formalities aside. "There's no need for that. Now, I imagine you have a lot of questions for me."

"Yes," I said, unable to resist. "It is not every day that one is introduced to one's own grandmother."

"Especially when our mother has been dead for over ten years," Ben added.

Lady Penelope frowned at his surly tone. "I apologize if you are somewhat inconvenienced by my arrival," she began, and then I cut her off.

"As Lady Cecilia might have failed to mention to you, we have been more inconvenienced by your absence, Madame."

"She did not need to mention it," Lady Penelope assured me, her voice still calm and level despite the anger within my words. "I have two perfectly good eyes; I can see it for myself. Cecilia is like a slow-acting poison; sweet at first, and then sickly, and finally too painful to hope for anything but a quick death. Your father must have been mad to have married her."

I looked over at Ben. He shifted his weight onto his straight leg entirely, hiding his begrudging agreement. I was suddenly glad he had left his crutch in the stables. I did not want to see our maternal grandmother cringe at the sight of it.

"I can assure you, your stepmother will be paid back for all the pain she has caused, down to the last little prick."

"She should," Ben muttered. "With interest."

"On that, we agree." With her gray hair and her frosty face, Lady Penelope suddenly radiated a chilly aura. But as she softened her smile, warmth suddenly shone in her blue eyes—eyes that mirrored my own.

Máma *had eyes like that, too.*

I nodded, barely able to contain my delight, but Ben huffed. "I would have preferred it ten years ago."

Lady Penelope looked at him, taking in every detail. Her eyes raked him up and down, before she let out a tired sigh. "And I would have preferred it that your mother stay at home, rather than cross the sea to come to London."

As Lady Penelope made her way over to us, walking around my father's desk, there was a small shuffling noise behind me. I glanced back to see the same man as before, straightening his shoulders and pulling at his cloak.

"Well," Lady Penelope said, "there is no point in questioning what happened back then. What is important is what we can do about the here and now."

"And … you will be staying with us, then?" I asked.

"Nora," Ben hissed.

Lady Penelope eyed him carefully. I watched her lips purse tightly, pinching her face into a scowl. "There is no need to be so hostile, Benedict. I am, after all, your grandmother. And you are correct. It is time I take up the duty my daughter's departure has left me. I intend to not only pay Lady Cecilia back for her trouble, but I will do what I can to make it up to you."

"Really?" My heart beat faster as she nodded. Ben and I exchanged a glance. I was hopeful; he was distrustful.

"What do you want in return?" Ben asked.

I was about to assure Ben there was nothing we could possibly give Lady Penelope when she gave him a wry smile "You're a clever young man, aren't you?"

My heart sank. "But we can't give you anything. "We have no money to offer."

"I'm not after money, am I?" Lady Penelope stood tall as she looked back at me. "You are so much like your mother, Eleanora. And I believe I may yet have a use for you."

"Pepé."

A guard spoke up and stepped forward. Ben and I watched as Lady Penelope frowned at him.

The man removed the hood of his cloak, revealing his tan face. He was a man who had clearly traveled the world, all the way from his home in the East Indies to the streets of London. From his crown of bright white hair, I would have said he was close to Lady Penelope's age, though there was something about him that seemed ageless.

"Pepé, I must object," he said. "These are your grandchildren."

Lady Penelope shrugged. "Then it's not your concern, is it, Harshad?"

"It is my concern if we are compromised."

"We need not worry about what might be."

"Your duty has higher demands," Harshad said.

"Is there any higher demand than family?"

Harshad's eyes narrowed. "You swore your life over to a different ideal."

"I made my vow to God, and God himself has given us the blessing of family. Fealty to one cause does not preclude another."

Up until that moment, I had only seen Lady Penelope calmly and coolly dismiss any arguments or objections at Cecilia's hysteria and Ben's distrustful sneering. As she battled against Harshad, she quickly lost her calm and fire replaced it.

At my inquiring gaze, she immediately switched to another language, still bitterly exchanging verbal blows with Harshad. Even as they spoke in what I guessed was an Indian tongue, I could tell they were nowhere close to a compromise.

Taking the opportunity, I took a moment to study Harshad; I saw he was slightly shorter than Lady Penelope, only a little taller than myself. His accent was distinct, and even when he had spoken in English, his heritage seemed to carry the essence of his past. From his tone, I could tell he was a stubborn man, deeply rooted in his beliefs.

Why is she traveling with an Indian? And what are they talking about?

When I heard Lady Penelope say "Artha," in her mix of lilted language, my heart jumped.

Why is my grandmother arguing about a dead man?

A second later, I frowned. That did not make sense. Was it possible I had heard her incorrectly?

Lady Penelope went back to ignoring Harshad. She returned her focus to us, and somehow she gave the impression that the argument with Harshad had never happened.

"Well, Eleanora, Benedict, there is no need to worry about all the details tonight. Now, I will need you to go and collect your things and bring them back to this wing of the house. You will have new rooms while I am here, and my servants will see to your needs."

Ben and I remained unmoved, and she seemed to be at the end of her patience.

"Go," she instructed. "It is for the best, after all. Your stepmother will be tempted to take her anger out on you, especially since she knows she cannot touch me. We should at least agree that for now, you will be safer with me."

Ben clenched his fists, and I had to wonder if he was upset at Lady Penelope for successfully making her point.

"You have already had a long night. Nothing good comes from talking business or making deals when you are tired."

We filed out of the room, passing the other guard. I watched as he shifted, burying even further into his cloak as I passed.

I was confused, but Lady Penelope and Harshad once more began to talk, and I forgot the strangeness of it all.

Remembering my time in the city, watching Dr. Artha's funeral procession, meeting with Ferdy and Mr. Clavan, fighting with the Turkish thief, and seeing Lord Maximillian and Teresa Marie, I decided there was a lot that was extraordinary about the day. Lady Penelope—my estranged grandmother—suddenly did not seem so unusual.

Unable to help myself, I let out a tired giggle.

"What are you laughing for?" Ben snapped. "There is nothing funny about this, Nora."

"You didn't see her battling with Cecilia and Alex." I wrapped my arm around his. "Come now, Ben, it might not be funny, maybe, but it is still not bad. Cecilia's angry, and there is nothing she can do about it."

"There doesn't seem to be much we can do, either," Ben pointed out. "We are dependent on Lady Penelope now."

I thought about the letter Lady Penelope had in her hands, the one she had given to Cecilia. She was clearly here on some kind of business. What it could be, and what it was, I was not sure. But she was our family, and I told Ben as much. "Surely there is nothing inherently dangerous about that."

"I don't know, Nora." Ben sighed. "Did you hear her, at the end? She's talking about making business deals. That hardly seems like the terms you would use to describe family matters."

He did have a point.

I hated how he had a point.

"But she promised us she would take care of us." I nearly jumped in excitement. "Just think of it, Ben. If nothing else, Liberté could be ours at last!"

"The devil always offers you everything you want," Ben said darkly. "But there is always a price to pay. Always."

"We have already paid it. All these years of serving in our own household, under a tyrant of a woman and a beast of our stepbrother, and not to mention the pampered princess who masquerades as our stepsister."

"Only to now find ourselves dealing with an even more dangerous woman." Ben sighed. "Our dream of opening our own bookshop and lending library is not worth the cost, as far as I can see right now. Liberté will have to wait, so long as we know there are invisible strings attached to anything Lady Penelope has to offer us."

"You certainly have a way of dampening my spirits," I muttered.

"I'm allowed to do that, since I am the only one who cares enough to raise them," he said. "Now, as much as I hate to agree with Lady Penelope on something, she was likely right about Cecilia. Go and get your things and come back here quickly. If Lady Penelope is interested in making a deal with us, she is unlikely to harm us."

I rolled my eyes. "How does it feel to be suspicious of people all the time? To always feel like everyone is going to treat you horribly?"

"I find it is easier to live with their derision than my disappointment. Being a cripple in a society that has no use for you will remind you of that every day."

"Oh, Ben. Please don't think that. You know I was only teasing … " Before I could embrace him, he twisted out of my grip and headed down the dark hall toward his own room.

I watched him until his shadow disappeared around the corner, and then I hurried out to the barn to collect my things. Ben was right to be worried, but I still believed I was right to be hopeful.

Wasn't I?

I glanced up at the ceiling, ignoring the fine craftsmanship of the stonework to look for the face of God behind the darkness. "Well, Lord, this certainly has been a long day," I said with a tired sigh. "I can only pray for your peace in the night."

6

◊

By the time I woke up the next morning, having barely slept at all, nothing had happened that made things seem any less surreal.

I doubted Cecilia felt any different. I did not know the specific details of Cecilia's pain, but through the stone walls of the castle, her muffled cries and disparaging howls rang out from the midmorning hour until noon. Even from my new room two hallways down, I could hear her constant wailing and gnashing of the teeth as she fought with Lady Penelope.

Sometime after Lady Penelope's servant brought a plate to me for lunch, there was another knock at my door.

"Who is it?" I called, quickly stuffing the book I had been reading behind one of the larger pillows of my bed. I frowned at my practiced movement; it was an old habit, but I was not sure if I would be able to break it.

"It's me." Ben entered, his own lunch tray in hand, and I hurriedly took it from him as he moved toward the window seat in my room. "I can take care of it myself," he said, annoyed by my help.

"I know you can. I'm just being polite, Ben."

"We're family. There's no need to be polite."

"Then choke on your food and see if I care."

It felt good to have things back to normal between us.

Ben grinned. "That's better. But if I do, you better hope I choke only after I finish telling you all the gory details of Cecilia and Lady Penelope's argument."

"You were eavesdropping?"

"This is my house, and I'm allowed to go where I want within it," Ben said. "Even if Cecilia and Lady POW are arguing over it, *Otec* was supposed to leave it to me, and Lady POW will leave it to me when she's gone."

"Lady POW?"

"Her full name is Lady Penelope Ollerton-Wellesley. I shortened it to Lady POW, for her initials. Her name's too long." Ben shrugged.

I smiled, nearly laughing as I recalled Ferdy telling me my name was too long, too. "Maybe it's a family trait."

"Huh?"

"Never mind," I said, brushing it aside. "Lady POW seems like a good name for her, anyway. She seems quite powerful as a lady, and one who is used to getting her way."

Ben nodded. "I'll give her that. She could most likely walk into Market Square and convince the vendors to give her their goods for free."

"From all the disruption I heard this morning, I'll bet Cecilia experienced something like that."

"She did." Ben chuckled. "Among other things, the engagement is off between Alex and Lady Teresa Marie."

"What?"

"His Grace was clearly much happier about it than Cecilia. He was still trying to curry favor with Lady POW as he left the library. He is going to stay with us another day or two, and then I believe he will leave."

"I can't believe it. That was all Cecilia had worked for these past ten years."

"Lord Maximillian told her to write to him if it became acceptable to discuss marriage at a later date."

"What did Cecilia say?"

"Nothing. Lady Penelope interrupted and told him that I was allowed to choose my own bride."

Ben's face was stoic and stubborn; he would not allow me to know how he felt about that particular topic. I thought about how he had believed, all those years before, that he would never marry because of his leg, and because he had no inheritance.

After a long moment of silence, I finally giggled softly. "Well, you said we were at her mercy, but it seems she will allow you to make that decision on your own at least."

Ben snorted. "Lady POW also said she intends to give you a Season or two before she will consider marriage a priority."

I was the one who ended up choking. "What?" I sputtered, sending a cloud of crumbs flying all over the floor. Ben thumped me hard between my shoulders before I was able to articulate my surprise better. "What did you say?"

"She's intent on giving you a Season," Ben said. "She's going to buy you a whole new wardrobe and send you out to the marriage mart."

I groaned.

"Calm down. You're already a lady. Now you just have to act like one."

"I guess," I said slowly, "with Lady POW as my example, that does not appear to be as bad as it sounds. If I can give scathing lectures to my stepmother in public, at a party she is throwing herself no less, that would make it worth it."

It was Ben's turn to scowl.

I flicked my nose at him, using one of Tulia's silent insults. "Come on, Ben, I don't think she's bad," I said, putting my lunch tray aside. I paused for a moment before I added, "And I don't know if she knew about us before, either. She called me 'Eleanor,' like *Máma*, when she first saw me. She did not seem to know about you, either, when I asked."

"She's still dangerous, even if she didn't purposefully neglect us. I overheard one her servants call her the Iron Dowager. Apparently, she is formidable, in addition to her impressive wealth and prestige."

"You say that like it's a bad thing."

"Of course it is bad for us. We are at her mercy."

"Not entirely. Cecilia's been banished back to half of the manor's rooms, right? She told the Duke I was going to have a Season, so that means she really does want to do something for us. And if you are worried about it, we just need to assert our compliance comes with a price, too."

When he said nothing, I tugged at his arm. "Come on. Let's go and talk with her. We're rested, and she's done with Cecilia. Surely we can discuss everything now."

Ben groaned, but he walked with me toward the library. From his dragging foot, I could tell Ben was only going along with my wishes. I scowled at him, silently reminding him the only other option we had was to do nothing.

Neither Ben nor I had ever been any good at doing nothing if we could help it.

As we passed by the doors to Lady POW's bedchamber, we could hear her arguing with Harshad again. Immediately, Ben quieted his footstep and shuffled up against the door.

I gave him a disapproving look, but he only rolled his eyes. Before I could tell Ben to ignore her and that everyone should have a right to some privacy, I heard my name.

"—Eleanora is clearly a fine young lady with spirit, just like her mother," Lady Penelope said. "She's just the element we need as a new cover."

Ben's eyes snapped to mine, and I knew he was silently telling me he had been right to mistrust her.

"Pepé, stop this nonsense. Dezda did not tell you about them, remember?"

"So?" I could almost see the angry snarl on Lady POW's face through the door.

"She likely thought it was for the best," Harshad said.

"Well, now she is dead, and it is up to me what we will do—both in regard to my grandchildren, and to the mission."

Mission? What mission? Ben and I exchanged a quick glance, before Lady POW and Harshad started arguing again.

"Amir was right," Lady Penelope said. "It *is* her. He was right about Eleanora. And I must honor my role as a grandmother, to both her and her brother."

"This will disrupt our mission."

"Hardly. This helps us, if anything. Dr. Artha was our lead contact, Harshad, and now he is dead. Lady Cecilia is in no position to be of any help. This is not the time to question the gifts of providence."

The world seemed to shift unexpectedly, as I realized my grandmother was interested in the death of my father's former doctor—and she was interested in us, for some reason. Before I could voice my concerns to Ben, Harshad began to speak once more.

"What will you tell them about their mother? And even if you tell them the truth, who is to say they will accept her legacy? They could easily reject us and leave us with a heavy liability."

"And what if they do accept our offer?" Lady Penelope countered. "It will be wonderful."

"It will be terrible."

"Likely a bit of both. Which will be all the better, if you ask me."

"Pepé, it will still be a liability."

"We've had worse!"

"But what would you have me do? Teach them? That will take time away from our inquiries. We do not have time for this. More lives are at risk, as Dr. Artha has shown us."

"Then we will just have make time for it. That is an order, and you will follow it, Harshad."

Harshad sighed, and I could hear his reluctant defeat. "The League is already not happy with you, Pepé, and this decision will call for a special council. The Order will not be able to help you this time."

"You can make the arrangements for that, then." Lady Penelope paused. "Assuming you have enough time."

"You cannot just alter our plans."

"The plans were already altered, long before we arrived."

"Dezda would not approve of this!" Harshad hissed.

"It matters not. She is not here. For now, I have heard your arguments, and I will take them into serious consideration, no matter how much I disagree with you."

"Your grief is blinding you to the truth," Harshad said.

"And your pride and arrogance have always blinded you," Lady Penelope shot back. "That is why we work so well together, despite our past. We know each other's weaknesses too well."

"Then you should consider listening to me more."

"What an appalling thought," Lady Penelope said. "As I've already listened to you for quite some time, and I've found no such reason to bend to your wishes."

"You should still let them choose. Dezda regretted it in the end."

"She did not regret anything. She just wanted more. And as we now know, she was able to get it, clearly. But we will not argue over that now. I am the appointed leader here, and what I say will go through in the end. Send a summons to Eleanora and Benedict. I will meet them in the library."

"You have always been too stubborn," Harshad said. "You are free to ruin your life, but I will not let you ruin theirs."

"It is *their* choice if I will ruin it or not. Besides, what would their alternative truly be? Cecilia seems to have done quite enough damage. Do you really think it is better that they stay here, under her authority? As I see it, better they are with us, than with her. And much better with us than being out on the streets."

Secretly, I agreed with her. I knew how terrible Cecilia was, and that alone was enough for me to hope for a better future with my increasingly odd, estranged grandmother.

"You are not the only one who owes Dezda," Harshad said.

At his icy tone, a shiver went down my spine. I tugged Ben's arm. "Come on," I whispered. "Let's just go to the library and wait for them."

It was clear Lady Penelope and Harshad would still need several moments to bark at each other. Their voices gradually faded as Ben and I approached the library.

"Well, that was intense," I said. "Even through the door."

Ben nodded. "What do you think their mission is?"

"I don't know for sure, but I have a feeling I know what part of it involves," I said, thinking of Dr. Artha. Before I could tell Ben what I suspected, I tugged open the door to the library. There was a shuffling noise and a grunt of surprise.

That was when I saw him again.

My eyes went wide and then narrowed in anger as I suddenly found myself staring at the Turk, the one who had stolen my father's book.

"You!" My mouth fell open in shock. There was no mistaking him. He had the same eyes, the same nose, even the same expression of registered surprise as he saw me.

"Nora, what's wrong?"

I barely heard Ben's question as I raced across the room to the bookshelf, lunging an attack at the man. In the brief seconds before contact, I saw that while his turban was missing today, his black hair was still elegantly combed back, his mustache was still immaculately trimmed, and he was still astonished that I would attack him at all.

My fist managed to strike his torso with enough force to send him slamming into the bookshelves behind him; I was gratified to see I managed to land a successful blow once more. He groaned in pain before falling to the ground.

"What are you doing here?" I demanded, preparing to strike again. "This is my home, and I will not let you steal anything else from me."

The man sighed. "Please," he said. His English was without inflection, and I stopped.

"You know English?" I asked.

"Yes, much better than I know Czech. But I can switch to French, if you would like." The Turk fell back on his bended knee in apparent surrender. I was disgusted to see there was a hesitant smile on his face as he looked at me, and I gritted my teeth at his gall.

"Nora, who is this?" Ben asked. "What are you doing?"

I pointed at the Turk accusingly. "This is the man who took our father's book from me yesterday."

"The one who accosted you?" Ben looked down at the Turk and frowned. "With the knife?"

"My apologies," the man said. He pulled out his curved dagger from underneath his cloak, presenting it before us as proof of who he was. "Yes, I am the man you saw yesterday."

"Why did you come here?" I asked again, my voice angry and loud. "Who do you think you are, to be here—"

"Eleanora, that's enough."

Lady POW's voice cut through my vicious triumph, severing its full life force with the power of her words.

I swiveled around to see her enter the library, with Harshad at her heels.

"Lady Penelope," I exclaimed, "this man is—"

The Turk reached out and took my hand, squeezing it firmly. "I am not an intruder," he interrupted. He moved quickly, standing up with my forced assistance. "I do believe I have startled Lady Eleanora."

"Well, you are a Turk, and I've heard there have been more Turkish thieves in the city of late."

"Eleanora, do not allow prejudices to cloud your vision," Lady Penelope said. "Skin and race are no more proper judges of character than wealth, health, or wisdom. The devil believes in oversimplifications, but I do not."

I blushed at her comments, knowing I agreed with her in principle. If the man had not stolen from me, I would not have said anything at all, let alone attacked him.

"Amir here is harmless, Eleanora, and I have good reason to trust him with nothing less than my life."

The Turk glimpsed over at Lady Penelope, rubbing his side where I had managed to hit him. "She has an impressive left hook, Lady Penelope."

"Does she?" Lady POW moved gracefully into the room, making herself home at my father's desk, just as she had the previous night. She sat down and smoothed out her skirts. "Well, I guess some good came out of her attacking you, then."

I had no doubt there was a befuddled look on my face as Lady POW tapped her fingers together. "Eleanora, this is Amir Qureshi, my medical consultant and confidant. He has been in my service for the last thirteen years, although we have known each other for much longer. What is it now, Amir? Nearly thirty years?"

"Twenty-five, Madame."

For the first time, I noticed the small threads of silver at the sides of his temples. Before, I would have easily guessed he was in his thirties, but it was clear he was at least forty. "*Enchanté*," I muttered, the barest amount above polite I could muster.

"Amir, allow me to properly introduce my granddaughter."

Harshad scowled beside her. "As you might have already seen, she is Dezda's daughter to the bone."

Dezda? I frowned. Was she talking about my mother?

Suddenly, the earlier conversation Ben and I had overheard made a lot more sense. And it made me a lot more suspicious.

"I have seen it is so," Amir agreed, "although there are several hints of her father."

I sneered at his too-proper tone.

"I'm hoping not too much," Lady Penelope said, making me further frustrated. I hated how she talked over me, as if I was not present. "Now that I've found my grandchildren here, I see it was a needless errand to send a servant for them."

"I'll attend to rescinding the order." Amir turned to me. "Will you see me out of the room, mademoiselle? So you may see I am not a philistine or mongrel of sorts?"

I glowered at him but took his outstretched arm. As we approached the doorway, he whispered, "Please, do not tell Lady Penelope about yesterday. I will explain myself at a later time, if you will only let me. You have my word."

"Your word means nothing to me. You took my father's book."

"Your father's book?" He frowned, and then shook his head. "Never mind. I will explain myself and my actions to you, and this I swear on the soul of your mother."

As he made his vow, Amir covered my hands with his, and that was when I noticed the burning white scribble seared into the skin of his right hand.

The stark white of the scar, a large half-loop dotted with a searing square, winked at me against the library light.

"Please, mademoiselle," he whispered. "There is much more going on than you realize."

I looked into his eyes and then back down at his hand. Seeing the crispy outline of the mark against his knuckles made me soften. It was an older scar, but it hid a deeper pain. I thought the shape of it looked vaguely familiar, but I had trouble recalling where I had seen it. "Fine," I said through clenched teeth. "But I will hold it against you if you give me any trouble."

"Not only your mother's daughter, but your grandmother's granddaughter as well, I see." The smile on his face was a sad, rueful one.

"Eleanora," Lady POW called. "What is taking so long?"

Amir's hands slipped out of mine. "She just wanted to make sure I was feeling well, Lady Penelope," he replied.

"Did I ask you something, Amir? I believe I was talking to Eleanora."

"My apologies, Madame." Amir's smile turned wry as he looked back at me. "Excuse me."

I watched him for a long moment as he left, eyeing the small outline of his dagger from beneath his cloak.

He had better keep his promise.

I was intrigued, if somewhat repulsed, by the man my grandmother trusted so much.

As I walked back toward Lady POW and Ben, I glanced over at Harshad. He was quiet and still, and he did not look back at me, even though I had a feeling he was still taking in everything from around the room.

"Now, then," Lady Penelope said. "To business."

Ben narrowed his eyes at me.

I pretended not to notice. He had been right, but the earlier conversation we overheard only added more mystery. I was interested, even if family came after business.

"I will start by suggesting you stay in this half of the manor for your own safety while Cecilia and I settle our legal disputes."

I briefly thought of *Máma's* locket and Táta's watch, still tucked away under the pantry floor. *I will have to go and retrieve them soon if I want to keep them safe.*

"What happens to us after that?" Ben asked.

"That is the question, is it not?" Lady Penelope mused. "I know I have neglected my duties as your grandmother for far too long. I know there is much hurt between us—"

"The hurt seems to just be with us," Ben interrupted.

"Not all pain is seen, Benedict." Her tone was distinctly soft, and I felt a hint of the feeling behind it.

Whether or not I believed it was a different story, however. I knew Ben was likely unsure of her sincerity. He grumbled and crossed his arms, but he went silent.

"I would first seek to make amends—should you choose to allow me. I have coerced Cecilia into allowing you to make that choice," Lady Penelope said.

I was not as interested in making amends as I was getting answers to my questions, which seemed to be accumulating by the moment. It was time to do something. "We heard you need us for something," I said. "You said I would make a good cover. What were you talking about?"

Harshad's mouth dropped open, before he glared at Lady POW. She shot him a smug look before turning to me. I was expecting her to explain herself, but even though she was clearly pleased by my admission, she waved the matter aside.

"You will see later," she said briskly.

Did she want *me to overhear their conversation?* I wondered. *Or is she just happy that I did?*

Before I could ask, Lady POW turned toward a stack of papers on the desk. "Now, Lady Cecilia was kind enough not to test my patience—much. She has shown me her budgets for the last several years, and I am prepared to restore your inheritance."

"Thank you," I said. "But—"

"That will include a new wardrobe for you, Eleanora. If you are in agreement, I will make arrangements for your introduction to Society at once. While we are here, waiting for my man of affairs to make settlements with your stepmother, we can send you out on several social calls. It is the perfect time, too, as the Diets are in session and the elites of Prague will be ripe for entertainment."

"But I'm not an entertainer," I cut in, tired of letting her interrupt me.

"You may not be an entertainer, but you will be a sensation. I will see to your wardrobe and your manners, and then we will go out and introduce you to the town. Even his Imperial Highness King Ferdinand V will be eager to meet you once I am finished with you."

"What? Why—?"

"It will be an adventure," Lady Penelope insisted. "And we can make up for our lost time."

I hesitated to object; I did not want to dampen Lady POW's spirits. She seemed much happier than she had the previous evening, and some part of me was secretly thrilled. All my years of yearning for my mother came rushing at me, and it pushed back against my fears and questions.

"Harshad is right—you are clearly Dezda's daughter," Lady Penelope said, flicking another snippy gaze over at her colleague. "She was a beauty."

"I do remember *Táta* saying so," I whispered. I glanced over at Ben, and my resolve found itself again. "What about Ben?"

"Yes, indeed. What is it that you want, Benedict?" Lady Penelope asked.

Ben stilled beside me. "I will have to think about it."

"What is there to think about?" Lady Penelope scoffed.

"It doesn't matter," Ben muttered. "If there is anything I want for sure, it's just Nora to be happy."

I was touched by my brother's concern, but Lady POW bristled.

"Believing that your own happiness is not feasible does have a tendency to limit it. You might already know that, from what I have seen."

Ben scowled. "What's that supposed to mean?"

"It's easy to be altruistic when there is no real sacrifice involved."

"I—"

"It's clear that you believe your life is meaningless," Lady Penelope said. "Is it because of your leg? Do you think you've become useless because of it? Or do you just want to be unhappy?"

Ben stared at her, speechless. I tried to speak up and defend Ben, but Lady POW stopped me. She held up her hand, making me think of Tulia briefly. "Stop, Eleanora," she barked. "This is not about you, despite what your brother thinks. This is about his pride, his damaged sense of honor, and how he can overcome his shame."

"I have no shame in who I am," Ben retorted.

"Not in who, but in what."

"This isn't something you should talk about," I interrupted. "Ben doesn't like—"

"The truth?" Lady Penelope turned back to me. "He doesn't like the truth, Eleanora? Is that what you were going to say?"

"No." I blushed. "I was going to say he doesn't like to talk about his injury, that's all."

"If only the world could work in such a way that everything we did not like would go away if we would only cease to talk about it." Lady Penelope threw Harshad a wry look over her shoulder. "That would do wonders for us, would it not, Harshad?"

Harshad continued to say nothing, even though I could tell there was nothing more he wanted in that moment than to speak up.

Lady POW shook her head at Ben. "I am asking you to allow me to make your life better. It is time I rectify my mistakes after all these years."

"Mistakes?" I asked.

Lady Penelope's lips suddenly tightened into a twisted grimace, and I blinked in shock, realizing I had caught her slip up before she did.

"Yes. My mistakes."

"Pepé, stop." Harshad lunged forward with a speedy grace that belied his age, gripping her wrist as she reached for something at her side.

"Enough," Ben objected. "We already know you're hiding something from us. If she is going to tell us what it is, I want to hear it. *That's* what I want."

"Me, too." I reached out and took Ben's arm in support. "Tell us why you are here. And tell us what it has to do with Dr. Artha's death."

Lady POW's eyebrows raised, while Ben and Harshad both whirled to face me.

"So, you know of Dr. Artha's murder?" Lady Penelope asked.

"I heard rumors in the city," I said, suddenly determined to keep Ferdy and Clavan out of any of my explanations. Her casual tone was disconcerting.

"Rumors are one thing, but truth is another."

"Then tell us the truth," Ben grumbled.

Lady POW sat down and folded her hands together in careful consideration. "Is that what you really want?" She briefly narrowed her eyes at Harshad, and I saw his face sour even more as he saw me look at him.

"Yes," Ben insisted.

Lady Penelope ignored the fury in his gaze. She turned to me. "What of you, Eleanora? You will not be able to go back to not knowing, once you learn the truth. Do you still want to know?"

Sudden fear and solid certainty took hold of me. "Yes," I said, unsure if I had the bravery to match my sudden bravado.

Lady Penelope cast another quick, triumphant look over at Harshad, who pursed his lips in further displeasure. A silent battle continued between them, but he stepped back.

"Very well then, Benedict, Eleanora," Lady Penelope said. "I will tell you the truth. But it does not start, nor stop, with me. I must tell you about your mother and the Order of the Crystal Daggers."

7

◊

Lady POW clasped her hands together. I scooted forward on my seat, dreading and anticipating what she would reveal. If hearing the truth was the price for our freedom, I knew telling us the truth also required a price from her.

"My Eleanor, your mother, was a member of an elite, secret society once known as the Order of the Crystal Daggers," Lady Penelope said. "Before she died, she handled several delicate assignments on behalf of certain kingdoms and governments."

Ben and I only looked at her, torn between reactions, as we waited for her to go on.

What could I really say? *Máma* had died many years ago. I remembered her the way one might recall a strange and vivid dream; sometimes I would forget about her for days at a time, and then I would smell a familiar scent, or recall a certain memory, and I would long for her embrace. Before Cecilia came to the manor, I would walk past the portrait *Táta* had commissioned of her, truly seeing her face stilled in the dried oil; at those moments, I would be caught back in that feeling of wondering where she was, and how I missed her.

To imagine her as a government worker, as someone who did not spend her days taking care of our family or seeing to our needs, was not beyond my capability; it just seemed beyond believability.

It seemed to be beyond Ben's, too.

"*Otec* never mentioned anything like that," Ben said. "And I never saw anything to indicate you are telling the truth."

"Your father was part of her last assignment," Lady Penelope said. "She was supposed to come down here with some others and take care of King Ferdinand V during the Revolution of 1848."

Ben and I exchanged glances. From his eyes, I could tell he was frustrated—and afraid. I was surprised to realize I was, too. The beautiful lady in that portrait had always been a loving, maternal memory, and it was troubling to hear she had led such a contrasting life prior to my birth. My childhood innocence had long been gone, thanks to Cecilia's callousness and my father's death, but I felt a secret pillar of my heart splinter as my memory of my mother, a relic born of ignorance and illusion, began to crumble.

"This was not an unusual task for a member of the Order to handle," Lady Penelope continued. "The Order goes back several hundred years, starting with the warriors of Constantine. When he converted to Christianity, there were several more threats on his life from those in the kingdom he had displeased. Everyone from the pagans to the Jews were upset at his conversion and his success as a leader. There were others, of course, who were upset with him long before that."

"Saint Constantine?" I asked, briefly recalling the church's Latin rites. "That is who you mean, correct?"

"Yes. Forgive my confusion. The Church of England does put a barrier between me and Catholicism. But Constantine had a particularly sharp intuition for betrayal," Lady Penelope said. "Under his rule, the Byzantine Empire commissioned a small, secret group of elite members to protect him. As time went on, and the empire collapsed in on itself, the last of the rulers, in a desperate attempt to gain allies, pushed the Order to protect more allies of the surrounding nations. The group decentralized, and loyalties shifted. Today, the Order itself spans many nations. Queen Victoria herself sent us out here to investigate the situation and keep the status quo."

"Why is the British Empire sending you out here?" Ben asked.

"Her Imperial Majesty wants to ensure the safety of the trade routes to the Orient and the Indies."

"Many consider her to be a powerful ruler, even in my home country," Harshad added. "Her vocal support has kept these lands, and others, stable during growing political divides. But not all are happy with her support."

"Is that who sent *Máma* out here the first time?" I asked. "Queen Victoria?"

"No." Lady Penelope shook her head. "Back then, it was the papal state government, under His Holiness Pope Pius IX himself, that requested aid, for Savoy's sake."

"Empress Maria Anna," Ben said. "King Ferdinand's wife."

I thought of the lady I'd only seen in small pamphlets, the one who had once ruled as my country's queen as well as the Empress of Austria and Hungary. She was rumored to be devoted to the church and her husband, with her only other love reserved for traveling throughout Bohemia during the summer and decorating Prague Castle in abundant Christmas decorations every year.

Briefly, I thought of the half-torn invitation to the Advent Ball Ferdy had handed me. Despite all the confusion of our present situation, I could not stop wondering if I would be able to go to the Empress' ball, now that I had the chance to be free from Cecilia. I clasped my hands together tightly, trying to keep the sudden excitement inside of me to myself.

Lady Penelope, oblivious to my inner delight, nodded. "Yes."

"The former empress was concerned about the revolution, and she had a right to be, in hindsight. That is why your mother came here. Dezda was very eager for another mission at the time," Harshad said.

"When she met her Dolf," Lady Penelope said, "she decided to stay and marry him."

There was something in her tone that told me she had been displeased by my mother's choice.

"And then she had us," I said.

The terse brunt of her response left me breathless. "Yes."

There was a long pause, before Ben finally said, "I do not understand why this information matters. Our mother has been gone for fourteen years now. What does an old society and Dr. Artha's death have to do with why you are here?"

"The society for whom she worked is still around," Lady Penelope said. She cocked her head to the side, glancing back at Harshad. "Mostly."

Realization dawned on me as I looked from her to Harshad. "And you are part of it," I said. "You're a member of the same society as *Máma* was, aren't you?"

"Excellent, Eleanora. The good Lord gave logical faculties to both male and female, and I am proud to see you use yours so well."

"Since you are here then," Ben said, "that must mean the society sent you on another assignment."

"Also very astute," Lady Penelope said. "You are correct. Harshad and I, along with the others under our command, have been ordered to come here on a special mission."

"Did they send you out here to investigate Dr. Artha's murder?" I asked. "Does this mean Ben and I will help with your assignment?"

There was no mistaking the satisfaction on Lady POW's face. "I hope so. I have a plan, and it includes you both."

Harshad cleared his throat. "Lady Penelope sees this as an opportunity to be with her family as well as serve the kingdom of Bohemia and discover the truth."

His tone was resigned, but it was how he used Lady POW's proper name that made me shudder. I wondered if it was an insult of sorts between them.

"What good would a cripple do this society of yours?" Ben asked.

I saw the small amount of fear in his eyes as he stared at Lady POW. Breathlessly, I waited for her response.

She smirked. "Plenty, given your spying abilities," she said. "Harshad and I were aware you were listening in on the conversation Cecilia and I had in the library this morning."

For the first time, Ben dropped his guard. "Really?"

Between Ben and Lady POW, I could suddenly see a lot more similarity.

Ben's earlier warning whispered through me; Lady Penelope was our grandmother, but she was clearly more dangerous than either of us had anticipated. What she was asking of us was not clear, and as I watched she and Ben began to discuss more about the Order, and I felt myself pulling away as Ben was pulled in.

"So we would be spies?" I asked, interrupting her. "That hardly seems proper."

"It is hardly proper for you, as a rightful lady, to be subjected to preparing an engagement dinner for your stepbrother, or selling your father's heirlooms at the market. Spying is not an honorable task, but that has never negated the necessity of it at critical times like these."

Lady Penelope's tone was sharp and shaming, and I blushed at her remarks.

"Protecting others is a calling, but each has to answer it. Some do not. That is what even God himself offered to man."

"So the Order protects people?" I said, still hesitant.

"Yes." Lady Penelope nodded firmly. "We serve truth. And the truth is, rulers are needed in order to keep the peace. We protect them at great cost. We investigate on their behalf. We seek to overcome and control chaos. We serve others in love and in hopes of peace. Is peace for our time not a noble enough endeavor for you?"

"It is a good goal," I agreed, "but—"

"—and just think, you would be taking up the banner of your mother's legacy in helping us. She worked hard to maintain peace here in Bohemia, before you were born. Wouldn't you like to honor her memory by helping us now?"

At the mention of my mother, all the wispy memories I had of her flooded into my mind. I heard her words, I saw her smile. I wanted to run to her and embrace her, to feel her heart beat against mine; I thought about what she loved, including my father, and about how she was proud of him for protecting the king during the revolution all those years ago.

The illusions of my mother were gone, but I could still know her in a real way, to walk through the steps of her life on my own.

"You do not have to help, of course," Lady Penelope said, her sudden flippancy repulsive to my pride. "You know the truth about your mother, and now it is up to you what you will do with it. Even those set free by the truth often choose to remain enslaved. And I know Cecilia would love the chance to remain your guardian, if you would let her."

"I want to be free." The words came rushing out of me before I could think through their implications and consequences.

"There are two things you need to know about yourself if you want to be free—what you stand for, and what you stand against." Lady Penelope held up her hands, brandishing a pair of daggers that had been hidden in her skirts. "This world lives enslaved to its destruction, and so long as you are living, as long as you are fighting, you will be free."

I gazed at the daggers, transfixed. Each blade was clothed in a leather scabbard, but the silver and obsidian of the daggers' hilts winked at me, as though it was calling for me.

Lady Penelope pulled the daggers free, revealing a pair of gleaming blades; each were an unusual shade of violet, one that held other spots of blue and green, and other colors, even as it encompassed them. The gemlike mosaic added to the overall power of the weapon.

"Beautiful, aren't they?" Lady Penelope ran her gaze down her blades, following the elegant curve of the daggers. Her fingers lightly stroked the weapons as she held them. "The motto of the Order is *In Hoc Signo Vinces*, or 'With this sign, you shall win.' It was the same message Constantine heard from God."

"What are they … " My own voice trailed off, hushed and full of awe as I looked on the mysterious weapons.

"This is the weapon of a member of the Order," Lady Penelope continued. "You bow to God alone, but the rest of your life will be a fight, in which you alone will have the choice of victor. It was my privilege to free you from ignorance. Now, it is my duty to teach you how to stand, and remain standing, even when you are tempted to fall."

I looked back at the daggers in her hand and swallowed hard. Lady Penelope was clearly offering me a choice between different lives of servitude, but only one offered meaning and redemption in the end.

My life would mean nothing, my mother's life would mean nothing, if I wasted my efforts to serve Cecilia and her household. I already knew I was insignificant in the eyes of the world, but I suddenly had a chance where my life would be about something greater. And I did want that.

So I reached forward and made my choice. It was the one I wanted.

Ben put his hand on my shoulder protectively as I took hold of a dagger. From the look in his blue-green eyes, I knew he was ready to stand with me. "We accept your offer."

Lady Penelope clasped her hands together. "Then it is time to get to work."

At her determined smile, I could not stop the rush of anxious excitement that washed over me.

8

◊

To my dismay, I soon found out my excitement was unwarranted.

"Are we finished yet?" I asked, grumbling as I stood on the small pedestal. "I've been here for hours."

"Let Jaqueline finish," Lady POW barked. "This is hardly difficult, Eleanora."

I groaned. For hours, I had been standing in the middle of a large parlor room, one that had been closed off to the other parts of the wing, all while three of Lady POW's maidservants worked to measure every inch of my body. Jaqueline, Amelia, and Marguerite doubled as seamstresses, and they were making me different outfits to wear.

"I don't see why a new outfit is necessary. I can work fine in my current skirts. Ben and I have been brawling with each other and battling our way around the manor since we were born."

"You have been wearing that oversized maid's outfit for far too long, Eleanora." Lady POW sat at a small writing desk in the corner of the room, jotting down notes and, from the looks of it, keeping up with her correspondence. "I thought you were much bigger than you actually are."

I bit my lip, irritated. It was bad enough I was naked except for my chemise and stockings, but Lady POW made the whole experience much worse. Every ten minutes or so, she would glance over at me, narrow her eyes, and call out some condescending judgment or shake her head with a sigh. Occasionally, she would come over to me and circle me, wearing a look of cold professionalism that unnerved me.

While it was tempting to whirl around to face her, if for no other reason than to remind her that she had flaws, too, I was stuck holding my arms out straight while Amelia wrapped them in rolls of a range of different fabrics, from velvet and silk to leather and suede. If I moved even the slightest, her pins would dig into my arm. I discovered this for the second time when I glanced behind me, surprised by another one of Lady POW's comments.

"You have good hips for birthing, Eleanora," Lady Penelope observed. "We will have to be careful, though; it seems one is a little higher than the other. It's not ideal for fighting."

I was just about to ask her what my hips had to do with fighting when she continued.

"Men like hips like yours; they make it easier to grab onto during intercourse."

My face went dark red instantly.

"It will likely be easy to coerce information from your opponents and informants if you use your bodily charms, should the occasion call for it."

"What?" My voice nearly squeaked.

Lady POW grimaced. "Oh, dear. It has been a long time since I have dealt with the sexually inexperienced. Marguerite? Add that to the list, please."

It was suddenly much easier to worry about fighting.

"Lady Penelope," I said, "I would rather learn how to beat the answers out of my opponents, please. I don't … I don't want to … " My voice trailed off as I felt the heat in my face rise.

"Spoken like a true innocent." Lady Penelope sighed. "In that case, consider yourself fortunate that we don't have time for a full review of the curriculum."

I did. I considered myself very, very fortunate.

"I will go over the basics, and that should be enough to suffice for our current mission," Lady Penelope said.

"Now?" My eyes went wide with horror at the thought.

"Come now, Eleanora, don't tell me you have never even thought of sex before?"

"I know what it is," I shot back through gritted teeth. "If that is what you mean."

"Any simpleton can look at a painting or sculpture and know that it is art. But only a true and trained master knows how to create such a splendid pleasure."

I squirmed. "This is hardly appropriate."

"One does what one must, Eleanora; propriety be damned." Lady Penelope returned to her desk.

"What do you think I will be doing that requires such … explicit … knowledge? I thought I was just to be a cover."

"And you will be," Lady Penelope agreed. "We will begin introducing you to everyone in Prague tomorrow, ordering clothes for you so you can attend socials and breakfasts and balls. Hopefully, it will not be too much longer before we can launch you into Society properly." She reached over and took a sip from her teacup. "God, I miss England. London is so wonderful this time of year."

"None of what you listed seems like it would require a discourse on manipulative sexuality," I said, ignoring my own stomach's grumbling as I suddenly wanted some tea for myself.

"There is more to your introduction to Society that we need to concern ourselves with," Lady Penelope said.

"You're not secretly auctioning me off to the marriage mart, are you? I can already tell you that I would reject such a fate."

"Hearing that relieves my nerves like nothing else." Lady POW rolled her eyes. "The Order takes its business seriously. There is no time for real romance in these instances. Relationships just cause problems."

For some reason, Ferdy's face flashed in my mind, and I felt sad at the thought of never seeing him again.

"Take it from me, Eleanor. It is best to use people as much as you can and then forget them."

At my mother's name, I winced, but that was not the only reason her statement shook me. From the harshness of her voice, I could tell it was a personal lesson she had learned.

"Eleanora," I corrected.

Lady Penelope did not seem to hear me. "Jaqueline, make sure we have enough material to hide Eleanora's hips, *s'il vous plait.*"

As Jaqueline filled in my corset with extra padding, giving me more of a boyish figure, I decided I would do my best to make sure that, even if I did learn how to use my bosom to get what I wanted, I never needed to employ it.

"What kind of outfit is this?" I glanced down at the full ensemble. It was made of all black, with different shades and different materials. As Amelia allowed me to lower my arms, I felt the smoothness of the leather as it hugged my body. My legs were nearly bare, with only short pants reaching to my knees. It felt like a long pair of delicates, even though I had on a pair underneath it. I felt better that there was a leather skirt hanging over my legs, secured at the waist with a belt.

"This is your stealth habit," Lady Penelope said. "The leather is sturdy and able to provide some protection. The lining is infused with silk, to provide comfort as well as smooth movement, and the linen wraps are there to provide padding."

"Padding for my hips?" I asked her, still annoyed by her earlier comments.

"Yes. Although the wraps are typically there more for your wrists and knuckles."

Marguerite came up to me. "Here, mademoiselle. This is a hood for you."

"A hood?" Before I could ask for specifics, she pushed the material over my head, briefly catching on my hair.

"It has a mask sewn into it." Amelia said, reaching toward my face. She wrestled with the material as I tried not to groan. When I could see properly again, I saw Jaqueline had brought a small hand mirror over for me.

I gazed into it and briefly wondered if everyone else could see how uncomfortable I felt. My eyes were a stormy blue, and my face was clearly pale. My hair had been shuffled free from my pins, so some of my disheveled curls were sticking out from under my hood.

"You and your brother both have such beautiful black hair," Marguerite said. "It matches the outfit perfectly."

"Put the mask on," Amelia said, before she did it for me.

A strip of thick, dark cloth suddenly pressed against my nose and mouth, and I coughed at the sudden interruption of fresh air into my lungs. No one else voiced any objection; the seamstresses all smiled and gasped, delighted to see my semi-finished self.

I had to admit, I liked it. The long tunic over the leggings made it much easier to move, and my arms were loose enough that I could move without tearing at my seams.

"*C'est parfait*," Marguerite cheered.

"Wonderful!" Amelia beamed.

I had to wonder what I was supposed to be doing in an outfit like that.

Lady POW made her way over to me once more. "It'll do. Now, ladies, we do not have much time. Please see to it that this is finished first."

"*Oui*, Madame." Their choral response was amusing, and it cheered me up some as they began to slide the outfit off me.

"Madame, what about the rest of her attire?" Amelia asked. "Should we get started on that as well?"

"We will need a walking dress for her; make it in the Parisian style." Lady Penelope looked thoughtful. "I will take Eleanora out to the city tomorrow and order other clothes. As much as I know you ladies are the finest talents with a needle and thread this side of the globe, I need to make Eleanora a sensation."

She turned to me. "Which means we will need to go over etiquette next."

I drew myself up proudly—or as proudly as I could, as Jaqueline, Amelia, and Marguerite were peeling away the pinned fabric. When my mouth was free of the mask, I said, "I remember a good bit of what *Máma* taught me."

I did not add the additional insight Tulia had provided me, considering most of it was counterproductive to acting like a true lady.

"You were only a child." Lady Penelope dismissed my concern. "I doubt Eleanor taught you how to flirt outrageously with a man and get away with it under the guise of innocence, or how to waltz, or any number of other important skills you will need to learn in order to stand out."

I could have used that chance to ask her about the mission, and why I would need to learn all of that, but something else bothered me more about what she said.

"Why does Harshad call *Máma* Dezda?" I asked. "My father always introduced her as Lady Eleanor."

"Your mother's first name was Eleanor, but Harshad and I often called her Dezda, for her middle name. It is not that unusual a practice; Queen Victoria's first name is actually Alexandrina." Lady Penelope waved her hand. "It is hardly a matter of concern."

"So it is a British tradition to call people by their middle names?"

"Do not be foolish, Eleanora. People often have names that are specific to their loved ones. Your own brother calls you Nora, after all."

I thought of Ferdy calling me "Ella," and smiled. I smiled even more as I faced the temptation to ask Lady POW if Harshad's name for her, Pepé, was an endearment.

But a long, thoughtful moment later, I decided since Lady Penelope had the power to make me suffer, it would be best not to provoke her—especially when I was already tired from the past several hours of wardrobe demands. "I suppose that is true."

"Of course it is. Now, stay still. Do not cause my lovely seamstresses any duress. One more dress for today, a riding habit for later this week, and then we will be finished here."

I kept my groan to myself and prepared to feel another hours-long session of aches and stiffness as I was prodded and poked and measured.

Watching her scribble notes on a small tablet of stationary, I realized Lady POW had yet to tell me anything specific about her special assignment—or why she was concerned with Dr. Artha's death.

"What is the stealth habit for, exactly?" I asked. "I can't imagine I will need to wear this while I'm dancing and flirting outrageously out in Society."

"You're so inquisitive, Eleanora."

"I wouldn't be, if you would answer my questions."

Lady POW gave me a sly smirk. "True. I don't know yet what this assignment will demand of you. I was not expecting you at all, and now that you are here, I feel as though I have our Dezda back."

Lady POW's gaze moved across my face and over my messy curls. I saw her sadness, and I mourned for my mother's loss once more. This time, it was not just for my own loss, however; I saw more than ever that her absence had removed me from an entire life I could have known, and one in which there were more people to embrace.

"But," Lady Penelope said, her voice snapping back to its professional tone, "luck favors the prepared. You might need such a suit if we need information or reconnaissance."

"You mean espionage?"

"You would be surprised at how often the right information has saved lives," Lady Penelope said. "It is easier to save lives with the right information than to simply take out threats."

I nodded. My only real experience with a threat seemed to be Alex, with his pretentious and licentious expressions. Kicking him and occasionally bloodying him up was simple, but then, he was really a simple villain.

"Will we begin looking into Dr. Artha's death?"

"You will not be worried about that," Lady Penelope said. "I will handle that. I have contacts sending me information. For your end of the mission, we will go out to shop and socialize. We will need to make arrangements to be invited to different houses and parties throughout the season."

"Dr. Artha's death seems like a bigger concern," I said. "Especially since he was your lead contact and he was murdered."

"You would do well to remember that murder is always a serious business. I will not involve you in this aspect of my mission, Eleanora. It is risky, even for an experienced spy."

"Dr. Artha was my father's friend," I said. "I remember him from when I was younger. If he was murdered, and there is something I can do, I should do it, should I not?"

"That question is now mine to answer, both as your grandmother and your direct leader, and I have told you what you will do about it."

"But skipping around Society seems … " I searched for the right word, knowing that Lady POW would likely not care if I feared boredom or vanity, especially compared to the threat of murder. "Inefficient."

"It is actually very efficient, in terms of my inquiries. Remember, the Diets will be meeting again before the year is out," Lady Penelope said. "We will need to keep the elites entertained to avoid suspicion. With my arrival, we will have plenty of it already. Especially since I will not be able to manipulate Cecilia into helping me as I had originally planned."

"Suspicion?" I frowned. "What are you talking about? There's no need to worry about anyone being suspicious of us. Unless it's possible you were lying about my father's will?"

Lady POW clapped her hands together. I had a feeling she was getting impatient herself, considering my previous concern for efficiency was marred by my own arguments. "You do not have to worry about Cecilia anymore, Eleanora. As I have said, you are free from her. You are under my protection now."

I stood there, wrapped in pins and measuring tape, wearing only my undergarments. I had to wonder if this was truly freedom, or if it was only a different kind of cage.

But there was one thing I wanted to know for certain.

"You had a message from Queen Victoria for Cecilia, but nothing for Ben or for me."

"Yes. When your mother moved out here, she married Dolf. He was almost bankrupt, and I bought the manor's property, as I said before, in order to help them out. When she died, I largely left it to my man of affairs. He had years in between her letters, as he was inquiring if she wanted to buy the property back. She never seemed to have the money for it. When Queen Victoria requested my presence here, I came with the intent to befriend her and settle our accounts."

"You are not going to do that now." There was no question behind my statement.

"Heavens, no. Now I will see she suffers in any way I can imagine. And I will stay here, overseeing your entrance to Society and Benedict's education. I will look for a new house in the city, but this one is suitable for now."

I felt my breath catch as I asked the question I had wanted to ask since she had revealed herself. "You really did not know about me or Ben, did you?"

"I see your powers of observation and deduction are well-honed. This is to our benefit. Even if you will have nothing to do with the murder, you will need to pay close attention to what you see and observe as you go about your role," Lady Penelope replied.

She was right about my powers of observation. That was proven once more as I noticed she did not answer my question. "When did you find out about us?" I tried again.

"It wasn't me, initially. Amir was the one who found you." She sighed. "When he saw you in town yesterday, he came rushing back to our hotel and told me he had discovered something of critical importance. I thought it was something related to the mission, but then … "

Suddenly, I would have given almost anything to have been there, to see the look on Lady POW's face, when Amir told her about me.

"And Ben?" I asked.

"You told me about Ben, just after I saw you myself for the first time."

"I remember that."

"Good. You will need to have a good memory," Lady Penelope said, trying to switch topics.

I did not let her. "*Máma* never wrote to you about me and Ben at all?"

She shook her head.

My throat was suddenly dry as I remembered meeting Amir. Briefly, I was torn between disgust at his thieving and my despondence over my mother's secretiveness; it was hard to decide which one felt worse.

"You mustn't hold it against her," Lady Penelope said. "Believe me, I could hold it against her enough for the two of us."

"Why did she—?"

"Everyone has secrets, Eleanora." Lady Penelope sat down at her small desk again, looking glum. "Everyone lies, everyone has secrets, and everyone has regrets. In the end, the truth cannot hide forever. But if you are to take your mother's place in the Order, you must accept you may never know some things. You will spend your life searching for truth, but there is no guarantee you will find it."

"I will," I insisted.

Lady POW gave me a rueful look. "Careful. Your naïve illusions will get the better of you if you let them. Thankfully, you will be following my lead on this mission."

"But surely that doesn't mean I will be running around and following your orders blindly?"

She gave me a look, and I knew at once that Lady POW was expecting *exactly* that.

I grimaced. "Really?"

"You've followed Cecilia's orders for years, from what the staff and others have told me," Lady Penelope pointed out. "And I know you do your best to follow the teachings of the church."

"My faith in God is not blind, and neither is my fear of Cecilia's wrath," I argued.

"True. But in regards to Lady Cecilia, I will say that you will need to unlearn what she has taught you. Being under another's authority is not necessarily something to abhor. A bad master, yes. But not mastery itself. She is not to be feared."

"I know you have taken care of her for the meantime," I said slowly, "but it might be a long time before I trust in it."

"And you have that right. But I would request you speed it up as much as possible. And not just for your own sake, but for your brother's, too. It is clear she has managed to do more damage to him than you."

There was no denying she was right about that. "You are correct. But that does not mean I will follow your orders without explanation."

"I am the leader of the Order, Eleanora. It is your job to follow my orders, whether you know why or not. My goodness, do you want me to put a formal request, as though I was petitioning the House of Lords? I will never understand your generation's comfort in bureaucracy." She gave me an assessing gaze. "But … "

"But what?"

"But you and I must find a way to work together. So I will tell you this much. I was telling you the truth that I have been sent to Prague by the request of Queen Victoria. She wants to make sure this area is secure, especially with all the trouble she is facing in India right now."

As Amelia began to pull the newer set of sleeves off my arms, I asked, "What's happening in India?"

"Trouble," Lady Penelope replied. "There are several in the government who are making an appeal to the queen to become their ruler."

"But India is on the other side of the world," I said. "How would she be able to rule it from England?"

"The same way she rules her other land holdings in the Americas and in Australia," Lady Penelope said with a sharp smile. "By good and gracious force, and the goodwill of God."

I frowned. "I guess that's quite an accomplishment. The Bohemians here cannot even rule themselves. The German Diet has been in power for so long. I do not know much about politics, but even I know their stalemates are legendary."

"Which is another reason why I have been asked to come," Lady Penelope said. "There are always people who look for something to be discontent over, and there are always people who seek to make their discontent the government's problem. The rule of law is precarious enough in this region, and the recent causes for alarm are particularly unsettling. If Prague was not experiencing an economic boom thanks to Bohemia's coal industry, we would see much more of a political uprising."

"I guess if the death of Dr. Artha was enough to disrupt the country, it is something to be concerned about."

"It is not just his death. The other two similar deaths were members of the Upper House of the Lords, who had a lot of influence in the *Reichsrat*, the German-speaking Parliament of Bohemia and Austria. The representatives from Mlada and Beroun were killed, supposedly by Jews."

I frowned. The death of Dr. Artha, and the other deaths that Ferdy and Clavan discussed the other night suddenly seemed even more sad.

A new thought struck me as I stood there. *I have a reason to go and see Ferdy again!*

My body prickled with excitement as I cheered silently, while Lady POW paced around the room.

"Of course, it is possible they are using the Jews as a scapegoat. Still, this is discomforting. There have been other deaths, too, where the Parliament members have likely been poisoned."

"Poison." I shuddered. "That sounds awful."

"It is. Especially since the Order has identified the poison in question. It makes it look like the individual has had a heart attack. It is only hours afterward that the skin turns blue at the fingers."

"If it works so well, why did they kill Dr. Artha in the street?" I asked. "And the others, too?"

"It is possible, though very unlikely, that the two Lords had a natural immunity to the poison," Lady Penelope said. "Thus, a different means of disposal would be required."

"And Dr. Artha?"

"We don't know yet if he was killed by the same people. That is one thing we are looking at in this investigation. But just because something looks a certain way, does not mean it is true. Once you see that, you begin to see everything else."

A small smile flitted to my lips as I recalled Ferdy's similar observations. "I suppose you're right, even though I have yet to see it."

"Then you must understand why this is too important for you to go about untested," Lady Penelope said. "There is more than your comfort at risk, Eleanora."

I snorted. "It's been years since I've had a life of comfort."

"Even in your life under your stepmother's cruelty," Lady Penelope said, "you have been sheltered from the world's pain. Do not think pain only takes something away from you. You have experienced things being taken away, but you have also been given things as a result."

I suddenly felt very small, as the world around me grew and I shrank.

In that moment, I did not know what was more overwhelming to me; the idea that my pain, as great as it was some days, was small compared to the world's, or the idea that the world's problems were much bigger and much more complex compared to mine.

As if she sensed my displacement, Lady Penelope nodded prudently. "You have lived your life here, on the outskirts of Prague and across the Vltava. As you grow older, you see more of the world and its politics, its hypocrisy, and its illusions. The trick is not to allow it to drag you down."

I was uncomfortable with the bitterness in her voice, but it was not enough to stop me from seeing that, despite her cynicism, Lady POW was still determined to accomplish her goal. "Yes, Lady Penelope."

She gave me an approving look, no doubt at my humble tone. "Whatever our association comes to be, Eleanora, I will always be your grandmother, and I am very proud to have that title. When Eleanor died, I thought all was lost. Now I know that I was wrong. Of all things I could have been wrong about, I am very glad it was that."

Looking me up and down with a critical eye once more, she added, "Which is why I am going to tell you now that you will need to go on a diet and begin an exercise regime as we make our way into Prague's Society. You are much too soft around your middle to be considered fashionable. The empress would be frightened if she ever met you in this state."

I groaned. "Empress Elisabeth is much too thin," I said with a shudder. "I have heard the rumors that she has a thirteen-inch waist, and if my hips are good for birthing, I doubt I will ever have her proportions."

"If you are going to add to your stepmother's comeuppance, we must make you a sensation, yes?"

She must have expected me to nod or voice my agreement, but my accommodating disposition was gone. "A sensation is more feasible than a stick, Madame."

Lady POW chuckled. "Oh, Eleanora. You do remind me so much of Eleanor. You will be a legend among the town within a fortnight."

Pudgy hips and all, I thought with a smirk.

9

◊

Before long, I had the distinct feeling that if I was going to be a sensation in less than a fortnight, I was going to spend at least half that time deprived of sleep and food.

"Come along, Eleanora," Lady Penelope called. "We have several more appointments to keep yet."

"Surely you are jesting," I muttered under my breath, as I hurried after Lady POW. We had just come from a milliner's shop, and I was certain I had seen enough hats and bonnets and caps to last me a lifetime.

I yawned as I caught up to my grandmother's spritely steps and decided to be grateful we were at least out in the city. Lady Penelope had spent the previous evening drilling pure boredom into my flesh in the form of etiquette review. I had been astonished to find whole books dedicated to discussing how a lady should walk and laugh and fold her hands and a million other useless things.

My mind felt so stuffed, I had several nightmares surrounding *The Ladies' Guide to Excellence and Etiquette*, easily the most loquacious offender. I decided once I learned enough for Lady POW, I would burn that hideous book.

"This has been a wonderful day for shopping, Eleanora." Lady Penelope glanced around Prague's crowded streets. I had to agree; there had been some snowfall over the past couple of days, preventing us from heading out for any significant errands, but today the sun was out, and the chill in the air added a shine to the whole city. "By the time we are finished here, all of Prague will know who you are and how much you are worth. No one will be able to resist talking about you."

"I hope it is not because you have paid them to do so," I said as a coachman offered me his hand. I climbed up into the coach and settled in the cushions across from Lady POW, while another one loaded some of our new purchases into the back.

"I guess this is the cover part of your plan?" I glanced outside, peeking through the silken coach curtains. As we passed by, heads turned, eyes widened, and mouths dropped.

Lady POW chuckled as I buried my backside even more into the seat cushions. "You will need to get used to this, Eleanora," she said. "You will need to command their attention, and not only keep it, but manipulate it to achieve your ends."

"I'll go ahead and write that down."

Lady POW only nodded curtly at my supposed diligence before starting another lecture of some sort.

Another reason to envy Ben, I thought. He was allowed to stay home in the shadows, while I was forced into the limelight. I did not get a chance to talk with him earlier, before Lady POW summoned me to try on my new walking dress, but I knew he was starting his own form of training with Harshad and Amir.

At the thought of Lady POW's associates—the sympathetic thief and the angry colleague—I decided not to envy Ben after all. Instead, I focused on my own good fortune.

It is rather nice to be in the city without having to worry about selling anything.

As we passed by the Old Town Square, I leaned closer to the window again, suddenly wondering if I would be able to spot Ferdy's faded hat among the crowds.

"Have you heard from any of your contacts here?" I asked Lady POW, unable to resist looking for my own.

"The Minister-President, Count Potocki, is unusually busy," Lady Penelope said. "He has not returned my inquiries, but I have secured invitations to a ball he is hosting for the political elite at Queen Anne's Royal Summerhouse."

"We are going to see him there, then?"

"Yes." Lady Penelope's eyes gleamed. "He is the newly promoted Minister-President, and lately he has been seen in the company of Karl Marcelin, a young man making waves in society because of his disdain for the Emperor."

"I see," I replied neutrally, beginning to realize just how little I knew of politics. "Should we be concerned with Mr. Marcelin? Did he know Dr. Artha?"

"I have not yet discovered an association with Dr. Artha. From what my informants have told me, Marcelin is highly educated, having gone to Oxford in London, and then studying at the university here in Prague. He is close to Benedict's age, but his ambition would suit a much older man."

"And that is a bad thing?"

"Not necessarily," Lady Penelope said. "He is ambitious, but he is looking for funding for his various campaigns. I am curious as to why. From what I have seen, he has always been able to afford quality items, including his education. I wonder if his family is not supportive of his political career. There is not much else I have heard."

"Are not politicians always concerned with money?" I said.

"True. But Marcelin returned to Prague a month ago, and that is when other political figures began dying mysterious deaths," Lady Penelope said. "Dr. Artha is just the latest, and Count Potocki is my best lead. Thus, we will investigate this new young friend of his."

"Do you believe Count Potocki will back Mr. Marcelin's career in politics financially?"

"Possibly, but it would reflect poorly on him as an active agent. His vocal support is enough. In regard to finances, Marcelin is single, and rumors have said he is looking for an heiress to marry." Her eyes glittered. "Which is where you will come in."

"You don't want me to marry him, do you?" I asked, suddenly frightened and appalled.

"Heavens no, Eleanora." Lady POW shook her head. "For now, I plan on collecting several invitations for various dinners, social calls, and balls in the coming weeks. I am sure you will get your chance to playfully ignore him, drive him mad, and then make him spill all his secrets."

"What?" I sputtered.

"Calm down," Lady Penelope said. "We are working with a short window of time, and we cannot wait for a full, fashionable courtship and wedding."

"Oh." I was relieved.

"A quick seduction might be all we need, should it come to that."

I started coughing.

"Oh, do grow up, Eleanora," Lady Penelope scolded. "I have no patience for this."

"But—"

"But what?" Lady Penelope looked down her nose at me. "You know I need the cover, Eleanora, and the cover I will have. But in the meantime, you will just have to trust me."

"Fine," I growled. "But I don't want to talk about intercourse."

"For now, you must focus on the task at hand. If you want to help, pay attention to the things you see, and what the people say. Learn your lessons well. Observation is a dying art, Eleanora, and you will never gain the upper hand on your opponent if you are too concerned with yourself." She glared at me. "Especially if you are worried I will auction you off to a suitor of my choosing."

I desperately wanted to roll my eyes, but I only gave her a contrite look. It seemed to be the quickest way to appease her. "Apologies, Lady Penelope."

My hands curled in the walking dress I was wearing. The bright yellow material had turned several heads as I walked through the various shops with Lady POW at my side. I had to give credit to her seamstresses, and of course to Lady POW herself. If she wanted me to stir up rumors and draw attention, she had certainly succeeded.

"That color is splendid on you, Eleanora," Lady Penelope had said, when I was unnerved at the thought of wearing it. "It brings out the blue of your eyes and complements your dark hair very nicely."

I was still unsure, but I felt better after she told me my mother favored yellow.

"So far things are going according to plan," Lady Penelope said. "You have captured the attention of Prague beautifully today. Even your slipups have been seen as endearing. I thought Madame Bourgeois was going to kick us out of her shop after you insisted on the roomier sleeves for your gowns, and then you convinced her that you intend to set the trends rather than follow them."

I laughed nervously. "Persuading others must be a family trait, since you were able to convince Cecilia to let me go."

"It was not persuasion that won over the dressmaker," Lady Penelope said. "It was sensibility mixed with charm and tact. I was impressed myself, Eleanora."

It was the first time I could remember her praising me for something I had not struggled to learn, and I allowed myself to savor my first taste of success.

"Convincing Madame Bourgeois to mix in classic Bohemian style with French influence was good for us, too, I think," I said.

Lady Penelope nodded, as her coach came to a stop at Market Square. "I am going to check with some of the vendors. Use this chance to buy whatever else you'd like, and have the bill sent to your stepmother."

"What?" All of my previous purchases ran through my mind. We had to have spent at least two years' worth of income from my father's tenants. "You didn't charge everything to her, did you?"

"Don't worry about the money, Eleanora. It is only to give Cecilia a good scare. That is all."

I laughed a moment later, remembering to do it that musical, charming way *The Ladies' Guide to Excellence and Etiquette* instructed, with a high pitch and my hand covering my mouth in a delicate manner.

As Lady POW strode through the flanks of people, her steps sure and direct as she headed away from me, I felt free once more.

I roamed slowly through the market, ignoring several gazes and open stares more easily, knowing I was supposed to command attention. It helped that I knew there was a footman trailing me, and Lady POW was nearby if I needed her.

I went up to Madame Balthazar's shop, and she greeted me with a confused and happy look.

"My dear Miss Eleanora. My, you look so lovely today!"

"Thank you, Madame," I said, giving her a small curtsy, despite remembering *The Ladies' Guide to Excellence and Etiquette* forbade such posturing to my economic and social inferiors. "I have come into an inheritance from my, um, grandmother," I said. "The Dowager Duchess of Wellington."

"I heard Lord Wellington had multiple affairs," Madame Balthazar said. "I did not realize he married again."

"Well, the title and the land all went to his sons," I said, glad Lady POW had prepared me for such questions. "It seems he married my grandmother and settled a handsome portion on her, as his second wife, when he died. They were not married for a long time."

Madame Balthazar looked impressed as I reiterated all the details Lady POW told me about her scandalous courtship and marriage to one of London's most renowned rakes. She also told me to make things up if I did not remember all of it, because people remembered general stories and key details, but never the full story.

"If you want to be remembered," she had said, "be clear in your speech and emphasize your talking points."

It sounded nice, but I was not sure reality agreed with her.

"This red silk will look lovely on you," Madame Balthazar said, as I began to look at her displays. "It is perfect for you, Miss. You must wear it to a fancy ball and tell all your new friends to come and see me."

It did not take much for me to agree with her. As she totaled up my expenses, the mention of a fancy ball stirred my memory. I thought about the ripped invitation Ferdy had given me to the Advent Ball hosted by Empress Maria Anna.

I wonder if Lady POW knows about the ball.

Thinking it over, I decided I would keep my invitation from Ferdy a secret, but I would talk to Lady POW about the ball. I did not think she would appreciate Ferdy's insistence any more than she would enjoy the ripped letter.

"Madame Balthazar," I said slowly, "do you know of a street urchin named Ferdy? He says he knows a lot of vendors around here."

"Oh, of course," she said. "He brokered a trade between me and a midwife just a few weeks ago, when my daughter became feverish after delivering her twins."

"He seems to be good at making deals," I said.

She laughed. "That he is, Miss. But he is, too, a very kind young man."

"Do you know where I might find him?" I asked, trying not to blush. "I … I actually had him help me sell something before, and I wanted to see about giving him his full pay."

"I have not seen him in a few days," she said. "He has probably been down by the riverbanks again. There are fights there every week, and there are plenty of men who enjoy watching a good fight and having a good gamble."

"Fighting?"

Madame Balthazar chuckled. "Young men easily get bored. If you are fond of him, be grateful the worst thing he does is attend fights down by the riverbanks. Well," she said, wrinkling her nose in distaste. "I suppose he does hang around the Jewish Quarter a lot, too."

"I see." After a quick moment, I decided to risk her scorn. "Why is it bad he associates with the Jews?"

"Oh, poor dear. The Jews cause trouble wherever they go," Madame Balthazar said. "Rumors have been circulating that they are starting to form their own political group here in Prague. And that is the last thing Prague needs now—another group of people who feel entitled to dictate our laws just because they live here."

"Aren't you a migra—never mind." I brushed the matter aside. "How much are my purchases?"

I walked out of the vendor after instructing Madame Balthazar to send the bill to the castle with a bad taste in my mouth. I did not like Madame Balthazar's opinion on the Jews, especially after meeting Mr. Clavan.

My heart swelled at the thought of Ferdy's kindness. He was clearly a man who refused to look down on any person, no matter their ethnicity, culture, religion, or even their social status.

Thinking of him proved to be an enjoyable distraction. I made my way through the market, glancing around, hoping to see Ferdy's cheeky grin and silver eyes light up in mine.

I hope he wasn't lying about wanting to see me again.

The sudden thought made my face flush with heat, and I struggled to dismiss the sudden mix of hope and fear inside of me.

I shook my head, trying to clear my thoughts. Even if he had been lying, I still needed to see him. He was the one who had information on Dr. Artha's death, and Lady POW and I needed it.

My steps came to a slow stop as my hands felt clammy. The footman who had been following me bumped into me as I stopped short, abruptly frightened. What if the reason I was not able to find Ferdy was because he was in trouble? He was the one who told me the details of Dr. Artha's death.

Suddenly, there was more than one reason I wanted to find him.

"Hurry. We need to get back," I ordered the footman, and we began to head toward the coach again, where Lady POW was waiting with a triumphant gleam in her eye.

"We have just been invited to several events," Lady Penelope told me. "A concert, a picnic, a house party, and more! We will be booked from dusk till dawn for the next several days, and I have an invite from Lady Hohenwart herself! This is excellent—"

"Lady Penelope, we need to talk."

"What is it?"

"I have some information," I said, and Lady Penelope quickly ushered me into the carriage.

"What is it?" she asked.

I quickly told her everything that Ferdy and Clavan had told me, desperately raking my mind for the smallest details. As I spoke, I left out their names, hoping she would not ask for them.

"I have received that information already." But then she paused for a moment, looking thoughtful. "You said he came out of the Church of Our Lady of the Snows?" she asked. "That is unusual. He was a patron of St. Nicholas for years."

"Yes, that was the church where he was," I said. "Or something like that, anyway. But I am more worried that the people who told me this are in danger."

"That is the nature of the job," Lady Penelope replied.

"I still think we should go and find the people who told me," I said, keeping my tone careful so I would not reveal anything. "We should warn them. What if we go over to the Jewish Quarter, around where I heard the news, just to see if everything is okay?"

I did not think it was possible to surprise Lady POW, but she blinked twice before she said anything. "There is a line between eccentricity and impropriety you do not cross, Eleanora," she began. "You hint and tease, but never promise anything—no stolen kisses in the gardens, no getting caught *in flagrante delicto*. Going to the Jewish Quarter is not a breach of propriety in Prague, but it promises only the worst sort of trouble for your reputation."

"But it would make people talk, and we might be able to find out more for me as a cover."

"That is a job for your brother and Amir to handle. It would be good practice for Benedict. I will assign them to take care of the task."

"But—"

"Enough, Eleanora." She shook her head. "There is no reason to believe that your source is in trouble. You are concerned for the well-being of others, which is a natural inclination you have, from what I have seen in how you care for Benedict. But you cannot—I repeat, you cannot—allow your feelings to cloud your judgment. For now, as you learn about the Order and work on developing your skills, just follow my orders."

Slowly, I nodded, even though I disagreed with her. As I sat there, I was strongly reminded of Cecilia's way of ordering me around.

I stared down at my folded hands, imagining Ferdy attacked or running from trouble, picturing the Cabal burning to the ground as the neighborhood screamed in panic.

My fingers tightened into fists as I made a decision.

If Lady POW was going to act like a spymaster version of Cecilia, I would do what I had done in the past. I would agree with her to her face, and then when she was not paying attention, I would do what I wanted.

And I will get Ben to help me. If it is his job to help gather information now, he should be able to take care of it for me.

"I am glad that is settled. Now, Eleanora, let us go over our upcoming schedule," Lady Penelope said. "The Hohenwart Ball is tomorrow, and this is our first chance to mingle among the political elites. We will have to make sure your gown is ready, your hair is washed, your shoes are … "

As Lady POW went through the details of the ball, I smiled and nodded. Inside, my mind was only thinking of Ferdy and our adventure into the *Josefskà.* I desperately wanted him to appear in the streets as we passed, even though I knew I could not step out and see him without causing a tidal wave of whispers.

But his smile would have brightened my mood considerably.

10

◊

The Hohenwart Ball was to be my official introduction into Prague's Society, and if I was going to move up in Lady Penelope's limited measurement, everything had to be perfect.

Where have I heard that before?

As Lady POW's carriage cheerfully rolled down the city streets as the moon made its appearance on the horizon, I remembered Cecilia's warning the night of the Duke's arrival. I had a feeling, especially after hearing the Duke of Moravia had left to stay at a friend's townhouse, she still would find a way to make good on her promise.

"Come now, Eleanora, make haste," Lady Penelope hissed. "This is your first ball, and I want it to go perfectly."

We arrived at the Hohenwart house in Lady POW's grand coach. I nervously gripped at my skirts as we stepped down and headed toward the grand manor.

As Lady POW began to list the various social niceties I had to remember, I grumbled to myself, swearing in French under my breath the way Tulia had taught me.

Lady POW likely heard me, because a second later she stopped short, whirling around to confront me. "Listen to me now, Eleanora," she said. "If there is any doubt—any whatsoever—that you are going to be able to do this, I will offer you this chance now. We will turn around, claim an illness, and opt for a soft launch at another ball. But if you stay the course, after tonight, there is no going back. You will reap the consequences of your choice."

She had not even finished speaking before I knew the truth, and I knew my answer.

It was already too late to turn back. Ferdy could be in danger. I had to find a way to make sure he was safe.

After all, Dr. Artha and many others were already dead. How could I go back to knowing nothing but my life under Cecilia? And even with Lady POW allowing me to be free of her, what was the point of being free if I used it to only serve myself?

"I'm ready," I said.

"Are you sure?" Lady Penelope arched her brow. "Last chance."

"I already said I was ready." I whipped out my fan and flapped it furiously. "Now, don't make me repeat it, or I might just change my mind."

At my show of spirit, Lady POW smirked. "Good. Now, we do not want to disappoint Lady Hohenwart. Hurry."

Easy for her to say. My toes were squeezed inside small-heeled shoes, and I had been stuffed into a tight corset. I wondered how my dancing would be affected, with all the petticoats and bindings and fluffy things I was wearing; my gown had to be at least a good fifty pounds by itself.

My hair was pulled back for the evening, while several of my curls playfully slipped free from their pins. I had a small amount of rouge on my face, and even with the little bit I had on, I knew why rouge was supposed to be scandalous. I felt like a mask had been painted on my face. I was literally wearing a lie.

The analogy worked in more ways than one, since my smile was blatantly false as I made my way up the entrance to the Hohenwart Ball.

It was a magnificent house. It stood on a small hill just outside of Prague, on the opposite side from my father's manor; it had taken Lady POW's coach a long time to weave through the city streets. While I had enjoyed the sight of Prague and its glowing nightlife, Lady POW relished the chance to give me one last session of etiquette review.

When I asked about being late, Lady Penelope had replied, "*Psh.* We are fashionably late, and I intend for us to only be fashionable tonight, Eleanora."

It seemed she was no longer content for that, I noticed, as she cajoled me up the stairs.

"Walk gracefully," she murmured.

This was my first big test, and I wanted to show Lady POW I could handle my part. But her orders, while I imagine she thought they would be helpful, were only making my nerves worse. I arched my brow as I glanced down at her feet. "Are you wearing heels?"

"Watch your manners, Eleanora."

"I'm so sorry, I forgot old people can't hear as well," I said more loudly. Another lady and her companion glanced over my way, clearly trying not to laugh at my assentation.

Lady POW frowned, but she said nothing.

I turned my attention to the grand house once more. Several glowing chandeliers and candelabras were scattered throughout; in the grand, gothic windows, I could see billions of lights shining like stars against the night.

I hope it will not be this cold inside, I thought, snuggling into my cloak.

"The red looks wonderful on you," Lady Penelope said. "Be sure to stay away from red wine tonight."

I rolled my eyes when I was sure she was not looking. When she whacked me with her fan lightly a moment later, I knew I had failed.

There is just no sneaking around her, is there?

"Get it out of your system before we get in. Remember your main objective tonight, Eleanora. Go in there and make people talk. I will be watching, but I will also be working. Now, do not fail me."

"I won't."

As the footman came and took our cloaks, I took a deep breath, trying to calm myself.

It was not just Lady POW I wanted to impress. I hoped to make my mother proud, and I wanted to protect my country. It was frustrating that my stomach was turning in knots, my feet were sore, and I was secretly worried for a street urchin who managed to charm his way into my life.

As I stepped into the house, seeing the throngs of people before me, I was relieved to be here in service to my country. *I could be here actually looking for entertainment, rather than here on a mission.*

"Over here," Lady Penelope whispered. "We will enter the greeting line and introduce you to Lady Hohenwart."

I followed her gaze to see our hostess for the evening. Lady Hohenwart was matronly, wearing a fashionable turban covering her whitening hair and a dress even more heavy-looking than my own. She wore the deep purple gown well, even though she was quite thick around the middle. Even with the corset, her gown was pulled too tightly across her bosom.

When she greeted my grandmother, Lady POW gave her a slight bow of the head, and she began giggling like a schoolgirl.

"Oh, Penelope," she crooned. "I'm honored, absolutely honored, that you decided to come. Imagine! The Iron Dowager in my ballroom tonight."

"We thought it was a prudent stop on our way around the city tonight," Lady Penelope replied, before turning to me. "Now that I have been reunited with my lovely granddaughter, nothing will make me so happy as to share the sights with her. May I introduce my Eleanora?"

"Madame," I said, giving her a perfect curtsy.

Lady Hohenwart giggled again. "Oh, you are just lovely, Lady Eleanora," she said. "Please, stay beside me. I simply must introduce you to my guests. We have some of the nation's finest coming tonight."

Lady Penelope pulled out her fan. "If you insist."

We stood there for the next hour, as more people began to gravitate toward us. Lady POW was practically radiating joy as I was introduced to several members of the Upper and Lower House of Lords. Soon after we joined Lady Hohenwart, I noticed that more and more young men were coming up to pay their respects.

I soon found myself surrounded by lords and ladies, members of the militia and the Diets, all of them asking me questions and telling me stories and fawning over me or my gown or anything witty I happened to say.

The attention was intoxicating at first; as I laughed and smiled with them, and as I made them laugh and smile back, I almost forgot why I was supposed to be there.

When I noticed how comfortable I was, it was as if a spell had broken. Thankfully, the crowds around us gradually thinned, as more people sought drinks and dancing, and others made their way to the gardens.

I learned too many names and saw too many faces, and I definitely had my hand kissed more than I would have ever liked.

Thank you, Lord, for allowing me to wear gloves.

Several of the gentlemen asked for me to dance, and Lady POW, despite all her trouble, declined all of them.

Until he arrived.

Long moments passed, and eventually several of the other men began to part the crowd. I looked over to see who was causing the disorganized shuffle.

It was a man; he was tall, with hair the color of night, with just a hint of brown mixed in. His features seemed a little hawkish, but not in a necessarily unattractive way. I could tell from the storms in his eyes he was a man of great passion, and he controlled himself with an iron will. If that alone was not enough to make me look twice, I saw he wore the elegant clothes of a traveled man, with the confidence to match. He stood out among the others instantly as a man who was walking among the world in hopes of leading it.

Even Lady POW seemed to straighten as he came before us.

"Mr. Marcelin," Lady Hohenwart said. Her voice was so squeaky with excitement I had a feeling this was going to be the climax of her night.

"That's Karl Marcelin," Lady POW whispered as she nudged me, and I nodded. I was supposed to see what I could find out about him.

"Lady Hohenwart," he replied. He took her hand and bowed over it reverently. "It is wonderful to be in your company again."

As he bowed, I saw he was glancing at me from the corner of his eye, studying me. I used my fan to hide my blush; so far, the other dandies had been overtly delighted by my appearance and charm, but none of them had seemed so intentional in their attentions. I took the moment to study him back, letting him know in my own way I would not allow him an easy conquest.

Lady Hohenwart also noticed his interest. "May I introduce my dear friend, Lady Penelope Ollerton-Wellesley, and her granddaughter, Lady Eleanora of Bohemia?"

"*Enchanté*," I murmured, as he held my hand. Even through my gloves, I could feel the solid quality behind his strength. "It is a pleasure to meet you, Mr. Marcelin."

"Karl here is a personal friend of Count Potocki and my husband," Lady Hohenwart said. "He has become a very prominent figure among the Diets since returning from London."

"The only reason I was invited tonight, I assure you," Karl replied.

"Oh, Karl, you are too much." Lady Hohenwart laughed before turning to me. "Is he not, Eleanora?"

"I confess, I am not certain," I replied, with just a hint of ennui. "I have only just met Mr. Marcelin."

"You have excellent judgment in such matters, my lady," Karl said, and at once, he was ready to meet my own challenge with one of his own.

I never lost his gaze as I gave him a small, thoughtful smile. "You have only met me just now yourself."

"Then you simply must get more acquainted with Karl, Eleanora," Lady Hohenwart insisted.

"He seems like a gentleman, but he is hardly duty bound to insist on my company."

"I only wish that I could," Karl replied, "but that would hardly allow me to be a true gentleman."

At his remark, I could almost feel Lady POW's excitement beside me. I knew he was on her list, and his acceptance of me proved my exhausting efforts to impress the right people worked well enough to give me a preliminary acceptance into their circles.

"If you want to convince me," I said, still playing coy, "perhaps a compliment or two would help?"

"Lady Eleanora," Karl said. "May I say, you are the most enchanting of flowers in this garden of beauty tonight?"

"I suppose," I said, "since you have just said it, it would be best for me to allow it."

Lady POW and Lady Hohenwart laughed.

"What spirit she has," Lady Hohenwart cheered.

"Indeed," Karl replied. He reached out for my hand once more. "May I then request the honor of your next dance?"

I looked to Lady POW modestly, even though I already knew what her answer would be. Still, it made me look like a dutiful heir, and one who was not necessarily impressed by manners or the man himself.

"Go on, Eleanora," Lady Penelope said. "You have my permission."

There was enough of a sneer in her smile that I decided she was really saying, "*You have my permission to make a fool of yourself.*"

I hated to admit, it was possible she was right. I told Lady POW before that I had learned to dance several years ago, when Priscilla was taught. The instructor, Mr. Binghamton, had caught me watching them several times, and after my stepsister retired for the day, he would allow me to match her success.

After all the shopping around and reviewing etiquette with Lady POW, I had not wanted to review dancing, too.

Lady Penelope pushed me forward, playfully laughing as a cover. "My Eleanora is so modest."

"Karl here has a wondrous reputation as a dancer." Lady Hohenwart glowed with such motherly approval, I wondered if she thought she was helping Lady POW play matchmaker tonight. "She will be in good hands."

"Yes," Karl agreed. "She will."

Grinning broadly to hide my discomfort, I finally allowed him to lead me down the stairs to the dance floor.

God, please help me. Knowing that while my grandmother was content to ignore my silent pleas, God had promised never to do so.

Whispers started immediately. The hushed tones and the soft words licked at my skin, sliding over me with their own sense of grotesque pleasure and perverse delight. The crowd's collective leering and gossip was inescapable; I had to focus hard on Karl's supportive arm as we made our way down to the ballroom dancefloor.

Everyone else seemed to fade as I stepped out onto the marble. As we walked toward the middle of the ballroom, I smiled up at Karl, remembering what Ferdy had told me when we first met.

"Everyone lies about something."

Lady POW wanted me to be a sensation. That meant I had to command attention and control the situation, just as she had taught me.

"Well, sir, I will give you credit," I said. "You do not seem to be overly upset at all the gossip you're sure to inspire."

"I might inspire the gossip," he said, "but you will inspire the poetry."

I laughed, tapping him with my fan playfully, hating myself every step of the way. "What an outrageous thing to say. After all, we haven't even danced yet. For all you know, I could wind up stepping on your feet for the next several moments."

He likely had no idea how much of a possibility it was.

Karl gave me a slow smile. "I'd still risk it."

"Well, quite the gambler, are you?" I needled him. "This is hardly a proper topic for conversation, sir."

"It is entirely proper for a man to be frightened by asking the most vibrant and lovely lady in the room to dance," Karl said. "Especially when you are the loveliest lady in any room I've seen in Prague."

"Well, thank you," I murmured, humbled more than amused. I prayed desperately I would not cripple his toes. While I was trying to decide if he had anything to do with a murder, I had to admit he did not seem like the type.

As the music began and we talked more, I saw he was very sensible, smart, and graceful on his feet. Even as he talked, he led me through the steps of a waltz perfectly. Karl lived up to his reputation as a stellar dancer, and the two or three times I tripped, he caught me with an easy grace I was sure even Lady POW would admire. I fumbled along after him, but I still felt graceful as he caught me.

The waltz was scandalous in many London drawing rooms, and even more so outside of the city. It was said to inspire the worst sort of sin, and as I allowed Karl to lead me, I realized it was very easy to slip into daydreams and lose sight of the task at hand.

Lady POW wanted me to be a sensation, but I wanted to find the truth. I had to protect Ferdy and his friends, after all, and others like Dr. Artha deserved justice.

"So, what brings you to Prague, sir?" I asked. "I might be the loveliest lady here by your judgement, but I cannot imagine I hold a candle to the ladies of Paris or London, or even Rome."

"Most assuredly, my lady, you need not fish for compliments. Especially when you do it in such a manner that it makes it hard for me to assure you I came here just for you."

"It would be hard to do that regardless," I said. "Especially when it is well known you are great friends with Count Potocki."

"Do you know of him?" Karl asked, giving me a dazzling smile.

For some reason, I suddenly had a much harder time concentrating. His smile seemed to tug at me, and I wondered suddenly if we had met before.

I quickly dismissed the possibility. Lady POW told me that he had just come back from his studies abroad, like Alex. If I thought he was familiar, it was likely because Lady POW had reviewed the politics of Prague for hours before so I would have something engaging to discuss, but I was hoping Karl would have other interests. I doubted it, as he warmed to the subject.

"I'm afraid I have not had the pleasure of meeting him yet," I said, realizing Karl was still waiting for an answer.

"Alfred—the Minister-President—is indeed a good friend and mentor of mine."

At least Karl is not hard to look at, I noticed, recalling that Minister-President Potocki was easily forty years my senior. I was not certain of Karl's age, but I doubted he was much older than Ben. If he had just finished his schooling abroad, he would be in his early twenties. Entertaining Karl, and digging down to his secrets, would be easier and likely more interesting.

"So you are here to amuse yourself with the Diets, perhaps?" I asked.

"Are you interested in politics, Lady Eleanora?"

"Only minimally," I said, wanting to keep the focus on him. "But surely that is not the case for you?"

He gave me a smile, one that was both rueful and playful. "Well, my lady, you are indeed correct. I am very interested in what is happening in Prague."

"I did not realize there were so many interesting things happening in Prague's politics. Enlighten me," I pressed, glad Ben was nowhere around to see me. Either he would be disgusted by my performance, or he would have laughed me off the dance floor.

Or he would have hit Karl, for the look on his face as he stared at me.

"I am here as an elected orator," he said. "I will be serving directly under Count Potocki while his successor is elected. He is set on retiring in the new year, due to his health and his interests."

"Are you hoping you will be on the ballot to replace him?"

"It would be the greatest honor of my life to serve Bohemia," he said, his words weighted with passion.

It sounded nice, but I wished he were less vague in his response. "So that is a yes?"

"It is of little consequence," he said, ducking my question once again. "I will say, as of now, I am merely attempting to fulfill the role I was born for. It remains to be seen if God should grant me such a privilege. I have great hope that I can broker deals that would fundamentally change the course of Bohemia's future."

"You must have a lot of connections," I said. "In politics, it is not what you know, so much as who you know."

"I do have the connections," Karl agreed. "But I am always open to more."

I knew he was flirting with me, but his words were infused with such intent that I could only laugh. Otherwise, I would have been frightened. "Are you proposing to me, Mr. Marcelin?"

"Karl, please," he said, this time more easily. "If you are so curious about my intentions, I insist you call me by my given name."

"Surely one cannot fault me for wondering, Mr. Marcelin," I said, intentionally addressing him formally as he spun me around once more. "My grandmother is searching for a husband for me, and she would be remiss in her duty if she did not see to my welfare."

"She is looking, then?" Karl gave me an eager smile. "I heard rumors that she would allow you a Season or two."

"She may be the one looking," I said carefully, "but I am the one who will do the finding."

"You are certainly clever. I must admit, that makes conversation with you all the more engaging."

The music fell to a close, and the audience applauded. I gave Karl a quick curtsy, but before I could excuse myself, he reached for my arm.

"Allow me to escort you back to Lady Wellington," he said. He tucked my hand around his arm and kept it there. "I would ask you for another dance, but I have a feeling your grandmother would object at the gossip."

I hid a smile; Karl's assumption was dead wrong.

"So many people are here, and this is such a beautiful place," I said, as we weaved our way through the crowded room.

"The view from the garden balcony is wonderful," Karl said. "You can see all the city's lights, even the ones down by the Vltava."

"I will have to see it for myself."

I looked back over toward the stairs, hoping Lady POW would give me some idea of what to do next. I blinked in surprise, watching as Lord Maximillian began talking to her.

"I wonder what His Grace is doing here," I said.

"Oh, you mean Lord Maximillian?" Karl followed my gaze. "I imagine he was invited, since he is staying with at the Hohenwart estate for the rest of the year. Lord Hohenwart is a close friend of his."

"He is?"

"Of a sort. Lord Hohenwart, along with Alfred—excuse me, Count Potocki—are avid beer enthusiasts. Both of them have stock in distilleries. But Lord Maximillian is from Moravia, with several estate vineyards. They have argued for years over which is better, but they also exchange bottles and harvesting information every so often."

"Do you also have an interest in such topics?" I asked.

Karl shook his head. "I have little interest in where my beer and wine come from, so long as it is enjoyable."

"I see." I started to feel a slight panic. We were getting closer to Lady POW and Lord Maximillian, and I still had nothing on Karl that seemed to help our investigation much.

"Lord Maximillian has generously gifted His Imperial Majesty with a full shipment of wine this year," Karl said. "It will arrive just in time for the Advent Ball Empress Maria Anna is hosting this year. I know she is most pleased. Several other representatives from around Bohemia are acquainted with his estate's reputation."

The Advent Ball? I thought of the ripped invitation Ferdy had handed me days ago.

"Will you be attending the Advent Ball this year?" I asked. "I have heard it is wonderful."

"I have attended it before, though it has been some years since my last attendance," Karl said. "It is indeed quite wonderful. Her Imperial Majesty the former Empress does an incredible job each year."

"You have attended it before, so that must mean you are from Prague, then?"

"Yes," Karl replied. "I have been many places, but I was born here, and I relish the chance to be back."

"Where are you staying?" I asked. "With your family?"

"I am staying with a friend," Karl replied. "Perhaps you have heard of him? Roman Szapira of Slavuta is hosting me for the first part of the season, until after the Advent Ball. He is a friend and confidant of the count's, and one of the most well-known architects in Prague. He is currently being commissioned to renovate Prague Castle's wine cellar."

"His name sounds familiar," I lied. "Who else does he know?"

"He would likely know of your grandmother," Karl answered. "She is quite famous."

I laughed in that fake, overly charming way. "Of course Lady PO—I mean, my grandmother—is well known. She is very rich and very difficult to ignore. Would she know your friend, Mr. Szapira?"

"I am not certain. Roman is very well known in other respects. Like Lord Maximillian, he has a large vineyard, and I know he and the count argue over the virtues of the vine quite frequently."

I will have to ask Lady POW about him.

As if she knew I was longing for her counsel, Lady POW suddenly stood before me—on the arm of Lord Maximillian. The Duke looked down his pepper and salt mustache at me with curious eyes.

"Eleanora," Lady Penelope said. "I have accepted His Grace's invitation to dance. Please wait for me with Lady Hohenwart."

"I shall watch over her for you, Madame." Karl patted my arm gallantly. "I am greatly enjoying her company."

I almost rolled my eyes as Lady POW profusely thanked him. What did Karl really think he was doing for me? Taking on a dragon? Slaying a witch? Rescuing me? Keeping me company as I stood with the hostess of the evening hardly seemed like something worthy of a grand announcement.

"I hope you are not enjoying her too much," Lady Penelope told Karl. "I have heard you are in the market for a bride, and I fear I cannot part with my Eleanora so easily, now that we have been reunited."

Karl smirked. "I assure you, I am up for the job of convincing you, should it be necessary, Madame."

Pardon me? I was too shocked to say anything. Was he joking? I wondered. Who really decided they were going to marry someone after one dance?

Before I could make my own statement on the matter, Lord Maximillian turned to me. "Perhaps you will say hello to my daughter, Lady Eleanora," Lord Maximillian suggested. "I do not believe you had much time to converse the last time our paths crossed."

It took no effort to remember Teresa Marie's entitled self-absorption and her churlish display at Cecilia's dinner party.

"Perhaps I will, Your Grace." I gave him a quick curtsy before Karl and I headed over to stand next to Lady Hohenwart and Teresa Marie.

It was hard not to feel like a novice standing next to her. Teresa Marie was expertly dressed, with her hair piled up on her head, with a few stray curls twisting free. Her amber hair gleamed under the chandelier and the pastel colors of her dress seemed to make her skin glow, while a string of ruffled flowers winded around her bodice like a vine, looping itself under her bustle.

In my bright red dress, with its simple French silhouette and lace trim at the sleeves, I easily saw the contrast between us. I had a feeling that, as we stood there, others did, too.

"Well, well, Lady Eleanora," Teresa Marie said. Her lips were tight across her teeth, and I knew at once she would have sold her soul for the chance to spew venom at me. "So nice to see you again. And what a lovely dress you have on. It is so … different … from the one you were wearing the last time we met. You must give me the direction of your new modiste."

Karl reached for her hand. "I do not believe we have been introduced," he said. "But any friend of Lady Eleanora's surely has the highest of recommendations."

Teresa Marie smiled much more warmly. "Lady Eleanora is too kind to introduce us," she said, shooting me a dirty look behind her flower-covered fan.

She cornered me into an introduction. Even though I was not interested in marrying Karl, I hated her for her deceit. "Mr. Marcelin, this is Lady Teresa Marie, Countess of Moravia."

Karl introduced himself as a new song began. I glanced back to see Lady POW and Lord Maximillian dance. From Lady POW's form and frigid smile, I could tell she was less than delighted with her choice, but there was a determination on her face that seemed to suggest she had a good reason for making herself suffer.

Karl saw me watching them and cleared his throat. "I must thank you once more for the earlier dance, Lady Eleanora," he said. "One account of thanks hardly seems appropriate for such pleasure."

"You're welcome." I gave him a teasing smile. "I will forgive your lapse of manners, and I am happy to have a chance to talk with you without worrying I will step on your toes. I fear I am not as experienced with the waltz as you are, sir." I used my fan to hide my face with graceful contrition.

Teresa Marie cleared her throat. "Perhaps you would find another dancing partner that is equally as charming, Mr. Marcelin?"

"I sincerely doubt it." Karl brushed her subtle suggestion aside and kept his attention on me. "Might I ask to share another dance with you later this evening, Lady Eleanora? Your grandmother had given me permission before, so I do not see why it would not be allowed."

"I have often been complimented on my own skill at the promenade and even the Scottish Reel," Teresa Marie remarked. "Perhaps you would be interested one of those?"

Karl did not seem to hear her at all this time. "Well, Lady Eleanora?"

I hesitated for only a second, before begrudgingly deciding that if I was going to talk to him more, it was best I accept his invitation. "I would be—"

"Excuse me, sir."

Karl whipped around to see a footman behind him, and I breathed a quick sigh of relief. I was getting tired of smiling, and I was glad for the break. I was also better able to enjoy seeing Teresa Marie, as she silently fumed at Karl for neglecting her. Given her churlishness, I felt my own delight at her anger was a forgivable offense.

I turned my attention back to Karl when I heard him snap at the footman. "What is it? Can't you see I am busy?"

I winced at his tone. His polite demeanor dimmed as he glared at the servant.

"Beggin' your pardon, sir," the footman said. "But a message of grave importance has come for you." He held out a small note.

Karl grabbed it and turned to read it in the small lamplight beside us. When he cursed under his breath and crumbled the note, I knew it was not good news.

"Thank you," he said, waving the footman away. He turned back to me. "I must profoundly apologize, Lady Eleanora. I find I must depart for tonight."

"Is something wrong?" I asked. "Where are you going?"

Inside his dark gray eyes, an angry storm was brewing. "Nothing you need concern yourself with." Karl took my hand and bowed, before kissing it gallantly. "I hope I will see you at other balls in the future."

"I have been invited to the Advent Ball," I said. "Perhaps I will see you there?"

"Yes, you will," he said. "I have been invited along with several of the other nobles and aristocracy. But I hope to see you much sooner than the Advent Ball. That is still a week away."

"My grandmother and I have been invited to several events."

"I will see to finding you again soon, then," Karl said. "So we might enjoy another dance. Farewell, my lady."

"It was a pleasure, Mr. Marcelin." I curtsied, and then I watched him go. I nearly laughed at Teresa Marie's pout when he forgot to give her his goodbyes.

Lady Hohenwart seemed to forget about Teresa Marie, too, since she patted my shoulder in a motherly manner. "Do not fret, dear. He seems most enchanted by you."

I nodded. Before I could respond by saying something witty and amusing and completely forgettable, another footman caught my eye.

I saw his shadow in the hallway behind us. His hand waved at me, motioning for me to come over. I could not see his face, but there was something familiar about him. Curious, I decided to investigate.

"Excuse me, Lady Hohenwart," I said. "I am going to … the ladies' withdrawing room."

After Lady Hohenwart's quick directions, I slithered off and then twisted around, ducking into the dark hallway.

The footman was no longer there. I continued deeper into the corridor, cautious, but still determined.

Several steps later, I realized I was in a private hallway used for servants. There were no decorations along the wall, and the dimmed lights hid a good deal of the poor cleaning.

"What that was all about?" I wondered if my imagination was getting the better of me. Silent seconds ticked by, and I suddenly felt foolish.

I sighed. "I should have stayed with Lady Hohenwart after Karl left."

"I hope you will excuse his impromptu exit," a voice said from behind me. "He received a note that his brother was down in the center of town, making a fool of himself with an actress."

I stopped short, turning back toward the source of the voice. "Who's there?"

"Over here."

I watched as a man came out of a darkened corner of the hallway. His roguish grin caught the small glimmer of the moonlight. There was no denying that smile, and I gave him one of my own. "Ferdy?"

"At your service, Lady Ella."

11

◊

Ferdy shifted out of the shadows, and I was unable to stop the rush of happiness inside of me. Before I remembered myself, I ran over and embraced him. I was so happy to see him, after wondering if he had gotten into trouble over Dr. Artha's murder.

"What are you doing here?" I backed away from him, noticing he was dressed in livery identical to the footman who had delivered the note to Karl, but as he stood before me, I saw he was missing the matching hat and his outfit seemed much too loose.

He bowed over my hand, and as much as I expected him to kiss it, I was disappointed when he did not. He kept himself at a respectful distance, and I found myself more irritated than relieved at his propriety.

I wonder if Ferdy has read The Ladies Guide to Excellence and Etiquette *too?*

He gestured down his clothes. "I'm working, clearly. But I've decided to take a break, now that I know you are here."

"Is that how you know what was in the note Karl received?" I asked.

"It's not too hard to figure out the secrets footmen carry. They're only too happy to share interesting tidbits of information between themselves."

"Is this another one of your jobs?"

"You ask a lot of questions," Ferdy said, and I blushed again. "But I don't mind answering them. This is not usually one of my jobs. They've hired some additional staff for the party tonight."

That would explain the ill-fitting garments. Extra hires don't have much time for proper fittings.

"But when I heard you had asked about me from some of the vendors in Market Square, I wanted to come and find you. Lately you have been the talk of the city, it seems, so it was not hard to find you tonight."

"So you decided to come and work here, all to see me?" I was flattered and embarrassed, but still pleased. "Don't you think one of your superiors will notice you are missing?"

"Someone will likely notice *you* missing before they miss me."

"That's true. My grandmother will likely be worried if I am not back with Lady Hohenwart soon."

"I actually meant that other guests would miss you. I certainly would, were I among them."

"We have a little time to talk," I said, daring myself to forget Lady POW would be upset with me for spending time away from the ballroom.

Ferdy reached out his arm, just as gallantly as Karl had moments ago. "Shall we take a quick stroll through the corridors, my lady?"

I took his arm with no regrets. "I am actually glad you are here," I admitted as we walked. "It is nice to see a familiar face."

"Familiar and fun," Ferdy reminded me. "Who else here would save you from a thief and take you through the city's forbidden haunts, all to find a new home for your lovely book?"

I tapped his arm with my fan at his teasing. "How is Mr. Clavan enjoying *The Prelude*?"

"He loves it. He devoted a whole hour to it at our last meeting," Ferdy said.

"It sounds like a job or club when you say it like that, instead of a friendly visit."

"It is more of a meeting, in actuality. Clavan and Eliezer are business associates," Ferdy said. "Clavan is the owner of the Cabal, but with Eliezer, he helps run a small publication company dedicated to discussing politics and current events. They hold meetings every week where they talk over different things, and I enjoy listening to them."

"Are they a political group?" I asked, remembering what Madame Balthazar had said.

Ferdy laughed. "No, but they discuss politics often. My friend Jarl works for them on the side, writing up pamphlets and articles that they submit to different newspapers and distribute to interested parties."

"I see."

"You should come. To one of their meetings, I mean," Ferdy said. "If you like books, you will like it."

"I am curious about it. Mr. Clavan seems like a good man."

"He certainly is," Ferdy agreed. "But never let him know I agreed with you. Clavan knows nearly everything that goes on in Prague, as it all filters through the Cabal sooner or later."

"Even news about specific people, like Karl Marcelin?" I asked, and Ferdy's smile suddenly waned.

"I suppose." His voice was still cheery but suddenly hollow. "Are you interested in him? Is that why you danced with him?"

"Do you know him?" I asked.

Ferdy scoffed. "Oh, I know him," he said. "But I don't like him. We have very little in common, and even the little we do, I'm sure he would be willing to argue."

"So you know him? Personally?"

"We've met," Ferdy said, his lips pursed with unpleasantness. "I know a lot of people myself, from working in some of the top social circles."

"He seemed very nice to me."

"That's because he likes you, clearly." Ferdy looked glum. "But he does not think much of people who disagree with him and people who inconvenience him."

I thought about how Karl had snapped at the other footman when he had come to deliver the note.

"He's very smart," Ferdy said. "He can make himself sound as though he agrees with you, even if he doesn't. He can quote a thousand and a half philosophers and poets, and even some Americans, but he can't see the wisdom behind all of his knowledge."

"So you do not agree with him in anything? Not even on politics?"

"Definitely not there," Ferdy said. "I'll admit I enjoy Clavan and his Cabal for the politics. There is something about a government that can't sign a whole country over to an Empire at the stroke of a pen. Even Empress Elisabeth has sympathetic leanings toward democracy. Karl's views on the matter are vastly different. He wants to return Bohemia to a full sovereignty."

"He seems to be quite popular," I said, even as I remembered Lady POW mentioning he disliked the current Emperor.

"The Federalists fear him, but they keep it polite, on the chance he actually will be elected to the Bohemian Diet or assigned to the Minister-President position when Count Potocki steps down," Ferdy explained. "The socialists on both sides can tolerate him, when they are not fighting amongst themselves. They think he is a nice enough man on his own. That will allow many people to tolerate his policies for some time, even if they are failures in the end. And the Nationalists, of course, love him. They are so happy to see some youth and energy coming into Bohemian politics."

"What of Germany and Prussia, and the Austria-Hungarians?"

"What of them? The Emperor has demonstrated time and again that Bohemia is hardly his concern," Ferdy said. "Other nations are too worried about their own to worry about us."

"That's interesting." I wondered if anything had to do with Lady POW and the recent murders.

"You're strange," Ferdy said. "Why so interested in politics?"

I shrugged, and then decided to turn the tables on him. "You seem interested in it as well. That is strange, for a street urchin such as yourself."

Ferdy grinned just as I realized I had insulted him. "First, I'm not polite enough to keep myself from talking to you about anything, even if we are talking about something as indecent as politics. And second, I know enough about politics that it amuses me," he said. "The world will never be a better place with people just talking about it, whether they try to shape the world into their vision, or they scrape their words out of the clay of the world itself."

"I don't know about politics much," I said. "Just a little, mostly from what my father taught me. But I like learning what I can from others."

Especially if they are going to help me solve a murder.

"Governments, according to the Americans, were made to secure the natural, inalienable rights from God," Ferdy said. "It gets to be a bigger deal when there is a government who is preventing the people from their rights."

"Did Mr. Clavan tell you that?" I giggled.

"Why, yes he did," Ferdy said with his usual guilelessness, and I laughed even harder.

"Good, I've made you laugh, and for real," Ferdy said. "None of that fake, flirty chittering you did earlier."

"How did you know that was fake? And how long were you spying on me and Karl?"

"Long enough to wait for the footman to deliver the message," Ferdy said. "And that took him enough time, to be sure. I should have waited until afterward to pay him."

Realization struck me. "You sent Karl the message?"

"Of course." Ferdy gave me his charming grin. "You know I would never miss the chance to rescue you if I could, Ella."

Mild shock sank into me, and I was just as surprised to find I was pleased. My steps slowed, eventually coming to a stop near a window.

"I know him well enough to get him to leave, and I would not have missed the chance to steal you away for even a few moments this evening."

I suddenly realized that we were all alone. There were no other people around, and the last warmth of the ballroom had long since been whisked away.

"Are you angry?" Ferdy asked. "I didn't want to upset you."

"No." I shook my head. "I'm fine. I am just surprised at—"

"—how much you missed me."

Despite being interrupted, I could only laugh. But after a moment, I had to admit Ferdy was right. Everyone else out in public was someone to lie to or someone to manipulate. Ferdy still knew me as the lady who was forced to do her stepmother's shopping, dressed in a maidservant's dress and accompanied by her muted neighbor.

"Well, I have been worried for you," I said. "My grandmother was concerned of all the dead politicians turning up, and I thought you would be in trouble since Mr. Clavan asked you about it."

"I see." Ferdy squeezed my hand. "There's no need to worry about me. I have been out in the city long enough to know how to take care of myself and cover my tracks."

"That's a relief, but I want you to promise me that you will be careful."

"I would never deny you anything." Ferdy stood beside me, and as I looked out over the view, I had a new appreciation for how peaceful and robust the city looked. The simple happenings during the day, and the darker stains of murder and intrigue of the shadows, seemed to whisk away into the light of its magic.

Prague had stood for hundreds of years, and the blood of my father's ancestors ran through me, bringing me to this moment in time, in all its vastness and mystery, watching as the kingdom and its housed traditions continued to stand against time's ebb and flow. The richness and the endurance of it all added something mystical to everything, and I wondered, glancing over at Ferdy, if there were things that really did last forever. The warmth of his arm brushed against my shoulder, and I was strongly tempted to lean into him.

"I must admit," Ferdy said, "that I have been worried for you, too. I was happy to hear of your grandmother's arrival, but I thought maybe you would forget about me once she came and took you out on all those fancy shopping adventures."

"I didn't," I said with a laugh. "If anything, I will need you more in the coming days, to remind me who I was before she came. I feel almost like a different person in all these fancy clothes."

"You are different. You are more beautiful than ever." Ferdy waited until it was clear I was too embarrassed to reply before adding, "But if it will make you feel better, I can steal something from you. I'm willing to bet you would chase me down, just like you did to the Turkish man."

I smiled at the thought of Ferdy running from me, clutching something against his chest as I tried to steal it back.

Looking up into his eyes, I suddenly had to wonder if he was not already stealing something from me; my heart seemed to beat faster as I stood there.

"You seem to like gambling," I said, keeping the conversation light as I pondered the depths of my heart, and what it held for the pleasant street urchin and job hopper I'd met only days ago.

"Some things are worth the risk," Ferdy replied, stepping even closer to me.

"Always the charmer," I whispered, before Ferdy tightened his fingers around mine and he drew my hand to his lips.

"And you, Ella, are always the enchanter," Ferdy replied. "But your spells would be even more irresistible if you were to only stop lying."

"Lying? About what?" I asked. His remark caught me off guard, and suddenly I wondered if he had found out about me, Lady POW, and the Order of the Crystal Daggers. I momentarily pictured Lady POW bursting into flames, angry with me for my carelessness.

Ferdy grinned. "How much you want to kiss me, of course."

I nearly laughed in relief, but then his eyes caught mine in the moonlight. Nerves of a different sort twisted inside of me as I saw his gaze slip down to my lips.

He was only a breath away from me. My heart began to beat faster, racing like a jubilant melody. In the distance, Prague Castle glowed with a mix of light from the moon and stars. Everything seemed to overwhelm me in that moment. I could smell the fragrance of the gardens below us; I could sense the barest edge of the wind … feel the tremor of my hand in his.

Ferdy's silver eyes were bright as he waited for my response, his breath warm against my cheek. My hand was still on his arm, and his other hand covered it gently.

I knew we were alone. It was a moment where I could be free to do as I pleased, and, as hard as it was for me to admit, Ferdy was right.

I liked him, a lot more than I should, and I did want to kiss him. That was why I stayed where I was, daring myself to be brave, daring myself to allow him so close to me—even as my logic warned me, and the expectations placed on me by others cried out bitterly.

He was a street lad, someone who was fast and loose with the truth, and he had just admitted to me that he had tricked one of the most well-known political stars of Prague in order to steal some time with me.

Everything seemed so strange. Even a week ago, Ferdy was someone I never would have expected, someone I never would have even dared to dream was real.

But here he was, standing next to me—and here I was, letting him, hoping he would close the distance between us. I could take half a step and find my body pressed against his. Our breath mingled together as I was overrun with confusion and curious longing.

"I won't force you to tell me the truth, Ella," Ferdy whispered. "I know better than most that some lies are preferable to the truth. But I can't keep aching for you like this."

Heat fluttered to my cheeks. "Do you really want to kiss me?"

He laughed and stepped back from me, making me miss the shadow of his warmth. "Oh, Ella, it's no wonder why I am enchanted by you. Of course I do. I might be the bigger liar between us, but I could never lie about that."

"Why?" I asked. Another thought struck me at his words. "What are you lying about?"

"Plenty," he said. "But not about wanting to kiss you. Even if I were to say otherwise on that matter, you would find the truth out easily enough. I am sure it is written on my face at this point."

My brain was limpid mush as I tried to focus. "Were you lying about your friends earlier?" I asked. "About Mr. Clavan and the others?"

"Why would I need to lie about that?" Ferdy asked. "No, they are intellectual, and yes, a little scary, especially considering how fast Eliezer talks, but they have nothing to do with this part of our conversation."

"I suppose you have a point. You're right."

Ferdy grinned. "About you wanting to kiss me?"

I blushed again, before glancing back down the darkened corridors of the Hohenwart house. "I should probably head back. My grandmother will be worried by now, I think. It probably does not take anyone this long to find a powder room, even if they are lost."

"Your chaperone will likely need her vinaigrette, especially since Karl left."

"Hardly," I scoffed, but I smiled at the thought of Lady POW fainting.

We walked for several moments in silence, retracing our steps back to the ballroom. All too quickly, the music grew louder and I felt my freedom shrink as my time with Ferdy ended.

"I would love it if you could come and see me again," Ferdy said.

"This time, you were the one who came to see me," I pointed out. "You seem to have better luck in finding me than I do in finding you."

He laughed again, but softly this time, as we were approaching the edge of the shadows.

"That's true," he said. "But come to one of Clavan's Cabal meetings. They're on Thursdays and Mondays, in the evenings. I'll be there. And you'll be able to see for yourself what the Cabal is all about."

It was so tempting to say yes.

So I did.

"I'll make arrangements," I promised, even though I had no idea how I was going to make it work.

"Good." Ferdy finally pressed his lips against my knuckles, and then against my palm, and I felt my legs go weak with strange wanting. "Next time, Ella, I will find a way to get you to admit you want to kiss me."

Unable to resist giving him a challenge, I arched my brow at him. "We will see, won't we?"

"You're not denying it," he pointed out, and I felt my heart flutter as he blew me a kiss.

I headed back toward the ballroom, sighing and smiling, unexplainably happy. Ferdy was safe, and I would see him again soon. And, I thought, feeling a little guilty, if I did go to the Cabal, I might be able to see if there was any more news on Dr. Artha's death.

My happiness was immediately interrupted by my grandmother, almost as if she could sense how forbidden it was.

"Eleanora."

I snapped to attention as I saw her in the doorway to the ballroom. "Lady Penelope."

"Where have you been?" she asked. "I have been waiting for you to reappear for the last thirty minutes."

"Um … I was looking for the withdrawing room," I said. "I had to take care of some … personal needs. I was lost."

Lady Penelope groaned. "I knew I should not have danced with Lord Maximillian. Leaving you on your own was clearly a mistake this early in the game."

"You could have refused Lord Maximillian," I said. "What did he want to dance with you for, anyway? Did he want a chance to ruffle your petticoats after you ruined his plans with Alex and Teresa Marie?"

"No." Lady Penelope frowned. "He seemed very thankful I gave him a way out of that arrangement. His daughter will be able to find someone in higher circles now."

"If she's charming enough," I said, thinking of how she had failed to take Karl's attention away from me.

"Lord Maximillian took the time to check up on you, to see how you were adapting to life outside of Cecilia. He said he was shocked and appalled to find out that you and Benedict were being treated so horrifically."

I crossed my arms over my chest. "I do not believe him."

"He also assured me that he and his daughter would refrain from speaking of your time as a servant."

"I don't care about that," I said. "If anything, maybe it would be better for people to know the truth. He is likely only refraining from saying anything to keep Cecilia from looking bad, and himself by extension."

"That is true," Lady Penelope said. "But you are smart enough to know that you are the entertainment for society, Eleanora. No one wants to feel guilty in seeing you as entertainment, either. Revealing the truth is counteractive to your efforts to enchant them."

I thought of Ferdy, and how he had called me an enchanter. Was it possible he felt sorry for me? A moment later, I decided he did not. He lived on the streets, working for a living. He was not the same as the rest of society.

Besides, I thought with a quick blush, it was clear he had other feelings for me than pity.

"Eleanora? What is it?"

"Karl told me that Lord Maximillian is a guest at the Hohenwart house," I said, changing the topic. I did not want to think of my role in society.

"Karl?"

"Mr. Marcelin."

"You were supposed to get him to like you, Eleanora, but there is no need for you to like him when we speak face to face, as we are now."

"Well, he was nice enough, especially to me," I said, remembering his kindness and patience with me and my subpar waltzing skills. "He mentioned several things to me about his high hopes for his political career and how Count Potocki shares an interest in wine with Lord Hohenwart and the Duke of Moravia. That was when he told me His Grace was a guest at the Hohenwart estate."

"Lady Hohenwart did not mention that to me," Lady Penelope replied in an irritated tone. "But it sounds like you have some information we might be able to use. We will discuss it later with Amir and Harshad."

"And Ben."

"Yes, of course."

"Does this mean I passed your test?" I asked. I thought of the crystalline blades of Lady POW's daggers, the chosen weapons of the Order of the Crystal Daggers.

Will I get the chance to wield them one day soon?

Lady POW sighed. "Now is not the time for this, Eleanora."

"But I did *some* good tonight. And if it's not good enough, you know as much as I do that it's hardly fair to test me when I don't even know what I am being tested on."

"On the contrary. It is the perfect time to test you."

"It's still not fair."

"Life is not fair, Eleanora, in case you haven't noticed."

"I assumed it would be at least somewhat better after you came and assumed responsibility of me from Cecilia. Her chores were harder on my body, maybe, but yours are completely mad on the mind."

"As I said, enough of this." She took my hand. "Come. We are leaving."

"Do we have permission from the social betters to do so?" I scoffed. "Or is this one of your orders that I must follow blindly?"

"None of that, Eleanora. If you must know, another murder happened earlier tonight. Amir and Ben are waiting for us outside. We must hurry."

Shame and silence weighed heavily on me as we made our exit.

12

◊

"Where are we headed?" I asked, as I settled into the carriage cushions. I pulled my cloak more tightly around my shoulders, regretting that I had to be in my evening gown the first time I joined Ben on a mission.

"We are going to the Church of Our Lady of the Snows." Lady Penelope pulled the carriage curtains shut and began tugging at the lacings and hooks of her gown.

"What are you doing?" I asked.

"Changing." She reached down under her seat and lifted up the cushion. I was amazed to see there was a secret drawer there, and I was even more confounded as she tossed me a pair of breeches. "Which is what you should be doing."

I gripped the soft material hesitantly, noticing it was cut in an older style. "Do I just change … in here?"

"Now is not the time for modesty, Eleanora. We only have a few blocks."

Carefully, I pulled off my own gown, alternatively cringing and sighing over the next several long moments. It was a simple ball gown, but it was so fine I hated the thought of ruining it. As the carriage jostled, I stumbled and shifted uncomfortably in the small space I had to change.

"You'll get accustomed to this," Lady Penelope assured me, before she pulled a shirt on over her own chemise. She seemed to all but slip out of her own gown.

I tried to ignore her, considering she had a critical gaze set on my middle, where I was trying to squeeze myself flat as I squirmed in my petticoats.

Finally, several more uncomfortable moments later, I bundled up my chemise and tucked it into the pants. My gown bubbled up on the empty seats, and as much as it irritated me, I regretted rolling it up into a ball and shoving it into the newly empty drawer. I winced as I shut the top down on its soft fabric.

"Amelia and the others will be able to tend to it," Lady Penelope told me, and I was grateful for her concern, even if I hated to give her seamstresses more work.

I looked over to see Lady POW was dressed all in black. She had on her slacks, a shirt, and even a greatcoat and hessians. She bundled up her gray hair and tucked it under a hat, before pulling out a walking stick and sitting down once more.

"You don't happen to have shoes for me, too, do you?" I asked.

She quickly tossed me an identical set of clothes and a fine walking stick of my own. "Pull up your collar to help hide your hair."

Moments later, I was wearing a set of man's clothes, and I felt deliciously sinful in doing so. I kept moving my legs, crossing them over each other, reveling in the freedom to move.

"This is great," I said, pulling the black greatcoat over my stays. "This is almost as good as my stealth habit. And it fits so well."

Lady POW smiled. "I had a feeling it would. You are close to your mother's size the last time she wore it."

My eyes went moist. I felt the soft material surround me in a new way, almost as if I now saw it as my mother's embrace.

"Oh, if only Harshad could see you, Eleanor."

"Eleanora," I muttered.

She waved my correction aside, quickly and meaninglessly apologizing before moving onto the next topic. That was when I realized I had not seen Harshad since the day Lady POW initiated Ben and me into the Order. I wondered why. Maybe it was because he was busy with Ben, or maybe it was because of something Lady POW had said.

Those seemed like good reasons.

But why would Lady POW get such delight at the thought of torturing him?

Eleanor.

It was jarring to realize Harshad had known my mother, too. If Lady POW was looking at me, and seeing my mother, she knew Harshad would likely see her, too.

I shuddered inside the large greatcoat. How much did Lady POW have to hate Harshad to enjoy torturing him that way?

"You will need to make sure you follow my lead when you wear those clothes," Lady Penelope was saying, as I drifted back into the moment. "Men are different from women in form and function. We walk differently, we carry ourselves differently, we even think differently. And we must adapt if we are to convince others of the truth of our charade."

"It's dark enough out I don't think people will notice much," I said.

"No need to be sloppy about these things, Eleanora."

The carriage rolled to a stop in a darkened street, and we alighted into the night.

Since we were still several blocks away from the church, we made our way through the dark alleys. During this time, Lady POW tutored me on my walk and using my hat and walking stick as a metaphorical sword and shield.

As a kind of game, I used the stick to hit different piles of garbage until I struck a pile of horse manure. After that, I stopped. I kept my frustration to myself as I watched Lady POW lead the way. I saw the twin hilts of her crystal daggers sticking out by her side.

Our earlier debate, just before we left the Hohenwart Ball, momentarily slipped back into my thoughts. *I hope she doesn't think she made a mistake in allowing me to join the Order.*

"I checked into your earlier information," Lady Penelope said. "You were right. Dr. Artha was last seen coming out of this church. But he has been a patron of St. Nicolas for years."

"It is possible he was meeting someone here," I said. "He seems to have a lot of friends who are not members of St. Nicholas."

"That is correct. He was meeting with Father Novak, who is now dead."

I said nothing. It was slowly dawning on me that Lady Penelope was comfortable with death and other uncomfortable topics, and if I wanted to prove myself to her, I would have to become accustomed to them, too.

That did not mean, of course, that I had to approve of them.

"Here we are," Lady Penelope called, as I attempted to fling the manure off the stick. "The Church of Our Lady of the Snows."

I looked at the building, marveling at its construction. It was constructed over two hundred years before, and its beauty was restored over the various generations.

"Admiring the scene, are you?"

"Hey!" I whirled around, and there was Ben, standing right behind me. "You scared me."

"Eleanora, hush. And Benedict, control yourself. This is no time to scare your sister."

"Apologies, Madame," Ben muttered. It was a little unnerving how much he sounded like Lady POW when she apologized to me for calling me by my mother's name.

"I don't even know how I missed your approach," I grumbled.

Ben pointed down at his misshapen leg, where I saw the gleam of new metal brackets sticking out from the bottom of his breeches. "Between my mechanical skills and Amir's knowledge of anatomy, we were able to design a new brace that's much more light and quiet than my previous ones. It's still a little harder for me to move around than others, but I am improving."

"Well, if anyone is up for a harder task, it's you," I said.

"I would say the same of you," Ben whispered, and I marveled at his genuine cheerfulness. I was glad it had nothing to do with keeping our stepsiblings in line or pilfering pastries from the kitchen.

"Mademoiselle."

I looked over to see Amir as he came up beside the rest of us. As my gaze met his, all the hardness of his face from our previous meeting melted away, and a look of frightful terror took its place. "What is it?"

He seemed to realize he was staring and quickly lowered his gaze. "Lady Eleanora." He quickly gave me a proper bow.

I curtsied in return, before I remembered I was supposed to be acting like a man. I attempted a bow instead. "Mr. Qureshi."

My voice was dull and hard, and Amir seemed grateful for the reminder that I disliked him.

"Amir, I am waiting," Lady Penelope called.

Amir nodded and began talking to her at once, making me scowl. I had wanted to remind him of his promise to me.

I nudged Ben. "Where's Harshad?" I asked. "Is he here, too?"

"No, he's not. He does not go with Amir when I am here. He says Amir draws too much attention as it is, and with my limp, we are already having trouble blending in. He goes by himself if he wants to make rounds."

"Oh." I wondered if Harshad was telling Ben the truth. "I thought maybe he was avoiding us. He doesn't seem to like us that much."

At Ben's sudden grimace, I frowned. "You're hiding something. Tell me."

Ben sighed. "He is not happy about having to train you. I overheard him arguing with Lady POW over it. That's actually why she probably brought you from your ball, since he is refusing to do anything for now."

"What?" Anger burst through me. "So he's not going to train me? How can I do a good job at this stuff if someone isn't going to teach me?"

"Calm down." Ben glanced over at the others. "This is business, Nora, and if it's one thing you should know from watching Lady POW by now, it's that business does not mean people need to get along to work together."

I snorted. "That's true. But still, Harshad can't just deny me the right to—"

"Eleanora. Benedict. This way," Lady Penelope called. "We are going to inspect the body."

"We can talk about it later." As Amir led the way into the side of the church, Ben gave me a smirk. "I don't know what is stranger, seeing you in a lady's gown or a gentleman's clothes."

"Hush, Ben." I smiled at his teasing, but I was still upset hearing Harshad did not want to teach me. What kind of person wanted his colleagues to fail? How could I trust him after hearing this?

How could I really trust any of them?

Lady Penelope changed from leader to grandmother and back again when it suited her. Harshad was aloof and distant, and even Amir had been careful to avoid me for the last week since our meeting in the library.

Walking behind them, I studied Lady POW and Amir.

What reason do I really have to trust them at all? I thought.

I glanced over at Ben, and suddenly I had an answer. Despite the darkness of our mission, my brother had lost the desire for pleasure in the pursuit of purpose. I thought about the past few days where we had quietly exchanged updates, discussing everything from Lady POW's too-literal translation of a Hungarian vendor's cursing to Harshad's questions.

Ben not only seemed more alive, he was a better man.

I knew I could risk trusting Lady POW and her cohorts for a little longer if it made Ben happy. If he trusted them, I knew I could trust them, too.

"You should prepare yourself," Ben said. "This is going to be unpleasant for you. It's nothing like my other ventures into the city with Amir."

From our stolen moments of brief conversation over the past week, I knew Amir had been taking him to meet with runners and traders recently; Ben had mostly been meeting with people who bought and sold information as much as goods or services around Prague. I doubted he had come across a murder since he had been exploring the city at night.

"Half of what I have been doing is smiling and nodding and laughing at things that are not funny," I said. I decided not to tell Ben about Ferdy. Karl's amorous interest alone would be enough to get my brother riled, I thought.

"You sound jealous."

"Well, I am, even if you are forced to work with Amir."

"Amir's not so bad, Nora. You might actually like him if you gave him a chance."

Amir and Harshad could not be that *different.* I wrinkled my nose. "I doubt it."

"Don't be so stubborn," Ben said. "He's really smart, and he has a good sense of humor. And he knows where all the best food is in Prague."

"Oh, so that's why you like him. Well, in that case—"

"You two need to keep it down," Lady Penelope hissed, as we walked through the winding hallways under the chapel.

"We're almost there," Amir said, leading us up a small staircase before entering main chapel.

Flickering lights greeted us as we made our way through the large chapel. The beautiful vaulted ceiling crisscrossed above us as I looked to the altar with wonder. The contrasting shine of gold and black on the portal spoke of so much more than worldly worship, calling back to the ancient battle of good and evil, and the resounding reward only goodness brought.

"This place is magnificent," I whispered.

"Yes," Lady Penelope agreed. "It is too bad Father Novak died in here. But then, perhaps it was a good place for such a fate. One last glimpse of worldly beauty, and then death's release."

I looked over at her, shocked by the simple horror of her words.

But then I looked past her; a limp body was lying at her feet, half-hidden behind the confessionals. The gray-streaked hair covering the sides of his head fluttered softly at our arrival, as our small group surrounded his prostrate form.

Amir knelt down at his feet. "He was sitting in the booth as he died. I pulled him out to examine him."

"It doesn't look like murder," I said. I stared down at the dead man, taking in the sad details of his form as I contemplated his fate. I felt a tenderness for the man, for even though I had never met him, I wondered at the sadness of dying alone. "There's no blood and no wound."

Táta's death was similar, I remembered. He died in his study, sitting at his desk, with his cup of wine from dinner still half-full. Dr. Artha had been called at once, and Ben later told me that he said *Táta* had likely died from a fit of apoplexy.

"You are correct," Amir said, surprising me. "But that does not mean it wasn't. Look at the tips of his fingers and the corners of his mouth. You'll see there is a small, blue tint, and it is a simple explanation."

Lady POW sighed. "Poison."

I looked over at Ben, who was staring at the body with his mouth gaping open in silence.

Amir sighed. "From the blue markings, it is safe to say it contained elements of the silver thallis. Likely a hefty dose, too, if its effects are already showing up on the corpse."

"Are you sure?" Lady Penelope asked.

"Yes. Xiana taught me well."

"Who is Xiana?" I asked, desperate to find anything that would keep me from shuddering. If Harshad did not want to teach me, it did nothing for me to show my weakness in other areas.

"One of the Order's other members. She is a trained herbalist who studied under Harshad. I know it will be a few weeks before she arrives."

"She might be too late," Lady Penelope said. "Poison, especially of this sort, is powerful. We can have Xiana mix an antidote when she gets here. I will have Harshad send her a message. If anyone can reach her, it will be him."

"Why, though?" I asked. "Why would someone kill him? Was Father Novak the one that Dr. Artha met with before he wound up dead, too?"

"From what one of the altar boys was able to tell me, he was," Amir said. "And that means trouble. Father Novak was one of our regular informants. He knew of the Order of the Crystal Daggers, just like Dr. Artha."

"That is not good news," Lady Penelope said. "That gives the murderer another motive."

"It does?" I asked.

Lady Penelope ignored my question. "Do we have time to search the church? I know the other monks and priests have given us a small block of time before they will need to summon the city authorities and see about disposing of the body."

Lady POW began searching through the priest's pockets. As Amir began to search the nearby confessionals, I turned to see Ben was still staring at Father Novak's body.

"What is it, Ben?" I asked quietly. "Are you well? You're the one who warned me it would be unpleasant."

"I thought it would be hard to see it," he said slowly, "because I am not used to death. But … I recognize this."

"What are you talking about?"

"His blue fingertips," Ben said. "The small tinges around his mouth. I saw the same things on *Otec's* body at the funeral."

"What are you … " My voice trailed off as I remembered that moment, at *Táta's* funeral, where I had seen the bluish skin of his fingers and the azure veins of his knuckles. I looked down at the dead reverend, seeing the evidence of his death in a new light.

"You know what I am talking about, don't you?" Ben asked.

I nodded slowly. "Do you think … does this mean … ?" I looked at Ben, unable to finish my sentence, though I was unable to say if it was due to shock or rage.

"I think so," Ben said. "*Otec* was poisoned."

"But why? And by who?" I was not able to stop looking at the poisoned priest. I watched through half-glazed eyes as Lady POW picked up his fallen rosary. "Do you think it was by the same person?"

"It is possible, but doubtful," Lady Penelope said, as she took hold of the large printed Bible beside the priest.

I gripped Ben's arm, though whether it was for his comfort or my own, I could not say. "What does this mean?"

"It means," Lady Penelope said, standing up and wiping her hands off on a handkerchief, "that this goes back much further and deeper than Queen Victoria suspected. If it goes back as far as your father's death, this is a political coup."

"No political party advocates for killing priests," I said. "Dr. Artha was a good man, too. The Federalists and Nationalists both agreed he was a good man."

"A good man is nothing compared to a man who will get you what you want."

"Well," I said, "at least there will be no way for someone to blame the Jews for this one."

"The Jews make a good political scapegoat, because there are plenty who would believe the worst of them," Amir said, as he came out of one of the confession booths. "I do not think this was a calculated death. Father Novak was collateral."

"So someone decided to kill him after Dr. Artha's death," Ben said.

"Good, Benedict. I agree." Lady POW nodded. "Dr. Artha's death was intentional. If it was poison, and one that he would have been familiar with, that is why he was stabbed."

"It could also be a strategy of misdirection," Amir said. "If a priest were to die with the same circumstances as the other politicians, it would likely reveal too much about the murderer's intent. Because we can link Father Novak with Dr. Artha, we are better able to discern their intent."

"Not to mention their identities," I added.

"Yes," Amir agreed. "Misdirection can be a powerful tool. Especially if this is something that goes back more than ten years. And it looks like it might."

"What did you find, Amir?" Lady Penelope asked.

Amir handed her a small note. "Father Novak had Dr. Artha's last message tucked away. Here you are, Madame."

Lady Penelope tore open the note and read it. Her eyes shifted along with the script, and I waited for her to react. She went still.

"What does it say?" Ben asked.

When Lady POW said nothing, Ben jerked the paper out of her hands. "It's in French," he said. "I can't read it."

"Let me look," I said.

Lady POW regained her composure. "I warned her. I warned her something like this would happen if she decided to stay."

I glanced down at the paper, looking over the words. "She?"

"It's a quick note. Translated, it read, 'Sent for the Light, made arrangements with my sweet *Míra,*'" Lady Penelope read. "It also mentions he is praying for protection and hopes this note is an unnecessary precaution."

"It is unfortunate for him that proved not to be the case," Ben said sadly, looking down at the corpse again.

"But not for us," Amir said. "He made arrangements."

"And Lady Penelope knows who it is." I turned to see her angrily pacing once more. I had seen this expression on her before, when she was facing unavoidable inconveniences.

Amir nodded. "*Míra* is a codename. She is a woman who was once your mother's companion. Her real name is—"

"Tulia?" A strange sense of foreboding took hold of me, as I realized another illusion of my lifetime was about to come crumbling down. "Tulia wasn't just my mother's companion. She was her assistant. Wasn't she?"

"So, you know where she is?" Lady Penelope turned on me, and I felt the fire and brimstone from her gaze.

"Yes," I said. "I've visited her frequently since my father's death, actually."

For a long moment, Lady POW seemed unable to process what I had said. Then she shook her head. "That lying witch." Lady Penelope let out a string of muttered curses, prompting me to make the sign of the cross. "I should have known she would be fine with betraying me, too."

Ben and I exchanged glances, and we both looked to Amir as Lady POW stomped away.

"What's her problem?" Ben asked. From the expression on his face, I could tell he was as concerned for Tulia as I was.

"You must forgive Madame," Amir said. "She has been somewhat disconcerted by the fact you both have managed to be hidden from her for so long. Your mother's companion would have known about you, so Lady Penelope is distraught over her deception. Now we have this concern to look into as well."

"Everyone lies, and everyone has secrets," I said.

"It is wonderful to hear you are taking our lessons seriously, Eleanora." Lady Penelope made her way over to us once more. She appeared much more calm, even if her tone was bitter.

"But just as there are secrets and lies, there are those who will strive to find the truth. I will summon Tulia in the morning," she said.

"Are you going to punish her somehow?" I asked, more curious than worried in that moment. Tulia was tough. She would not submit to Lady POW without a fight.

Lady POW smirked. "Somehow," she replied. "But for now, you need to make another round of appearances, Eleanora. There is still plenty of time to drop in on one or two balls tonight."

"But we'll be out until dawn."

"That is the point of Society."

"Can't we just go and see Tulia ourselves?" I asked. "If we can figure out who murdered Dr. Artha and now Father Novak, and the others as well, we might be able stop them."

"It is not just about stopping the murders," Lady Penelope said. "This is a matter of kingdom security. If these same people poisoned your father, whoever they are, there is a long-awaited *coup d'état* underway. Taking down one man is not enough. This is a coordinated effort against the Empire."

"Ideologues do not usually murder people," Amir said.

"But their adherents might," Ben said. "Just look at the Revolution of 1848. The protestors were willing to kill King Ferdinand. He abdicated rather than face their wrath, and my father was poisoned by someone who would undo his work."

"I thought you hated *Otec*," I said.

Ben glared at me. "I hated him, but I will not allow the little good he did in his life be disregarded, especially by someone who thinks killing politicians and priests is some kind of worthy game, like four-dimensional chess."

"That's enough for now," Lady Penelope said. "We must return to the social scene, Eleanora. I will discuss things with Tulia tomorrow."

"Good," I said. "I want to hear what she has to say myself."

"You will be busy." Lady Penelope brushed me aside with the wave of her hand. "I will take care of it."

"What do I possibly have to do that is more important than talking with Tulia?"

"You'll have plenty to do," Lady Penelope insisted. "You'll see."

13

◊

Much to my chagrin, Lady POW was right; I was busy the next day. But it was not until later that I realized being busy did not mean I would be doing something important.

By the time Ben came to my room with the lunch tray, I was desperate for relief from my assigned task.

"Oh, thank God you are here," I said, as I reached for a new cup of tea.

"Are you talking about me, or the tea?" Ben asked,

"Give me a few moments and I'll let you know." I saw him smile before he sat down and relaxed into a chair. For the next several moments, the two of us indulged in our grand lunches, allowing me to reconsider the annoyance I felt at Lady POW.

Even if I was not good enough to be trusted to help more in her assignments, I was grateful for what I did have; I had good food and I was free to read anything I wished, and Ben and I still had the comfort of each other's company.

He sat with me, sighing happily as he poured more tea for himself. "Sundays are the best. No training today."

"Not for you." I wrinkled my nose. "Lady Penelope accompanied me to church today, and it was a miracle God did not strike me naked for all the attention I was stealing away from him."

"I'm sure if he did that, he would have lost a lot more attention."

I laughed. "True. I'd be crowned a saint on the spot."

"Or condemned as a witch, since you would have been showing your unholy flesh in church. The Pope would have had a fit of apoplexy reading that letter from the bishop."

"That is also true."

"So that was Lady POW's big assignment for you?" Ben asked. "Going to church today?"

"No. These are." I gestured toward my desk and the area surrounding it. Several arrangements of flowers, including a large bouquet of roses from Karl, cluttered the desktop and mixed with various calling cards and other notes from admirers. "I have to send thank you missives to everyone who sent one. And I can't just say something vague or polite. I have to be specific and elusive. She says that will increase my popularity."

"And help with her cover."

I huffed indignantly. "*Our* cover, you mean."

"So you've just been writing letters all morning?" Ben arched his brow. "Why didn't you just go and see if Betsy and Mavis would be able to help you?"

Irritation and inspiration struck me at the same time. "That would have been a good idea. It would have given them a chance to practice their Czech. I wonder if Lady POW would let them come over here? Or would Cecilia's wrath be too great?"

"I guess I don't know if it would actually work," Ben said with a shrug. "They are Cecilia's servants, after all. Lady POW has no claim on them."

"I hope they are doing well." I thought of Betsy's frailty and Mavis' hesitancy. "Alex will be a handful for them if he is not watched carefully."

"Amir told me Alex and Priscilla are both under watch from Lady POW, in addition to Cecilia herself."

"That's a wise move."

Ben nodded. "I suppose it is better she is wise. If she's dangerous, I mean."

I agreed with him, and I would have cheerfully commiserated over that topic until nightfall. But there was something I wanted from Ben, and I finally had the chance for the perfect opening. "Speaking of dangerous, Ben … I have a favor to ask."

"Why do I get the feeling that this is something you'd rather not discuss with Lady POW?"

"Because you know me so well, obviously."

Ben crossed his arms. "Well, now I know I should be worried. What do you want, Nora?"

I bit my lip, before forcing myself to follow through. "I wanted to see if you could meet me in the city tomorrow night and take me somewhere."

"Without Lady POW?"

I nodded. "Yes. Lady POW told me Count Potocki is throwing a ball at Queen Anne's Royal Summerhouse tomorrow night. It is supposed to be packed with the aristocrats and nobles. I'm sure I can slip away before she realizes it."

"I don't know about this. You really don't have a lot of practice at reconnaissance, Nora," Ben said. "Maybe you should practice some this week and try some other day."

"What about all those years dodging work from Cecilia and bullying from Alex?" I objected. "I know how to sneak around."

"That's not quite the same thing."

"But I don't want to wait," I said. Ferdy told me the Cabal held its meetings on Monday and Thursday, and I wanted to go and see him again sooner. The thought of waiting was worse than even the thought of Lady POW's wrath. "Come on, Ben, help me. Please."

"Why do you want to go so badly?"

Quickly, I turned my gaze away from Ben. "It is … mostly for a private reason."

It was true, even if it was a reason I did not even fully understand. I liked Ferdy. I envied him, even. He was free to be himself and do what he liked, and I was touched and even excited that he wanted to spend time with me. And despite all his joking and his lying, I could tell he was a good man. He was poor and homeless maybe, but he was someone who could understand me in ways that no one, especially men like Karl Marcelin, ever could.

"Now I know this is not a good idea," Ben said. "How can a reason be 'mostly private,' Nora?"

"Well … " My fingers curled into fists, tightening around my skirt. "You remember that boy who helped me sell *Táta's* book?"

"Now I especially don't like where this is going." Ben shifted forward in his seat.

Despite his vacillation, I told Ben about Ferdy—specifically, about how he worked with Mr. Clavan and the newspaper, and how he had been investigating Dr. Artha's murder when we first met.

I did not mention how I felt about Ferdy, or about how he felt about me.

Ben was quiet as I told him about Clavan and the Cabal, and Ferdy's other friends. When I mentioned their meetings on Mondays and Thursdays could possibly help us, giving us clues as to who was behind the recent string of murders in Prague, Ben finally interrupted me.

"So this is for the mission?" he asked. "How is that a private reason, Nora?"

"Just think about it." I ignored his question. Misdirection could work in my favor, just as it could for others. "We could find more information on our own, and Lady POW would see that we were serious about being part of the Order."

"When you put it that way, it sounds like you want to prove her wrong."

"Can you blame me?" I asked. "Harshad has yet to teach me anything. And as much as you like Amir, I don't want to go begging him for anything."

"I don't think you would have to beg him," Ben said, his voice hardened and sad at the same time.

"Either way, I'd rather ignore him. Besides," I said, nodding toward the wardrobe, which was overflowing with dresses and hats and accessories of all sorts. I reached under a nearby pillow and pulled out the gentleman's clothes Lady POW had given to me in the carriage the night before. "I'd much rather get another chance to go around the city wearing these instead."

"I can't fault you for that," Ben said with a small chuckle. "Some of those contraptions look like a nightmare. I'm glad I don't have to worry about such matters."

"Another reason you'd rather not get married?" I teased, hoping the small amount of levity would further distract him from asking about my feelings for Ferdy.

Ben snorted. When he said nothing else, I decided to risk his wrath with my prodding. "Don't you want a wife of your own, now that Lady POW can provide an inheritance for you?"

"Please, Nora. No woman would want me," Ben said. "I am not fit to provide for her. As much as I hate to say it, Cecilia was right—"

"No! Never say that! She is wrong on every account when it comes to you."

"Be fair, Nora. You and I know the truth. A beautiful woman would never look my way, except out of pity or amusement."

"That's not true," I insisted. "You deserve someone to love you. You watch, the most beautiful woman in the world will find you and beg you to marry her. I will pray for just that to happen. If for no other reason than to make you recant your awful words." I wrinkled my nose. "Imagine, Cecilia being right. Ha!"

"Well, if you believe that God will hear your prayers," Ben said, "I'd rather not have a beautiful wife."

"Why not?"

"Beauty fades and often hides the hollowness behind it. Give me a wife who is unique. As the years go by and the beautiful fade into the background, my wife will only grow more vibrant."

I stuck my tongue out at him. "You'd better hope she isn't mad then."

"I've had plenty of experience with that, between our stepmother and Prissy and Alex."

"True enough," I agreed. In that moment, it was hard not to wonder if my father had lived—if he had not been poisoned—how he and Cecilia would have gotten along.

Would things still be this bad? Would I still be this desperate for my own independence, my own freedom?

I could never know the answer to that. But I was grateful, despite all her thoughtless comments and insistent prodding, that Lady POW had come into our lives. Even if *Táta* had lived, I would have wanted something more of *Máma*.

As Ben shifted his leg restlessly, I shrugged. "I'm glad we haven't had to worry much about marriage until now."

"But you are, indeed, thinking about it now?" Ben asked.

It crushed me to see the somber look on his face, and even more when I realized I was blushing. "Not really, Ben, but Lady POW has mentioned it as a ploy enough to make me worried."

"It's fine, you know, if you want to get married, Nora," Ben said. "I'm glad that you are thinking about it, at least. I don't want you to end up alone and hating me for it."

"I won't end up alone if you are with me. And if I do end up hating you, it will be for other reasons. You have my word on that, *brácha*."

"You won't hate me if I decline to participate in your desired venture, will you?"

I gave Ben a rueful smirk. I had to admit, he was good at catching me at my own game. He had distracted me enough that I did not see his counterargument coming. "I never thought you would decline, so we will have to see. Would you risk that fate?"

"I've never been much of a gambler." Ben sighed. "So it appears to be in my better interest to take you. If for no other reason than if I do not accompany you, I have a feeling you would try to do it yourself."

"Yes!" I bounced over and gave him a hug. "Thank you."

"But when we get there, I want to meet your new friends," Ben warned. "Especially the one you're pining for."

Before I could vehemently deny that, there was a knock at the door. We both turned and watched as Amir appeared.

I groaned to myself. His mustache twitched, and I had to wonder how much of our conversation he might have heard.

Amir looked much the same as he had when I first saw him, with a formal shirt and pressed pants. His shoes gleamed, and the dagger at his side was tucked behind the folds of his coat. "Ben. Mademoiselle," he said, greeting each of us with a polite nod.

I gave a cool, polite curtsey. "Mr. Qureshi."

He caught my tone and straightened. "Lady Penelope has requested mademoiselle's presence in the west parlor. She sent me to find you."

"Why?" I asked.

"She said after the Hohenwart Ball, she needs you to practice the waltz."

I did not know why, but the way Amir said it made me feel even more foolish. I had been hoping Harshad was ready to teach me, or that I would begin to learn more about surveillance or reconnaissance.

No, instead I would be dancing. Dancing, when murders were happening all over the city and Bohemia's political situation grew more precarious.

"No," I grumbled, "I meant, why did she send you?"

Amir's patience never faltered, even as Ben gave me a blunt kick in the shin.

"Because it was efficient, no doubt," Amir replied. "But one does not question Lady Penelope's decisions too often, of course."

His response was perfectly polite. But I was certain he knew of my reluctance to follow orders without asking questions. If he really was Lady POW's trusted confidant, there was no telling how many hours she had complained about me to him.

Ben nudged me with his leg, this time more gently. "Go, Nora," he said, with a teasing smirk. "We'll talk later. I have some relaxation to tend to."

I nearly whimpered at Ben's good fortune, but I settled for pouting as Amir escorted me to the west parlor. I gave my brother one last angry look, and then I brushed past Amir.

Leaving the room when I was with Ben was already hard enough, but I was appalled when Amir followed me. He caught up to me quickly, his long steps shortening into an easy rhythm as we headed for the library. He started to offer me his arm but backed down when I glared at him.

A few moments passed in silence, save for our footsteps, before Amir spoke. "I have heard Lady Penelope is pleased with your performance so far," Amir said, as we walked through the hallways of the castle.

"So far? Does that mean you think I'll fail at some point?"

Amir pursed his lips. "No," he said. "Although it is a possibility, and one that should be considered in its proper context."

"How about we consider the context of other things?" I purposefully provoked him. "Such as when you attacked me and stole my father's book?"

Finally, I saw a quick flash of emotion on his face. He said nothing and silently turned away from me.

"Lady Penelope is waiting for you, mademoiselle. We do not have the proper time to spend on such … an enlightening tale."

"Well, when are you going to tell me about that day? Are you going to go back on your promise?" I asked, as a cloud of thick tension increasingly surrounded us. "Or are you hoping I will just forget about it entirely?"

"We have other things to concern ourselves with, mademoiselle."

"Such as?"

"Miss Tulia has refused to answer Lady Penelope's summons. She is not in good humor today," Amir said quietly, and I had to wonder if he thought he was being slightly treasonous in saying so.

"Tulia's smart enough to know not to come here if Lady POW is upset at her."

Amir cleared his throat, as if he was holding back a laugh. "Lady POW? Oh. I see Ben's endearing nickname for Lady Penelope is catching."

"It is an appropriate one," I argued. "And it is much easier to say her name that way. I don't care if she hates it."

"I don't know if she does. She's never said anything about it to me. But it would not surprise me to find out she enjoys it. She has a fondness for pet names."

"I still wish she would stop calling me Eleanor." I wrinkled my nose in irritation.

Amir went quiet. I saw he was staring straight ahead with a faraway look in his eyes. His expression seemed to suggest he was suddenly no longer there.

As his eyes cleared and he looked back at me, it was almost as if we shared the same, single thought.

"Naděžda."

At that moment, I finally understood. He had known my mother, too. Amir had called out her name when he saw me for the first time, face to face. When he first saw me, he recognized her.

I stumbled a little and stooped for a moment to fix my shoe, struggling to think through everything.

Lady POW had mentioned that to Harshad, I recalled, thinking of the conversation Ben and I overheard before any of this began. Harshad called my mother "Dezda," and Amir had met my mother. Clearly, he called her by her full middle name.

It was strange to think that my mother had been so much to so many people.

I was still stunned as we walked into the west parlor. Lady Penelope called out to me, and I was immensely grateful for the distraction. "Ah, there you are, Eleanora."

"You sent your servant here to find me," I said, pointing my thumb at Amir. "Why wouldn't I be here?"

Lady Penelope frowned. "I know better than most the complexities of sarcasm and wit, Eleanora. It is best to keep your good humor out of the former and concentrated on the latter. There is no need to insult anyone. You know Amir is not my servant. We are on the same side here."

Yes, the side of espionage. How comforting.

"Thank you, Amir," Lady Penelope said. "Please await us in the ballroom. We will be there shortly."

"Ballroom? We?"

"Your gown for tonight's ball is here," Lady Penelope said. "We need to be sure that you can dance properly in it. As much as Karl Marcelin might have found your clumsy footwork attractive, I prefer we stir the pot with your exceptional skills."

For a long moment, as she went on about social politics, I felt a new sense of weariness come over me. There was nothing that exceptional about me. Not really. If I had been smarter, I might have found a way to be free before Lady Penelope's arrival. If I had been stronger, I might have found a way to stand up to Cecilia. If I had been more aware of the world surrounding me, I might have been able to find my place in it. And if I had been more faithful, maybe God would have erased all my doubt of who I was and what I was put in this world to do.

I was none of those things. I was a simple girl playing dress up, chasing after my mother's shadow, longing to be free when I was not brave enough, strong enough, smart enough, or sure enough to face freedom's cost.

"Come, Eleanora. You will be practicing with Amir." Lady POW looked me squarely in the eye, demanding my full attention, before she put her hands on her hips. "And while you are practicing your dancing, you can also practice being a proper lady. That includes *not* insulting your dancing partner, and pretending to be civilized."

I gritted my teeth angrily, saying nothing as Amelia, Marguerite, and Jaqueline began suiting me up inside my new gown.

It took longer than I expected, but at the end of their frittering, my hair was combed back, my feet were placed into small silk dancing slippers—I thanked God for his goodness that they were not heels—and I had the stays around my waist groaning as my figure was pulled in place.

"Eleanor, you look lovely," Lady Penelope said as I twirled for her final inspection.

"Eleanora."

"Yes. Apologies, once more."

"Maybe it would help if you called my mother 'Dezda,' like Harshad does," I said. *Or Naděžda, like Amir.*

Her gaze softened, ever so slightly and ever so briefly, and I felt guilty, as though I had struck her. "I don't like to call her that as much as he does," Lady Penelope said quietly, before the hard, stoic mask came down again. "That was always his name for her when she was … "

Lady POW let her voice trail off, and before she could say anything else, I took her hand. I did not know if I was trying to comfort her or not.

"I'm sorry," I said. It was part of who I was, to be curious, but I would not want to impose her with my questions if it pained her.

She seemed to understand as she nodded. "Yes. Of course." Then she marched forward, as if our quiet moment had never happened. Soon we reached the ballroom, where Amir was waiting for us.

He was in the middle of the empty ballroom, standing tall and awkwardly straight. As I approached him, he held out his hand. "Will you do me the honor to dance with me?"

"I don't know that I should give it to you." I was aware of Lady POW's standards, but I decided I did not have to be cheerful when I was forced to be polite. I gave Amir a gritty smile. "But my grandmother demands it of me, doesn't she?"

"She demands it of both of us, I'm sure," Amir replied, and I was close enough I could hear the bitterness he was hiding in his voice.

At his tone, I knew Lady POW was watching us intently, waiting for me to accept Amir's hand. I could already hear her voice in my head, reminding me of *The Ladies' Guide to Excellence and Etiquette*, telling me it was not polite to refuse when a gentleman asked for a dance.

It did nothing for me that I did not consider Amir a gentleman, no matter how much he had insisted before that he was not a mongrel.

Reaching out, I settled my hand into Amir's.

An old memory of my father came to the forefront of my mind. He would dance with me when I was younger, before he died. *Táta* loved to indulge me with his kindness and his kisses, and as Amir's hand swallowed mine, I could not help but feel sad and nostalgic for those days.

"Just follow me," Amir said as he stepped closer to me.

I had practiced the waltz with Karl at the Hohenwart Ball, so I was not surprised by the steps that followed. But I was grateful the speed had slowed as I relearned how to anticipate direction and center my balance. Amir led me around the room in slow, lulling steps, and his gentleness never faltered.

I was more surprised that all the details of the room disappeared as Amir guided me through the slides and twirls of different dances. As I shifted my gaze from my feet to Amir's eyes—a glittering brown, with speckles of gold peeking out near the edge of his irises—I felt an unusual rush of compassion and warmth, and I did not like it.

"What is it?" I asked him, noticing that he was staring back at me.

"It seems you have remembered your dancing quite well," he said, and I shook my head at once, keeping my forced smile steady as we passed by Lady POW.

"The practice helps," I replied neutrally. "And it did help that Karl was a good dancer last night. Some of the others I danced with were not as good, but fortunately they blamed it on their own poor performance."

"They were likely distracted by your beauty."

"You don't have to talk to me like that." I rolled my eyes. "Besides, you might distract me now with your false flattery."

"Flattery is always false, mademoiselle. I was speaking truth." Amir smiled. "You may have that problem in the future, when other men are dancing with you."

"I can learn to handle it later, then."

"You can also learn it now. There is nothing efficient about wasting time, after all."

"I'd rather not, thank you very much. There is no need for you to continue talking to me." My tone was frosty and bitter, every part a perfect complement to the kindness in his eyes. "Unless, of course, you'd like to tell me why you stole my father's book from me when we unfortunately met?"

"I would not say it was unfortunate."

"What would you say it was, then?"

Amir's mustache curled around the corners of his mouth. "God's humor at work."

"What's that supposed to mean?" I asked, frustrated and infuriated. "Are you insulting me?"

"Never, mademoiselle."

Before I could accuse him of lying in addition to insulting me, or before I could "accidentally" begin stepping on his toes, Lady POW began calling out instructions, making me feel even more insulted and infuriated—and even worse, isolated, and unable to do anything to escape.

"Hands up, Eleanora," she called. "Yes, take a step closer. Now, remember to smile. Watch your timing; men are supposed to lead. And show your interest. Pretend you are dancing with a prince!"

Between Amir's dancing and Lady Penelope's snappy judgements, I felt trapped in a world of soft tyranny. It was a world where the truth was too impolite to be spoken, and even if it had to be, it had to be dressed up in clothes as strange and as ornate as the ones I was wearing, and it was likely as unrecognizable as I was in the end.

I certainly felt nothing like my usual self.

The others did not seem to believe it was me, either.

Amir held me at a polite distance as we danced, but I was still close enough I could see the pained delight in his eyes as he watched me, and recalling Lady POW's earlier mistake of calling me by my mother's name, I suddenly wondered if he was thinking of her, too.

The last note of the waltz rang out, and we finally slowed to a stop.

"Why did you take my father's book?" This time, my question was quiet but harsh against the growing silence. Amir seemed surprised, but he did not refrain from responding.

"It was not your father's book, mademoiselle."

I slowly dropped my hands from his.

Already, I knew what he was going to say.

"When I saw you, it was like falling into a portal to the past, twenty-six years ago. I saw the book, and I knew it could only belong to my Naděžda."

"You knew my mother." The words were chunky and foreign to me as they came out of my mouth. I knew I had no reason to accuse him of something I already knew to be true.

"Yes. She was my dearest friend for many years before … " Amir said quietly. I saw his gaze lower to the scar on his right hand. "And when she … left … I was angry."

It plagued me, knowing that Lady POW was not the only one who seemed to prefer my mother to me.

"When she left the Order, you mean?"

"She did not leave the Order," Amir whispered. "She left me."

It took me a long moment to process everything. Amir and I were still standing in the middle of the room. Somewhere, a thousand moments and a million miles away, Lady POW clapped and praised us, telling us I was already much better at the waltz than before. She was calling for another song, but I barely heard any of it, as I watched while Amir's eyes swam over with memories and emotion.

There was suddenly no denying the full truth of the matter.

Amir had been in love with my mother.

As his eyes cleared and his mind returned to the present moment, I did the only thing I could think to do.

I reached out and slapped him.

The smack of my palm on his cheek echoed through the now-quiet room. My hand seemed to fall against his face with much more force than I had meant, but it was over all too quickly just the same.

He just stood there, looking at me. And when he looked at me, he saw her—and his own heartbreak.

"Eleanora!" Lady Penelope gaped at me in shock.

I fumed as Lady POW stepped forward. I was too angry and confused and frustrated to care. I ignored her and stood my ground in front of Amir, who did not say anything as he only gave me a wounded look.

"Stop," I hissed at Amir. "I am not my mother, and you had no right to steal what I did have of her away from me."

Before Amir could say anything, I already knew there was nothing I wanted to hear from him.

So I ran away.

I brushed past Lady POW without any regard, throwing her off balance by my sudden and ardent desperation to escape.

"Eleanora!"

I struggled not to show my regret and confused rage; I did not want to show Lady Penelope my own weakness any more than I wanted to admit it to myself.

So I ran away.

I ran away from her, I ran away from Amir, and I ran away from the truth, as another one of my childhood illusions was stripped away from me.

"Eleanora, get back here at once, young lady!" Lady Penelope called. She was no longer surprised, but now she was angry. I heard her start to run after me, but Amir called after her.

"Let her go, Lady Penelope," I heard Amir say. "Please. I made her uncomfortable."

"We have to be ready for tonight. This is no time for her to be fighting with you over trivial matters."

There is nothing trivial about this. I stopped for a quick moment, leaning against the wall outside the door. My breath came quick and shallow while I forced myself to hold in my tears as I listened to Amir's response.

"I fear that is not all she found offensive," Amir replied. "You must forgive her, as I do, Madame."

Lady Penelope huffed. "But you did nothing wrong."

"Even so, my lady, I am not without my shortcomings."

At his insufferable forgiveness, I took off once more, hoping that his little speech would be enough to keep Lady POW from breathing hellfire and damnation down my neck the next time she saw me.

For now, I decided, it was enough just to run away and be free from them, even if it was for only a few moments.

Even if it was ultimately futile in the end.

I could not run from the truth.

My mother and Amir had been friends—and he had been in love with her. Had she been in love with him, too? And if so, why did she leave him? Did she even care for my father at all? I was surrounded with more and more questions, and everything I had grown up never questioning seemed to fall apart as I made my way to my room.

Outside the window, a strange midday fog rolled in. The outline of Prague and its proud castle had become more mysterious and ethereal, and I wondered if it was truly real, too. Before, everything about the city had a celestial touch to it, as if I could walk down a street and suddenly find myself in Heaven.

In that moment, I could not say that; my paradise was suddenly full of poison, and I had to wonder what parts of my life it had touched.

I entered my room, confronted with the terrible sadness of this reality. I flopped onto my bed, burying myself in the covers, letting my eyes swell over with tears.

It was only then that I allowed myself to admit the deepest part of my pain.

"*Máma*," I whispered into the silken sheets. "I miss you."

While I missed her because I loved her, I missed her more for the questions I had, the ones I knew could never be fully answered.

I missed her, and I had missed her whole life. How would things be different had she lived? Would I have known Lady POW sooner? Would Amir still be a strange man on the streets, thieving books, or would he be a friendly visitor of sorts?

Would anyone look at me and just see me? Would I be able to find my mother and not lose myself in the process?

"*Máma*." I curled up in the bed, feeling small and alone and silly.

I missed her, but I could never be her. I did not have her strength, and the strength I did have was only there because of all the pain I had endured without her.

14

◊

I gradually fell asleep in my bed. No one came to bother me, and later I would wonder if Amir had interfered, since Lady POW apparently canceled our evening entertainments. I slept so deeply that nothing woke me up until the earliest hours of the morning.

It was the rain that woke me up, long after the night had saturated itself in gloominess. I awoke feeling rested, more rested than I had felt since Lady Penelope's arrival. Sleep had renewed me, and my questions as well. I sat up in bed, curling my legs under my chin as my thoughts, as varied and complicated and deliberating as they were, kept me preoccupied.

I glanced at my door. I did not have to open it to know there was a heavy silence about the manor.

I felt surrounded in darkness in more ways than one.

I wondered, briefly, if Lady POW would be upset with me when she woke up, or if she would be relieved we were not out on the town while it was raining. We lived on the city outskirts, close enough to see the city skyline, but she would be upset if her coach was stuck in the muddy lanes that surrounded my family's farmland.

I rubbed my face, wincing at the scratchy tearstains. They were rough patches on my skin, hinting at the previous, ongoing pain in my heart.

I knew very little of *Máma's* life before Ben and I had come along, and from what Lady Penelope told me about her time with the Order of the Crystal Daggers, the little I did know was likely a cover of sorts.

My mind settled on another memory of *Máma.* I saw her wearing the locket she had worn each Sunday to church. She would brush my hair, and I would tug at it. She would open it and show me the miniatures of Ben and me, and the one of my father on the opposite side.

I thought about the locket as Ben's earlier comment came back to me. *"You really don't have a lot of practice at reconnaissance. Maybe you should practice some."*

That was what I should do, I thought. *I should go and retrieve it from under the pantry floor.*

Giving myself a task, even as it was nothing that would put me back in Lady Penelope's good graces—if indeed, such a thing was possible—helped me immensely.

I slipped out of my sheets and put on the breeches I had pilfered from the previous night. If I was going to sneak off to meet with Ferdy, I had to prepare myself. Retrieving my mother's locket and my father's pocket watch was a secondary pleasure to my ultimate purpose.

Thinking of Ferdy energized me, even if I knew I would be risking Lady Penelope's temper once more. I began to undress as I pushed that concern out of my mind, reaching for memories of *Máma* and Ferdy instead. I stuffed my chemise into the pants and bundled up, pulling the coat tightly across my body to hide any slits of white that might be visible. Pulling on the men's shoes, I felt free again, in a new way.

Women did not have as much power as Queen Victoria made it appear. Even in Prague, where there were artists and inventors and people of all backgrounds, the ways of London and Paris led us to be slaves to fashion, and fashion did not stop with our constraining clothes.

I made my way through the halls of my home, working my way to the end of the west wing with ease, trying not to feel a sense of despair. I had tumbled throughout the manor before my mother's death, reigning free as a queen in training and a princess in my own place. I was free because of my security, in my parents' love and our titles and income. Once Cecilia moved in and *Táta* died, I found a new sort of freedom, hiding in the shadows of the servants' quarters and their assigned hallways. Now, even though Lady POW had freed Ben and me from Cecilia's charge, I knew my freedom was limited.

I had learned, after the long years, that freedom was a precious, fragile thing, and easily overturned by power. That did not stop me from wanting it; in fact, I was certain I was even more anxious to secure it.

As I made my way toward the kitchens, I heard footsteps dashing about in different rhythms, according to the early morning routines. The cooks were preparing breakfast, mixing up ingredients for meals and gathering tools they would need; the laundry had to be prepared, and the stables had to be cleaned and the horses and other animals fed.

I was just calculating my odds of being able to get some freshly baked bread when I heard new footsteps start to come down the adjacent hallway in loud, angry stomps.

"I can't believe this!" Cecilia's screeching rubbed my ears raw. It seemed that no matter how long it had been since I'd heard her say anything, her voice was still shrilly enough to make me cringe.

I stopped short, hoping she would not pass by me on her obvious tirade.

"That bastard! How could he do this to me? To all of our plans?"

"Isn't there anything that we can do?" Alex was walking behind her, keeping up with her infuriated pace.

At the sound of his voice, I scurried to a nearby doorway and smooshed myself as flat as I could. I did not want another confrontation with Alex for more than one reason.

"What can we do?" Cecilia's voice dropped to a quiet whisper, but in the night, I was able to hear each word clearly. "The only thing would be to turn him in. Tell the king everything, destroy any chance of bettering our lives and ruining the little we do have."

"Surely the king would be grateful?"

"Grateful for what?" Cecilia spat. "Planning his overthrow? Funding it with our investments over the last twenty years?"

My heart began to pound inside my chest, so loudly I could feel the pulse behind my ears. Their footsteps began to move away, and I tiptoed closer to the edge of the corridor, hoping to keep up with them as they carried on their conversation. I was also glad to see they were heading toward the kitchens. I would be able to make an easy detour and head back to my room.

"I meant he would be grateful for your information. Why not place the blame on His Grace?" Alex asked. "Tell him he tricked you, forced you into it. Maybe we can say he even blackmailed and threatened you?"

"Have you seen King Ferdinand at all since he was forced from the throne? He is ignorant and simple-minded, and his only power remains because of the benevolence of his nephew. He will not be able to protect us from Max."

"What of the people?" Alex asked. "Surely their benevolence is also necessary?"

"The people are fools as a collective. They can do nothing, other than what their betters tell them to," Cecilia muttered. I could hear her cursing that followed. "I will need to contact Max's foreign benefactors. But I don't know what to tell them yet."

"Mother," Alex said. "Maybe instead of stopping the plan, we should be ready to act if it succeeds. The others are already dead, remember? What is one more body, especially if everything else is in place?"

I held my breath, waiting for her to respond. There was something going on, and Cecilia was part of it.

When she said nothing, Alex pressed her. "His Grace has extended us his fullest regrets about Teresa Marie. There is no harm in playing along for now."

"He will discard us. If we turn on him, he will find a way to assign us the blame. He has all the advantage now, Alex."

"We do not need to just sit here," Alex hissed. "This is what got us here in the first place. You allowed that British lady to destroy my marriage contract! If she had not come, none of this would have happened."

I smiled. It was good to see Lady POW, for all her trouble, was living up to her promise. She had clearly ruined plenty of Cecilia's plans by dissolving the engagement between Alex and Teresa Marie.

"Don't you see? Max found what he was looking for all those years ago. He would have broken the engagement himself, now that he's found King Ferdinand's son and heir."

My eyes went wide. *King Ferdinand has a son?*

"There's no need to be obtuse about this, Alex," Cecilia continued, as my world kept reeling from the news.

"We have to do something," Alex insisted. "I will not let your inaction stop us from getting what we want."

"We have already lost." Cecilia shook her head. "Max has what he wants. He has the advantage. There's nothing we can do, and if we oppose him, he will come after us."

"What can he really do to us?" Alex scoffed.

"People have died, if I might remind you. You've asked what one more body would cost. It costs something entirely differently when it is your own."

Alex went mostly silent as they turned around another corner. I heard their muffled argument continue as they walked further away from the kitchens.

Before I could trail after them, I heard an exclaimed gasp from behind me.

"Nora!"

I jerked around to see Betsy, her apron full of apples. It was the first time in more than a week I had seen her, and even though I knew Lady POW would be upset at me for shirking my spying duties, even if they were unassigned and impromptu, I raced toward Betsy with open arms.

"Betsy," I said, hugging her. "I'm so glad to see you."

The apples fell from her apron as she hugged me back. "It's wonderful to see you, too," she said. "Mavis and I have been lonely without you and Ben around."

"How are you and your sister? Are you faring well?" I glared back toward the shadows, where Alex and Cecilia had disappeared only a moment earlier.

"Her Ladyship has been in a rage," Betsy said, as we began to pick up her fallen apples. "She seems unsure of doing anything, however. Her Grace's servants pass us in the halls when we do chores, so she knows if she takes any of her anger out on us, she will be the one in trouble."

"Thank God for Lady Penelope," I said with a small laugh.

"Oh, I do, Nora. I'm so happy you and Ben have escaped her Ladyship's claws."

"Even if you are still her prisoner?" I asked, shaking my head. "You are too kind, Betsy."

"Your stepmother was cruel to you," Betsy said. "But believe it or not, she saved me. And Mavis, too. She hired me as an orphan with a younger sister and brought me here. She is cruel, sometimes, but she has saved me from a greater cruelty."

"That's still not good."

Before I could say anything else, Betsy noticed my outfit for the first time. I enjoyed the surprise in her eyes as she looked me up and down.

"Oh, my! What are you wearing?"

"It's one of Ben's outfits," I lied. "I thought it would be easier to sneak down here and see you. And I wanted to get something from the pantry while I was here."

"Your mother's locket?" Betsy asked.

When I gave her a quizzical look, she giggled. "You told me about it before. Come on. I need to take these apples to the pantry myself. I'll help you in."

"Thank you," I said, grateful to have a friend by my side once more.

It was strange to see Betsy, and even stranger to have her remind me I once was able to share secrets with her. Ever since Lady

Penelope told me about the Order of the Crystal Daggers, I had felt like a new person. I had secrets of my own now, and I would not be able to tell them to her. As I watched Betsy help me duck around other servants and sneak into the pantry unnoticed, I mourned for the loss of our sisterly bond.

When Betsy handed me my hidden treasures, I forced myself to smile. My mother's golden locket gleamed in the dull pantry light, and *Táta's* pocket watch shined as I opened it up. The clockwork screws were still, but I could see the familiar, delicate design.

"Thank you for helping me," I said to Betsy, sincerely and somberly, knowing it was likely one of our last adventures together, if not *the* last one.

"Oh, it's no trouble," Betsy said. She gave me a friendly smile. "I am glad you were able to sneak down here and talk with me. I know from the other rumors I've heard you have been busy, dancing in all them fancy ballrooms with proper gentlemen and dining all over Prague."

I laughed nervously. "It's not as fun as it sounds."

"It sure sounds wonderful."

"It is," I said, and as Betsy's eyes lit up with dazzling interest, I decided to tuck more secrets into my heart. I wanted to tell her so much about how the polite world was beautiful but hollow, and how I knew that I did not belong there.

Instead, as we walked back toward the west wing, I told her of the Hohenwart Ball, and the different parks around the city, all the new buildings that were being built. I allowed her to think it was a magical sort of world, like the one I used to believe it to be.

When we came to the last hallway before the west wing, I gave her a hug and wished her well.

"Please tell Mavis I miss her, too," I said.

"Will do, miss."

I smiled. "It'll always be Nora to you, Betsy."

Betsy giggled and headed off, and even as I waved goodbye, I wondered if I was not a hollow person, too.

My old life as a servant had never felt comfortable, but I missed it enough to mourn it as Betsy's bubbly shadow scurried back to the kitchens.

Entering the west wing was almost like stepping into a new world. The darkness, while it was still silent and heavy, seemed to carry more vulnerability and hope. I gripped my mother's locket and my father's watch closer to me. I prayed for God to hear me once more, to fill my heart with comfort, and, if he would, to send me a new friend—someone with whom I could share my new life without reservations.

It seemed like a reasonable request. After all, I had enough reservations about things. After Lady Penelope largely dismissed my theories about Lord Maximillian earlier, I had stumbled into a reality that would have seemed even less plausible only an hour earlier.

I felt a strong urge to go and wake Ben up, just so I would have someone to tell. But before I could turn back and head to his room, I saw that there was someone waiting for me beside the library door.

My feet stayed put as I tried to make out the features of the dark figure before me. I was just wondering if Alex had spotted me after all and had come to ensure my silence when the shadow spoke.

"I was wondering when you would return, mademoiselle."

15

◊

My eyes squinted at the darkness, before they found the familiar shape of Amir before me. He was standing upright, with his hands clasped together behind him, so unnaturally I wondered if it was a military stance. As I took a tentative step closer, he stepped back into a sliver of light peeking out from the library. He seemed to have been waiting patiently, although I had no idea how long he had been there.

"Amir. I mean, Mr. Qureshi. What are you doing here?" My fingers curled into fists, tightening around my parents' trinkets.

"I was just waiting on you to return from your outing."

"Why?" I frowned. Was he going to tell Lady POW? I could not say if she would be happy or not, but if I had to bet on it, I would have said she would have been less than pleased. Especially since Amir had caught me.

"I was on my way to return this to you." He pulled out the small book from behind his back. "I am somewhat surprised—but not entirely—to find you coming back from an unauthorized outing."

"It wasn't like I left the house." I shoved my father's watch into my greatcoat pocket before reaching for the book.

It was the same book, of course. The etching of the book's cover was clear, with its elegant and intricate design carved into the leather. I held it between my hands as my mother's locket dangled from my fingers, and for a moment, I wondered if I would feel closer to her by merely holding it, in just seeing it as something she had once owned.

Nothing staggering or supernatural happened as I stood there—as far as I could see, anyway. But as the moment passed, slowly and quietly, I remembered I had asked God for a friend before, and I wondered if this was God's way of convicting me as well as answering my prayers.

He would do this to me.

I looked back at Amir.

"You have my sincerest apologies over the matter of its theft," Amir said softly. "As you no doubt know, from our earlier encounter, I loved your mother very much. Seeing you—and her book—brought out the worst part of me that day. I pray you will forgive my lapse in manners and judgment."

I looked back at the book, opening it up, only to see scrawls of finely shaped letters, written in nearly perfect lines. It was my mother's handwriting, though I did not recognize the language or the words she had written. My eyes lingered over the preciseness of her hand, before looking up once more at Amir.

I do not want to like you.

"If it makes you feel better, your mother did not like me at first, either."

"Huh?" I blinked, and I blushed, realizing I had spoken my thoughts aloud. I sighed. "Oh."

"I cannot imagine Lady POW tells you a lot of stories of Naděžda," he said. "Would you like to hear one?"

"Lady POW?" I arched my brow appreciatively. "You are calling her that, too?"

"You were right. It is more efficient."

"You don't have to call her that so I will like you." I slipped my mother's locket into the other pocket of my coat.

"I was not doing so with that intention. I had to work to win your mother over, too, you know. If you talk with me, I'll tell you the story of how we first met."

I said nothing, and even in the dim lighting, I could see Amir was smiling, letting that mustache of his curl upward along his upper lip.

"I know you are very curious about her, mademoiselle. You need not allow your pride to get in the way of your happiness."

"Do you want me to talk with you or not?" I scoffed. "You shouldn't tell me how you are going to make me do what you want if you want me to do what you want."

"I only want you to do what you want."

I wanted that, too.

"Fine," I said, before pushing open the library door. The room was lit to full brightness, with candelabras flickering at me as I walked toward my father's desk. The fireplace was full of dying light, the dulling embers offering more comfort despite less warmth.

"Your mother loved books," Amir said. "It was one of the reasons she wrote as much as she did. Some of the books she read have notes along the margins. I found a few the other day when I was in here."

"The second time we met?"

He nodded. "The book you have now was the last journal she wrote before … before she passed."

I opened the book, looking down at the written lines. Just like before, I was not able to decipher the writing. "I can't read it."

"I was up all night with it," Amir admitted. "I wanted to give it back after earlier. But I could not tear myself away from it without finishing it. I hope you will forgive me this intrusion, too."

"It is written in a language and script I don't recognize. I didn't even realize it was written instead of printed before." I thumbed through the pages, carefully at first and then more comfortably, as I looked for numbers or any sign that I would be able to translate some part of the message. "I do not know why my stepmother thought I would be able to sell it if it was her journal."

Amir came up beside me, looking over my shoulder. "It is written in Arabic, but it reads from front to back. It was an odd system of compromise Naděžda and I worked out when we became friends. She would work on her Arabic while I learned to read books from left to right."

"So you've read all of it?" I asked, looking back up at him accusingly.

"Not all of it." He shook his head. "I know I stole the book from you, and I know stealing is wrong. I'm here to make amends. But before you get angry, you should remember that you are not the only one who feels robbed since her death."

Amir's sadness suddenly reminded me of my father. When my mother came up in conversations, the rare times that she did after her death, he wore the same downcast expression as Amir, right down to the same glittering eyes and softened gaze.

I leaned back against the desk. "I wasn't about to get angry," I lied.

"You were, too." Amir crossed his arms. "I've known you now for close to a fortnight. Your nostrils flare open and you clench your fists when you are angry."

"I can do that for other reasons." I held up my hand in protest, and it was then I noticed it was indeed curled into a fist.

Amir was kind enough not to laugh at me, although it might have made me feel better. I was grateful that I did not have a mirror to show me what my nose looked like.

"Nadězda had similar foibles. She would also stamp her foot and tap her toe if she was impatient. When we worked together on her business for the Order, we had more than one captive who would complain. One even broke down at what he called the torture of her incessant nature."

"You worked with her and the Order of the Crystal Daggers?"

Amir nodded. "That was originally how we met. She was fifteen and visiting India with Lady POW and Harshad—"

"How long have they known each other, anyway?" I asked. "How old is he? Seventy?"

"Seventy-two, next spring," Amir said. "Lady Penelope is only a few years younger. They have known each other since at least 1825, when your mother was born."

"Forty-five years is a long time to hate someone."

"This likely has more to do with love than hate."

The familiar turn of phrase took me back into the world of *The Tragedy of Romeo and Juliet.* I thought of all my trips into the library. "You have read Shakespeare?"

Amir smiled. "I have lived in London for many years, under the service of Lady Penelope and the League of Ungentlemanly Warfare. Yes, mademoiselle, I know my Shakespeare."

"The League of Ungentlemanly Warfare." I frowned at the foreign name. "So you are not actually part of the Order of the Crystal Daggers?"

"No, I am not. But I remain Lady Penelope's fiercest ally." He put his hand on the curved dagger at his side. "This is a *Wahabite Jambiya,* a special dagger that comes from my homeland. It is our choice of weapon, when it is needed."

"Such as when we first met?" I asked, cracking my knuckles. I decided to circle the conversation around to the League again later.

"Yes, mademoiselle." Amir took the dagger out of the wooden sheath and held it out to me, hilt first. Curiosity compelled me to take it.

"When Lady Penelope succeeds in making Harshad teach you, weapons such as this will be among the first ones you master. A sword is commonplace, and while a rapier might serve you best, they are often cumbersome for the spy and subtle attacker."

"It's beautiful." Studying it, I saw the inscription down the side, in foreign letters and unusual markings. Some of them were similar to the writing in my mother's journal.

"Arabic," he explained. "This is the language I was speaking with your beloved, when we first met."

"My beloved?"

"The boy who interrupted our battle, back in the alley."

At the mention of Ferdy, I forced myself not to blush. "He's not my beloved."

"He seemed to think he was," Amir said, making me frown.

What did Ferdy say to Amir?

As much as I wondered, I decided to worry about that another day. I turned back to the dagger. "What does it say?"

"A blessing for the wielder's protection from Allah."

"Allah?"

"The Arabic word for God, although there are significant differences between the religious views on God himself. Many in the Ottoman Empire follow Mohammadism."

"Oh," I said. "Bohemia is mostly Catholic, although there is more Protestantism here in recent decades. And there is the Jewish population, too, across the Vltava."

Amir nodded. "I've become very familiar with the Anglican Church, serving Lady Penelope. And you are right. In the Western world, there are not many Muslims."

"Are you a Muslim?" I asked, before realizing I was being more than a little too upfront.

"Not anymore." He shook his head. "I once was lost, but now I am found."

Another familiar phrase. "John Newton."

Amir nodded. "I grew up with an affinity for music, despite my father's disdain for it. Never has my soul been so gratified than by Handel's *Messiah*. But that story is for another day, as I have this one to tell first."

"Sorry," I murmured. "I did not mean to interrupt."

"It is no trouble. But this story is more enjoyable than that one, I can assure you, and it is less complicated. The differences between Eastern and Western minds are extraordinary."

"So tell me then." I wanted to hear about my mother.

"When I was much younger, even younger than you, I was working near Constantinople as a medical student, under my father," Amir said. "My Abba, my father, met Harshad as he cared for some of Harshad's … sources, most of whom were not so willing to tell their secrets."

"You mean after Harshad beat them, he sent for your father." I smiled at the thought as he nodded. "And you followed your father in medicine."

"I followed my father in every aspect of my life, until I met Nadězda."

I said nothing. His tone said it all. My mother had driven a deep wedge between Amir and his father, and Amir had chosen *Máma* in the end.

"The day I met her, my life changed." He looked over at me, and I did not have to guess that he was thinking the same thing of meeting me. "I had never seen such blue eyes before. And she was so spirited, unlike any other woman I had met before. She could argue with me in a way that was smart and charming, and even after I admitted my infatuation with her, her arguments still stood better than mine in a way that was uncomfortable."

"I don't remember her like that at all," I said, looking around the library as if I was suddenly in search of her ghost. "She was very gentle and soft. She taught me how to read, and she would spend long days with me while Ben was off with my father. He probably followed him around like you did yours."

"That is why I think your brother and I get along so well," Amir said. "Both of us understand the pain of a father's rejection over something we could not help."

I saw his gaze fall to the looped scar on his hand, and I wondered if that injury had been what had turned Amir's father away from him. Glancing down at the book in my hand, I saw that Amir's scar was the same shape as the design on the cover.

Amir cleared his throat a moment later. "But we were talking about your mother," he said. "I met her in Agra, a city in the northern part of India. Harshad had asked my father to join him as his medic when he returned to India for a business trip of sorts. I doubt my father would have accepted his offer, if it was not for the political unrest facing the Sultan at the time."

"But he did accept, and you went along with him."

"My father learned his trade from the Ottoman Army. After he retired, he was a devout man of faith. When he heard Harshad was going to Agra, he was eager to go and see the Taj Mahal so he could worship in its legendary mosque."

"I've seen some drawings and maps of the Taj Mahal," I said. "It is beautiful. I did not know it was also a place of worship. I thought it was just a tomb."

"It is that and more. And it is beautiful, but I barely noticed it at the time, of course." Amir's eyes looked off into the distance, and I wondered if he was somehow meeting my mother all over again.

"Harshad was introducing me and my father to his business partner there. By then, my father was devoted to Harshad. He was a good man, if not a Muslim, and a rich one, too. Abba was hoping to convince them to pay for my remaining medical education. He had known Harshad long enough to know our family could earn much more if I was trained in Western and Eastern medication."

"It did not go as planned, I take it."

"No." Amir smiled. "Abba was annoyed to find Harshad's business partner was a woman, and a British one at that. I only found that out later, of course. When you are young, the complicated nature of politics, and what it does to people, is elusive. I did not understand my father's concern over the British Empire at the time; I was taught they were the enemy, but one that we could get along with, if they would only play by the rules."

"I take it Lady POW made her usual impression."

"She did. She has her own rules."

I laughed. "That's for sure."

"When they met, Naděžda and I also met. She was angry with me quickly enough, just as you were."

"Did you steal a book from her, too?" I asked, this time with a small, teasing smile.

"No." He laughed. "I'm afraid the reason is much worse. My manners were somewhat lacking, especially in British terms. This was her first trip into the East, and from what she told me, it was to get away from her father. Lady POW corrected her behavior, but Naděžda was unsettled by my 'mongrel ways,' and the moment our parents were distracted, she did not hesitate to tell me so."

"I don't know why you even liked her." I thought of all the diverse communities in Prague. If I were offended at every little slip in manners, I would have had to stay home.

"I am not sure I did like her, at first," Amir admitted. "But there was something about her that … something I recognized. Eventually, we grew on each other and became inseparable, especially when I was done with my education and she was initiated into the Order."

"Did you go on adventures together?"

"That is one way to say it." Amir smiled, and from his expression, I knew he would refrain from telling me the whole story. I was not sure I wanted to hear it, either, from the sad joy I saw in his eyes.

"We worked through London and Germany, protecting emissaries and investigating murders and other crimes. We did this for many years, before we … before she left for her last mission to Prague."

I hugged the book in hands to my chest. I wanted to ask him why she left, but there was something too cruel about that question. "You don't have to tell me anymore."

"Yes, I do." He nodded toward the book again. "I owe you the truth."

I could not argue with him, even though I wanted to.

"She left at the end of 1847, and I never heard from her after that. It was only after the Revolution concluded the following year that I heard from Lady POW. Your grandmother told me that Naděžda had married and resigned her position from the Order. That was all."

"She did not even tell you why she stayed in Prague?"

"Another reason I was more eager to steal the book," he admitted. "We did not end our friendship on a cordial note."

I was not able to stop myself from putting my hand on his arm. "I'm so sorry. I hope whatever is in here has given you peace."

"Thank you."

I waited for him to tell me what he had found, but he said nothing more.

As I looked at Amir, I no longer saw a Turkish book thief. I saw a man who was desperately in love and unable to stop himself from any act of depravity if it would bring him closer to the answers he sought. In some ways, we were both searching for her; I was looking to find the woman that she had been, and he was determined to find out the woman she had become.

"Thank you for telling me," I said quietly, trying to give him a brave smile.

There was a rustling sound outside the door, and Amir reached out for my hand. "It seems that the morning has come. We should get you back to your room, mademoiselle."

"That's true." As I took his arm, I saw the scar on his hand and stared at it. "I suppose you can call me Eleanora now. There's no need for formalities, right?"

"Are you saying you prefer the casualties?"

I gave him a small smile, grateful for his levity. "Maybe. We'll have to see how it goes when Harshad and Lady POW allow me to begin fighting."

"As much as it is something you might want, I hope you will not rush into it too eagerly. Death is not something to be eager for."

"I think it is more that I want their approval," I admitted, somewhat surprised I said it aloud. But after a moment, I decided it was not so strange.

In some ways, it is much easier to be honest with another person than it is to admit things to even yourself.

"Do not allow your desire to acquire that get in your way of being free. If you want to be free, truly free, you should know that you answer to the truth, not to Lady Penelope or Harshad. Not even yourself at times."

I thought about that for a long moment, before deciding Amir was right.

"If you do want to progress in this field, I believe you are doing the right thing by practicing. I have studied many years as a medical student, but I would not have learned even half of what I know if I had not been paying attention to the condition around me, and if I had not been proactive in seeking out new knowledge."

Amir's logic impressed itself on me in that moment. He was right. Whether I failed or succeeded was not up to my teachers; it was up to me, and I had to take that responsibility seriously.

And, I thought, that was what I was doing earlier this morning. And that reminded me of my own discoveries.

"Wait." I gripped Amir's hand under my own. "That reminds me. I did actually learn something helpful today, and it is very important. It's about our mission."

I quickly told Amir what I had heard from Cecilia and Alex, about how Lord Maximillian knew there was a secret heir to the throne of Bohemia, about how he was threatening Cecilia, and how Alex and Cecilia were likely plotting something in revenge.

When I was done, Amir looked back at the fireplace.

"Well then, I will send for tea. Lady POW and Harshad will want to hear this news for sure."

"You don't seem surprised by this," I said.

Amir nodded to the book in my hands. "Your mother detailed her last mission in her journal, among other things. It seems Empress Maria Anna was pregnant when she arrived, which is why she worked so hard to persuade your father to protect the king."

"She would have done that." I thought of my mother, how gentle and wonderful she had been with me when I was a child. "She always wanted children."

"I know." There was something new and broken in Amir's voice. He cleared his throat a moment later. "I was going to inform Harshad and Madame when they awoke this morning."

Before I could ask him another question or say anything else, he slipped his hand free from mine. "Go and change, Eleanora. I will summon the others."

"Wait." I slowly held out my mother's journal to Amir. "I can't read this anyway. You might as well have it."

"Are you certain?" he asked.

"I have other things of hers," I said, gripping my mother's locket inside my coat as he took the book from me. The design on the book and his scar seemed to align as he held it. "And if there is proof in her journal that what Cecilia said is true about the king's son, maybe we can use that to find him."

"Thank you." Amir clutched the book to his chest, and, as much as it hurt, I knew I was doing the right thing. "If it is agreeable, I would rather keep the matter of her book between us. Your grandmother will be willing to investigate Lady Cecilia's claim, just by virtue of her saying it."

"Maybe you should say by vice instead of virtue." I wrinkled my nose.

Amir smiled. "This does mean that you will have to tell Lady POW of your nighttime adventure."

I bit my lip. If Lady POW learned of my adventure, it was possible that it would be harder for Ben to sneak me away from the Royal Summerhouse. I did not want to miss meeting Ferdy and his friends. "Maybe we should wait to tell her then."

"Are you worried about Lady POW's response?" Amir asked. "There is nothing to worry about. She will be pleased once she learns of your information. Tulia has still refused to meet with us, and Harshad is still looking for a doctor or apothecary who sells the silver thallis herb in Prague."

"I will tell you why I'd like to wait, but I want your word that you will not say anything to Lady POW about it."

Amir's mustache twitched in amusement. "You really are your mother's daughter, Eleanora. Tell me what your plan is, and I will find a way to help you."

16

◊

"You're in fine spirits tonight, Eleanora." Lady Penelope handed me a glass of lemonade. One of my many dance partners had recently fetched them for us, and I was grateful for it as I returned from the ballroom floor.

We had arrived at the ball only an hour before, and I had stepped into dancing almost at once. I had to cause a stir, and from the way the Royal Summerhouse was set up for the evening, the dance floor took me to the middle of everyone's attention.

"You're the one who insisted I would become a sensation," I said. I took a long drink, hoping she would not notice my extra enthusiasm. "This is a good place to do it, with Count Potocki here."

"Are you trying to make Mr. Marcelin jealous?" Lady Penelope asked.

"He can have my next free dance, if he is interested," I said. "Assuming I have any open dances at all."

I glanced over to where Karl was standing. Underneath a brightly lit chandelier, he stood talking with Lord Maximillian and some other gentlemen, including Count Potocki and Lord Hohenwart. I saw that Teresa Marie was standing with them, too, but Karl was not paying attention to her.

Almost as if I had whispered in his ear, he turned.

From across the room, our eyes met. At first I blushed, embarrassed to be caught staring, but I boldly stared back. From where I was, I could see his gray eyes were stormy and somehow sad. I nodded toward Teresa Marie, giving Karl a look that clearly asked him if she was the reason for his displeasure.

He gave me a rueful smile and a small shrug, before Teresa Marie tugged his arm and forced his attention back to her. I felt a twinge of sympathy for him, and in more ways than one. I was also a little afraid for him, as I knew Lord Maximillian was up to no good.

"It seems he is otherwise preoccupied," I told Lady POW, watching Teresa Marie scowl at me from behind his back.

"Count Potocki is a good friend of his, and if we want the Minister-President to pay attention to us, we should give him good cause," Lady Penelope replied.

"I agree, but Count Potocki is the one who invited you. You don't need me to get his attention."

There was no denying I had a lot of success in that chore. I heard the whispers—all of them, ranging from hushed awe to snippy criticism. The crowd questioned each other about everything from my hair to my shoes to my dancing partner; they would discuss my dowry and make bets over who would be the first to be rejected as my suitor.

"I was invited out of courtesy by his office," Lady Penelope said, drawing my attention from the glittering room before me. "I will not be able to ask him about his safety or anything relevant to our mission if I don't have an excuse for a private meeting with him."

"I've been dancing and smiling and flirting tirelessly since we arrived. I think I can survive long enough on my own for you to go and make your introductions," I said. "And if you wanted, I could do something that would give you more time."

"Is that so?" She gave me a thoughtful look, tapping her fan against her chin. "What is your plan?"

Quickly, I told her my idea. I did not tell her I had thought of it hours ago, with Amir's help. It sounded strange as it came out of my mouth, even though I had rehearsed my plan to myself so many times.

For a long moment, I was worried I had overplayed my hand, but when Lady Penelope arched her brow at me, I could tell she was genuinely interested in my proposal. "Are you serious in your offer?"

"What's wrong with that? I'm supposed to be a fast learner."

"You are also a troublemaker."

The way she said it, I had to wonder if Amir had broken his promise and told her about my plan to leave early. Though I had not informed him of the specifics of my intended destination, I stressed that it was a mission to collect more information and Lady Penelope did not need to know about it. The more I talked to Amir, the more I felt like I was trying to convince myself I was not asking for anything unreasonably outlandish.

Maybe I was. But I did really want to see Ferdy, and I wanted to prove to Lady POW that I was a good investigator. If I could manage to do both at the same time, it was only efficient.

Amir and I could agree on efficiency.

That was probably a large part of the reason he agreed to keep his silence. He also offered to help Ben smuggle me out of the Royal Summerhouse. They were waiting for me outside, near the carriages. Ben would escort me while Amir waited to inform Lady POW of my departure.

Giving him that book was the right thing to do.

Although I had to wonder if giving him a fair chance was also the right thing to do.

I glanced up at the clock. If I was going to make my move, it would have to be soon. It was time to move forward with my plan.

"If I am a troublemaker, it only goes to show that I am truly your family," I said, watching Karl intently as I whispered in soft tones.

He seemed to realize I wanted to dance with him, playing right along with my plan as he unlatched himself from Teresa Marie.

"Just watch and get ready to abduct Count Potocki. I'll take care of the rest. I'll head out to the carriage when I'm done so you'll have plenty of time."

"You have a good plan," Lady Penelope said. "Let's see if it works."

The approving smile on Lady Penelope's face was gratifying, even if her comment was irritating. Both elements gave me the courage I needed as Karl came up beside us. I could sense his delight as he bowed over my hand.

"Mr. Marcelin, we meet again," I said coyly. "What did you say to Lady Teresa Marie that allowed you to slip away from her?"

"I lied to her, naturally." Karl confessed his sin with an ease that almost reminded me of Ferdy. "I wanted a dance with you."

"So you will get your penance for your sin after all," I replied, and he laughed.

"I would gladly pay it. I regret I was not able to locate you last night for another dance."

"Oh, you know how it is, running from one place to the next," Lady Penelope said. "But we have missed you as well, Mr. Marcelin."

Karl seemed to have not heard her, as his eyes held mine. "Not as much as I have missed you."

I felt bad he seemed so sincere in his efforts. Other gentlemen had expressed their pleasure at my acquaintance, but Karl's admiration seemed starkly genuine compared to theirs.

"It is to your good fortune that I am free to dance then," I said. We joined hands, and thanks to all the practice I had with Amir and at the previous ball, we easily slipped into a comfortable waltz. I gave Lady POW a quick nod, telling her to make her move, and then turned back to Karl, batting my eyelashes.

"You were right, of course. It is indeed my good fortune that you were free to dance," Karl replied.

"I agree." I almost giggled, seeing the boyish enthusiasm that lit up his face before he squashed it back under a mask of austerity and regality. "But there is no need to be so serious about the matter, sir."

"This is an honor and should be treated as such."

"But it is fun and one should treat it as such, too."

His gray eyes twinkled. "You are indeed very clever, my lady."

"I can't imagine why you would think otherwise." I whirled around in a spin, and then came up next to him again. "I am dancing with you, after all. I suspect many other young ladies have been clambering after you for such an honor."

"If they have, I have only noticed you."

I tapped his arm with my fan. "I do not think I am doing what can be described as 'clambering.'"

"Then I shall make it my mission to convince you to do so in the future." Karl offered a smile, one full of genuine appreciation and admiration. For a moment, the innocent eagerness in his expression almost reminded me of Ferdy. I nearly tripped at the thought, but Karl caught and steadied me.

Too early! I yelled at myself.

"Are you well, my lady?"

"I'm fine," I assured him, squeezing his arm more tightly. He seemed to brighten even more at my closeness.

As we danced, I wondered if I would have been able to stay above the seas of Karl's spell if Ferdy had not stolen my attentions. Karl was handsome and intelligent, and his passionate nature was dominated by a strong will. He was serious and grounded, but it was not hard to see that Karl would make an excellent husband.

"I suppose I should not blame all of those ladies calling for your attentions, sir," I said, giving him a flirtatious smile. "You are among the better dancers here, as your reputation stated."

"Thank you. I have always been a conscientious student. Since my father was less inclined to indulge her, my mother used me as her dancing partner quite frequently as a child."

"That's sweet." I imagined a small version of Karl prancing around with his mother. "Is your mother in town?"

"She is, though she is busy. She is preparing for the Advent Ball this week."

"That is another reason for you to go, if your mother is excited for it."

"Yes. You and your grandmother will also attend, will you not? I fear it will not be fun at all without you there."

"I am certain my grandmother would be willing to go."

"I hope you will come. I do not want to be left alone with Lady Teresa Marie's attentions."

"Lady Teresa Marie?" I asked.

"She is here, and her father is, too."

"Do you suspect they are following you, sir?" I asked, curious, even though I kept my tone blasé.

"Oh, I doubt that," Karl said, "but Lord Maximillian has expressed interest in furthering my political career. He is a new friend of Alfred's and he is eager to support me."

I wondered if that meant that Lord Maximillian also hated Emperor Franz Joseph's neglect of Bohemia.

Does this mean Karl knows who the king's son is? Does His Grace see Karl's leadership as a step in taking over Bohemia's government?

I needed more answers.

"Lord Maximillian is a wealthy duke. His support would help you in your aspirations, surely."

Before I could remark on the Duke's vision of the future, I realized Karl was blushing, ever so slightly. "What is it?"

"I was rather hoping you would be more interested," Karl admitted, and I realized his flirting was taking on a more serious tone.

In all of my trappings of apparent wealth, and even Lady POW's actual wealth, I knew that there were plenty of men interested in pursuing courtship. I was my mother's daughter, after all, and I was a great beauty among the crowds.

I wanted to scream in frustration. My charm was an act and my grace was the result of education, and my reasons for indulging the crowded ballrooms of Prague were part of my quest for answers in a murder.

I did not really want to worry about relationships. Not like this, anyway, I thought, as Karl continued talking, mentioning marriage in the most obscure ways.

I wondered how my mother had faired when she came to Prague. Was this what she had experienced? Did my father fall in love with her at first sight? Did he fawn over her, dance with her, compliment her, treat her the way Karl treated me? Or was he more like Ferdy, hiding out in the shadows, waiting for the moment to come and rescue her from boredom, offering her real moments of laughter and truth, even if it was cloaked in secret?

At the thought of Ferdy, I turned and glanced along the ballroom walls, wondering if he would come and rescue me from Karl again.

"What is it?" Karl asked. "Is something wrong?"

"Oh, uh, no," I stammered. "I just … was curious where my grandmother went. That's all." I glimpsed back to where I had left her, only to catch sight of her talking with Count Potocki.

At least she got that far.

"Oh, I see." Karl nodded. "I would want to discuss matters with her as well, but I believe it is better that we are in agreement ourselves, first."

"Matters?"

"Marriage." For once, he hesitated. "I have not explained myself very well, have I?"

"Why would you want to discuss marriage?" I asked, genuinely curious. "We have only danced a few times. We barely know each other."

"I know you better than you think," Karl said. "Lady Teresa Marie told me some of the … the more unpleasant aspects of your life."

I arched my brow. Of all things, I had not expected that. "Shouldn't that disqualify me as a future Minister-President's wife?" I asked bluntly. "I can't imagine it would make good press for you."

"No," Karl blustered. "Of course not. If anything, I was … inspired, to be honest. Even before I found out about that, I have always known of your kindness to your brother, and to others, and of your bravery in facing your parents' death."

I faltered, nearly falling on accident. *How did he know about Ben? Lady Penelope had never said much about him to anyone.*

"I don't know what to say. I still don't know you very well."

"But you like me, don't you?" Karl asked.

"I think you are a very fine gentleman. And a good dancer. But … "

As I stood there, I felt strange. I should have been thrilled or touched to have Karl's affections, especially since he knew the truth about me serving under Cecilia. But all I could think of was the Order, and Ferdy, and how this was all very strange.

"You will not completely dismiss me, will you?" Karl asked, the hope fading from his eyes.

I smiled, forcing myself to play along. "Of course not."

"I'm glad to hear that." Karl pulled me close and held me tight. I shivered against him, surprised at his gentleness. I took a moment to look up at him, and I felt myself caught off guard.

"Perhaps I am not used to how society arranges marriage. My parents had a marriage based on mutual feelings," I said.

However, now that I think of it … I don't really know that, do I?

Karl nodded. "Thank you for your honesty, my lady."

At that point, the music began to swell into its ending crescendo. I was ready to leave Karl's side. The whole dance had been lovely, but the dialogue had been awkward and unsettling.

As I stepped back, I slipped my foot halfway from my one shoe and twisted it into my skirt.

"Oh, my!" I shrieked as I fell over, finding every way I could to make a scene.

Ben had taught me at a younger age how to duck and roll. Admittedly, it was harder to fall gracefully in a ballroom surrounded by other dancing couples, but when I landed on my backside with only a small bump, I knew I had achieved my goal.

From the stunned look on Karl's face, I could tell his reaction would be the perfect way to garner sympathy and concern.

I hurried to rearrange my skirts, but my stockings were still sticking out as other dancers stopped and hurried over to help—or just stare, which is what the majority of them did, as Karl and a few other gentlemen offered me their hands, and other ladies called out asking me about my condition.

When asked if I was well, I answered, "I will be, once I manage to get back up on my feet."

The crowd laughed nervously. I took Karl's hand, but reached for others' support as I worked to find my balance.

As I began to brush the wrinkles out of my gown, I glanced over the crowds to see Lady Penelope steering an astounded Count Potocki out of the ballroom.

"Are you hurt, Eleanora?" Karl asked.

For the moment, I ignored his use of my first name. Instead, I slowly pretended to put weight on my foot.

"Ouch!" I whimpered. "I do believe I have twisted my ankle, sir."

"Allow me to escort you," Karl said, as several other gentlemen reached out and offered me their hands as well.

"Thank you." I looped my arm around Karl's neck as I pretended to limp. We walked through the hoard of people together. I felt simultaneously guilty and grateful, glad my intended trickery had not led to actual injury.

"I apologize for this. I should not have startled you in such a manner."

"It's not so bad. But I doubt I will be able to dance for the rest of the evening," I said. "I believe I will head to my carriage, so I might return home and rest for the evening. If you would be so kind as to escort me?"

"Of course." Karl patted my hand. "If I cannot prove my affections to you on the dancefloor, I will be content to do so in other manners."

I barely heard him, as others we passed began asking questions about my injury. Once we were out of the Royal Summerhouse, we made our way through the large pillars of the building to where I knew Ben and Amir were waiting.

"As much as I am sorry for your injury," Karl said slowly, "I am grateful for the chance to speak with you alone and without everyone watching."

"Oh, I'm sure we have plenty of people who are watching," I said, looking back toward the entrance where more people had gathered.

"They love you."

"They love a good story," I scoffed.

"No, it's more than that. They really do admire you."

"I know you want to make a name for yourself in politics, but there is no need to presume the masses are so adamantly—"

"It is true that I am versed in politics, my lady," Karl said. "And that is how I know they truly adore you."

Between the way he said it and the way he looked at me, I almost believed him.

I shrugged. "Well, it's no matter now. Tell me, what was it that you wanted to say to me that you cannot say in public?"

Karl sighed. "Lord Maximillian has offered to support my political ambitions. He and Count Potocki are supportive of my election as the next Minister-President."

You already told me that.

I gave him a brilliant smile. "That's wonderful. You are so young, too. This must be very exciting for you."

"It is," he agreed. "But there is a condition to accepting Lord Maximillian's endowment. He has requested that I marry his daughter."

"Lord Maximillian wants you to marry his daughter?" I repeated his words slowly, and it was at that moment that the pieces all began to fall into place. "How old are you, exactly?"

"I am two and twenty."

"You were born in 1848?"

"Yes." Karl frowned. "Why do you ask?"

My mother's mission, Cecilia's screechy outburst—everything seemed to run through my memory all at once.

"Max found what he was looking for all those years ago. He would have broken the engagement himself, now that he's found King Ferdinand's son and heir."

The Empress had been pregnant when my mother arrived in early 1848.

Karl was determined to fulfill his duty to Bohemia, and thanks to Ferdy, I knew Karl wanted to return the kingdom to its own sovereignty, free from the Emperor.

Karl is King Ferdinand's son.

I stared at him, studying his face in the moonlight, as if I was seeing him for the first time. I did not recall much about King Ferdinand's face, or Empress Maria Anna, but nothing caused me to question the notion he was their son. With his dark hair and narrow chin, combined with the Hapsburg eyes and straight nose, I suddenly wondered at how others had missed this for so long.

In any other reality, he would one day be my nation's king.

"Does it bother you that I am so young?" Karl asked, interrupting my mental spasm. "I was rather certain you enjoyed my company and the closeness of our ages."

He slowed to a stop, as we drew near to my carriage. I saw Ben disguised as a footman, and Amir settled comfortably on the perch.

"I have enjoyed our dancing," I replied, my voice struggling not to betray my astonishment, "and your company as well, sir."

"I am relieved to hear that. I was rather hoping I could convince you to marry me instead."

At that, I stopped moving completely.

"I apologize if it is improper," Karl swiftly amended. "But I could not marry Teresa Marie without the hope I could convince you to marry me instead."

"I … don't know what to say."

For a long moment, I was flattered. Karl was the rightful heir to the Bohemian throne, or he would have been, if it were not for the Revolution of 1848. And here he was, telling me that he wanted to marry *me*.

Me—someone who had been a servant in her own home for the last ten years of her life, someone who longed for books and freedom, someone who spent her days dreaming dreams and commiserating miseries with her brother.

But as I thought through it, I was suddenly curious. "Why do you even like me?"

Why did he like me enough to have him turn his back on Teresa Marie and her father's significant financial support? If he wanted the Minister-President position so badly, why was he willing to risk it all for me?

Karl seemed as surprised by my question as I was. "Because I do. I do like you. And plenty of others do, too. You're clever, and funny, and you're beautiful. I … think you would make an excellent wife and mother. You are a true lady, in every sense."

"Oh." I nodded slowly. "I see."

"Please, Ella, consider my offer. I have a promising career, and significant holdings I am to inherit from my family one day."

He started listing other reasons I should marry him, and all I could concentrate on was how he called me Ella.

"My name is Eleanora," I said, still stiff with remaining shock.

Karl blushed. "I apologize. Your name is quite long." He bowed gallantly over my hand. "I don't have much time before Teresa Marie and her father demand that notice be sent to the papers. Unfortunately, I need to know your answer soon. I would not put you in this position otherwise, I swear. Count Potocki is to announce his support for me to become the next Minister-President at the Advent Ball. I need to know I will have your support by then."

"I see." I chewed on my bottom lip, thinking it over. If Karl was the heir to the throne, but he needed financial support, I suspected he did not have his family's support, as Lady POW had said before.

Another thought struck me. Was Karl somehow connected to all the strange murders that had happened? Had he needed to dispose of Dr. Artha and Father Novak?

"I would be happy to come and call upon you and your grandmother to formally ask for your hand. But I would not want to do so without knowing you are in agreement."

I had to stop myself from flinching. "Thank you." Karl was more mercenary than I liked, but he was polite about it.

"Please," Karl said. "I like you. Very much."

Quietly, I detached myself from Karl. "I will think about it," I promised.

I knew I could say that honestly, too. I would think about why someone like Karl would pledge his lifetime to someone who was smart and clever and funny, especially when I was sure that Teresa Marie would be more than willing to act the part of the perfect wife and mother for him. I appreciated he knew the truth of who I was, and my background, but I was still too shocked to do anything but curtsy.

"Send me word through a messenger when you make a decision," he said. "I will call upon you and your grandmother and we can discuss this more."

"As you wish, Mr. Marcelin."

"Karl, please." He kissed my hand. "Farewell … Ella."

I nodded tepidly as Ben came over beside me. Together, we watched Karl walk away. He was as confident as ever, with his head held high and his eyes remaining forward.

"I told you," Ben said, "you have *Máma's* charm and beauty. It was only a matter of time before gentlemen all around started to propose to you."

I would have laughed and agreed if there was less riding on the situation.

"Karl is not just any gentleman," I said. "He is King Ferdinand's son."

"What?" Ben blinked. "Are you sure?"

I nodded. "I'm fairly certain."

"But the king was declared medically unfit to have children," Ben said. "This is … that's not … how?"

Amir came up beside him. "What did you learn, Eleanora?"

"Karl has to be the king's son," I told him. "Lord Maximillian is offering him money for his political career in exchange for marrying Teresa Marie. From what I overheard Cecilia say, and given Karl's age, that means he has to be the true heir to the throne of Bohemia."

"Wait, what? What did Cecilia say? When did this happen?" Ben asked. "Did Marcelin tell you this when he asked you to marry him?"

"He asked you to marry him?" Amir repeated. "Well, this has certainly been quite a night for you already, Eleanora."

"She was asked by the king's son," Ben said.

"Is he the one?" Amir glanced over his shoulder, looking back at the entrance to the Summerhouse.

"I'm almost completely positive it's him," I said. "From what I know about him and what others have said, he's the right age, and he has the right connections. And it makes sense. His family—his mother and father—would not support an uprising against Emperor Franz Joseph. They are happy in their retirement, by all accounts."

"Do you have proof?" Amir asked.

"I can't even believe you think he's really the king's son," Ben said.

"I'll explain everything I know to you, Ben. But first, we have other plans. Lady POW is distracted for now. I managed to secure her an extremely private session with the Minister-President, and now I want to get to the Jewish Quarter before it's too late."

The Royal Summerhouse still swelled with music behind us. The early evening moon was shining on the alabaster of the columns behind us. I shivered at the touch of wind, even as it sifted through my hair like a loving hand. I turned away from Ben and Amir, looking out across the city. Prague was starting to light up with little flickers of light, and I felt it call to me.

"I can't believe you still want to go." Ben crossed his arms. "If what you're saying is true, we need to talk to Lady Penelope right away."

"Of course I still want to go." I threw up my hands in exasperation. "Besides, Amir is right; we need proof. And if anyone would know the truth about Karl, it is Mr. Clavan. Ferdy himself told me that everything filters through the Cabal sooner or later."

Ben still looked skeptical.

I tugged on his arm. "Please, Ben. Amir will be staying here and he can fill her in on the details. I don't want to disappoint Ferdy, and we might be able to learn more to help us. Besides, you promised."

"Fine, Nora." Ben sighed. "Come on. If nothing else, I want to meet this Ferdy person. If you're so enamored of him, especially when it appears a prince is asking for your hand, it is my duty as your brother to make sure he is worthy of you."

I flushed red, but I said nothing. Ben had a way of ruining my good mood, and I knew I would only get in trouble if we ended up arguing over Ferdy. Karl might have liked me very much, but I knew without even thinking that I liked Ferdy much more. Even if Ferdy had lied to me about things before, I had a feeling he would never lie to me about wanting to marry me for my dowry.

17

◊

Ben and I made our way through the evening streets of Prague swiftly, crossing the Vltava and sneaking our way through the tighter streets of the Jewish Quarter.

Clavan had said it right; there was a sad history between the Christians and Jews, and I felt the truth of the segregation's pains as Ben and I headed for the Cabal.

The streets of the *Josefskà* were cluttered with tiny townhouses and small rooms. In the darkness, the shuttered windows and the chipping paint made the neighborhoods collectively dreary. I gripped my old maidservant skirts. I had changed into them in the carriage, before stuffing my hair under a simple bonnet and pulling on my old work shoes. The rough stitching was already foreign to me, but I had a feeling that the downtrodden figures shuffling into the alleyways to avoid my gaze would have welcomed their itchy warmth.

"I've never been here at night," I said. "Is it always like this?"

"Like what?" Ben asked.

"I don't know. Quiet. A little sad. A little strange. It's hard to describe."

"The Jews have always been foreigners outside of the Promised Land," Ben reminded me. "Just as Christians are aliens this side of Heaven. You shouldn't be so surprised to feel like you are out of place, and that this place is, too."

"I suppose. But it seemed a lot more welcoming in the daytime the last time I was here."

"That's just an effect of night," Ben assured me with a laugh. "You don't go onto the streets of a city like Prague unless it's for balls or parties. Now that you can see past the gilded cover, you'll see poverty and other trials that exist in the city's crevices."

Ben was right. As we skimmed across shadows toward the Cabal, I saw the city was not just a wonder of light and magic; it was a place of darkness and sin, crying for deliverance.

My heart softened, witnessing plight of so many others, the ones I could see now that the daytime crowds had dispersed and the night had called out society's undesirables. "I wish we could help more people."

"That's part of the reason I like working for the Order," Ben admitted. "With Amir's help, and Lady POW's income, I've been able to see the world more for what it is than what I thought it would be."

"I know what you mean. Quite a few things have changed since they've come into our lives."

"I've noticed you've warmed up to Amir."

"He apologized and brought me back the book he stole," I said. "It was *Máma's* journal."

Ben nodded. "He told me about it when I asked, the first days we worked together."

"Why didn't you tell me?" I asked, slighted. "You're the one who wanted me to get along with him."

"He said it would be better if you asked, so I said I wouldn't say anything. And … "

"And what?"

"And you were younger than me when *Máma's* ship was lost at sea," Ben said. "You probably don't remember her the same way I do. She loved us, and even *Otec*, too. But there were days when she would disappear, locking herself in her room. I found out later she suffered from bouts of melancholy."

"Where did you hear that?" I asked.

"Cecilia mentioned it once or twice in her list of reasons I should be glad to be alive, even if I had to work in the manor." Ben shrugged. "Amir said that *Máma* and Lady POW had quite a falling out. He said he was certain that at least one of the reasons she left

Prague to go to London was to apologize to her. I didn't say anything to you earlier because I didn't want to tell you anything you weren't ready to hear."

I did not tell Ben that as much as I was grateful for his earlier consideration, it almost prevented me from finding out the truth. I knew that was a large part of growing and learning, and I did not want to be left behind because of childish matters. Thanks to Lady POW, and now Ben, I knew that the woman I remembered as my mother was as wispy and insubstantial as the wind.

We said nothing else until we caught sight of the Cabal. Torches flickered at either side of the doorway. Through the windows, I saw clusters of friends and family gathered together.

We made our way to them. As Ben shuffled beside me, I took his arm. "Ben?"

"What is it?"

"Promise me that we won't let anything come between us like *Máma* and Lady POW did."

Ben took my hand and squeezed it affectionately. "I promise that won't happen to us."

"Are you sure?"

"I'm certain, *ségra.*" Ben sighed and looked back at the Cabal. "But I'm warning you, if this Ferdy character is as much of a charlatan as I think he is, the limits of my patience and your forgiveness will be tested."

"It's better that way," a voice said from behind us. "Such things become more precious in the end when they are tested."

Ben and I whirled around to see Ferdy walking toward us. He had his cap on over his hair, and his scarf looped around his neck in a poor attempt to ward off the chill in the air. In the evening darkness, I might not have realized it was Ferdy at all, if I had not seen his slightly crooked grin.

Everything seemed instantly more vivid. My heart raced and my stomach twisted with happy nerves.

"Ferdy." I smiled and waved, and it was hard to quell the joy—and relief—inside of me.

"I'm glad to see you've made it to the Cabal tonight," he said, taking my hand and bowing over it before turning toward my brother. "And you've brought a friend?"

"This is my brother, Ben."

"I'll admit I'm relieved," Ferdy said as he bowed to Ben. "I've heard Ella's quite the sensation on the dancefloor—even if she falls over."

I laughed. "How did you hear about that already?"

"I know a few people," Ferdy teased. "And some of those people were very excited to see your stockings."

"Excuse me." Ben coughed. "Do you want to repeat that?"

"Later, my new friend," Ferdy said, giving me a quick wink. "But only if you insist. I know from Elie and Clavan that the news cycle can get quite dull."

Ben cracked his knuckles. "Is that so?"

"And this is one of the reasons I vastly prefer a brother to an admirer." Ferdy slapped Ben on the back in a friendly manner, ignoring Ben's threatening posture. "If I am going to fight someone for her, it's better that it's her brother than an admirer. That way, if we end up broken and bleeding, I can at least gain your respect in the end, if not your friendship."

Ben glanced over at me, and I could tell he was unsure of what to say.

Ferdy reached out to me and offered me his arm. "Well, Lady Ella, why don't you come in and see what's going on? Jarl is here with his Faye, and Helen cooked up a mutton stew that will keep you warm until next month."

"Sure. Come on, Ben."

"Yes, Ben, you too," Ferdy said with a smile.

"Ella?" Ben whispered behind me.

"That's what Ferdy calls me. He said Eleanora was too long." I thought about telling him that Karl had said the same thing, but Ferdy opened the door and the inside warmth called to us.

"I still like Nora better," Ben grumbled.

"I think both have their charm." I could tell he did not like my answer.

He frowned, but the atmosphere of the Cabal instantly overwhelmed our senses. I smothered a laugh as I looked at Ben's face. Right away, I saw he was impressed with the surroundings; after telling him how Ferdy had brought me here the first time, Ben had likely expected it to be a seedy place, full of drunks and criminals.

Candles decorated all the small tables as circles of friends surrounded them. The air was full of pockets of smoke and brandy, all layered with a warm ambiance coming from the kitchen at the back.

Looking around, I saw there were a lot of men and women in pairs, the men wearing their dark suits, and the women wearing long skirts and scarves. Most of the men wore hats or yarmulkes, but some had no caps at all. I was surprised there was a priest. He was sitting at a table near the bar, reading a Bible.

"Jarl," Ferdy called, waving toward a table tucked into the corner beside the bar.

"There you are, Ferdy. Where have you been?" A German man with dark hair and a smoking pipe gave Ferdy a brotherly hug, before he blew a stream of smoke out in greeting. "Faye and I have been here for hours."

"We have not." The young woman sitting beside him rolled her eyes before she laughed. "We just got here."

"They don't need to know that, Faye. I was hoping to leverage that into getting Ferdy to buy me another round."

"Oh, so you're not in your cups already?" Ferdy pulled over two more chairs for Ben and me.

"Of course not. Dad's been keeping his eye on him," Faye said. She looked behind her chair, where I saw Clavan scowling down at Jarl. I was glad to see Clavan gave Faye a wink a second later, and I realized he was in on the joke.

Ferdy laughed and then introduced us. "This is Ella, and her brother Ben," he said. "They're new to the Cabal."

"So you brought them over to meet us first, so we'd scare them off?" Jarl asked.

"If anyone could do it, I figured it would be you."

"Don't forget about Eliezer," Clavan said from behind us. He was carrying a tray full of beers, and when he sat it down on our table, he turned to Ferdy. "I've got a new tab started for you."

"Excellent," Ferdy said. "I didn't even have to tell you. Sometimes I think you can read minds, Clavan."

"It's a mark of a good businessman," Ben said, as Ferdy handed him his glass.

Ferdy and Ben seemed to get along after that. I smiled into my own glass as they began talking, Ben asking some questions and Ferdy jokingly answering them. I was introduced to Jarl and Faye, and even Clavan's wife, Helen, when she came out of the kitchen to meet us. It was clear there was an air of comradery and familiarity to the group that seemed to add to the open warmth of the atmosphere.

"So, Ella," Jarl spoke up, "Ferdy tells us that he rescued you. Is this true?"

"Ferdy has a reputation for being quite a liar," Faye said. "But he insists he is telling the truth this time."

"He is right to do so." I began to recount the tale of how I met Ferdy. I did not mention that I found out who Amir was later on, nor did I say anything about the book. Jarl was still skeptical of Ferdy's account, but Faye had misty eyes as I told her how he brought me to the Cabal and treated me like a princess.

As Jarl and Ben began talking about cigars, and Faye, Ferdy, and I all discussed Prague's latest social season, I lost track of time. The sounds of friendship and comradery around me blurred into a single confection of comfort and welcome, and I tasted the opportunity with relish.

It was only when the door opened and another man walked in that the atmosphere changed into one of business. He was wearing the dark suit of an Orthodox Jew. His yarmulke sat atop his head, the dark, loopy ringlets of a devout man framing his bearded face. As he entered, several men lifted their glasses to him.

"Elie!" they cheered, and the man waved their praises down.

"It's fine, folks," Eliezer said, greeting the crowds. "It's fine. I'm here, you can all settle in."

"Any good news this week?" a man called.

"If there was only good news, there wouldn't be news at all," Eliezer replied. "That's the way the news works. There's only news if it's bad."

"So the bad news is that there's news? That's good news to me!"

The crowd laughed, and I chuckled at their banter as it continued.

"Eliezer runs a news network of his own throughout the city," Ferdy explained to Ben and me. "I get to be part of it from time to time, passing along information I hear. I enjoy it. Jarl helps with the printing, when he's not working at the factory down the river, and Faye even helps by cleaning the bar here. Clavan provides the beer and offers his own insight, while Elie usually interrupts him."

Faye smiled. "I also help with some of the pamphlets," she said. "I take notes every meeting and help Jarl with the deliveries."

"That's wonderful," I said. "I'm looking forward to hearing the news tonight."

"It's mostly about politics now," Faye said, "since the Diets are in session. But Christmas is coming, so we might have something more religious, too."

"Most of the people in here are Jewish," I said. "Why do they want to hear about Christmas?"

"There are plenty of Jews here," Faye said. "But my father has friends who work as artists and writers who come in to hear the political and cultural commentary. And Elie studied law before he went into business. With his political analysis and Dad's cultural insight, there are plenty of Christians who come to hear them. As it should be. It's not good for people to focus on the little things that they forget about the greater calling around us."

"And they do this every week?"

Faye nodded. "Maybe one day politics will be so engrossing that there will need to be daily meetings, but so far politics is just a small sliver of our lives."

"So, folks, let's begin," Eliezer called. "Thanks to the end of the American Civil War, it seems that there is chance that republics will become more commonplace among the nations of the future. This could be either good or bad for Bohemia, but likely there will be a lot of good and bad that comes with this. As the Americans have proven in the last five years, revolutions are not bloodless, and settling disputes can take generations."

Over the next hour, Eliezer continued to talk about the life of empires, and how the Bohemian people were recklessly embracing nationalism at the oppression of the German Diet; Clavan talked about art and freedom, and the struggle for beauty despite the ugliness of the battle. Even Jarl, an artist of sorts when he was not at his job, chimed in with insights and occasionally insults.

Ben was mesmerized by Eliezer, as he began talking about a shipment of wine that, somehow, had exploded on its way from Hradiště, a small town in Moravia. When Ben called out a question, Eliezer answered him, never losing any of his enthusiasm.

I was about to congratulate Ben when I looked over and saw Ferdy, who was just staring at me.

I stared back, silently trying to remind him to pay attention.

He gave me a smirk and turned back to watch Eliezer and Clavan discuss the failure of the Minister-President to bring the German and Bohemian Diets to any meaningful compromise or agreement regarding regional transportation laws. But not even a moment later, Ferdy took hold of my hand.

And I let him.

There was no hesitation in me as I laced my fingers with his under the table.

After that, it was difficult to remember the rest of the meeting. The heat of our hands distracted me; excitement ran through my whole body, and I kept reminding myself not to blush as the discussion continued.

Eventually I gave up, deciding I would ask Faye if she would have a pamphlet sent to my house so I could hear what I missed.

Sitting here and holding hands with Ferdy was a relief my heart never seemed to know it needed. I thought of how intently Karl had looked at me while we danced and talked, remembering how I had wondered how someone could be so sure of wanting another so quickly.

But here I was, sitting here, slowly but surely allowing myself closer to someone I had really only met, someone who was a mystery and an adventure, a jokester by all accounts and a liar by his own.

When Clavan finished a reading from Wordsworth's *Lyrical Ballads*, discussing Edmund Burke's influence, and mentioning a slew of other names I did not recognize, the crowd clapped.

Ferdy and I exchanged a secret glance before he let me go, and we both clapped along with the rest of the crowd.

"That was brilliant," Ben whispered to me, almost making me jump. I had nearly forgotten he was there with me.

"Yes," I hastily agreed. "It was."

"I can see why you wanted to come. I'm not sure if there's anything that will help us, but it is good to be informed of local sentiments."

"Maybe we can ask for specific details. It's better we ask in secret anyway."

Ben leaned closer to me. "You go and try then. You know Clavan better than I do."

"Was there something you wanted, Ella?" Ferdy asked. "Or you, Ben?"

"Nothing," Ben and I said at the same time. When Ferdy arched his brow at us, I took a drink and smiled up at him. "I was just wondering if Mr. Clavan would give me another beer."

"Oh. Of course. He's already gone back to manning the bar," Ferdy said. "Maybe I'll tell him to bring a cup of coffee here to Jarl. He looks tired."

"I'm not tired," Jarl objected. "I've been working all day, not running around the streets like you."

"See, I would think that work would *make* you tired," Ferdy said. "Running around the streets means I can take breaks. From the sound of it, you also have to fight off some jealousy, since you can't come and join me."

As Ferdy and Jarl continued to argue the semantics of a full day's work, I slipped away and stepped up to the bar.

Clavan came up beside me, already pouring me a new drink. "Well, Lady Ella, what did you think?"

"I loved it," I said, trying not to let him see I had been distracted through most of it. "I especially thought your reading was wonderful."

"Well, as you know, Wordsworth is a favorite of mine," Clavan said. "Maybe next time I'll read something from *The Prelude*."

"Can I ask you a question about something else?"

"It seems you already have." He picked up a bottle of whiskey and poured himself a small shot. "What is your question?"

"Ferdy mentioned that you know everything about Prague," I said. "Is that true?"

"It depends, not on me, but on my information." He gave me a roguish grin. "What do you want to know?"

"I was wondering if you had heard rumors about King Ferdinand and Empress Maria Anna having a son," I said. I kept my gaze on his face, watching as his eyes shifted from interested to wary and then back to speculative.

"A son?" he asked.

"Yes." I frowned, wondering if he was trying to buy some time to respond. He seemed strangely uncomfortable all of a sudden. "You know something, don't you?"

"There were whispers of the Empress and King having a son a long time ago, back in the 1850s," he said quietly. "So I would not be surprised to see if it were true."

I nodded. "I was wondering, with the Nationalists fighting with the other parties, if they were trying to reinstate the monarchy."

"On the surface, it would seem like a good goal for them," Clavan said, "but the people like having power. That was proven in '67, when the Emperor reorganized the Minister-President's office. The Bohemian Diet is here to stay, even with a new monarch and a new governmental structure."

"Even if it's constantly deadlocked by the German Diet?" I asked, unable to stop myself from glancing at Jarl. It was strange to see a German getting along with so many Bohemians, and even more to hear him discuss the growing economy in Prague, now that the Diets were moving onto other matters in their sessions.

"Most certainly. The Nationalists would gain nothing," Clavan said. "And the other parties, and the Minister-President, might agree with a new king like that in the short-term. But in the long-term, it would fail."

"What do you mean?" I asked.

"The Nationalists are happy with the progress they've made, even if it is small. The other main parties are not as happy, but they are learning how to use the system to gain more power."

"So no one would like it if there was a new king on the throne of Bohemia."

"Not long enough for it to matter." Clavan shook his head. "The Revolution of 1848 brought an end to that line's power. Even if it were true, he would need to be elected to the throne now, and even that would take a large disaster to set in motion."

"But if the king's son wanted to get elected to the throne," I mused, "he would need the votes."

"For starters. He would also likely need a full-scale disaster, or an act of war from the Emperor himself, in order to make his argument." Clavan shook his head. "I don't see Franz Joseph allowing that to happen. He has his weaknesses as a ruler, but he is smart and sharp when he needs to be."

I nodded and took another sip of beer.

"Why so interested in the topic?" Clavan asked.

I looked at him, and then back at Ferdy and Ben as they struggled through an arm-wrestling match. "I heard the rumors while I was out at a party," I lied. "I thought, perhaps in light of the murders of Dr. Artha and the others, something was going on."

Clavan said nothing for a long moment. And then he took another swig of his whiskey, draining the small cup before refilling it. "It's strange that you did hear such rumors. Most who talk of that particular nature end up dead."

"Really?" My eyes went wide. "Why aren't you, then?"

"I only listen to those rumors." He took another drink of whiskey and gave me a small smile. "I don't report on them. Officially."

"I did enjoy the reports. Eliezer is a good lawyer, from the sound of it," I said, switching topics. "I enjoyed his analysis of the Diets and Bohemia politics, especially in light of events happening around the country."

"He's my brother in all but blood." Clavan nodded toward Faye and Jarl. "And that will be my son, after my daughter marries him next year. He's a knucklehead with charm. Not unlike your own admirer."

"I've noticed," I said.

"Ferdy's good at moving when he has to," Clavan said. "Which is why I will tell you, when he gets your brother to argue with Jarl over something inconsequential, he will slip away to see if you want to go on a walk with him."

I glanced back to see Ferdy was still watching me.

"If you like him, go with him," Clavan said. "Jarl takes Faye down by the Vltava and I've been assured by Helen I don't have to worry. And seeing how your brother watches over you, you won't have too much time alone with Ferdy."

I laughed. "I'll be surprised if he manages that," I said. "Ben is pretty smart—"

Before I could assure Clavan that Ben would not fall for such tricks, Ferdy was suddenly standing directly beside me, close enough I could feel the warmth of his body. "Ella," he said, "I hope Clavan here isn't boring you."

"I certainly am," Clavan said with a small chuckle. "Ah, I see Hermann Kavka has arrived. I have business I want to discuss with him. Excuse me."

As he had predicted, or warned, I was left alone with Ferdy.

"You aren't going to seriously ask me to go on a walk, are you?" I looked back to see Clavan pull Helen into a quick twirl as she came out from the kitchen, before greeting a robust man at the other end of the bar. "Mr. Clavan already warned me."

Ferdy laughed. "Of course not," he said. "I'm here to rescue you. If that involves walking outside for a little while, that's not the same thing."

"I don't exactly need to be rescued," I pointed out.

"If you don't exactly need to be rescued, and I'm not exactly rescuing you, then you can come with me for a few moments." Ferdy offered me his arm. Seemingly sensing my hesitation, he stilled, waiting for me with a gentle expectancy on his face.

After only a second's worth of uncertainty, and seeing Faye was now battling with Ben and Jarl as they discussed values and the finer points of the news, I laughed. "Maybe I need more rescuing than I thought."

"At this point, you would be rescuing both of us, Ella." Ferdy grinned.

18

◊

Winter was only a few weeks away, and I felt the chill in the night as we stepped into the small alleyway behind the Cabal.

"Well?" Ferdy asked. "What do you think? You can see why I come here."

"You were right," I said. "It's fun, even if it is a little more than I am used to. It's almost like going to school, I imagine."

"Oh, Eliezer would love to hear that. Keeping up with him as he talks is more than half the battle, but we love him for it." Ferdy wrapped my hand more tightly in his, pulling it into his coat as he led me down the alleyway.

"Are we headed toward the Vltava?" I asked.

"We can go anywhere you'd like," Ferdy assured me. "I'm just happy to be with you."

I thought of Karl once more, and I decided if I could be blunt with anyone, it was Ferdy. "Why?"

"Why what?"

"What is so special about me?" I asked. "Do I look that different in my usual clothes, without the gown and dancing slippers?"

"It's not that." Ferdy playfully batted at my bonnet. "You're beautiful no matter what you wear. I've been waiting for another chance to be alone with you again."

I laughed. "I can't imagine why."

"Can't you?"

He stopped in front of me, and I went silent as I met his gaze.

It was just like before, I thought, remembering those stolen moments at the Hohenwart Ball.

It was just like before, only everything felt even more vivid. The warmth between us, and the coldness of the wintery world around us;

the dark of the night, and the light of the stars; the comradery of the pub beside us, and the world only we shared before us.

"I believe I made a promise last time," Ferdy said, "to get you to admit you wanted to kiss me."

Terror and hope, that odd combination of emotion and feelings I always felt when it came to Ferdy—all of it leapt at me at once, and I took a moment to enjoy the rush before the inevitable hesitation came rushing in.

"Mr. Clavan told me that you would do this," I said, pulling my hand free and crossing my arms. "So I assume you've done this before, possibly more than once. And I don't know you very well. After all, I just met you."

Ferdy did not step back from my objection. "That is a fallacy, you know. Time never plays as much a factor as people think when it comes to situations like this." He met my gaze in the moonlight, and I felt vulnerable and exposed.

"Like this?" I stiffened, and he continued.

"Haven't you heard the tales of love at first sight? The stories of friendships that suddenly turned into love?"

"I have. But those are just stories. Things like that don't happen in real life."

"There is no such thing as 'just stories,'" Ferdy said. "Behind each story is truth, feeling, and experience." His gaze dropped to my mouth. "Just as the magic of a kiss is not in the kiss itself, but in the heart behind it."

"You just met me," I insisted, but my inner resolve was crumbling. There was something inside of me that wanted to respond to him, something that wanted to believe his words—and something that already agreed with him.

"No," Ferdy said. "I did not just meet you. I recognized you."

At his words, I felt my breathing falter. The beauty of the night fell away from me, and the last of the cold was whisked away as his hand reached out and cupped my cheek. Instinctively, I leaned into his touch. My mind was racing with incoherent thoughts, but the sound of my pounding heart drowned out any possible argument or objection.

"How brave would you be tonight?" he asked. His silver eyes held mine, and I could not help myself from leaning into their brilliance. "Brave enough to glimpse at the heart of a man who sees into yours?"

I thought of my mother. "I am nothing if not brave," I whispered softly.

"Good. I don't think I can wait any longer to kiss you." And then his lips pressed against mine, and what was left of my defenses shattered.

His kiss was at first warm and soft; he tasted like freedom and fun, just a little roguish and rebellious, both dangerous and safe. Ferdy reached up and pushed back my bonnet, letting his fingers find my hair. I fell into him, unable to fully process the pleasure running through me, as the warmth burned into searing heat.

We fell into a desperate rhythm of kissing and being kissed, a dance as old as time itself. The strangeness of the experience transformed into a welcome rush, as my arms wrapped around him and drew him closer to me. I heard him whisper my name and I felt my knees weaken.

It could have been hours or moments later when he finally pulled back. The chill of the night caught our heavy breathing, and I was tempted to laugh.

Ferdy beat me to it. "I'm not laughing at you, I promise," he said. "I'm just so happy. I can't seem to stop myself." He pulled me closer to him, trying to protect me from the chilly air.

"I know," I whispered back, unable to stop myself from winding my arms around his neck, forcing our bodies even closer. "I know how you feel."

He kissed my cheek before I curled into the crook of his shoulder. "You've always been kind," he whispered. "Tough, but kind. I'm glad you understand."

"I do, even if I don't." I leaned over and kissed him again.

I could not explain it. I could not explain why I was so drawn to him. I did not know him well, even after glimpsing at his heart. He was flippant but serious, teasing but friendly. He was caring in a way that made perfect sense, even if it seemed selfish. He was insightful and astute, always polite even as he was passionate. He knew me for who I was, not what I was nor how much money I had or how much beauty I displayed.

I attempted to think through everything, but I knew the individual reasons were not enough to account for the reality. It was terrifying but freeing, and I desperately wanted to embrace freedom.

Ferdy pulled back from me. "I was right, then?" he asked, his voice too husky to take as one of his usual taunts. "You did want to kiss me."

I had to drag myself away from him in order to reply. "*Absolument*," I murmured, teasing him back.

"Now all I have to do is get you to admit you love me," Ferdy said with another laugh.

At his words, I went still, staring at him for a long moment. My hands brushed against his cheeks, feeling the small stubble on them. I was enthralled and elated, and the heat between us added an edge to every emotion I could process. "You admitted you wanted to kiss me first. Maybe that strategy will work again."

He leaned into my palm before kissing it smoothly. "Oh, Ella, I've already told you how I feel."

"You did?" I pulled back from him, suddenly terrified I had insulted him.

"I did." He kissed me again. "And there, I just did it again."

I giggled. "You can hardly expect me to answer your kisses with words. Besides, you seem content with my kisses in return."

"I would be a fool to be anything other than content with the time I have been given with you." Ferdy loosened his grip on me and sighed. "Which means I'd better get you back inside. I'd hate for your brother to be upset with me already."

"Ben would be upset. But I don't think he would hurt you, if that is what you are concerned about. At least, he wouldn't hurt you too badly."

"I'd suffer any trouble in the world for another taste of you," Ferdy said, as he leaned in and kissed me once more. "But it is early yet. I'll take the pleasure of testing your brother's limits over time, rather than pushing him past the point of no return right in the beginning."

"Maybe I should have let you kiss me before, back at the Hohenwart Ball," I said, sad to see our time together end already. The hesitation I felt earlier had transformed; No longer was I unsure of meeting Ferdy—now I was unwilling to leave him.

Even if he was right about Ben.

"It won't be long before I do it again," Ferdy assured me with his characteristic aplomb as he led me back up toward the Cabal door. "Now that I know what I'm missing, I can promise you it's taking a good deal of self-preservation to take you back inside."

"Just how many other hearts have you looked at like that?" I asked, realizing he never denied coming outside the Cabal with other girls.

"Plenty," he admitted with his guileless grin. "But yours is the only one I have been searching for, and it is the only one that has proven irresistible."

I felt like a fool for smiling, but Ferdy had a way of making me feel incredibly happy. I barely noticed as the door opened before us.

It was only when I saw Ben in the doorway, glaring at us with an irritated look on his face that I snapped back to attention.

"There you are, Nora," Ben said, clearly aggravated. "I've been wondering where you were."

"We just took a little walk," I said, blushing again.

"It's getting late," Ben said. "We need to head back now."

Somewhere in the distance, I heard the *Pražský orloj* chime. It was midnight. Somehow, the long hours of the evening in the Royal Summerhouse had shortened once we arrived at the Cabal.

I glanced back at Ferdy ruefully. "Thank you for the lovely stroll." I reached for him once more.

Ferdy nodded and took my hand. He kissed it gallantly, keeping his usual respectful distance from me as Ben watched him. Despite all the confusion and strangeness, I missed his closeness; but in seeing the scowl on my brother's face, I understood Ferdy's reservations.

"Will you come back again soon?" Ferdy asked, as Ben steered me away from the Cabal.

Quickly, I looked at Ben, who gave me careless shrug. It was a small, silent movement, but I knew Ferdy had earned Ben's initial approval.

"*Absolument.*" I smiled as we said our last goodbyes.

"*C'est parfait, ma chérie.*" Ferdy leaned back against the wall of the Cabal before blowing me a kiss. "I will wait for you."

"Not too long, I hope."

Ben groaned. "Please stop, before you make me change my mind."

19

◊

"Are you angry with me?" I asked Ben as we walked across the bridge, heading out over the Vltava.

"I feel better knowing that Lady POW will likely scold you enough for the two of us," Ben admitted.

"Does this mean that you like Ferdy?"

"You like him enough for both of us."

"I still want your approval," I said, unable to stop the heat from rising to my cheeks.

"If you like him enough, my approval shouldn't matter."

"If your ambivalence is punishment me for walking with him for a few moments, you have made your point."

Ben stopped. "I didn't mean it like that, Nora," he said. He gave me a small smile. "Maybe I should start calling you 'Ella,' too, huh?"

I took his arm. "Ben—"

"Don't worry about it," he said. "I know you are growing up, and things have changed. Things will always change, but I will always be here for you. And if you like Ferdy, you really should not let me get in your way. I know you well enough to know that's not going to happen anyway. But you don't need my permission to love someone else."

I stood there, quietly amazed. My brother was right, and I knew he was telling me the truth. But I did not expect the sudden sadness that came with it.

"Besides," Ben said, tweaking my nose. "I know you'll punish him enough for loving you."

"Hey!"

Ben laughed and took off running. I heard the click of his brace as he hopped over the bridge cobblestones, and I hurried to keep up after him. It was a game we had played more than a million times, it seemed; by the time I came close to catching him, we were both laughing.

We reached the end of the bridge, and then he stopped.

"Ah-ha!" I cried, nearly tackling him, before I realized there was a familiar coach.

The door opened swiftly, as though it had been kicked open, and I found myself looking at the flaring nostrils of Lady POW.

Briefly, I wondered if that was what Amir saw when I was angry, too.

"I should have known you would be doing something inappropriate." Lady Penelope stared down at me.

Ben stepped in front of me. "It was my—"

"None of that, Benedict. I know Eleanora is responsible for this. Get in, both of you, before anyone sees you."

Despite his earlier teasing, Ben gave me a sympathetic look as we complied. We both knew Lady POW was anything but happy. And just in case we did not realize this on our own, she said so as soon as the coach began moving again.

"I am not happy about this, Eleanora," Lady Penelope fumed. "I cannot believe you thought it would be good for you to sneak away from the Summerhouse Ball. I felt like a fool, trying to find you and introduce you to Count Potocki."

"My apologies, Madame." I did not like that I had disappointed her, but I refused to regret stealing away. Besides having fun at the Cabal, Mr. Clavan had given me enough hope to believe that my instincts were correct.

"I had enough of a struggle in talking with him," she said, ignoring my apologies. "He asked about you, but was interested in little else."

"Karl is the son of King Ferdinand," I blurted out, angry she was not listening to me. When I managed to shock her into silence, I continued. "If Count Potocki knows the truth about Karl, that might be why he was concerned about me."

Lady POW just stared at me, blinking.

"Karl likes me," I said. "He is upset that Lord Maximillian is willing to sponsor his bid for Potocki's position only in exchange for Lady Teresa Marie's hand in marriage. I heard Lady Cecilia complaining that the Duke of Moravia was happy to end his daughter's engagement to Alex because he had found the heir to the Bohemian throne."

There was another long moment of silence, before Lady POW cleared her throat.

"Amir?" Lady Penelope turned to Amir, who was sitting beside her in silence. "What do you say to this?"

"We can easily get proof, Madame," he said. "But Eleanora's logic is sound. And it would not be unheard of to keep an heir a secret."

"Karl was born just after the Revolution of 1848," I said. "My mother would have known."

"Tulia." Lady POW nearly spit out her name in disgust.

"That is one way to know for sure," I said, grateful Amir would not have to reveal my mother's journal. As much as I knew Lady POW loved my mother, I wanted to keep that a secret; for once, it was nice to share a secret with someone, and in many ways, I felt that I owed Amir for the trouble I had caused him earlier.

"Tulia is also the one who Father Novak alerted," Ben said. "She might be able to tell us more about what happened to Dr. Artha."

"I think it is time we made a stop at her cottage, then," Lady Penelope said through pursed lips. She tapped on the roof of the coach, calling for the driver. "She cannot avoid me forever. Amir, you might have to restrain me. I suggest you prepare yourself."

"I am always prepared, Madame." He gave me a smile, and I felt a sense of relief as we headed for Tulia's house.

Several moments passed while Lady POW settled into deep thought, a disgusted look on her face. Amir and Ben were also silent. Both of them were content to stare out into the darkness.

It appeared only I was restless. I tapped my foot on the floor, agitated, until Amir looked over at me. He raised his brow at my foot, and I did not know whether to be insulted or delighted I was reminding him of my mother.

"Why don't you like Tulia?" I finally asked Lady POW.

Her answer came at once, much more quickly than I would have expected.

"Do I have to remind you that she kept you and Ben from me for over a decade?" Lady Penelope scowled. "She could have stopped Cecilia's reign of terror in your lives. If anyone should be angry, it should be you, Eleanora."

I thought of Tulia's silliness and her silent kindness, of how she had stayed close to watch over us for the past years. It was hard to imagine that she had refrained from contacting Lady POW for so many years out of malice.

"Maybe she had her own reasons for failing to do so," I said. I could not think of anything else to defend her, but I was determined to do as much as I could.

Beside me, Ben crossed his arms over his chest. "I'd like to know what they were, if that is true."

"Maybe *Máma* did not want her to say anything," I said.

"But after your mother died, there was nothing stopping her from doing just that, was there?" Lady Penelope bristled in her seat. "Of course, there are likely other reasons for her silence on the matter."

"If you're talking about how she is a mute," I snapped, "let me be the one to assure you I will be the one to give you an answer myself."

"I did not mean silence literally. Goodness, Eleanora, calm down—"

Outside, there was a large popping sound.

The coach rumbled to a quick stop, but not before we were all jumbled together. I grabbed onto the cushions for support, while Ben slipped onto the floor between the seats.

Lady Penelope groaned. "What is it, John?" she called, pushing open the coach window.

"There's been an explosion, Madame." I heard the muffled reply of the coachman as I moved closer to Lady POW. "Straight ahead."

The instant I heard the news, I pushed past Lady POW and opened the door. I hopped out of the coach, struggling with my skirts to keep from falling on my knees.

"That's Tulia's house." Ben came down after me, landing hard on his feet. In the dark of the night, with the small moon in the sky, I saw he was right. Tulia's small cottage, perched on the horizon, was alight with fire.

"Get back inside," Lady Penelope called.

"We have to go help," I argued.

"It will be easier to get there and help if you are inside the carriage!"

"Come on, Nora." Ben helped me up, and I was grateful all over again that I had changed back into my maidservant's outfit as the driver clicked on the reins and hurried toward Tulia's house.

I was already moving when the carriage came to a stop several yards from Tulia's house.

"Tulia!" I called, hurrying toward the cottage. I saw the roof flickering with flames and felt fear choke me as much as the soot in the air.

"Stay back," Amir said, reaching in front of me.

"We have to make sure she's safe." Before I could argue more, Amir pushed me down on the ground as a shadow jumped out of a window. There was a weapon held high in his hand.

My eyes adjusted to the inconsistent light, watching as a gleaming blade appeared before Amir, who had already unsheathed his curved dagger.

There was a small clash of the metal on metal. The noise of the battle faded into the crackling fire, as flames consumed Tulia's cottage.

I struggled to move out of the muddy grass, watching as the attacker met Amir in battle. In the firelight, I could see Amir's adversary was no taller than Ben, and he was wearing a footman's uniform, along with a black mask that hid the bottom half of his face. Seeing it, I was reminded of the mask on my own stealth habit.

Behind me, Lady POW jumped down from the carriage, and her drivers pulled out a pair of pistols.

Ben grabbed me from behind and lifted me up. "We have to help," he said. "We've got to see if Tulia is inside."

I did not hesitate at his words.

"When we get in, watch your skirts," Ben ordered, as he slammed his shoulder into the front door. It shuddered against his force but did not budge. I could feel the heat behind it as we pushed together, bashing our bodies against it in hurried desperation.

It did not move.

"Tulia!" I cried again, hoping for any sign that she was alive.

Ben tapped my shoulder, nodding at my hair. "Give me two of your pins. I can pick the lock."

I hurriedly plucked two longer pins from my hair. My curls bobbed free and added to the heat on my cheeks. "Here. Hurry."

Never had I ever been more grateful for Ben as he fiddled with the lock. He had learned to do some smithing work in order to build his leg brace, and I felt like all of his pain was suddenly worth it in that moment as I watched him, amazed at his calmness as much as his skill. Just as he turned the knob, Amir cried out behind us.

"Watch out!"

I whirled around, just in time to see Amir ram the attacker into the house beside us. The attacker's head smashed into the cottage hard, and Amir used the chance to drive his dagger deep into the man's shoulder.

I screamed, covering my eyes. "Did you kill him?"

"It's fine, Nora," Ben said. "Amir just got his coat. The man is fine."

"Really?" I peeked out from behind my fingers, only to see Ben was right. Amir's blade had snagged the man's jacket.

As I watched, the attacker narrowed his glazed eyes at Amir. He launched out a kick, and Amir responded by punching his face.

A dark wet spot began forming at the side of the man's mask. Behind the cloth, I could hear him sputter and squeak with pain.

"Nora," Ben called. "I got the door."

"Stop!"

I whirled around as Amir hollered. His opponent had slipped free from his jacket, renewing the battle between them once more.

He lunged toward me.

My instincts kicked in, and I was already stepping back as another dagger came rushing through the air between us. I heard the attacker cry out in anguish as Lady Penelope's dagger slit through his shoulder. I watched as the purple-tinted blade splashed with crimson blood.

The dagger of the Order.

I hurried forward and kicked him, tearing Lady POW's dagger free from him. He yelled again, lashing out at me.

Hurriedly, I stepped back; from the momentum of my movements, I fell; the attacker brushed past my skirts, before slipping around me. We were both caught off balance long enough that Amir and Lady Penelope both came forward, shielding me from him.

"Here," I said to Lady POW. "Here's your dagger."

She took it from me quickly. As it passed from my hand to hers, I already missed the comfort its legacy of strength and protection offered.

"Go and get Tulia." Lady Penelope held up the blade again, looking deadly as she aimed for the attacker once more.

Before I could object, Ben tugged on my sleeve

"Come on," Ben yelled at me. "You've got to focus now!"

"Sorry." I knew he was right. We had to save Tulia.

I allowed him to pull me after him as we hurried into the burning cottage with nothing to protect me but a prayer.

Immediately, I was flooded with the burning shadows of the fire. I coughed, breathing in the sooty air, and put my hand over my mouth to stop my tongue from tasting the ash.

"Tulia!" Ben called, as he made his way around the small house.

"Do you see her?" I asked, my mouth suddenly very dry. The wooden beams around me cracked, and I jumped closer to Ben at the sound.

"Ouch." He grimaced, grasping at his leg briefly. "My brace might need some adjustments after this." His latest model had metal springs, and I wondered if he would be able to manage in the heat.

"Can you move?" I asked.

"I'm fine. You check over that way," Ben said. "I'll look over here."

I was proud to see Ben was taking his role seriously. I held my hand over my mouth as I headed deeper into the house, heading toward the heart of the flames.

Outside, I heard a gunshot go off, and I gasped.

"Keep looking," Ben called. "Don't stop unless you're hurt. And even then, keep going if you can."

I hurried through the house, carefully sidestepping flames and broken boards. I frowned. The house was a mess. As I jumped over a toppled table in her parlor, I realized that the house had been ransacked.

That man must have attacked her and then lit the house on fire to cover his tracks. He must have been looking for something. We would not know whether he found it unless we caught him.

I desperately hoped we would catch him.

As I was heading out of the room once more, circling back to the front of the house, I caught sight of Tulia's hand.

Then I saw the rest of her. I moaned at the sight, and quickly called to Ben.

"Ben!" I called. "Over here; I found her."

Tulia was tucked behind a fallen chair, passed out on her stomach. Seeing her unconscious on the floor made me feel sick, but I forced my sudden queasiness down as Ben arrived. Together, we pushed the chair out of our way and Ben began checking for signs of life.

As we carefully turned her over, my mouth dropped open. There were several shards sticking out of her hands and face, gleaming in the firelight. Little trickles of blood and sweat ran together from the numerous tiny cuts in her skin.

"Tulia," I wept.

"Keep your focus," Ben snapped, and I tried to stifle myself. I knew he was feeling poorly too, or he would not have been so curt with me.

I lowered my gaze in shame, realizing this was not a situation where a member of the Order would get emotionally sloppy. As I glanced down, I saw a trail of glass shards spanning out on the floor all around, with several more small pieces littering the nearby area in a strange circular pattern.

Had Tulia been drinking? I gently touched two fingers to her forehead, where one particularly large shard was laced into her wrinkles. It was searing to the touch, and I almost gasped at the sudden burn on my fingertips.

"Eleanora! Benedict!"

From outside, Lady Penelope was calling for us. She might as well have been calling from the opposite side of the world, rather than from the other side of the door.

I wanted to yell back, but I inhaled too quickly and felt the smoke gather inside of my mouth. I ended up coughing before Ben knelt beside me.

"Take her right arm."

Carefully, I knelt at Tulia's side and hauled her up, suddenly grateful for all the years Cecilia had forced me to work with my hands so much. Despite the dizzying heat and the sharp sweat drops running down my face, I was able to balance her weight against my own and Ben's.

"I have her." I nodded as another loud crackle of fire whipped around us. I coughed and began to feel choked by the sweltering atmosphere.

Together, Ben and I managed to make it to the doorway. Amir was quick to relieve me of duty, and Lady POW breathed a sigh of relief. I felt her exhale rush past my cheeks, still warm against the chilly winter air that soon settled on me once more.

"What happened?" I asked, my voice croaking and cracking as I breathed in all the fresh air I could. "Where is the attacker?"

"He slipped away while Lady Penelope and I were calling for you," Amir told me. He looked away. "Lady Penelope managed to injure his arm and I took his weapon. That will be enough of a victory for us tonight."

"I'm surprised," I said. "I thought for sure you would win. Aren't the good guys always supposed to win?"

"This is not a play or a novel. You will find, in real life, there are more times than we would like that failure finds us."

Hearing his words, I almost wondered if Ben had been keeping him company too much lately. Ben was more likely to be the pessimist.

"Besides," Amir added with a small smile, "Lady Penelope had one of the footmen take off and follow him. With any luck, we will be able to find his local haunt and his boss while we are at it."

That was more like Lady Penelope, I thought with a grin. "Good."

"We already have some clues. Here, Eleanora," Lady Penelope said, as she stuffed a handkerchief into my hand. "Use this to help you breathe some."

All I could do was nod, before coughing some more. I looked down at myself, smelling of decay. *Well, now I am* really *glad I changed outfits.*

"What kind of clues did you find?" Amir asked.

"A handkerchief of his own," Lady Penelope said, pulling out a soot-covered scrap of fabric. "It's been embroidered with a coat of arms. I do not recognize it, but I will see what Harshad says."

I studied it, and I was glad to know Harshad would be analyzing it later. I did not recognize the loopy 'S' that marked it, any more than I could identify the wavy lines or the prancing horse embroidered into the fine cloth.

"What about Tulia?" I asked.

"She needs medical attention," Ben called. "Amir!"

Amir and I hurried over, and I realized Ben had blood on his hands.

"Don't try to move her." Amir came running up to us. He tore at his shirt, hurriedly making bandages for Tulia. "Let me stop the bleeding first."

"She is going to get better, right?" I asked. Behind me, the fire burned brighter as the house began to collapse.

"We will need to get some better bandages," Amir said, "and I will have to sew her up."

"I will make room in the coach," Lady Penelope offered. "Eleanora, come along and assist me."

I nodded dumbly, otherwise frozen by fear. Glancing back at the scene, I watched Ben and Amir grapple with blood and glass; as the house behind me burned to the ground; watched as my world became intensely more intimate with fear and all its oppressive power.

The next several minutes—perhaps hours—seemed to pass by in a feverish dream. As we transported Tulia to the manor and settled her into her own room, I struggled with all the powers around me and inside me. I felt helpless to curb the anxiety and its accompanying trials that crippled me. My mind raced quickly, running from Tulia's kindness to the world's ugliness, jumping from the realization I could do so little to stop the world's bleeding, before finally crashing at the aching hatred that the world should be so full of evil in the first place.

Why, God? Why? Why give me a problem I can't solve, a burden I can't bear?

I did not know how life could go on without Tulia.

Once she was settled into her bed, with the fireplace roaring and the dawn breaking through the windows, I took hold of her hand and grasped it tightly. Amir carefully removed many of the glass shards in her face and hands, while Ben reapplied new bandages, and Lady Penelope and Harshad worked on finding out who was behind everything.

All of this happened while I sat there, holding her hand, watching her sleep. I felt useless, needless. I did not know if there was anything else I could do, or if I would be able to do anything anyway.

20

◊

I was dreaming.

In my dreams I was flying, and then I was falling, and then I was flailing.

And then I slammed into the waking world.

"Huh?" I woke up, nearly shooting out of my chair. At once, I noticed the uncomfortable ache in my back and my neck; the smell of soot shot across my senses and pain pierced through my forehead. I was unable to process how much time had passed since I had fallen asleep.

Blinking, I looked around and steadied myself. I had fallen asleep in a chair next to Tulia's bed after we had brought her back to the house.

At the small tapping on my knee, I rubbed my eyes clear of the morning blur to see Tulia looking up at me.

The speckles of dots across her face had scarred over, but I saw no signs of permanent trauma in her eyes.

"Tulia!" I cheered, carefully reaching over to embrace her. "You're awake."

She smiled weakly, rolling her eyes, as if to say with all of her regular spunk, *"I'm alive."*

"I'm so glad. We were worried for you."

The eyes crinkled again, this time with curiosity.

"We, including Ben and … Lady Penelope, too," I said, answering her unspoken question. "My grandmother."

Her eyebrows crinkled again, and then she exhaled, defeated.

"I won't let her hurt you," I promised.

Her fingers, stiff with bandages mixed with dried blood and healing herbs, flicked at me. She was not afraid of Lady POW.

I hesitated for a long moment. Part of me knew I should go and call for Amir and let the others know Tulia was awake. We needed to know what happened to her, and who was behind it.

But . . .

"Why didn't you tell me about her?" I asked.

Tulia reached over and took my hand, gently squeezing it. Our eyes met, and for the first time in a long time, I had to guess at what she was trying to tell me.

"Did my mother want you to keep us from her?" I asked.

She nodded.

"Why?" I asked. "Was it because of Lady POW—er, Lady Penelope? Or because of the Order?"

Her expression gave me the answer long before she did. Tulia knew about the Order; I did not have to explain it to her. As I mentioned it, she closed her eyes, as though to stop any tears she might shed.

She nodded again. Her hand tightened in mine, as she slowly signaled her answer to me.

"The Order has many enemies."

"Enemies? You mean like the person who attacked you last night?" I bit my lip. "And the people who killed Dr. Artha?"

For a quick second, I saw the surprise on her face, and then I saw it transform into tired resignation. Tulia nodded again.

I sat back in the chair, slumping over with a sigh. It was easy to see what had channeled *Máma's* decision to keep her children a secret from her mother, especially if Lady POW was as relentless a leader back then as she was now.

Tulia slowly moved her hand, placing her palm over her heart. She patted it twice, before nodding to me.

"I am sorry."

"I know." I closed my eyes and sighed. I would forgive her, of course, just as I had forgiven my mother. It was hard to say if Lady Penelope would forgive her, and I was petty enough to hope she would not. Lady Penelope's anger seemed to be more of a punishment than my rejection.

I jolted upright in my chair as the door opened behind us.

"Well, you're awake." Lady Penelope's voice was as sharp as ever, leaving me to wonder if she was talking to Tulia or me.

Tulia's speckled face twisted into a grimace.

"I was hoping that we would not meet again, either. Family reunions have never been pleasant for us."

"Family?" I asked.

"Just how much have you kept from them, Tulia? Were you just acting under Dezda's orders? Or maybe Jakub's?"

"Who's Jakub?" I asked.

"Your grandfather," Lady Penelope replied with a disdainful snort. "Tulia is his half-sister."

Tulia nodded as I looked at her. She gave me a small, rueful smile. Her fingers moved over mine. *"A bastard child."*

I said nothing. And nothing happened. I did not ask any questions, nor did I start spewing accusations or lashing out in anger. I was getting tired of being surprised, but I continued to sit there, still and silent, somehow waiting for more surprises to come along.

"Which is why I'm not terribly surprised that she has betrayed us, come to think of it," Lady Penelope continued.

Tulia rolled her eyes, and I just stared blankly between the two of them. I was numb to the tension around us, even though I could sense it.

"Since she has neglected to tell you our wonderful family history, it would be better for you to wait with the others in the library. Your curiosity, Eleanora, as endearing as it can be when it is not inconvenient, would only keep us from getting down to business."

"But if she is family," I objected, "then I should be here for her."

"Operating like a business is better, when your family is full of secrets and lies."

"I'm part of the business, too, now that I am a member of the Order." I stood up, facing her, prepared to fight her objections.

"And as such, you should listen to my commands." She crossed her arms in front of her and shook her head. "Your anger right now is exactly the reason you should leave. You struggle to keep your focus enough."

Tulia brushed her fingers against my skirt. I turned and watched her nod, telling me she would be fine, and it was true that I should go.

"I want Amir in here first," I said slowly. "He needs to check her injuries."

"Go and send for him, then. I can trust him to remain silent."

Tulia made a small movement, telling me she was still tired and wanted to rest longer. I began to translate for Lady POW, but she shook her head.

"There's no need. I know what she is saying. It has been many years, but we have not forgotten how to communicate."

"Fine. I won't bother trying to help you again," I muttered, irritated at her lack of graciousness.

As if to prove it, Tulia signed a vicious insult, and Lady Penelope scowled. For a long moment, they stared daggers at each other.

When they finished their silent battle, Lady POW turned back to me. "Go and get Amir. He might as well tend to her for a few hours, and then we can ask her our questions. I will stay here until he arrives."

I frowned.

"There are a few questions I have for her." Lady POW arched her brow at me. "And besides, we will need her for our investigation, Eleanora, so you need not worry that I will allow any further harm to come to her."

"I didn't think you would," I said with a sigh, before moving around her and heading out the door. "But when she has rested enough, I am coming back with Ben. We both deserve to know the truth, especially after last night."

Lady POW scowled, but she said nothing. I had to wonder if she was more frustrated I refused to do what she wanted or if she was more upset she could not bring herself to correct me.

I took comfort in the opportunity to escape. My body ached from sleeping poorly, my mind was fuzzy and full of too many possibilities to worry exclusively about one reality. My clothes smelled of pungent smoke, and my hair was falling from the last of its pins.

But most of all, I was weary.

It seemed everything that had changed since the night of Lady POW's arrival ran up to me, catching me all at once. Since then, I had a completely new life; I struggled to imagine what life would have been like if Alex and Teresa Marie were still to be married, if I had never been freed from Cecilia's servanthood, and if I had never learned the truth about my mother, my work, and my home. My life.

All I knew was things were different, and there was no going back. There was only going forward, and there was no guarantee that there would be any rest or renewal.

The magic of Prague's far away city had dimmed, and in my disillusionment, I encountered a terrible plot to overthrow the kingdom. I had watched as one of my dearest companions almost burned and bled to death, and I saw that same companion turned into an unrecognizable family member. I was constantly being pulled in all sorts of directions.

Sighing, I shook my head. I was not just tired of being surprised. I was tired of being disappointed.

Hours later, we were still waiting for Tulia to wake up again. Despite the delay in the investigation, I was glad for the break. I was able to get a bath and wash my hair, change my clothes, and take a proper nap. I was also glad that Lady Penelope sent out our regrets for the evening, citing my twisted ankle from the previous night as the reason I would not be in attendance for Society's delight.

She informed me of her decision when we were in the library together, still waiting to hear from Tulia.

"Thank you," I replied, clutching the book in my lap. I was ignoring it as Lady POW worked at my father's desk, but it helped to feel I had some protection from her direct study.

"That was good thinking on your part last night, you know." She gave me a reluctant smile. "It gives us an excuse to stay away, and it will still make people talk. Perhaps their pity will be even more useful than your presence."

"I'm glad it helped. At least I am good at something, even if it is lying."

Lady Penelope's hands tightened together. "I suppose I should apologize to you, Eleanora."

The book dropped to the floor. "What?"

Lady Penelope smirked. "I know. Shocking, isn't it? And you have already had quite a few surprises lately."

"That is an understatement," I agreed. "But not one worth your apology."

"I do not want to apologize for the truth," Lady Penelope corrected. "You are doing well as a member of the Order, and I am proud of what you have done so far. If I do not express it, it is usually because I am not accustomed to surprises, either."

"Is it a family trait?" I asked with a small smile.

"Probably," she replied. "Just as curiosity is, no doubt. But my apology is more for the matter of our instruction. You are family first, and it has been a very, very long time since I have had to worry about family before work, if, in all fairness, I have ever done so."

I watched her as she said it, and it was hard to fault her as anything less than genuinely repentant.

Ben had said before that everyone was devastated by *Máma's* death, and it looked like the truth; but much like the truth, I did not realize it affected others as much as it did me.

"I'm just glad I am not a failure," I said.

Lady Penelope cleared her throat again, clearly uncomfortable. "These are early days between us, Eleanora," she said. "Our time will stretch out into eternity, and we must make it count. If there is any failure between the two of us, it is with me."

Lady Penelope met my gaze, and I felt a small ripple of approval from her. "Thank you. I did not want you to be angry with me."

"You should never fear my anger," Lady Penelope said. "Not as long as we are on the same side."

I nodded.

"From what Amir told me about your adventure earlier," Lady Penelope continued, "I can understand the reasons for it. I am glad to hear that you have good friends in the city. I cannot imagine Cecilia has made it easy for you to meet with them since your father's death."

Was she talking about Ferdy? I frowned, wondering if Amir had embellished our relationship in order to protect me. Lady POW would not fault loyalty, especially if there was good cause for it. Amir did not know the exact nature of my interest in Ferdy. Was it possible he had misread my interest when I told him? Or maybe I had given too much of my affection away?

I shrugged. "Oh, well, I really just met—"

"And it does help that they are apparently well informed of the city's secrets and news. Imagine the surprise when people find out there is an actual heir to the Bohemian throne. Tulia confirmed the report."

When she saw my troubled look, she added, "I told you earlier, Eleanora, I had a few questions for her. When you left, I asked them."

"So you know the truth, then?"

"Yes. Empress Maria Anna was pregnant when your mother arrived in Prague. That was the reason she was worried about the kingdom, primarily. She did not want the Revolution to claim her son's life, even if he could not inherit the throne."

"It also makes sense that she called for the Pope then," I said. "She would have been very concerned about her situation, as a Catholic mother."

Lady Penelope shrugged. "All mothers worry for their children. I know your mother must have worried for you."

There was no doubt in my mind that Lady POW was right. I was not happy with Tulia and my mother's deception and secrecy, but I was sure of their love for me.

"You suspect Karl Marcelin is the heir," Lady Penelope said, changing the subject.

"He is the right age, and Lord Maximillian, the Duke of Moravia, is interested in working with him. Karl told me that His Grace wants him to marry Lady Teresa Marie. And it makes sense, from what I heard, if their plot is to free the kingdom from the empire."

Lady Penelope snorted. "Freedom from the empire would only lead to its death. But I commend them on their vision. It is a noble goal, even if it carries great risk and flawed methods."

"If Karl does get the position of Minister-President," I said, "he would be able to push for his election as King of Bohemia, wouldn't he?"

"In theory." Lady Penelope looked down at the scribbled mess before her. "The king would have to be ratified by the constitution of Bohemia, which would require acceptance by the Upper and Lower Houses, including the Bohemian and German Diets, and by the *Reichsrat*. That is a lot of votes."

"Is there any way he could do it without all those?" I asked. Karl did not seem like someone who would worry about defeat when it came to getting what he wanted.

"Only if the majority of them were killed," Lady Penelope said. "Many people have died in the recent string of murders, but it is unlikely he would be able to continue using that method. If, indeed, he is behind the murders at all."

"If he is the heir, and working toward the crown, it is something to consider."

"To consider? Absolutely. To accuse? Maybe. But judgment at this point is early. We would need something that directly links him to the killings."

The door to the library swung open, and I was surprised to see Harshad enter. I had not seen him much over the past few weeks, and when I did, it was only for moments, if not seconds, at a time.

"Well, Pepé, you know what the Scriptures say," Harshad said, as he made his way over to the desk. He held out a small square of linen before her. "Ask and you shall receive."

"You know who it belongs to," Lady Penelope cheered. She stood up in triumph, snatching the handkerchief out of his hand. "Tell me who the unlucky bastard is."

"The man in question was a worker in the household of Mr. Roman Szapira," Harshad said. "While John was not able to follow your enemy into the house, he did see our culprit go into the servant's entrance at the Szapira mansion across town."

"Szapira?" I repeated. The name sounded familiar. Only a second passed before I remembered where I had heard it. "That's where Karl is staying for the season, until the Advent Ball."

"Well, then, we have our proof." Lady Penelope smirked. She clapped her hands together eagerly. "It seems that Mr. Marcelin is determined to gain his throne, no matter what he has to do."

"I don't think he is like that," I said, suddenly flushing over as I thought of his sincerity and eagerness in wanting to dance with me. There was nothing sinister about him that I had seen. "Maybe there is another reason why our attacker was at Mr. Szapira's house."

"I do not believe in coincidences," Lady Penelope said. "And that is not just because of location. There is timing to consider, too, and opportunity."

Harshad met her gaze, and rather than switching to another language, I watched as they communicated with their eyes. I saw the thrill of discovery in Lady Penelope's, and the grim hesitation in Harshad's eyes.

"I give up," I groaned. "I can't read your minds, as you two apparently can."

"Roman Szapira has recently completed renovation of Prague Castle's wine cellar," Harshad said. "He would know his way around the castle very well. And he would be able to infiltrate it. Marcelin has only recently struck up a good friendship with him since he returned to Prague."

"That minimizes Szapira's role," Lady Penelope said. "Marcelin must have a plan to take care of his adversaries at the Advent Ball. That is when Count Potocki is supposed to announce his official last day as Minister-President. He told me so himself at the Summerhouse Ball."

I had been wondering if Count Potocki gave Lady Penelope any useful information after Karl escorted me out of the ballroom.

"We have received more than one invitation for the Advent Ball," Harshad said. "So we will be there without cause for suspicion."

"Good." Lady Penelope pursed her lips together. "Now we just have to plan what we will do once we are there."

That is also when Lord Maximillian wants to announce Karl's engagement to Lady Teresa Marie. I thought about what Karl told me when he had escorted me out to my carriage the previous night.

As Lady POW and Harshad continued to discuss the likely scenarios, I was briefly taken aback, realizing it had been less than a day since I found out Karl was the heir to the Bohemian throne, and that he was infatuated with me to the point he was almost risking his political future.

It had also been less than a day since I had seen Ferdy—and less than a day since I had kissed him. My cheeks burned at the thought of him and my heart began to beat faster inside my chest.

Then, just as quickly, all color and blood drained from my face as I realized that if Karl did do something at the Advent Ball, Ferdy would be there, too. He was going to be in danger.

I can't let anything happen to him.

My heart lurched, imagining Ferdy poisoned, his body still like Father Novak's, surrounded by any number of other corpses. Or maybe it was possible he would be stabbed, I thought, thinking of Dr. Artha.

I stood abruptly, so fast even Lady POW and Harshad turned to face me.

"What's wrong, Eleanora?" Lady Penelope asked. "You have a strange look on your face."

"It's … it's … " I stammered, trying to put my thoughts into words properly.

Before I could manage, there was another knock at the door, and Ben poked his head inside. "Tulia's awake," he said. "She's ready to answer more of our questions."

Ours, not yours.

Lady POW looked at me once more, silently asking me if I was going to say anything. She wanted to know what concerned me, and I did not want to share with her the newfound fear in my heart.

While she had just commended me for my quick thinking, I did not want her to see me as weak for caring so ardently for a boy like Ferdy. From what I had seen of her, she would only see it as an unnecessary complication.

I could not risk losing him to Lady POW any more than I could willingly risk his life at the Advent Ball.

I shook my head, and Lady Penelope allowed me to keep my silence on the matter. As we walked toward Tulia's room, I decided to talk to Ben once we were able to learn more from Tulia. Between the two of us, I knew we would be able to come up with a plan to save Ferdy.

21

◊

If Tulia was upset at the small crowd of people that appeared in her bedroom an hour later, she handled the situation with enough grace I did not notice.

It was possible I did not want to notice. I was too distracted by other things; I was worried for Ferdy, for one, and I was also concerned for Karl. As much as Lady Penelope was ready to believe he was involved, I was still hesitant to think he would murder anyone, let alone his own parents and colleagues.

If Tulia had any information that could save Ferdy and distance Karl from suspicion, I wanted to hear it.

She was propped up on her pillows, sitting up. There were new bandages around her arms, but those on her fingers were unraveled. I could see several cuts and scrapes sticking out from the strips.

"Let's start this from the beginning," Lady Penelope said. She narrowed her cold gaze at Tulia. "Feel free to chime in when something comes up you can contribute."

"Please, Madame, have mercy," Amir said. "I have not yet removed all the wine bottle shards from her skin. She is still in a great amount of pain."

"The laudanum should be enough for that," Lady Penelope insisted, although her tone softened ever so slightly. "She has already proven she can handle—"

"Enough, Pepé," Harshad interrupted. "The beginning, if you please. Or I can start, if you prefer."

Lady POW turned her ire on him, while I said nothing. I was content to watch out for Tulia, but I was beginning to enjoy watching Lady POW and Harshad torment each other. It was a poetic sort of justice, and it made me feel better about all the irritation the two of them caused me.

"Let me begin," Amir said, before either Lady POW or Harshad could start a new argument. "We were called here by Her Imperial Majesty, Queen Victoria, when she asked the Order of the Crystal Daggers to secure this area. There were rumors of deep political division, and there were enough mysterious occurrences to give her cause for concern."

"You're not part of the Order," I said, remembering what he had told me before. "Why did you come along?"

"He is my confidant and medical advisor, even if he is not part of the Order," Lady Penelope replied. "Amir has proven himself to the Queen separately, so he is an honorary member of the League of Ungentlemanly Warfare in her kingdom."

"The Order has more of an international reach," Amir said. "And it is fitting for me, as I will never be a citizen, nor a gentleman, in Her Imperial Majesty's court."

I felt the sadness in his words, before Lady POW let out an impatient groan.

"I am also a member of the League, Eleanora," Lady Penelope said. "It often works with the Order for assignments such as these."

"Oh. I see."

"It probably makes it easier for Queen Victoria to fund you if you work in both," Ben said.

Lady POW nodded, giving Ben a smile.

I still did not know a lot about politics, but I knew money was at the heart of a lot of debate in the Bohemian government. The Diets especially fought over budget deals and spending, and the only thing they could consistently agree on was increasing their own fortunes. Ben's explanation gave me a good idea of why Amir and Lady Penelope had both come.

"Her Majesty is more concerned about unrest in India," Harshad said, "but she does not want this area to collapse while she pursues other international settlements. When we agreed to investigate, we headed for Prague, where several of our contacts were able to provide information."

Tulia flicked her fingers, signing out a name. I saw the letters she made and deciphered it for the others.

"Dr. Artha included," I said.

"Yes. Sigmund was very well informed of political division, being an instigator of sorts," Lady Penelope said. "He had great friendships with all parties, and even collaborated with the Jews from time to time. Needless to say, the Bohemians and the Germans did not like this, even if they liked him."

Tulia nodded in agreement.

"And then he was murdered," I said. "And that led to Father Novak's murder, too, at the Church of Our Lady of the Snows."

"What information did he have that made him a target?" Lady Penelope asked, turning to Tulia.

For several long moments, I watched her as her fingers and facial expressions spelled out her story.

"He was working on creating the antidote recently, especially after discovering the herb had been used for political deaths in the past."

"Did he find out who was purchasing it?" Lady Penelope asked.

Tulia shook her head, before running her fingers over my hand.

"There is another seller, but not an enemy of the Order."

"Who is it?" Lady Penelope's eyes glittered. "Tell us."

Tulia shook her head, shrugging, and Lady POW let out a frustrated groan. "You should know this, Tulia!"

She gave a few more signs, and I knew that she did not have a name for us.

Our clues were leading us nowhere.

I thought of what Ferdy had said. "Dr. Artha was stabbed by a man outside of the church, dressed in a servant's coat. Some people thought it was a thief, but it wasn't."

"I wonder if that was our fire starter last night?" Lady Penelope looked back at Tulia, who exhaled slowly.

"After Dr. Artha was murdered, Father Novak was, too," I said. "Someone knew he had left a trail of information that led to you. It makes sense it would be the same person."

"The attacker was young," Amir said. "Youthful and energetic. He is a good fighter, which is why he was able to slip away. But he is not a seasoned fighter. I landed several blows of my own before he escaped."

"If he is that agile, it would explain why he was able to get such good information, too," Ben said. "It would have to be someone who was used to finding information. Especially since we were the only ones who could make the connection to Tulia."

"He might have other sources," Lady Penelope said, and Tulia nodded.

While the others debated the identity of the attacker, Tulia met my gaze. She peered at me intently, and I remembered what she had told me earlier.

The Order of the Crystal Daggers has many enemies.

"So if Dr. Artha is dead," Amir said, "we must find the new source of the silver thallis herb. Whoever it is, he will be able to lead us to the people trying to kill off the politicians with it."

"We have tried to find someone all over town," Ben said. "Harshad did not find anything, either."

"Xiana has contacted me," Harshad said. "She is coming here to help investigate, as this is her area of expertise. But she will not be here for another week at best. She did tell me that Dr. Artha was our only contact with the silver thallis in his reserve. He told her that there was only one other person in Prague who would sell it."

"If he was able to tell her that, it must be true," Lady Penelope said. "Benedict, this is a good task for you."

"What I want to know is how this connects to Lord Maximillian and Karl Marcelin," Ben said. "Lord Maximillian would have known about the silver thallis from my father's funeral. He does not live in Prague now. He is just visiting."

"Visiting while he arranges for Lady Teresa Marie to marry the heir to the throne of Bohemia," I added.

"Karl Marcelin's ambition does play an interesting role as a catalyst," Lady Penelope said. "He finished his schooling in the summer, before he headed back here. That is when the politicians began to die strange deaths and others were elected."

"He does appear to be the mastermind," Harshad said, remaining still as Lady POW moved around the room restlessly.

"What do you mean?" I asked. "How is Karl the one behind the murders?"

Amir cleared his throat. "I have received some information from a source," he said. "He is a fellow league member. He contacted me regarding this matter. Apparently, Mr. Marcelin has made contact with others to help him work to free Bohemia from the empire."

"What?" My throat went dry.

"This makes sense," Harshad said, "given that we know from your own information from Lady Cecilia that Lord Maximillian has foreign contacts. We believe these foreign influences put the two of them in contact with each other."

"There is still no way to be sure who is the mastermind, then." But even as I spoke the words, the narrative began to come together in my mind. Lord Maximillian had been in contact with others for years. Karl wanted the throne. There were foreigners who were coordinating with them. The timing even seemed to make sense, I realized, thinking of how Karl told me of Lord Maximillian's friendships built over vineyards.

"Lord Maximillian would not have known about Karl until he came here, correct?" Ben asked. "Why murder other politicians beforehand?"

"Maybe he found out about Karl later on," I said. "He could have been considering a political career before. Karl told me he was a good friend of Count Potocki's, and he is staying with Lord Hohenwart right now."

"If he found out about Karl this season," Lady Penelope said, "he could have made some adjustments to his plans."

"Yes, precisely!" I said. "I don't think Karl would actually murder anyone."

"And Lord Maximillian would?" Ben scoffed. "Come on, don't tell me you're serious? You can't let feelings influence your opinions on Karl and this case, no matter how much you might like him."

"I don't like him," I insisted, blushing slightly. Of all people, Ben should have been the one to know that I did not like him. At least, not in *that* way. "But I'm the one who knows Karl the best out of all of us."

"You know the image that he has striven to project to society best," Lady Penelope said.

"It doesn't matter. He wouldn't have done that. And we just agreed the murders and threats started before he returned to Prague."

"So that means he's paying someone to do it," Ben said darkly.

"Maybe Lord Maximillian is doing it. He's the one with the money, remember?" I fought back.

"That's enough, you two," Lady Penelope interrupted. "There is no need to fight about it. We need proof."

"Lady Cecilia should be enough proof," I said. "She was the one I overheard talking about how Lord Maximillian found King Ferdinand's son."

"Maybe we should go and get her," Lady Penelope murmured. She tapped her fingertips together thoughtfully.

"We would be better to watch her," Harshad said. "There is no telling if she would tell the duke of our interest if we question her."

"That is true." Lady Penelope frowned, drawing her frosty eyebrows together in thoughtful consideration. "The Advent Ball is at the end of this week. That gives us four days to find out how they plan on massacring the masses. They still need a disaster to spark a revolution, and the timing is too convenient to ignore."

As Lady Penelope, Amir, and Harshad began to trade theories and suggest different routes of action, Tulia signaled to me again.

She gave me a secretive look, and I took her hand, pretending to comfort her while she used her stiffened fingers.

"The attacker came as a messenger. He had a gift for me."

"What was it?" I whispered.

She cupped her hands and twitched it, moving like it was a shot glass. I saw the gleam of the glass shards, some of them still stuck in her flesh.

"Wine?" I asked, and she nodded.

Her hand tightened around mine.

"He said it was from the Cabal."

I felt my heart drop and my breath catch in my throat. Was it possible … Mr. Clavan and Eliezer, all of them … was it possible they were working for the enemy? Was it possible they *were* the enemy?

Or were they in as much danger as we were?

Tulia pinched my palms. *"He smashed the bottle, attacked me, and started the fire."*

I nodded again, before squeezing her hand. "I'm so glad you are safe," I said. "You are my family, and you always have been."

She smiled, and at that moment—as the plans were being made and the tasks were being assigned, as Lady POW and Harshad argued while Amir injected logic into the conversation, as Ben and I exchanged worried glances and Tulia fell back asleep—I resolved to protect the ones I loved, no matter what I had to do.

22

◊

While I was determined to do whatever I had to do to protect my friends and family, I was faced with any number of impossible challenges. As the Advent Ball crept closer, I was certain I would go mad before it was all over.

The first problem I ran into was Ferdy.

Or rather, I thought bitterly, the problem was that I was not able to run into him.

In keeping with my earlier excuse, Lady Penelope made it known throughout all of Europe I would be attending the ball, but I had to rest up if I was going to be able to dance and enjoy myself. I had an enormous pile of cards come to the house wishing me well, and little notes from different ladies and gentlemen, all ranging from friendly to flirty.

I was stuck at the manor, unable to escape the house. There was no way I could go and warn him. The whole world seemed to conspire against me, because even when I sent Ben out on his own investigations, he was unable to find Ferdy.

"Even Clavan and the others at the Cabal have not seen him this week," Ben said when I came around the morning before the Ball. He handed me my note, the one I had written days before. The paper was still carefully folded, as though my prayers for its protection were so effective it had failed to be delivered.

"You went there?" I asked carefully. "To the Cabal, I mean?"

"Yes." Ben shrugged. "Jarl and Faye are there most nights, and they are able to answer some of my questions. I never ask them directly or tell them why I want to know. They are closer to my age so I think they think I am there to be their friend more than I am trying to get them to be my source."

"What about the wine from them? The one that Tulia's attacker used to get her to open the door?" I asked.

"It was obviously a ruse, Nora," Ben said. "Do you really think they are part of the plan to free the country from the Emperor?"

I thought about what Clavan had told me before, about how freedom was found in the struggle. "I … don't know what to think," I admitted.

"But you're ready to leave Karl Marcelin out of everything, but Ferdy and his friends are not above suspicion?" Ben asked.

His words cut into me as I realized he was right.

"You're right," I said. "I don't know what is wrong with me."

"Tulia's going to be fine," Ben said. The look in his blue-green eyes softened, and I was briefly reminded of our father as he reached out and patted my shoulder. "You have a soft heart, Nora. If I worry for you, it is only because that's something that can be easily bruised. That's why I was worried about Ferdy, and that's honestly why I am worried about Karl."

"You think he is innocent, too?"

"Not exactly." Ben crossed his arms over his chest. "I meant more how I worry that you like him more than you might want to admit."

I felt myself flush. "I don't like him. At least, not the way I like Ferdy."

It was a rare moment of vulnerability as I admitted I cared for Ferdy to my brother. Of all the people in the world, I loved Ben the most, and I did not want to face a world where I would have to choose between him and someone else.

"That's fine," Ben said briskly. "And that's even more cause for worry for me, frankly. I know you like Ferdy. He's fun and exciting and immensely distracting. He can tell a story that will make you forget about everything else, and he can argue with you until you are mad with rage. All while he just sits there, laughing at you. Or," Ben added thoughtfully, "he gets his friends to."

I might have smiled at the reference to Ben's own experience with Ferdy's friends and their collective craftiness, but I had a feeling more was coming. "But?"

"But it is hard to say if there is anything meaningful about him," Ben said. "Is Ferdy serious about anything? If not, he's not someone who would make you a good match in the long run. At least, not from what I have seen."

I said nothing, wondering if Ben was right.

I thought about why I liked Ferdy. He had rescued me from Amir before, that was true. Ferdy was sweet and goodhearted, even if he was too much of a jokester sometimes. He was clearly able to support himself, or at least enough so that he could rely on Clavan to open a tab for him, so he was clever as well as charming.

And he claimed me as his, even if I had yet to give him permission to do so.

Karl would never have charmed a kiss out of me, or called me out on my own secrets.

Karl might as well have been Ferdy's polar opposite. He was still charming, but he was dignified and intelligent, passionate about making the future a better place, fighting to get what he wanted.

"When you danced with Karl," Ben said, "and I saw you talk with him, I thought you might like him. He is someone you would have been able to meet properly, if our parents had lived. He would have been the kind of man you would marry, if our lives had been different."

I did not know what to say. Ben, as always, had solid reasoning. He was right on so many things.

Sighing, I crumbled up the note I had written, the one I had written warning Ferdy to stay away from the Advent Ball.

"I still do not want Ferdy to get hurt," I insisted. "If Karl is trying to kill everyone between himself and the throne, he will have to find a way to survive the party. I don't want Ferdy caught up in that."

"And if Lord Maximillian is the one behind everything, as you'd prefer," Ben said, teasing me some, "he will find a way to protect Karl."

"Exactly. Karl is safe no matter what. I need to make sure Ferdy is, too." I leaned against the wall behind me. "We only have hours left before the Ball."

"Once we arrive, I promise I will go and find Ferdy and tell him," Ben said. "If that will make you feel better, *ségra*."

I reached out and embraced him, letting myself breathe in his warm strength like a tonic.

"Thank you," I whispered into his shoulder. "It would make me feel better. It seems I have done nothing this week but pace through the manor. I can't sleep well, or for very long, thinking about it. Even Cecilia's part of the house has gone quiet by the sound of it."

"I'm surprised Lady POW did not make you work on something," Ben said.

I scowled. "She said I should learn how to wait. Can you believe that? Amir lets me help him tend to Tulia's wounds, and that is the only reprieve I have had from worrying for the last several days."

"You mean talking with me is not enough to ease your mind?" Ben gave me a grin. "It will be all right, Nora. Or maybe I should call you Ella, since Ferdy and Karl both refer to you as such?"

I shook my head. "I will always be Nora to you," I said. "No matter what happens."

"We will see," Ben said. "You can't stop some things from changing."

"Yes, you can," I argued. "And even if you're right, there's no need to change how we react to it."

"Well, your resolve relieves me," Ben said, patting my shoulder, "as it always has."

He gave me a quick kiss on the forehead, much like *Táta* used to do. "Be safe tonight. I have faith in you, but don't take any unnecessary risks if you don't have to."

"You, too." I gave him a brave smile. As he walked away, heading to his room to change for the night, I found that his faith in me gave me peace.

I clasped my hands together, as though I was trying to hold onto that moment and that feeling, letting it submerge me in its comfort. "Thank you, Lord."

As if he had granted my prayer, I felt the fullness of that moment settle on me. Even as I slid into my stealth habit, even as Jaqueline, Amelia, and Marguerite sewed my gown on top of it; the scarlet silk was just dark enough to hide the black suit underneath, and it was loose enough I could move easily. Several ruffles and an elaborate sash of ribbon hid the seam at the side, the one I could easily rip if I needed to make a quick wardrobe change. Jaqueline instructed me carefully on how to slip out of my stays, and I went over it twice, just to make sure I was ready.

Even as my hair was curled and piled onto my head; even as I faced myself in the mirror, getting one last look of myself before we disembarked, I knew I was going into battle, and I knew I would face it with resolve. My blue eyes were clear, and I swore I could almost see my mother looking back at me and through me.

"You look beautiful, Eleanora."

I turned away from the mirror to see Lady Penelope behind me. She was dressed in resplendent holiday colors, with fur lining her gown layers and her neckline.

"Not Eleanor?" I asked, only teasing her slightly.

She shook her head. "No."

I felt a twinge of guilt at her saddened expression. "I'm sorry," I said. "I shouldn't have said that."

"We are family." Lady Penelope stepped closer to me. Her tone was brusque, but I knew from the look in her eyes she was still concerned for me. "And as such, the pains and pleasures we give each other will always be interconnected. Besides, it is much better to remember Eleanor than to allow her memory to slip into the darkness."

I nodded. "You are right."

"Of course I am." She gave me one of her haughty smiles, and I gave her one right back.

"I am not just Dezda's daughter," I said, remembering what Amir had said before. "I'm your granddaughter, too."

"Which is why I have two things for you tonight," Lady Penelope said. She came over to me and held out her hands.

Inside of her outstretched palms sat a dagger, sheathed in black leather.

"This is the first," she said, while I just stared at it, my eyes wide with reverence and disbelief. "I think you have earned the right to carry it."

"Really?" I asked, reaching for it.

"Well, not entirely. I still have to insist that Harshad will instruct you. After tonight, we will have more time to devote to such matters."

I did not trust myself to say anything. I was upset Harshad had to be forced to do what I saw as largely his job, but I had been waiting for this moment, the moment I would gain the right to bear my mother's weapon and legacy. I was overjoyed and fearful, eager to please and terrified to fail. My inner mix of emotions only settled as I took the dagger from Lady Penelope. I pulled it out of its snug pocket, allowing the violet blade to shimmer in the evening light.

"Honesty is better than lying in matters such as this," Lady Penelope said. "You don't know how to use it, I might remind you. And you know this, too. You would not believe me if I said you were ready for it. But you are ready to embrace the responsibilities of the Order of the Crystal Daggers."

I curled my fingers around the hilt, the old weapon full of ancient strength, tense with passion from its previous wielders.

"If there comes a time tonight," Lady Penelope said, "where you must reveal yourself and the Order, the King will recognize this as a symbol of your authority."

"He will?" I asked.

Lady Penelope nodded. "We do not reveal ourselves unless the situation calls for it, when death or defeat are the only other options."

I studied the blade again, testing it in my handling. I believed in destiny; I believed in God, and I knew he had his plans for me. At that moment, it struck me as odd how right this seemed, to be here, standing on a precipice, standing before a moment when I had the chance to do something greater than I could have ever imagined. It was humbling and awing, and I was floored with the tension between looking up in faith and glancing down in fear.

Lady Penelope watched while I looked at my eyes as they reflected darkly in the blade.

"What is it?" I asked.

"You should know this is your mother's dagger," she said. "I have carried it beside mine all these years, since she resigned her position. It is not something I would pass to you lightly, but I welcome the chance to share her legacy with you."

I felt my throat clog as I tried to imagine my mother holding her dagger for the first time. I could see her rising to the challenge, sharing her adventures with Amir by her side, looking for approval from her mother with fiery determination.

"Which is why you must listen carefully now," Lady Penelope said. "As the following information is the most important thing for a lady in the Order to know."

"What is it?" I asked, eager to hear.

"Eleanora, when you fall in love with someone," Lady Penelope began, "it is important that you do not lose your head in the process of letting go of your heart."

I nodded. "I think I can remember that."

"That's not it," Lady Penelope said. "I'm telling you that when you decide to have sexual intercourse, you must remember to indulge in it according to your monthly courses."

"What?" My voice squeaked.

"This is the rule of twos. You can have as much sex as you want in the two weeks following the end of your monthly cycle, but you cannot have sex in the two weeks before. If you engage in intercourse two weeks before your period, you can get pregnant." She arched her brow at me, intently staring into my soul, as though instilling inside of me a permanent sense of discomfort. "Do you understand this?"

My voice was gone. I only nodded.

"Good. When was the last time you had your monthly courses?"

At her intrusive question, I balked. "I'm not going to have sex tonight," I sputtered. "There's no reason to ask that."

"I have plenty of reasons," Lady Penelope snorted. "The Order is sworn to serve the truth and protect the innocent. That includes our children. I would hate to have you live up to our family's reputation in this matter."

"This matter?"

She grimaced, realizing her mistake. "Never mind," she said. "But you should start keeping track of your monthly courses. We can't afford any slip ups."

Lady Penelope turned and walked away as another round of questions came rushing up from inside of me.

"What do you mean by family reputation?" I asked. "Did you—"

Lady Penelope glared at me. "That's enough on the subject. Amir and I do not wish to discuss such things. Now, finish getting ready and hurry downstairs. We need to make sure we arrive early tonight. We will need the extra time to secure the castle."

She shut the door to my room hard enough that the dagger in my hand quivered, and I sighed.

Was that the reason my mother had resigned from the Order? That did not make sense; at least, not to me. Lady POW had not known about Ben or me before she came here. Was it possible she was talking about herself? Had my mother been an "unnecessary surprise?"

And why mention Amir? I stared back down at the dagger. I could only wonder for now.

Other things needed to be done.

Tucking the dagger into the hidden pockets under my gown, allowing the sheath to sit around my stealth habit, I felt an old sense of comfort.

It seemed that I was used to the stress of fulfilling my intended role at parties, I thought with a smirk. As much as that was true, I was glad to be armed with more than my wit and beauty this time.

23

◊

The crystal dagger was a gift that seemed to christen the night, giving me a supernatural sense of purpose and preparation.

It also helped keep my stomach from turning over into knots. As I sat up straight in Lady Penelope's coach, the hilt leaned into my side, giving me something to focus on, something other than how if I failed tonight, the majority of Prague's aristocracy and nobility would be dead, along with me and likely everyone I ever cared for.

Ben, dressed up in a footman's livery, squeezed my hand as he helped me descend from the carriage.

"Remember your promise," I whispered to him.

"I will," he assured me, and then he quickly let me go.

Lady Penelope and I hiked up our skirts and headed up into the entrance to Prague Castle.

If I had been there under any other circumstances, I would have thought I had died and gone to heaven. A heaven, I thought with a smile, where it was Christmastime all the time.

Since Queen Victoria had taken up the tradition of decorating trees for the season, many others had followed in her example. Empress Maria Anna had gone further, hanging wreaths and silk all over, presenting many images of the infant Jesus, surrounded by his holy mother and the shepherds who gathered at his birth. At the front of the room, there was even a mock manger scene, complete with sculptures of angels and shepherds. Tall trees lined the walls of the room, each of them lit with small candles and decorative ribbons and other little ornaments.

The ballroom was filled with light, so brilliant it was hard for me to look up at any of the chandeliers without shielding my eyes. I stood atop the staircase before it, wondering if it was wrong to feel as though I was descending into Elysium rather than Hades.

The dagger at my side, underneath all my skirts, slanted against me, even though the rest of my outfit seemed weightless all of a sudden.

It was as though I was an actual princess in this moment, and I smiled at the thought of seeing Karl. The voice at the back of my mind reminded me that if I wanted, I could be a *real* princess.

"Remember our plan," Lady Penelope hissed at me, as she walked down the stairs beside me.

I glanced around at the footmen, wondering if Ferdy was already working. "I remember," I said, hoping she would not realize how I intended to add some small changes to what we agreed upon earlier.

"I see Lord Maximillian is here already." Lady POW pointed to the receiving line, where he stood before King Ferdinand and Empress Maria Anna.

I was shocked to see the king. I had not seen him since my father's funeral, but he seemed to be the very same as I looked at him. He had the high forehead, the uncertain gaze, and the kind, weak smile. I studied him for a few moments, as Lady Penelope was surrounded by her friends—or at least, the people who were familiar with her.

I stepped back to look over at Empress Maria Anna. Her black hair had grayed over the many years, and I saw she was wearing a large crucifix among all her pearls. She seemed like such a little old lady, one who seemed content to look down as if she was in perpetual prayer. She was so different from Lady POW, who had very little jewelry but still carried herself with a regal sense of being, despite her older years.

A soft whisper of footsteps approached me from behind. "Would you allow me the honor of your first dance tonight, my lady?"

I whirled around in disbelief to see Ferdy behind me. But this time, he was not wearing a footman's uniform. He was wearing a fine suit and pressed pants, paired with boots that gleamed with a shine and a simple cravat. I barely recognized him, with his hair combed back and the shy stubble of his beard gone from his face.

Seeing Lady Penelope was busy receiving effusive praise from Lady Hohenwart, I grabbed him by the wrist and whisked him away quickly, before anyone else could see him.

"What are you doing?" I hissed at him. "This is not the time to pretend that you're a lord or something."

He grinned at me. "How could I resist?" he asked, testing the limits of my patience as he took over my lead and turned me toward the marble dancing floor.

Ben's earlier comments came back to me, and I felt another round of frustration. "Don't you take anything seriously?"

Ferdy took a step closer to me, closer than he should have been. "Of course I take some things seriously," he said. His eyes twinkled under the ballroom lights. "I have wanted to dance with you ever since I rescued you from the Hohenwart Ball."

"Enough to steal some royal's clothes?"

"I can assure you, the royal in question is close enough to my size that he won't notice, and he won't miss one of his suits. Though he will be upset, if he ever figures out what I've done."

I gaped at him incredulously. "Why would you do this?"

"Does it make you mad to see me risk so much for you?" Ferdy asked quietly as the music began. I was too shocked at his daring to realize that he was a confident dancer.

"Yes," I admitted, too brazen to care. "I need you to leave here at once, Ferdy. You're in danger."

"I know."

"What?" I glared at him. "What do you mean, you know?"

"I know that I'm in danger," Ferdy said. "But I have been in danger for a long time, Ella. From the moment I first saw you, I've been in love with you."

It was then that I noticed Ferdy was indeed a good dancer, since he caught me as I tripped.

"Have you fallen for me, too, then?" Ferdy asked, holding me too close as he looked into my eyes.

I was so tempted to scream in frustration. I wanted to so badly. Ferdy was wonderful. I cared for him deeply, more than I knew why, and here he was, dressing up like a noble, stealing me away from my grandmother, and passionately declaring that his heart was mine, all in the middle of my imaginary kingdom, where heaven touched the earth and flooded me with pure wonder.

I would have given anything, anything at all, to have been able to respond with more than a stunned look and a rush of heat running through my body as it pressed into his.

"Ella?" For the first time that night, Ferdy frowned. "What's wrong?"

"I need some air." I flushed, silently cursing myself for my befuddlement.

Ferdy quickly obliged me, twirling me toward the back of the ballroom. Together, we slipped into the shadows of a dark hallway, and I was reminded of the time that we shared before at the Hohenwart manor.

"Better?" he asked, the eagerness waning from his voice.

"Yes, thank you." I leaned against the coolness of the walls. "I'm sorry."

"Sorry for what?" Ferdy asked. He gave me a friendly pat on the shoulder. "I did not mean to take your breath away."

"No, that's not it," I said, shaking my head. "I need you to leave now, please."

"Will you come with me?" he asked, and at his flippancy, my patience broke.

"Enough," I snapped. "I need you to be serious about this, Ferdy. There's danger here. Something is going to happen here later, and I don't want you to be around when it does."

"What is it?" Ferdy asked. To his credit, he did look more serious all of a sudden.

"I can't tell you," I said. And that was the truth. I did not know what was supposed to happen tonight. All I knew was that something was supposed to happen, something that could possibly kill people, and no stretch of my imagination allowed me to believe Ferdy would be safe just by virtue of his humble status.

"You can tell me anything, Ella," he whispered.

I grabbed his coat and tugged him closer to me. "We don't have much time here. Right now, I just need to know you're not here. That you'll be safe, please. I care for you too much to let anything happen to you."

"So you do love me, then?"

"Of course I do," I snapped. "But this is—"

He cut me off, along with all my complaints and concerns, as he kissed me.

The taste of him was lightning across my senses. I felt the shock of our lips pressed together, the ache in my heart as I wanted him. I closed my eyes, unable to resist, as the longing inside of me stood strong, and all my feelings came rushing out, pushing reason to the side.

I had been so worried for him over the past few days, and I was suddenly more desperate than ever to cling to him. I was so worried the Cabal was in danger, and I was so worried when Ben could not find him and warn him. I had been prowling around the manor like a caged animal, and now that I was with him again, I was free.

Ferdy's hands trapped me next to him, and I could only revel in the chaos, clinging to it as I claimed his heart as my own.

He is freedom, I thought, as I let out a small moan. Ben was right; Ferdy was flippant and fun, but he was freedom, and he was more than able to frustrate me. Karl might have proven to be the more stable one, but I would never feel such power and passion.

Ferdy pressed against me, driving me into the wall behind us. The solid coolness of it sent another shockwave of pleasure behind me, as the space between us collapsed and my body melted against his.

It was only as his hands slid down my body, roaming over my side where the crystal dagger was tucked away, that my mind insisted on reorienting itself.

He seemed to sense the change and slowly pulled back from me, breathing heavily. "I cannot tell you how long I have waited for you," he whispered. "I knew you were meant to be mine."

I breathed in deeply, letting my hands run through his hair and down his face. I was shaking. I did care for him. I did love him. I did not want him to be hurt. I did not want to think about what my life would be like if he was gone.

How could the world exist if he was gone?

"Then," I said, still breathing irregularly, "please, promise me that you will leave this ball now."

"I would not worry about anything if I were you. If there is any danger, we will face it together," Ferdy said. "Besides, I think I might be able to help you, if you let me stay."

"No!" I shook my head. "Please, no—"

"Do you think after all these years of searching for you, I'd risk losing you now that I've found you again?" He gave me a grin, and I was suddenly aware of how odd his words were.

I frowned. "What are you talking—"

A new voice called out from down the darkened hall. "Ella?"

"Ella?" Ferdy frowned. "Who else calls you Ella? That's my name for you."

I groaned. This was a whole evening of poor timing. "It's Karl Marcelin," I said. "He likes me. He said my name was too long, too."

Ferdy began to growl. "Why—"

"Please go," I said. "He can get you in trouble. I don't want anything to happen to you."

"But, Ella—"

As Karl made his way closer to us, I shoved Ferdy behind a nearby corner. "Stay here and don't say anything," I hissed. Even though there was very little light in the corridor, I hoped he would be able to see the grim look on my face.

After he remained quiet for a long moment, I hurried away, determined to meet Karl halfway.

"Ella. I thought that was you," Karl said. "I'm pleased to have found you here. I did not see you in the ballroom."

"Oh, I was … looking for the ladies' withdrawing room." I made a mental note to find a new excuse as I thought I heard Ferdy smother a laugh. It would not be long before someone noticed I was apparently going to the bathroom too often to be normal.

"I can give you directions, if you still need … " Karl's voice trailed off politely and I quickly shook my head.

"Oh, I am perfectly well."

He offered me his arm. "Then might I request the pleasure of your company?"

"Yes, you may." Under the guise of tucking in a loose curl, I glanced back to see Ferdy was still out of sight. I sighed, glad I had found him, even though I was still worried he was going to refuse to leave.

"It's a pleasant night," Karl said. "The Advent season is always magical."

"Yes," I agreed. "And the castle is so lovely. Her Imperial Majesty has clearly done a wonderful job decorating."

Karl beamed, and I wondered if part of it was familial pride. "She always does an excellent job," he said. "But this year, nothing compares to your presence."

We were walking down the hallway toward the ballroom when Karl veered off to the opposite side.

"Come this way," he said. "This is one of the king's gardens."

With Ferdy out of immediate danger, I was hoping I would find a way to escape from Karl soon enough. But as he opened the door and I was able to see the indoor gardens, I momentarily forgot the mission.

Large windows glowed with opaque lighting. Outside it was winter, but inside it was the height of spring.

It was an indoor garden, where several rows of plants were crawling with vines and blossoms. Walls held pots full of draping ferns and cluttered flowers. In the moonlight, it felt like walking into the Garden of Eden, just before its twilight.

"This is beautiful," I said, my voice hushed with awe.

"The king is very fond of his botanicals." Karl led me through an aisle of planted blooms. I was grateful to feel the warmth of the room. "He is in here a lot of the time, experimenting with different crops and planting methods."

"It sounds like you know him very well," I said, doing my best to keep my tone unsuspecting.

Karl smiled. "I do. It is a shame he is not as supportive of me as Count Potocki is, in terms of politics," he said. "But His Imperial Majesty has been most kind on other accounts."

"That is his name among the people," I recalled. "Ferdinand the Good."

I eyed Karl carefully out of the corner of my eye. "It is a shame he did not have any children of his own," I said. "Bohemia is poorer for it."

"I could not agree more," Karl said, startling me with his tone. It was a mix of anger and longing, and it was one I could recognize myself. I knew what it was like to live with the feeling life was not what it was supposed to be.

"How is your situation with Lord Maximillian coming along?" I asked, changing the subject as I moved away and glancing down at a bed of orchids. "He would be upset if he knew you were with me in here, wouldn't he?"

"He would," Karl agreed. "But it is worth the risk. Especially if you have thought about what we talked about before."

I sighed. "I must be blunt, sir," I said, pretending I was trying to be brave. "I do not wish to marry for anything but love."

"Have I not confessed to my love for you?" Karl asked.

I shook my head. "No."

"Then I love you."

There was the chime of the clock in the distance, and I was taken back to the night when Ferdy had kissed me for the first time. That night had been over far too early for me.

And this one could be over at any moment. As long as Karl is here in the castle, nothing can happen.

"Thank you, sir," I replied quietly. "But I fear your love for me is quite shallow compared to your ambition."

"Others are depending on me, Ella. Lord Maximillian is ready to announce my engagement to his daughter tonight if I tell him to. He has plans for us, and I won't be able to go forward with any of them if I am not completely dedicated to my calling." His tone was much harsher all of a sudden.

And then I had an idea. If Lord Maximillian did not have Karl's agreement, maybe the rest of their plans would fall through.

Is it possible?

"If your love for me is true," I said carefully, "then go and tell His Grace that you will not marry his daughter. Tell him that you want to marry me instead."

"He is very insistent on supporting me. I do not feel it would be wise to upset him."

"You cannot have me as a bride if you are already betrothed," I pointed out.

Karl raised his eyebrows. "So you will marry me, then?"

"If you love me, you will go and tell him the engagement between you and Lady Teresa Marie is off," I said, sidestepping the question. I did not want to commit to anything. Lady POW's warning came back to me.

"You hint and tease, but never promise anything—no stolen kisses in the gardens, no getting caught in flagrante delicto*."*

Karl reached over and kissed my hand. "I will do as you say, my lady. You have made me the happiest man on earth."

Before I could stop him, he drew me close and kissed me.

Karl's kiss was soft and gentle, completely polite, both passionate and restrained. I went still, paralyzed by the unexpected tenderness as much as the unanticipated guilt. I had not wanted him to kiss me, but I felt like if I stopped him, it would be impolite.

After all, he might have kissed me out of excitement, but I was the one who was lying to him. I did not want to marry him, and I did not want to kiss him, either. I felt nothing of the fire I felt for another, and only my desire for Ferdy's safety kept me from pushing him away.

Karl pulled back, oblivious to my disenchantment, with a satisfied look on his face.

I gave him a bland smile back, unable to do anything else, before he stepped back, bowed, and headed toward the door.

"After I am finished talking with the Duke," he said, "I want to introduce you to my parents."

I nodded, waving as he headed out of the room. "I'll meet you back in the ballroom."

Karl was still grinning when the door finally closed between us.

I squeezed my eyes shut and sighed. For the first time, I felt the excitement of being a member of the Order transform into poison.

My love for Ferdy, in all its innocence and purity, made me feel wretched. Kissing Karl had not been altogether unpleasant, but I felt more like a mistress of politics, a member of the demimonde who sold her time, body, and mind to the preservation of the state.

I reached down toward my dagger, wondering if my mother had ever experienced a similar feeling. *Maybe that was why she quit.* If she was in love with Amir, she would have been unwilling to do certain things for the sake of information.

I rubbed my eyes and temples, grateful I had succeeded. I had agreed to nothing, technically, and Karl was off to buy us more time before Lord Maximillian could execute his plan. "Thank God that's over."

"Yes, I couldn't agree more."

Ferdy's voice echoed in the spaces between us as he appeared behind me, and I jumped, my heart beating with sudden fear and adrenaline.

"Oh, my God. Don't scare me like that." I was angry at his sudden appearance, but then I saw the look on his face and forgot everything else.

I did not have to ask him to know he had overheard everything. *Everything.*

My head fell into my hands. "Oh, no."

24

◊

A long moment passed before I felt like I would be able to withstand the shame. When I looked up, Ferdy met my gaze squarely.

The shame was hard and fast and left me breathless, and even worse, it stripped Ferdy of all the fun and joy I loved about him.

"Well, I guess you were right."

"What do you mean?" I asked.

"Something terrible was going to happen tonight." The harshness of his tone was unbearable, and I heard every splinter of his heartbreak in each syllable.

"I can explain," I said, trying to find my bearings.

"You can explain," Ferdy said. "But I don't think I will wait around to hear it."

"Ferdy, please—"

"Good day to you, mademoiselle," he said, giving me a quick bow. "I hope you'll be very happy in your engagement. Mr. Marcelin offers you such wonderful prospects, much more than I could ever hope to offer you—"

"That's not it!" I stepped up in front of him, trying to stop him as he made for the door. "I'm trying to save people's lives—"

"By destroying others'?"

"That's not what I meant." I took a hold of his arm. "Ferdy, Karl is King Ferdinand's son."

Ferdy finally stopped. "You know?"

"You know, too?" I blinked. "I found out a few days ago."

"After he talked about marrying you before, at the Summerhouse Ball?"

"Yes," I said. "He is—"

"So that is why you want to marry him?" Ferdy asked. "Because he's a prince?"

"What? No," I argued. "Listen to me, I'm trying to tell you—"

"I'm not going to listen to you," Ferdy said, struggling to free himself from me. When I would not let go, he pulled his arm away even more, pushing me away with his other arm. "Let me go!"

I felt the last of my strength leave me at his bark, and I ended up tripping before slamming into the wall behind me.

"Ouch." My shoulder scraped hard against the brick wall behind me. I sucked in my breath as a small trickle of blood oozed out from my skin.

I glanced up from my blood-speckled fingers to Ferdy's face. He looked shocked and apologetic, and for a long second, I was certain he was going to run back and embrace me.

But a moment later, he pulled out a handkerchief from one of his pockets and tossed it my way. "My apologies. I must return to the streets for the night. It is for the best. That's where I belong."

His words cut into me deeply and the second he left, I slipped down to the floor, trying not to cry. My fingers were shaking, this time out of grief, as I reached for the handkerchief he had left behind, resting the soft silk against my cheek. The cut on my shoulder hissed with softly searing pain, but I ignored it. It felt better to bleed.

I knew I only had a limited amount of time to myself. Even if Karl did manage to convince Lord Maximillian to change their arrangement, there was still a chance that something was going to happen. I knew from our plans that Lady Penelope was keeping an eye on the King and Queen, and I knew that Ben was searching the castle for any signs of suspicious activity, especially from the Szapira household.

I was supposed to be the distraction, keeping an eye on Karl.

"For all the good it did." I pulled out my mother's dagger and looked at it again.

Now that he was leaving, I knew Ferdy was safe, even if he hated me. I managed to get Karl to discuss terms with Lord Maximillian. I did not know if the assassination plot was foiled, but if nothing else, I had bought time.

Even if I had broken Ferdy's heart and my own in the process.

The door opened again, and I nearly jumped. "Ferdy?" I was unable to stop myself from hoping he would come back for me.

"Nora?" Ben's voice was a welcome one, and if it had to be someone other than Ferdy, I was glad it was Ben. He was a friendly face I could count on.

"I'm over here," I said, hurriedly wiping my eyes once more. It was time for me to find something more useful to do than cry over my pain.

"Lady POW was looking for you," he said. "She just saw Karl Marcelin leave."

"Why? He told me he was going to go talk to Lord Maximillian."

"He's gone, too."

I felt fear seize hold of me and determination move to cut through it. "Then something must be happening somewhere."

Ben sighed. "I'm not sure where. But I followed a footman from the Szapira household down this way when I thought I saw Ferdy storm out of this door and head toward the kitchens."

"That was probably where he came in."

"So it was Ferdy?" Ben asked. "I saw his face, but I wasn't sure when I saw he was wearing those clothes."

"That's the way he sneaked inside the castle," I said. "He danced with me for a song, and then … " I waved my hands, unable to say anything else. It was better to let Ben assume things.

"Is something wrong?" Ben asked.

I shook my head. "Nothing that can't wait. We need to get to work. If Karl and Lord Maximillian are both gone, we have to work quickly to make sure nothing will happen to all the people here."

Standing up, I stripped off my gown, tearing at the stays and ripping the fine fabric, just as Jaqueline had taught me. I stuffed the gown into a fireplace before quickly lighting it. The simple but thick layer of the dress began to burn, and while I was sorry to see such finery be destroyed, I felt much more like myself.

The smell of burning fabric, too similar to the aroma of Tulia's house, chased me away. But I jerked my mask up and readied my dagger at my side.

"Are you finished?" Ben asked.

I nodded, reminding myself to be brave. "I'm ready."

Ben and I made our way to the hallway, and then I sighed. "Wait," I said. "Give me one moment."

"Hurry," Ben said with a quick nod. "I'll head for the kitchens. Amir might be there already, checking for signs of the silver thallis herb."

"If nothing else, the head chef will be able to tell if there's something wrong with the food. We could warn them that way."

I turned back to the fireplace, now smoking with the remnants of my dress. Taking the handkerchief Ferdy had thrown at me, I prepared to settle it on top of the pile. I would talk to him later, so there was no need to be so sentimental over his souvenir.

But just as I was about to let it go, the embroidery in the corner caught my eye.

The trotting horse, and the squiggles symbolizing wheat and waves were all too familiar.

He got this from the Szapira household.

I froze.

Is it possible … ?

All those moments of Ferdy telling me he was a liar fell through my mind. He was well informed. He knew how to sneak around. He had a variety of jobs that allowed him to find out information on different people, sometimes very quickly.

He knew about the Cabal, and he would know that Tulia would recognize it if he talked to her about it.

Was it possible Ferdy was the one who attacked Tulia?

Surely not. I shook my head. *But* …

"But if it was, I'll kill him myself," I muttered, before I turned around and hurried to catch up to Ben.

25

◊

"What's wrong?" Ben asked, as I crept up beside him. He was standing in the shadows, just outside the main entrance to the kitchen. As we watched, several lines of servers and maids rushed about, working on preparing plates and refilling drinks.

We had been careful to sneak quietly through the servant corridors. Prague Castle was known throughout the kingdom for its intricate hallways, and I was surprisingly relieved at the reality. Combined with the busyness of the Advent Ball, Ben and I were able to keep the shadows without much trouble, and any serious scrutiny we might have faced was negated by the event's demands.

"Nothing." I peeked out over his shoulder, watching for any hint of Ferdy.

"You're really not going to convince me nothing's wrong if you use that tone."

"Be quiet," I muttered. "I'll tell you later, when we have more time to worry about killing people rather than saving them."

Ben raised his brow in surprise, more likely at my temper than at my words, but said nothing. We both turned and watched.

"There." Ben pointed at a taller figure, who was slinking toward the far end of the kitchen. "I'm certain that's the missing footman."

"How can you tell?" I asked, looking him over carefully. He was dressed in a large coat, and it was hard to make out his features from where we were standing. I could not tell if he was the same height as Ferdy or not.

"Remember what Lady POW did?" Ben asked. "She managed to slice through his arm. If you look, there's a slight bulge just under his right shoulder."

"That could be his shirt," I said.

"I saw him earlier in a different outer coat, and the same thing."

"I still don't know."

"He's going into the wine cellar. That should be proof enough, as far as I'm concerned."

"Why?"

"Because Roman Szapira's the one who renovated the wine cellar here," Ben reminded me. "He would be the one who knows how to get into it and how to use it. They have been planning this party for months, so there is no telling how easy it would be to hide it."

"The wine."

The words left my mouth before the idea had fully formed inside of my mind, but there was no stopping it. I grabbed Ben's arm. "Ben, it's the wine."

"Yes, I just said that's where it might be."

"No, not in the wine cellar, it's the wine. It has to be. Karl told me before that the wine had been shipped in from Lord Maximillian's vineyards for this year. He was supposed to be in town and attending the Advent Ball."

"He poisoned the wine?" Ben asked. "If that's the case, we have a major problem on our hands, because it's been pouring steadily since the guests started arriving. Some of them are already tipsy from what I've seen."

"That can't be it then, I guess," I said.

But it had to be something like that, I thought. There was the wine cellar designed and renovated by Karl's host; a footman from his house was linked to Tulia, and even she had mentioned the wine before the fire exploded …

"It *exploded.*"

"What is it?" Ben asked.

Buried inside my mind, cloistered between the moments of Ferdy holding my hand and holding me close, another memory called for my attention.

"It's the wine," I said.

"We just had this discussion." Ben rolled his eyes.

"No, remember what Eliezer said at the Cabal? There had been a shipment of wine that had exploded," I said. "It was coming from Hradiště. It's close to the border of Bohemia, and Lord Maximillian owns several vineyards throughout Moravia. That's got to be it!"

"So the wine is supposed to explode?" Ben glanced around nervously.

"I don't know how," I said. "But that's got to be the plan. Think about it. What better way to say the Emperor is incapable of leading Bohemia? He's already ignored us. With a major attack escaping his notice, especially after he paid for the renovation of the wine cellar? His project would literally blow up."

"And Karl's role?"

"He's the heir. He could offer leadership to a revolution, like Harshad and Lady POW said."

"But he's supposed to be set on getting the Minister-President position."

"Maybe that's a front." I thought about the way he was eager to marry me instead of Teresa Marie. He needed the support to look good. Was it possible he did not actually want the position?

"I don't know," Ben said. "That sounds like circumstantial evidence to me. There might be another clue down in the wine cellar."

"Come this way," I said, tugging Ben's arm toward the left. "This is the kitchen area. We're close to the wine cellar."

"If you say so."

Together, we headed down the stairs, slowly and quietly making our way through the empty corridors. Ben's brace tapped noticeably on the stone stairwell as we moved through the underground halls.

"Where are we?" I whispered.

"Probably underneath the kitchens," Ben said. "Look. There's a door up ahead. The wine would not be too far away from the kitchen. They would need it for cooking as much as serving."

I wrinkled my nose. "True enough. I remember all too well some of Cecilia's cooking needs."

"I try very hard to forget everything I can about her," Ben replied, and despite the enormous amount of fear we were facing, I smiled at his remark.

"Good," I said, as we stepped into the wine cellar entrance. "Hopefully, we will never have to worry about her—"

"Watch out!"

Ben pushed me aside as the shadow of the footman came rushing out the wine cellar door at us. Our attacker had his mask back on, but I could see his dark eyes widen in surprise as Ben fought with him.

He quickly threw my brother off him, but I stepped in to distract him before he could attack Ben again.

"Here," I called, pulling out my dagger before I remembered that I had not been trained to use it properly.

The attacker took the bait, regardless. He had his own knife in his hand, and I felt all of my breath rush out of me as he slashed through the air, barely missing me. If I had been wearing my fancy clothes, my petticoats would have been sliced open. My stealth habit's short skirt managed to whip around him as I dodged his attacks.

Ben stood up behind him and hurried over to help me.

I heard a small crackle; Ben's brace caught on the uneven floor. He went skidding across the stone floor, managing to trip just behind the footman.

"Ben!" I lashed out a quick kick. Triumph shot through me as my aim proved true, hitting the footman in the groin.

The footman fell over and yelled in pain. His mask covered his mouth, so I was unable to tell if I recognized his voice or not. Ben knocked him down and he fell, hard, before I held my dagger in line with his heart and Ben pinned him to the ground.

"Got him?" I asked Ben, my own voice muffled through my mask.

When he nodded, I carefully reached down and pulled off the attacker's mask.

And then let out a sigh of relief.

It was not Ferdy.

"Who are you?" I asked.

The attacker glared up at me in the darkness. "It's not your concern."

"We captured you," Ben insisted, tightening his grip on the footman's arms. "Tell us who you are."

"I don't think so," our enemy declared. "All I'm going to tell you is that it's too late. I've done my job, and this place is going to be destroyed in a matter of moments."

Ben and I exchanged worried glances.

"That's right," the footman said. "And if you were smart enough, you would let me go and get out of here as fast as you can."

Ben thrust a knee into the man's back. "Tell how to stop it."

"You can't." The footman smirked. "That's the power of fire. It's destructive, breaking everything down until there is nothing left. Once the wine cellar explodes, it will take half of the castle with it. And then the rest of it will fall, too."

For the first time, I noticed that there was a large cloud of smoke flowing from the wine cellar door. "Ben," I hissed. "Look."

As Ben turned to look, the attacker launched another punch. His fist caught Ben in the stomach, but I launched myself at him.

The impact was harder than I would have ever expected, but when our attacker slumped over, unconscious, I did not feel the least bit sorry for him.

"Thanks," Ben huffed, trying to breathe properly. He wavered as he stood up and grabbed my hand for support. "Let's go see if there's a way to stop the fire—"

Boom!

A burst of fire and noise poured through the wall and covered the stone halls with fire around us. Ben and I struggled against the fire, coughing in the smoke and debris. Behind us, I squinted through the fire to see our attacker was writhing around in pain as he screamed.

I felt sick as Ben pulled me to the staircase and pushed me forward.

"We need to get out of here, and fast. This is bad, Nora," Ben said. "That had to be enhanced gunpowder. Maybe even nitroglycerin."

"What is that?" I asked.

"It's an ingredient found in a lot of explosives." Ben glanced around us uneasily, looking down at the large barrels of wine and the walls lined with countless bottles. "This is bad. The alcohol in the wine will only make the fire more difficult to put out."

So I was right, I thought. *It was the wine, even if it is not directly the cause of the explosion.*

"So there is no stopping it?" I asked.

"I wouldn't even know where to begin. But maybe if I can take a—"

"No!" I argued. "No, we have to get the others out of the castle, and fast. There's no way of telling how much time we have."

"I'm guessing that the footman was the one who was supposed to set the trigger."

"We don't know for sure," I said. "You need to go outside and get Amir. I'll go and get Lady POW and then we will get everyone else out of the castle."

"You go get Amir. I'll retrieve Lady POW."

"No." I shook my head. "I'm the better runner."

Ben paused for only the slightest second before he nodded. "Well, you know I don't gamble with risks—"

Another explosion rocked the floor around us. I felt pure fear as the ceiling began to crack and the castle walls next to me suddenly shifted.

"Go, Nora," Ben yelled at me. "We will do it your way. Go and get Lady POW. I will get Amir. I'll see you outside."

His tone was hard and unyielding, and I squeezed my eyes shut as in a second of frustrated, fervent prayer.

And then slowly, I nodded. I did not want to leave him, but Ben was right. We had to get the people out of here, and we would do better if we split up.

I put a hand on my dagger. I needed to go and find Lady POW, and we would have to save King Ferdinand and the Empress. *I guess it's time for me to go and meet Karl's parents. Although I doubt this is what he had in mind.*

"Be careful, Ben!" I called back, as I made a run for the ballroom.

Making my exit from the wine cellar was much easier and quicker than getting in. I gripped my dagger, holding the hilt in my left hand as I eagerly charged through the hallways, telling everyone I could to get out of the castle.

The cook looked confused, but when I explained to her that it was the king's wishes to protect his people, everyone seemed to follow much more smoothly.

I raced through the halls, only mixing up my location once. I struggled not to think of Ben. I hoped he was not lying to me about getting Amir. I did not want him trying to enter the wine cellar, even if he thought he might be able to stop more explosions.

I prayed for him fervently as I headed up the steps and worked my way back to the ballroom.

I pulled my mask up more tightly around my face before I entered the room of glittering light.

The ladies and gentlemen all turned to stare at me, but I was thankful once more for the mask. I had pulled the hood over my hair, and it was a relief to hear their concern. I saw several back away from me, and some left the room entirely.

"Halt!" A guard blocked me, but I skirted around him. For all his armor, he moved slowly, and I was able to dodge him much more easily than I anticipated.

I came to a stop before King Ferdinand and Empress Maria Anna, before I bowed. At that moment, I gave them the full view of the purple blade in my hand.

There were whispers and shrieks behind me, but I ignored them as I waited for the king's response.

I felt rather than saw Lady Penelope as she came up behind me, shielding me from the others' scrutiny.

"Your Imperial Highnesses," I said. "I will need a private audience with you. And quickly," I added, daring to look up. "Everyone here is in danger."

After he exchanged a quick glance with his wife, King Ferdinand ducked his head toward mine. "Come … with me," he stuttered.

Immediately, several guards beckoned me toward a large tapestry. Behind it, I saw there was another hidden hallway. I thought briefly of Ferdy, desperately afraid I would never see him again all of a sudden.

I barely noticed Lady Penelope had made her way to my side.

"What happened?" Lady POW hissed beside me. "There's no need for you to reveal yourself to an entire ballroom of guests."

I gritted my teeth as I told her what had happened. "The other guests did not see my face, and it was important to get here as quickly as possible. I don't know how much time we have."

It disturbed me that Lady POW went quiet all of a sudden.

"Please tell me you have a plan," I whispered back. Hearing my voice was an attempt to hold onto my sanity. We were likely moments away from disaster, and I had no way of knowing if I would make it out alive or not.

"Are you worried for your life?" Empress Maria Anna turned around to face me.

"No," I lied. But I thought of Ferdy again, and I decided I could die happy knowing he was safe, even if he hated me. Even if he would never believe the truth about me.

"I see." The Empress' dark eyes glittered, and I thought I saw a hint of Karl as she smiled.

The room we came to was open and large, almost like a hidden coronation room. There was a pair of thrones at the forefront, and I tried not to fidget too much while King Ferdinand and Empress Maria Anna sat down.

Why do they still worry about all these formalities at a time like this?

"Now, what is all of this?" King Ferdinand asked me.

I took off my hood and pulled down my mask. "Your Imperial Highness. I am sorry to report this, but you must order everyone out of the castle at once. There is an assassin here who prepared an explosion in the wine cellar. This wing of the castle will be likely destroyed, and all the people in it could suffer greatly."

Lady Penelope nudged me. "Show him your dagger again, Eleanora."

I reached out, but King Ferdinand waved it away. "Eleanora?"

"Yes, Majesty. I am Eleanora Svobodová, of Bohemia."

"Adolf's daughter."

It felt strange, hearing my father's name, but I nodded affirmatively, praying the king would not go into a lengthy dialogue of my father's deeds or something similar.

I was surprised when he chuckled. "What is it?"

"You're the one my son is in love with." The king's small chuckle blossomed into a throaty laugh.

"I understand he has feelings for me," I said slowly, "but this is not the time to discuss it. We have to get everyone out of the castle now."

"I will send the guards." The king clapped his hands. "But you must go and retrieve my son for me. I know he was upset about something. He is likely moping around the library in the east wing. Go get him, please, Lady Ella."

Lady Penelope stepped up beside me. "There is no need to worry about him, sire. I saw him follow the Duke of Moravia when he left earlier."

"I know Karl wanted to talk to him about his engagement to the Duke's daughter," I said. "So he is safe. There was an assassin dressed in black running around the castle earlier, but Karl left before the assassin made his way to the wine cellar."

"Karl?" King Ferdinand repeated. Then he laughed. "No, not Karl."

"What?" I frowned. "What do you—"

Before I could finish asking him, a strange look suddenly appeared on the king's face. It was a look I recognized, and instantly I could see it all once more inside of my mind. I remembered my father's funeral, when the king had experienced a seizure, and I saw him beginning to flail back and forth.

"He's having a spell," Empress Maria Anna cried. "Come help, quickly, Heinrich."

"Yes, Your Imperial Highness." A tall attendant appeared at the king's side as the other guards were dismissed to carry out the king's orders. Lady Penelope took off after them.

"Eleanora," Lady Penelope hissed, pushing me out the door. "You heard the king. I will alert Amir and help the other guests evacuate."

But I stayed where I was, watching the attendant as he tended to the king, much like the other two assistants had all those years ago, trying to give him medicine and pinning him down to the chair while the spasm continued.

It suddenly struck me as very odd that the king had brought two young assistants with him to my father's funeral. They would not have been able to keep the king pinned down while he had an episode.

I remembered the dark gaze of the one boy as he glared at me, telling me in his own way to mind my own business while the king was experiencing an episode.

Karl.

"Oh."

The king continued to fall apart before me as I stood there. Empress Maria Anna took charge. "Heinrich, please call another guard, so we can escort the king out of the castle," she said. "Lady Eleanora, I must ask you to go and retrieve my other son. His father is right; he is likely in the library further down toward the east wing. He has recently come home from Silesia to celebrate with us, but he does not enjoy social events."

I could only nod, already hurrying off.

The pounding in my heart might as well have been a doomsday clock of sorts as I hurried through the complicated maze of hallways around the castle. With each moment that passed and I found myself not only still alive and the castle intact, I found reason to hope.

As I made my way in the direction of the east wing, all I could think of was Karl and the king.

Karl had been at my father's funeral. He would have known who I was, and he would have recognized my name when he was introduced to me. The king remembered my own father well enough, and the Empress had met with my mother at least once, to the point where my mother knew she was pregnant with an heir.

Or another *heir,* I thought, as the focus on my memories shifted to the other little boy who attended the king at *Táta's* funeral. He had been shorter than Karl, I remembered, and his hair was more brown, and he had different eyes.

It was so hard to remember that, but it had been over ten years since that awful day. And it was not like I wanted to remember that day so well in the first place.

I turned down another hall and saw a door ajar. A light was on, and I could see glimpses of bookcases inside. *That must be it.*

As I watched, a young man came out of the room. He was about the same height as Karl, with brownish hair. As I got closer to him, he jumped in surprise, and I could see freckles dotted his cheeks.

That must be him, I thought, suddenly realizing I did not know the other prince's name. "Your Highness," I called, waving my dagger high, hoping he would recognize it.

He apparently did not, because he pulled out his sword a moment later.

"There were rumors that there was an assassin dressed in black in the castle," the man said. "I see they were correct."

"Your Highness, please," I said, skidding to a stop. "I am not the assassin, that was—"

"No one would admit to being an assassin." The man lunged at me with his sword.

I almost smiled. In many ways, the young man reminded me of Alex. I ducked and jumped, landing a quick blow to his knee. He yelped in surprise, before I punched him across the face and elbowed him in the side.

"Oy!" He fell back against the wall, gripping himself, winded from his injury. His sword fell out of his hand as he fell over.

Certain I was safe, I hurried over to him and quickly bowed. "I'm so sorry, Your Highness," I said. "But we must go. I was sent here by your mother, Empress Maria Anna. I am a member of the Order of the Crystal Daggers. I'm here to protect you."

"I'm—"

"I'm sorry," I said again, as an expression of pain flashed across his young features. "I promise we can get some bandages for you if you need it. I have a friend who's really good at fixing people up."

The man shook his head. "I'm not … "

"Not what?" I asked, starting to get irritated. I quickly sheathed my dagger and tried to pull him upright.

It was only when he stood that he took a deep breath and tried again.

"I'm not the prince," he said.

My mouth dropped open. "You're not?"

"No, he's not."

The voice behind me was too familiar.

While everyone was clambering to safety outside, I had been sent to find the king's second son. Little did I know, I had already found him.

I had already found him, and I had already fallen in love with him.

And when we finally met this time, I found myself staring at him, unable to take my eyes off him, as he held a sword up between us. His silver eyes no longer gleamed with stars, but instead held a dangerous mix of lightning and sadness. The light of the grand hallway teased out the copper-colored undertones in his chestnut hair. He stood prepared to fight, the princely attire no longer a costume he wore but a sign of his true self.

I could only stand there, as my mind put it all together. The Hapsburg features, the straight nose and the defiant chin … I had seen Karl's sharp features transform into the face of a prince, and this time, it was even harder for me to acknowledge my ignorant blindness.

"Ferdy."

His name was a whisper on my lips, but I knew he heard me; he flinched and faltered in his stance ever so slightly.

"Ella." I could tell from the grim look on his face that he was deadly serious. The sword held steady. He glanced at the dagger I had at my side. Recognition flashed through his eyes, but his gaze only hardened. "You've already managed to wound me enough tonight. There's no need to try to kill me, too."

"I'm not here to kill you," I said, trying to regain my focus. It was hard to move; of all the surprises I had faced in recent weeks, I had never imagined this one was possible. "I came to save you."

Ferdy arched his brow. "And why should I believe you?"

It was the wrong thing to say.

"Excuse me?" I snapped. "You're the one who always insisted he was the better liar between us. And clearly you were telling the truth about that, *Your Highness*."

"There's no need for formalities," Ferdy muttered as a small blush came over his cheeks. "I am a prince in name only."

"Just like your brother?" I asked, my voice even more acerbic.

"Exactly," Ferdy said. "Although I am the one who is more content to keep it that way."

I took a step toward him. Beside me, the servant I had initially mistaken for the prince stepped back.

"Philip," Ferdy called. "Stay where you are. There is no trouble here."

"You're wrong," I said. "We have to leave the castle. You are in danger here. Someone is trying to destroy the castle."

"Oh, is that so?" Ferdy narrowed his eyes. "Who is it? Would it be Karl? Do you really think he would go so far as to claim the throne from our cousin?"

"I'm not sure about him," I grumbled, tightening my grip on the hilt of my dagger. "You're the one who's been carrying around an assassin's handkerchief. For all I know, you could be behind everything."

"You really think so poorly of me?" Ferdy asked, genuinely surprised.

"You lied to me about being a prince!" My hands were suddenly shaking as I relived every interaction I had ever had with him, trying to figure out how I had missed something as important as this.

Every single encounter only proved to make me more frustrated with myself. I saw Ferdy as a young boy, not even a year younger than Ben, at my father's funeral as he looked over at me, staring as he tried to control his father's seizure; I heard him speaking fluent Arabic to Amir in the streets; I saw the quickly borrowed footman's clothes at the Hohenwart Ball; I felt the learned grace of his dancing from back in Prague Castle's ballroom.

How did I miss so much?

Ferdy lowered the sword to his side.

I looked at him now, realizing *this* was who he truly was. He was a prince.

I tried to shove my memories aside, but seeing the distrust in his eyes, I found myself unable to bear his derision. But I did not want to admit how deeply he still affected me.

Lying to me would not have been so bad, if I had not fallen in love with him.

"Surely lying about being a prince is different from lying about being an assassin." Ferdy met my gaze with a challenge, much as I had done to him the first time he had seen me.

"That's not the only thing you've lied to me about." I put my hands on my hips. "You never told me that you saw me at my father's funeral."

Ferdy frowned. "I'd rather not discuss that. Obviously, falling in love with you was a mistake, and at this point, I'm allowed to keep my pride."

His words were sharp, like a slap to the face.

"Especially if you're going to stand there and accuse me of being a killer," he added, seemingly out of spite. "We've heard the rumors of an assassin running around in black."

"I'm not the assassin," I nearly shouted. I held out my dagger. "I am a member of the Order of the Crystal Daggers, and I have pledged my allegiance to your protection."

"You freely admit to being part of the Order?" Ferdy arched his brow. "That gives you even less credibility. From what I know, they've done more than their own share of murders."

"That's not true," I said, but my voice was suddenly much weaker. I did not know much about the Order, other than what Lady POW had told me. It was not enough to deny such charges, and I felt, impossibly, even more foolish.

"Are you going to kill Karl, too?" Ferdy asked.

"Right now, you're the one who is putting us in more danger," I shot back. "You're standing here, arguing with me, when we could be escaping the castle."

"You're not answering the question, I see."

"Sire," Philip, the servant behind me, spoke up. Both Ferdy and I seemed to jump at his voice; it was clear we had both forgotten the servant who was watching us.

"Perhaps she is right, sir," Philip said. "Maybe we should leave, especially if your life is in danger as she says. There is an assassin that is rumored to be here, after all."

"Yes, thank you!" I grumbled, before turning back to Ferdy.

"I do not fear death," he said. He walked up to me and looked me directly in the eye. "Or little girls, no matter what weapons they might wield against me."

"So far I have only managed to wound you with the truth," I said quietly. "It might not have hurt so much, if you had simply given it to me earlier."

We stood inches apart, while there were so many worlds between us; but even in that small moment in time, I felt as though I had the faith to bridge the distance, if only he would meet me in the middle. As we stood there, face to face, unable to ignore the truth between us, I silently begged Ferdy to trust me, to let me keep him safe this one last time. As much as I knew we could never be together, I knew I still could not imagine a world without him.

I could not stop myself from gazing at his mouth, remembering the soft texture of his lips against mine. "Please," I whispered, suddenly unsure of what it was I was asking of him.

As if he sensed my thoughts, Ferdy relented. "Ella," he murmured, so softly only I could hear.

There was a rumbling noise behind us, but I was already lost.

The explosion began to crescendo. A storm of breaking walls and crashing stones exploded, rippling into a tidal wave of sound and wind.

In those precious seconds, I launched myself into Ferdy, grasping onto him tightly. No matter how much he had hurt me, no matter how much he had lied to me, I was still determined to protect him.

We were thrown back at the impact. Seconds passed before I realized I had screamed.

I felt a sharp pain against my head before everything started to slip away.

In those moments, I felt the entire kingdom's heart break along with my own. I screamed and yelled, even as I was jolted and pressed on all sides. The power from the eruption burst out like a tidal wave of stones and dust, stripping me of the last of my illusions and innocence, crashing down all around me before burning up into piles of ash and soot.

In the last seconds of my consciousness, I thought I heard Ferdy call to me again.

I did not know if I responded or not.

Everything, I thought as darkness fell, *everything had been a lie all along.*

AUTHOR'S NOTE

Dear Reader,

Welcome to another new world of mine. Once more, it is a world that has stewed inside of me much longer than it would have liked, and like a demon being exorcised, I am relieved to finally have freed it for you.

Freedom really is at the core of this novel, and will continue to play out as a core part of the series. As it is in real life, it is an idea that is bound to much more than itself. Ella wants to be free, but under her stepmother's authority, she really has no idea what it means to be free. Under the state, she has no certainty of maintaining freedom. Under the Order, she has the tools to fight for it, but they are given to her in exchange for responsibilities.

I've been wondering about freedom and liberty myself lately, and what it means for growing up. Is there such a thing as true freedom? I am continually dependent on air and food, and even coffee, no matter what my doctor tells me not to consume. I've found, after all my "philosophical reflection," which is what my one professor in college referred to it as, that there is freedom, and it is real, but it is not something we can see as we might see an object. It is an idea, and it is something that my life will spell out for others through my actions and reactions, unbound by time and unguided by circumstance.

What that means more practically, really, is that I'll write stories about it. And that is, for me, proof of my own freedom. I know it does not come free. Writing these stories provides me an outlet of freedom, but it still takes time and effort from others in order to come to life. And that is the great lesson for me in all this. Trust, love, and freedom are all interdependent on each other. That is why I must thank all of the people who have dedicated such care to my work, including my (Almost) Famous Readers, my "book doctor" team, and my family.

Ultimately, true freedom has always been found in Christ. We are shown the Truth, and the Truth has set us free. We are able to recognize our chains for what they are—our inner fears, the power struggles around us, the individual forces, both natural and spiritual, interacting around us—and we are, through that recognition, able to choose the right ways to struggle for our freedom. We can, like Ella, choose to be brave, to be kind, and to be determined to fight for what we love.

I hope you have enjoyed your introduction into Eleanora's life, and all the complicated quests and inquiries that it has presented. Please look for the next book in this trilogy, *Prince of Secrets and Shadows*, where Ella must face the reality that truth has shown her—despite all the pain it brings.

Until We Meet Again,

C. S. Johnson

SAMPLE READING

Chapter 1*from*

PRINCE
of
SECRETS and SHADOWS

BOOK TWO OF *THE ORDER OF THE CRYSTAL DAGGERS*

◊ ◊ ◊ ◊

C. S. Johnson

1

◊

"Ella."

The whisper of his voice inside my mind was enough to jolt me free from any dreams and propel me into the waking world.

I gasped as I woke, gripping the fine sheets I found surrounding me. The silken softness beneath my fingers was a foreign feeling, one that became clearer as I sat upright on the bed. I blinked, glancing around as moonlight glowed outside the window in front of me.

Squinting, I saw the view was completely unfamiliar.

Where am I?

My nose wrinkled, as the scent of lavender and mint wafted around me, and I began to feel a pounding pain in the back of my head. Reaching under my loosened curls, I felt a small bump.

The pain seemed to spread as I became aware of it; my muscles were sore, and my body ached. I took careful inventory of myself, finding a bandage wrapped around my right leg, just above my knee, and another around my shoulder. I was still in my stealth habit, with its short skirt, black bodice, and armored sleeves, tucked between fine sheets in a bed that was not mine.

As my eyes finally adjusted to the night, I could make out my surroundings.

My hand covered my mouth in shock.

I was in a bedroom, alone, seemingly surrounded by every creature comfort imaginable. The bed was grand, with intricate carvings and covered in delicate drapery. There were rugs on the floor from the East Indies, and a messy bookshelf tucked beside a window seat. Other items—chests and chairs and lamps of all sizes—dotted the room, shining in the retreating moonlight.

Despite the glory of the room around me, my gaze went immediately back to the window.

The dwindling starlight reflected through the glass as morning rapidly approached. Outside, the remaining walls of Prague Castle gleamed, taunting me with their unmoving stasis as my last memories trickled into my mind.

"The fire," I whispered hoarsely, struggling to orient myself to reality's bitter welcome. I did not know if the sound of my voice against the emptiness of the room would keep me from going mad or send me there sooner. There was a singed quality to my throat, and the taste of smoke was suddenly on my tongue.

I licked my lips and cleared my throat. Then I shifted out of the bedsheets and forced myself to find a cognizant starting place.

The last I remembered, I had been at the Advent Ball, the yearly event hosted by King Ferdinand V and his wife, Empress Maria Anna. It was the first time in over a decade I had seen the former rulers of the Austria-Hungarian Empire, which included my home nation of Bohemia, and it proved to be just as devastating as the last time.

"If not more so," I whispered, as my head fell into my hands. I rubbed my forehead and raked back my hair, the dark curls feeling frayed and knotted between my fingers.

It was almost like a bad dream, and my current surroundings did nothing to make it less surreal. The room I was in was crowned with high ceilings, the walls were decorated with splendid paintings and lined with silk wallpaper, and books of all sorts were scattered around, while a half-open wardrobe and several unlit, half-melted candelabras leered at me from the shadows.

On a nearby table, there was a basin filled with lavender-scented water. The fragrance caught my attention before I saw the folded dress beside it.

After only a second's hesitation, I went over and picked up the gown. The fabric felt as soft and pliant as liquid when I held it up to me, surprised to find it was my size. There was even a new set of matching combs on the table beside it.

Is this for me?

It was too much. Everything about the room was too much, I thought, spying a copy of *Morte d'Arthur* on the floor, splayed upside down, carelessly forgotten. I picked it up, briefly noting it was a different copy than the one my father used to own before I clutched it to my chest and looked around again.

The elegance of the castle room was something my stepmother would have sold her soul to have, even if it was just for a day.

I looked back at the dress, noting the fine stitching and the ornate design. My fingers fiddled with some of the ruffles, marveling at the elegance.

Cecilia would probably sell the souls of both her children for this dress.

Not that the devil would take them, I added, allowing myself a small giggle despite my uncertainty.

As I made my way back to the bed, my eyes scourged over everything; the room was elegant and beautiful, resplendent with treasures I had never seen and could never earn. But it was a kind of illusion—just like the heavenly city of Prague outside my window.

The room was still a prison, and I was its prisoner.

I was *his* prisoner.

I slumped back against the pillows as the onslaught of memories ran through me. I relived those last moments of terror all over again. In many ways, they kept me captive more than the sturdy locks on my door.

Fresh wounds scraped against the flesh of my heart, as I drifted back to that night, to that moment—the last moment before everything fell apart, and nothing seemed like it would ever be the same again.

I remembered running as fast as I could through the hallways of the castle, my breath coming in small pants. I knew I only had a limited amount of time before the walls would fall, thanks to the wine cellar collapsing. The castle's cellar had been set afire, and it was only a matter of time before it spread and wrecked its way through the castle.

It was an act of treachery courtesy of Lord Maximillian, the Duke of Moravia, his nefarious henchman, and possibly Karl Marcelin, the secret heir to the throne of Bohemia.

On the other side of the ballroom, guests were quickly evacuating the castle under the orders of the King, aided by the oversight of my grandmother, Lady Penelope Ollerton-Wellesley, the Dowager Duchess of Wellington and the leader of the Order of the Crystal Daggers. My brother, Ben, and our small team of spies were working to save as many people as possible.

I had been sent to find the second heir to the kingdom—only to discover I already knew him.

"Ferdy."

In my mind, I heard myself speak his name. I saw him, standing in the hallway outside the ballroom. He was regal and serious, nothing like the boy I had fallen in love with. We sparred verbally, fighting with our feelings, arguing over secrets and lies, before the castle rooms behind me echoed with oncoming destruction.

The last thing I remembered was grabbing onto him and trying to pull him away from danger.

There was a small part of me that felt him grip me back, that heard him call my name.

I clutched my arms, trying to force myself to distinguish between dreams and reality after that. It was too much to hope for that he would call to me, after everything else that had happened.

My shoulder shifted against the pillows. I saw it taped up, covered with medical bandages. Carefully, I reached up and began to unwrap the wound, flinching as the bandage tugged at my skin.

I was prepared for the worst, so I was surprised when, underneath it, I only saw a small cut across my skin. Immediately, my eyes squeezed shut, trying to ward off the memory.

It was hard—there were a million moments I wanted to forget, but they were all still there.

Ferdy dancing with me in the ballroom. He had worn a lord's jacket and combed back his coppery hair. There had been a distinctive shine on his boots and a twinkle in his eye. He was utterly irresistible, and never more so when he told me he was in love with me.

Ferdy kissing me with grand and growing passion as I unremarkably admitted I loved him, too.

Ferdy overhearing me discuss marriage with his brother, before confronting me, assuming I was only after Karl because he was a prince.

Ferdy trying to run from me before I could explain. Then him struggling as I tried to speak before he finally pushed himself free of me. I had scraped my shoulder at the time, causing it to bleed.

I barely registered the pain then, and now there was none left as I carefully touched the clotted blood scabbing over in a thin line and a patch of red, roughened skin.

But the bandage was soaked with herbs and medicine, and it had been tied back with care so evident it could have been a silent apology.

Does this mean he still loves me?

I could not stop myself from hoping he did.

For several moments, I allowed myself to indulge in my feeble hopes. I wondered if he would come and see me again. As the eerie light of dying night transformed into blossoming day, I finally shook my head.

I was being foolish—a lovesick servant girl and spy, pining for a prince.

"I shouldn't even want to see him," I said to myself. "He *lied* to me! And about so many things. Who's to say he was even telling me the truth about loving me?"

My memory tried to contradict me, and it was at its rebellion that I pushed myself out of bed and began to get ready to leave.

I *had* to find a way out of there.

"I still have a job to do," I reminded myself.

I needed to find out what happened to Ben and Amir, and the others, too. Admittedly, I was not as worried about Lady Penelope. My grandmother was a spymaster, no doubt one used to dangerous situations. She was probably used to finding a way out of a mission's complications, even ones like half of a castle collapsing. She might have been used to losing people, too.

After all, she had lost my mother.

Deep down, I knew it was possible Lady Penelope would be happy to see me when I returned to my father's manor. But I could already hear her chiding me for even needing to recover as I washed my face and brushed out the knots in my hair.

As I contemplated changing into the new gown, the locks behind me chimed, and the door opened.

A shadow stepped forward. "Good morning, my lady."

Disappointment crushed me. It was Philip, the servant I had originally believed to be the Prince of Bohemia. For the first time, I recognized the smothered accent of the streets, the hidden Bohemian harmony, tucked underneath his proper tone.

There were other things I noticed now, too; Philip was close to Ferdy's height, only a little taller than myself. He had a similar color of hair, but his eyes were brown rather than silver, and even in the darkness of the morning hours I could see the string of light freckles on his face.

I could also see the hesitation in his gaze as he looked at me.

Carefully balancing a silver tray in his hands, he cleared his throat, clearly embarrassed to be caught staring. "How are you feeling, my lady?"

It was hard to give him an answer when I did not know myself. "What is today?" I sidestepped the question altogether.

"It's the seventh of December," he said. "Two days after the Feast of St. Nicholas."

Two days since the attack on the castle.

"How did I get here?"

"His Highness and I brought you here after you fell unconscious," Philip replied. He cautiously made his way to a bedside table and set down the small tray. My stomach grumbled at the smell of freshly baked bread and herbal tea.

"Can you tell me what happened?"

"After you found us and argued with His Highness," Philip began slowly, "the floor in the ballroom collapsed in on the castle's underground hallways while some of the nearby walls and ceilings fell."

He looked up me, clearly overwhelmed with gratitude. "You pushed His Highness out of the way and protected him. Some debris fell on your head."

The small bump on my head twanged with remembered pain, as if in agreement.

"I see. So then you brought me here."

"Yes, my lady."

One of the lessons Lady POW had taught me was to observe things, and knowing how traumatized I was by Ferdy's deceit—how I failed to realize he was a prince in disguise, I would never fully understand—I vowed to be extra careful in the future. As I watched Philip, eyeing his quick and careful movements, I saw no immediate reason to distrust the freckled servant who apparently served as Ferdy's royal stand-in.

Admittedly, I was not willing to distrust him when I was as desperate as I was for news.

"What happened to my brother? And what about the ballroom? Did everyone… survive?"

Philip stood, straight and rigid, as he informed me of what he knew. There was no way for him to answer some questions, but even then, I already knew some of the answers.

As Philip remarked on the damage, the Empress' pain, and the king's proclamation of sorrow regarding the loss of life, worry for Ben started to override my concern for Ferdy. I had to get back to my home, find Ben, Lady POW, and my other friends. Then, if I was still allowed to help after all of my mistakes, we had to find out what to do next.

Lady Penelope will be upset with me when I see her again.

I decided I would welcome her ire, if it meant Ben was alive and the Order would allow me a chance to redeem myself. And then Lord Maximillian would pay, I vowed, gripping my fingers into fists as my failure tormented me.

"Please," Philip said, stepping forward as I began to pull on my boots. "You are not well."

"I'm fine," I insisted. It was at that moment I realized my dagger, the one that marked me as a member of the Order of the Crystal Daggers, was missing. "Where is my dagger?"

Philip hesitated again. "Please, just rest for now, my lady. His Highness only wishes for you to recover."

"I am feeling fine," I repeated angrily, shooting him a threatening glance. "Give me back my things. I need to be on my way, and I won't let you—or him—stop me."

Philip did not seem to be very brave—or at least, he was not willing to anger me. As displaced and determined as I was, I supposed I could not fault him for that. He gulped and nodded slowly. "As you wish, my lady. I shall return."

He paused briefly when he opened the door. "I know I should not tell you this," he said quietly, "but His Highness wishes for you to stay here. You are safe, and so are your secrets. We are indebted to you for what you have done."

Heat poured through me. As Philip left, relocking the doors, I finally caught sight of myself in the mirror. My cheeks burned bright crimson as my heart began to beat faster inside my chest.

He wants me to stay.

But a long moment later, I forced myself to move. I could not stay. I had my family to find, my work to finish.

My dignity to salvage, my honor to restore.

I grabbed at the dress left out for me and tugged it over my head. With the stays laced loosely, I could easily wear it over my stealth habit. I hurried to secure it, grateful it would be a suitable disguise. Just as I was contemplating how to get home, even if it meant walking the whole way there, the lock clicked again.

The door opened as I pulled my hair free and tucked my hood down beneath a line of ruffles.

"You can put my dagger down on the table, Philip." I tugged the sleeves down off my shoulders, grimacing as the lower neckline brushed over the small cut. "I'll get it in a moment."

"I suppose it shouldn't surprise me that you hardly pay attention to me when we meet like this."

My spine tingled with sudden awareness, and my heart began to race at the sound of his voice. It was not Philip who had come.

It was Ferdy.

Thank you for reading! Please leave a review for this book and check for other books and updates!

CPSIA information can be obtained
at www.ICGtesting.com
Printed in the USA
LVHW041453270720
661633LV00001B/79